PATERNAL BONDS

THE HIGH COUNCIL WITCH CHRONICLES

5

JULIE CATHERINE

PATERNAL BONDS

THE HIGH COUNCIL WITCH CHRONICLES
BOOK 5

JULIE MEE

Edited by
ALLANA STUART

GCMW PUBLICATIONS

For Bub and little Bub

ONE

THE KONYA THOMAS SPECIAL COLLECTION

"HERE." Beck urged me out of the way and eked himself in front of the locked door. "Let me try." Frustrated, I handed over the tools.

"Sorry I'm not an expert lock picker," I grumbled, crossing my arms in front of my chest.

"Well, I am!" Beck said with flourish.

"You got it open?"

"No... but wouldn't it have been cool if I did?"

I swatted his back. "This is serious."

"I know." He winked. He raked a hand through his mousy brown hair in that 'I got this' thoughtful manner that I seriously loved, then bent back over the tumblers. "Just give me a minute." Beck thrust the bobby pin straight into the hole like we'd seen on internet videos. He tried his best to feel for something to click or to move, or to do *something*. When they did it online, it always went quickly. It looked pretty easy. When we tried... nothing.

Beck stuck out the pink tip of his tongue in concentration. For a moment, I just enjoyed the view. The urgency to the task was all our own doing. No one was breathing down our necks. There wasn't much chance we'd get caught. After finding a letter from Lady Mauve addressed to this building, we'd staked out the Konya Thomas Special Collection several times to see the location, but the records hall and the adjoining parking lot were always deserted. There was no one here. And a person wouldn't just stumble in from the street. You had to know that the file warehouse was here, down a long, winding road, remodeled in the bones of an old farmhouse. The building was remote.

And locked.

"We should have borrowed keys from Blue Moon," Beck said. His attempts at lock-picking didn't appear to be any more fruitful than mine.

"It wouldn't have been borrowing. It would have been *stealing*. And you know, I don't-"

"-want others involved. I know."

Touchy subject.

Involving family and friends in my coven business in the past had had some pretty serious negative consequences. I wasn't about to tempt the hands of fate with another go. If we were gonna break into the Special Collection, we would do it alone.

Beck sat back. "Well, this isn't working."

"We can't give up!" The panic jumped out of my voice. I clamped it down, but too slowly. Although I tried to play it cool, I was desperate to get into the building and learn all its secrets. Information about my mom, about my father, how he probably (but definitely) could be a murderer. How he killed my mother. Maybe. His identity was still uncertain. Exactly who he was... there was a lot to learn. This was the one clue we had.

"No one said we'd give up," Beck squeezed my shoulders, standing and looking up at the red brick building. He offered a reassuring grin.

"We already tried the doors and windows." I followed his gaze.

"Down here." He agreed. They were all locked from the inside. "What about up there?"

We looked up at the second story. On the upper level, there was a Juliet balcony and four windows. Any one of them could be open, but from here we'd never know.

"Higher up, people tend to be more careless..." He raised an eyebrow. I remained unconvinced but Beck shrugged. "It's worth a shot."

Dubious, I nodded. "Alright. Hey, thanks for doing this."

He leaned down and pecked my lips, a tingle running through me. "I'll get the truck. Be right back, parabond." He snuck a second kiss. This one lasted longer. I let him feel a hint of my desire. The attraction was mutual. We broke apart with a grin.

Parabond.

I loved that nickname from him.

My one fated partner.

Beck and I were forged by destiny. That much was sure. I didn't know how I'd gotten so lucky. But he was right beside me in every challenge that we faced. No matter the circumstance. Even today. Beck was here, trying to help break into this building. A misdemeanor crime. He wouldn't get anything out of it, except for helping his mate.

I'd make it worth his while, I thought to myself, stifling a blush.

We'd parked his pickup truck off the main road on a nearby dirt lane so it wouldn't be discovered. Even though we knew the Collection was deserted, Beck and I weren't taking any chances that our research mission would be seen. At least, we'd taken those precautions upon first arrival. Now that we'd been here for almost an hour, I wasn't much worried we'd be discovered. The dirt path was overgrown and the soft sand only showed the tire tracks and shoe prints we'd made. In the last month, since I'd heard of the place and we had started our secret visitations, there had been zero visitors to the Konya Thomas Special Collection. Nobody cared about this old assortment of paperwork. The only person who wanted to know more about the legacy of the High Council coven was *me*. Well... me and by proxy, Beck.

It would be fine to drive right up to the door.

I swept up my long brown hair into a bun. For the thousandth time, I planned out our attack. We knew the approximate year when my mom left Plumpkin High School and parabonded out of the public system, so if this file system was organized by calendar years, we could find her quite quickly by date and proper name: Sierra Kingsley.

Members of the council were referenced by their given and family names for the first three years of their training (after that they became Lady and/or Fellow Somebodies, picking a shade or color for their coven identities), so we would have three years of record-keeping to make use of. From there, I felt certain we could deduce other things.

Like the name of her parabond.

My father.

I felt certain she and my dad were once a fated pair.

Like me and Beck.

The pull of desire I felt for my bond made me physically ache. I hoped for her sake, the same had been true for my Mom. Of course, pairing off with your bond had its challenges. Beck and I were lucky we found our way to each other. When we first met, he'd been Josie Jiu's boyfriend. Sweet, forbidden fruit. Totally off-limits and I wasn't the kind of person who would steal another girl's man. In fact, I was stuck with a terrible potential partner. Spade Polari. The guy who thought we'd become better witches by jumping into bed. He liked to manipulate me, which he tried to do often. He nearly drove me crazy, although I *tried* to make it work. It just didn't. Nor did it work with Josie and Beck. We're still friends with her, but some moments are weird. Just part of the territory when you hang out with your boyfriend's ex. Spade and I parted on a harsher ending. Which opened a clear path between me and my man. That was our story.

I wanted to know Mom's.

A lot of witches fell in love with their partners. Some parabonds were romantic. Others were forced. It was an aspect of the fates no one could explain. I was a little biased based on my own experience, but I felt confident Mom's parabond would be romantic. Even if I was wrong and her official parabond wasn't my father, I was excited to learn who he was. I knew in my heart, he could tell me much more. Now that I'd learned about the Konya Thomas Special Collection, Beck and I were *thisclose* to learning all my family's secrets... that is, once we broke down the damn door.

At the sound of a coming car, I instinctively ducked into the nearby landscaping to protect my identity. But there was no need to hide. The approaching truck was just Beck, returning to the scene of the crime.

Now with physical reinforcements.

He pulled the old truck as close to the building as possible, making his vehicle a de facto ladder on wheels. "How's that?" He asked through the open cab window, staring up at his handiwork, trying to decide how much closer to go.

"It's perfect. Think it'll work?" I wondered.

"Only one way to know."

We climbed into the truck bed and Beck clamored up on the cab frame. The metal let out a little groan as it shifted under his weight. Nothing the auto body couldn't handle. We looked up to the window above. Still out of reach.

"If you climb on my shoulders?"

I nodded, scrambling over, above him, hugging his neck with my thighs. Then he started to rise. "Easy," I warned.

He held onto my ankles to stabilize. "Ready?"

"I think so..."

Beck stood up slowly. I held my arms out in front of us, widely spread as he straightened. As we got higher, I reached out above me. I could grasp the bars of the Juliet balcony frame, but there was no way to pull myself inside. The second-floor terrace wasn't big enough to stand in. Just a kind of architectural flourish jutting out on the wall. Since my earliest lessons at the coven, I'd become a fairly well-practiced participant on the climbing wall at the castle. Vince had taught me a lot about body position, and proper footing and such, but it would have been a far cry statement for anyone to claim me as a climber. No one would say that.

Especially not Vince.

This lithe ascension was beyond my abilities. Maybe I should've asked for his help?

Since we'd almost died together battling a sea creature and racing against a river of boiling, skin-melting lava, the snarky boy and I had become pretty good friends. In fact, I liked Vince a lot. Near death experiences would do that.

I should know. I've had a lot of them.

But, if I was gonna ask anyone for help on this mission, it would have been Lady Blue Moon, not Vince. After all, Blue Moon likely had a key to this house. And that wasn't happening. I'd bent the rules and called in too many favors before. Getting into the house of records wasn't nearly as immediate or necessary. I would figure out this quandary all on my own.

Well, on my own and with Beck.

"It's no use. I need more reach," I told him.

"I could lift you up?"

"You're already grunting."

"I thought you wouldn't notice."

"Oh, I noticed. A groan over a girl's weight isn't ideal."

"Cuz this is an awkward position. My shoulders are super strong. In a better spot, I can do it. Just... Which is your stronger leg?"

"I have a stronger leg?" He sounded like Vince.

"Well, which leg would you use to swing over a fence?"

I could have easily pointed out that I don't go around willy-nilly fence-hopping or swinging legs over items, but I was sitting on his shoulders, trying to break into a building to learn the secrets of my parents and the boy was trying to help. I kept the comments to myself. "Right leg, I guess."

"So I'll press you up with your left. You hold the bars for balance and swing up, over when you can."

There was maybe a foot of space between the wrought iron holding the balcony on the wall and the brick building. I could maybe stand on it? At least cling to it? In theory, it sounded like a reasonable plan. But in practice...

"All this on the off-chance that they left one of the windows open," I muttered. "Alright." I gathered my nerves. "Don't drop me please."

"I wouldn't dream of it. You might dent the truck."

Har. Har.

"Just-"

"Up we go." Beck transferred all his strength to my left ankle and calf and pushed me straight up like I'd seen college cheerleaders do. Luckily, I didn't have to hold my body straight with my core strength like they did because I already had the bars in grasp. They took some of the weight. And Beck was right. As his arm straightened out, the proportions of my body beside the tiny balcony evened and I was able to swing my free leg up and over the railing. I scrambled between the iron and the brickwork and squished safely into the small surrounding space.

"Holy crap!" I held onto the balcony bars, just happy to be on something solid again. Adrenaline coursed through me. Beck stared up at me, smiling and squinting into the sun.

"You did it!"

I caught my breath. "*You* did it." I laughed. "I just held on."

He looked so sweet, pride swelling in his cheeks. He too was flushed from the effort, it was obviously hard work to clean-and-jerk lift me above his head, although we both let him play it cool.

Now, to make the athletic feat worth all the sweat.

I turned and tried the balcony's door.

"Locked." I frowned. "Hold on." I leaned out and pushed on the first pane I could reach.

It didn't budge.

I looked back down and shook my head at Beck. He frowned. No door and no window access. That was two of the four upper level entries. There was a window on the far side of the building that we both knew wasn't happening, but there was one nearer that I might be able to reach if I really tried. I had to lean out from the far-side of the Juliet balcony to touch it, but, after the feat we'd just accomplished to get me here, I felt I could do it with ease... and some luck.

A lot of luck.

I crossed my fingers it would be unlocked, because, although we'd been quick to get me up here, neither one of us had considered how, if the windows didn't open, we'd get me back down.

"Careful," Beck worried.

"I got it," I climbed onto the far side of the railing, no longer safe between its curves and the building, and I concentrated on the task. The final, reachable window. I checked my feet. They were safely on the ledge. I held on tight with my left arm. I gripped the balcony railing then leaned out on the right. "Almost..." I strained for the distant window ledge. "Hold on- I-" My fingers barely scraped it.

The window pane budged.

It moved.

It shifted from where it was.

"Oh my god." I slid it further open. "Holy crap!" I pushed it as wide as I could reach. "It's open. Beck! We did it!" I turned down to see that playful exuberance on his face.

"Yes!"

He beamed up at me. For a moment, we just grinned. I was so hopped up on adrenaline, if an eight foot drop hadn't spanned the distance between us, I would have flung myself down to him, kissed his face with a thousand kisses, and lunged into his arms.

So strong and secure.

"There's a screen," I realized, the balloon of excitement deflating, the adrenaline rush starting to wane.

"I can chuck a rock through."

"No! That might rip it! We don't want anyone to know that we've been here. Remember? That's the whole point. If we were gonna smash and grab I could've done that from the ground. Get me a stick or something."

"Like a rock?"

"No *rocks*! Like a pole. To poke it."

Beck hopped down from the truck frame and went to the edge of the nearby forest to forage.

I looked at my next task. Popping out the screen shouldn't be hard, but after that... I would have to leap into an open window two feet away from the safety of the balcony irons. It wasn't an easy chore. The window was on my level, but I'd have to stretch to reach over... and magically scale to the second story window, with only a hedge beneath me to break my fall. But we got this, I hyped myself up.

"Here," Beck passed up a good sized stick. I quickly maneuvered it to pop out the screen without so much as a tear. Easy peasy.

Now came the hard part.

"Uh, Mae?" In his own head, Beck seemed to be doing the same geo-spatial arithmetic.

"I got it," I told him before he could object too finely. "I got this," I told my own internal worries trying to silence my fears.

Remember why you're doing this.

I steeled myself.

Your father killed your mother.

He's never been held accountable.

If you want him to pay for his transgression, then it's up to *you* to track him down.

The first step was to learn his identity.

And that could only be done if I entered this second story hole.

"I'm going."

"Just be careful. I kind of like you."

"I like you, too," I grinned down.

There was no way I could get in the window with the brute strength of a grab and transfer, so I took a sort of triangle-body rotation approach. Holding on to the bars slightly out from the building, I swung out my right, stronger leg and wedged it beneath the window pane. Two feet of space hung between my grip on the rail and my leg. There was nowhere to go but down. Next, slowly, methodically, I spun my body around, transferring the weight from the safety of the hand rails to the precarious ledge on the far wall. I twisted as far as I could and wedged my body weight anew in the wonky triangle position. The transfer went smoothly. I felt pretty solid. So far so good.

Now was the hard part.

In order to move forward, I would have to release the hand rail and reach for the wall. At that point, I could put my fingers around the window ledge, and pull myself in.

I took several deep breaths, willing myself to move past the point of no return. I frowned. "Sure wish Ferris was here with her trusty blue mat."

"You can do this," Beck encouraged.

I can do this, I mirrored the confident words.

We both knew the longer I stalled, the weaker my legs would become. It was now or never.

"Here I go." I pushed off the rail and swung towards the window frame. I grabbed the metal border and tightened my grip.

"Yes!" Beck cheered.

For a second, I really did it!

I transferred my body. I grabbed the window. I moved myself forward.

But my foot hitched.

Or my knees.

Or my hip.

Something snagged me, and gravity didn't trifle. The moment I lost connection, it pulled me straight down to earth.

"No!"

I heard Beck shouting.

For a moment, I was falling.

"Beck!" I might have yelled back.

Then everything went black.

TWO

WELCOME TO THE REAL HIGH COUNCIL

OHHH.

"You're alright. Don't move." Beck ran in, hovering above me.

"Ohhh, my-"

"Head? Back? Leg?"

"Yeah." I groaned. "Everything."

"Mae, where does it hurt?"

"Everywhere," I complained. *My pride*, I thought first and foremost, starting to come around. I tried to get up. "I'm alright."

"Well, don't move!"

"No, I'm good."

We both knew until I actually tested my arms and legs for myself, that platitude wasn't really accurate. But I was able to move things. At least that was a good sign. I tried to sit up. Beck gingerly helped me off the shrub that had broken my fall. "I'm alright," I said again, this time feeling more sure. I stood beside my man on the ground and tried to dust the sprigs of greenery from my clothes and hair. "Now what?"

"You don't want to try again?" He asked gingerly.

"'Cuz my first attempt was so great?"

"Well, maybe I can get across. I'm taller than you." He gauged the distance.

I shook him off. "I don't want you falling to your death either. I like you not dead."

He tucked me under his wingspan. "And I'm glad you're not dead too. I kind of like you, Mae Kingsley." Hearing his low voice saying my name gave me shivers of pleasure. His exact intention. For a moment, we both smiled. "So, what? We regroup another day?"

"Umm..." He'd sounded so delicious, I had to pull my brain back to the task. "What? No. We can't leave with the window open. Someone would definitely know we were here. And if they're gonna know no matter what, we might as well break in." I shrugged. The die was cast. We were bound to be discovered. If that were true, we might as well take what we came here to get. "Look around. See if there's something we can use to gently encourage a window to open."

We split apart searching for rocks.

"Gently encourage a window," Beck chuckled. "Your way with words."

I smiled. I did have quite the vocabulary. I came by it quite honestly. "You know I get it from my aunt."

We searched the space.

"Got it!" Beck called. He'd disappeared around the back of a second out-building.

"A big rock?"

"Something better!" He re-emerged from the structure's flank carrying a long ladder.

"Oh no," I laughed and moaned all at once. "You're kidding. We couldn't have found that *before* I risked my life?"

"On the ground against the back of the garage." He grinned. "We didn't think to look." How did we miss that? We'd been so concerned with the main structure... I rolled my eyes, but Beck was undeterred. "Be happy we found it now." He leaned it up against the wall. "Perfect fit. You want the honors?"

The ladder *did* reach the open window, but the distance made the apparatus look flimsy and unsafe. I shook the base, the whole thing shuddered.

I squinted up to our destination. "I've had enough of the skies for today."

"Sweet, my turn to lead." Beck climbed to the second floor with ease. As the ladder wiggle-waddled under his weight, he didn't even flinch. I held the base. Not exactly sure what my tiny bracing would do, but it felt good to play some part in the task. At the second story window, he braced himself and slipped inside the building. Success!

"Be right down," he winked then was gone.

I ran to the farm house entrance and waited the seventeen seconds like it was three hundred years, but in a flash, he was there. I heard the front lock jiggle and he opened the main entrance from the inside.

"Welcome to the real High Council," he joked, flourishing his arms like Lady Gray and Lady Mauve had done introducing us to the castle. Giggling, I poked his gut. His arms collapsed with a laugh. Eyes wide, I looked around.

"So this is the Konya Thomas Special Collection."

Excited, I stepped inside. We flipped on the house lights and walked over the threshold. Aside from the basic exterior locks on the doors and windows, there wasn't any security to worry about.

No cameras.

No high tech vault system.

If there *were* secrets to learn about the coven or its members in this collection, no one seemed to be worried about keeping them.

To the left of the foyer, there was a small office with several computers, behind that, an empty kitchen. (Beck opened the fridge and several cupboards just to be sure. He had worked up quite an appetite.) There were another four small rooms converted to hold nothing but files. The paperwork was housed in giant shelving units built from floor to ceiling. All the furniture had been removed and in its stead, the organized rows filled the entire room but for one small space between two giant shelves. The racks were attached to large tracks, each one on rails, letting you roll open or closed the rows simply by turning a single large wheel. The contraption allowed at least two more shelves full of paperwork to be crammed into the room. It also implied, if you weren't careful, you could be crushed between the shelves.

"Paperwork heaven," I muttered.

"Or hell," Beck suggested.

"What do you think are the chances that Lady Blue Moon organized all this?" I asked with wonder. It was an impressive feat. We both looked at each other and grinned. "Pretty good!"

I pulled a random file off the shelf. It was both alphabetized and dated. I took it back with me to the office. There, I found a bundle of papers on the desk, still waiting to be filed. In Blue Moon's writing, a note said 'to do'. It was a stack of the most recent contracts the students at the castle had endorsed. The ones that claimed the pupils of the coven wouldn't involve ourselves in the Damocles' drama or leave the castle without permission. The contracts that I, my parabond, and most of our friends had signed.

And broken.

Several times.

I rifled through the pages and found mine. My signature was there. The ink was dry. I traced the outline of my name.

"So where do we start?" Beck asked, popping in behind me.

I looked up, surprised.

"There are even more rooms like these upstairs," he noted, waving towards the files. "One full, one half-full and two more empty but ready to fill."

I nodded. I left our contracts where I'd found them, and shoved my random file back in its rightful spot on the shelves. My eyes focused on the small date tabs the paperwork was organized by. I pointed out one to Beck. "We go back in time."

Beck and I searched through the rooms until we located the right approximate timeline. The three years that I knew Sierra Kingsley had been in her training at the Judicial School. In our first year, Beck and I were signing so many contracts, learning so many rules, and leaving such a large imprint with our arrival at the coven, I felt confident that Sierra and my unknown father did too...

But that wasn't true.

Going back five or six years in High Council history, the paperwork was thick and plentiful, but ten or twelve years before that, the contracts started to grow thin. Folders espousing dates twenty years in the past or further were practically empty. The files and book-keeping got thinner the further back we went. At the time that my mom would have been inducted into the coven, some of the file folders had only one or two measly pieces of paperwork. A printed and faded newsletter. Scattered photos. Some folders held nothing at all.

"Do you think that back then they just didn't keep very good records?" Beck also clocked the difference. "Not everyone can be at Blue Moon levels of consistency."

"I don't know." I agreed, but then located the file I

wanted. I pulled the folder off the wall. "This is it." The notations for the students in the season my mom joined the High Council. This was the start. As I opened the flimsy cardboard folder, I held my breath.

There wasn't much.

A list of ten names written in pairs.

Terry Takehiro and Bristol Antwon
   Alistair Samir and Latisha Crash
   Matthew Galene and Eva Nimo
   Sierra Kingsley and Wesson Zaid.

I didn't even read the names of the final row of students. Instead, I re-read his name again.

Wesson Zaid.

"Is that him?" Beck asked over my shoulder.

"That's him," I said, quietly.

Wesson Zaid.

Sierra's parabond.

My mother's murderer.

The one we'd been looking for.

Dad.

I took a picture of the list with my phone, then slid the sheet back into the files. Beck poked ahead in the folders. I went back to the office to search for more. In the front room, I'd seen a computer. There might be more information in the database. For a moment I worried I'd need a password, but like the rest of the files in the farmhouse, the computer had no protection. I simply had to open a search tab.

First, I typed in my mom's name, Sierra Kingsley.

Twenty-three files.

I clicked on print all. The machine whirred to life.

Next up, Wesson Zaid.

Thirty-seven files.

Again, I printed. Page after page poured out.

Mae Kingsley.

Three files.

I printed those too.

I started to search Templeton, but Beck, who'd come up behind me, watching, put a hand on my arm. Surprised, I looked up. I'd fully intended to print all his parents' files. Maybe his sister's too. Didn't he want to know about them?

He shook his head. "I'm good."

I frowned.

It wasn't just my family who had secrets, didn't he-

"There are some things that are mine, some are theirs."

My face fell.

"It'd be different if I was searching for something or someone. Besides, your family's gonna run the printer out of ink," he joked.

A pit opened in my stomach. Was I being creepy? Like some nosy jerk? His words stung. I could see he was trying to soften the blow, but, not wanting to know? It went against everything we were doing here. What did he mean he was *good?* Not *knowing?* If it was up to me I would have grabbed Josie's and Spade's files next, maybe all of our paperwork. Even our friends'. It could give us so much insight into where they'd come from. Who they were. Why was Rick so silent and stoic? Why'd they choose Nicolette to be a part of a pair? Who thought she'd go well with Vince? What an awful partnership. We could learn the full backstory of Lady Mauve. Didn't Beck want to know any of these things? It was all there. Ripe for the taking.

He and I could print their files and no one would ever know we were here.

Was it so wrong to wanna know?

Not about my parents, I decided. I deserved that information. But on the others... I felt sheepish. Maybe Beck was right. That was crossing some imaginary line. He didn't want to know. Or he didn't think it was our business. I didn't push. Instead, I forced myself to chuckle.

"What can I say? We're a prolific family."

I closed the search engine, letting the others keep their secrets for now. I was about to close the whole system, when something on the desktop caught my eye.

It was labeled 'master list'.

Whoa.

I slid the cursor over and clicked on my mouse. A spreadsheet popped up on the screen.

Names.

Induction dates.

Parabonds.

Witch powers.

Current locations.

It was all there.

"Jackpot." I clicked on print all. I didn't check with Beck. Didn't even look back.

He cleared his throat. "I'm gonna reset the window upstairs and open one of the ones on the ground floor just in case we need to... come back... for more." He eyed the large stack of printouts I was generating.

"Okay."

After Beck stepped out, I couldn't help myself. I clicked the search engine open once more. Just one more little probe. Strictly related to my own family. I typed Abeline Kingsley. Maybe I could learn why she didn't get in? She would want to know.

Zero files located.

Huh. That was weird.

Overhead, I heard Beck's footsteps. He was moving back in my direction. Fearing his arrival, I shut down the system as quickly as I could. I replaced all the elements in the office exactly as I'd found them, or tried to, then scooped up the large batch of paperwork I'd printed and took it out to the truck. Better to grab it now before Beck saw exactly how much information I'd taken. I was no longer sure he'd approve. I dropped the bundle on the floor of the front passenger seat, out of his direct view, and went to repair the shrub under the window. The last thing we needed was my butt print in the foliage leaving a clue we'd been here. I perked up a couple branches to remove the evidence of my fall.

And of course, the ladder Beck used to climb through the window would have to go back to the garage. I moved it prominently in front of the entrance to the Collection so we wouldn't forget it. I looked up at the second story window. The screen was back in place and the window was sealed, so I knew Beck would be back truck-side soon. Time to jet.

I dusted off my hands, about to drop myself into the car, when a big gust of wind blew through Beck's wide-open window and into the cab. The print outs whirled to life on the breeze.

"No!"

They fluttered in every direction, losing proper order. Spanning out into chaos.

"Shoot!"

Twenty or more sheets spilled right out of the car. More followed before I could slam shut the door. Several papers really took flight, blowing straight across the gravel parking area and into the woods behind.

"No, no, no!" I hurried to grab all the sheets in reach and stuffed them hastily under the protective floor mat. The weight held them firm. Having secured the majority, I raced out for the others now blowing around.

Beck was already there, hunting them down.

As he left the building, he'd taken in the scene of spreading papers and discerned what needed to be done. He raced off to catch the most distant fodder. He crashed into the forest behind the building, giving chase as I tracked down the closer stragglers, weaving left and right.

"Got 'em all," I told Beck, looking back. A fistful of papers in both paws. "Beck?"

He should have caught up with the final fly-away papers by now. But he and the missing files were no longer in the gravel lot.

"Beck?" I squinted to see within the forest. Out of the sunlight of the parking lot, the trees and shadows grew dark. I squinted harder. "Beck?" I shoved my last few papers under the mat with the others.

Where was he?

I started to walk towards the trees where I thought I'd seen him duck in.

"Beck? If you lost one or two, don't worry about it," I called. I had no idea which papers had even blown in this direction. Whatever we'd lost, we'd make due. With a window secretly propped open at the collection, we could always print them again. "Seriously, Beck. It's no worries."

For a moment, I hesitated, thinking he might emerge any second. But he didn't. I stepped inside the outstretches of forest, under the cover of branches. The world drained of sunlight and joy. The trees were cool and quiet. An array of blues, deep navy shadows.

"Where are you? Beck?!" This time, the words were more insistent.

A chill went through me.

Where could he be?

Suddenly, there was a clatter of branches. On my left, Beck burst through the shrubs. His hand clutched the remaining wayward papers, but he paid them no mind. His eyes shone wild with excitement.

"Mae, wait 'til you see..."

THREE
THERE'S SOMETHING BACK THERE

WE SECURED the final printouts under the mat in the truck and propped the two-story ladder back in its rightful spot behind the garage, then Back took my hand and led me back into the wooded area. He refused to say more about it, but like a gentleman, as we got deeper into the forest, he pushed branches aside and helped clear a path.

"Where are we going? The papers blew this far?"

"Kind of," he nodded. "Just wait, you'll see it."

"Beck, I-" Behind him, I frowned. We'd finally gotten a whole world of information on my dad, his real name, and thousands of pages to glean for more details. I wanted to dig in and read every factoid, not traipse through the forest to see... what? A funny mushroom? An animal den? Whatever it was, I couldn't care less. But, Beck looked so pleased with what he'd found. Like a kid in a candy store. And I had to admit, he'd been pretty generous with his time. Such a big help. My co-

conspirator and my biggest cheerleader. I knew I should follow him happily, giving him the same sweet energy he'd given me. The best I could do was plod behind.

It would be dinner time soon. We were expected at Aunt Abeline's. That was the excuse we gave for leaving the castle. Our weekly visit. At this rate, I wouldn't be able to look at this stuff we'd just acquired until super late in the evening, and we had a spell-caster test in the morning as well.

"How much further?" I trudged heavily.

"Almost there." Beck glanced back. I forced out a smile, but he wasn't fooled. "I promise, it'll be worth it." He pulled up and kissed our conjoined hands then looked over his fingertips at me and wiggled his eyebrows.

I couldn't help but giggle. "Fine."

He turned to keep going, but this time, he pulled me up with him. I hurried to catch up, but that just encouraged him ahead. Beck picked up his pace, so I did too. Soon, we had both quickened into a run. We were crashing through the branches. His energy was infectious. I gave into the playful joy of being with him. I always gave in to Beck. Then I realized where we must be headed.

The *sound* of the water reached me before I saw it.

Gushing.

Running.

Folding and crashing.

"Ready?" Beck pulled up, grinning like a Cheshire cat. I nodded. He pulled the branches aside.

A waterfall.

In the middle of nowhere.

A beautiful crystal blue pool. White, splashing, splendor tumbling down. A rainbow in the droplets that we saw.

"Oh, wow." I broke away from his handhold to explore the magical setting.

"Right?" Beck grinned. Happy. So vindicated. And proud.

A magical waterfall that only he discovered. We both went right up to the shore. All the world was drowned away in the sound of the falls.

"And look." Beck picked up several smooth stones. He skipped them across the water pool. The first two bounced several times, then dropped into the water, but on the third, the skipping rock flew across the small pond, into the falls, and disappeared. "There's something back there. Maybe a grotto or cave?"

"No way." I started to move around the pool. Was there an opening? The river fell into the lagoon in perpetual motion. Was there really something back there? Behind the water flow? It was impossible to tell. From every direction, the waterfall covered the rocks behind.

"Maybe," Beck shrugged. He clearly thought it was true.

I knelt and touched the surface of the pool. The pond was a good size. The gently lapping water was cool. "Either way," I murmured. I watched as the ripples my fingertips made pushed back against the current from the falling water. The whole place looked untouched, like it had never seen a human hand. It was so beautiful. I didn't want to disturb it, but I also longed to rush in. If only the temperatures hadn't so drastically cooled. Winter was now on its way. "What a perfect place to swim."

Beck grinned. He had thought the same thing.

Suddenly, the sun in the sky shone brighter. Warmer. I felt the heat on my hair. The water was dappled by the rays. I spun back to see Beck, holding his hand in a fist, generating a weather harness, watching me enjoy his perfect sunlit patch of land. The cool blues of the forest gave way to sparkling, sunny reflections.

"*Now* it's the perfect place for a swim." Beck's witch powers enabled him to control the weather, and he'd turned the late fall into a hot summer's day. "You wanna?"

"But we don't have our suits..."

"That never stopped Greg and Marcy." He grinned.

I flushed. Any chance to strip, those two always jumped right in.

Would I go scantily swimming with Beck? The world's most beautiful boyfriend? Here, in the world's most beautiful venue? Manufactured to precisely the most beautiful weather?

Hell yeah, I would.

I yanked off my sneakers with a wild grin. Delighted, Beck laughed. He tugged at his hoodie. Holding the harness in his hand while he undressed was awkward, but he managed to strip the sweatshirt off his chest. It tumbled to the dirt. Next, he dragged his t-shirt over his head. I unzipped my pants and kicked them aside to safety, freeing my plain gray undies. Cotton, with just a touch of lycra.

No lace.

Not even a pattern.

Just a comfy and practical pair.

At least they were clean. No rips or holes. Thank god. But they weren't sexy like Marcy's. I wasn't trying to show off. I'd had no idea Beck might see them. Even now, while we readied for swimming, I stripped as quickly as I could, planning to jump in the second I was disrobed... but that was before I snuck a peek at Beck.

He was having trouble with his shirt.

To keep our sunny vibes in place, Beck couldn't release his balled-up fingers. He had to keep his fist harnessed. But being one-handed while undressing was a little harder and more awkward than he'd anticipated. The jersey he was removing had become stuck around his head. The material bunched up over his ears and he couldn't free himself. The boy was a mess. Adorable and ridiculous. Clothing was stuck everywhere. And underneath, his sleek chest was revealed. His flat abs were on display and so was that fine dribble of hair that journeyed from his belly button into the depths of his pants.

I couldn't help but giggle.

In another strong undressing choice, he'd already unbuttoned his bottom half. The top button and flaps of his pants hung dangerously open on his hips. Beck was half naked and trapped.

"A little help?" He flopped around.

I quickly folded my pants and my t-shirt on top of a large rock. I had wanted to run into the water, knowing full well that my black bra and my cotton undies also revealed a lot of skin, but Beck was so terribly trapped in his clothing he had missed any opportunity to leer. Even though I wanted to run, I couldn't leave him twisted up as he was. He might never get free. As he shook and shimmied his torso, the unbuttoned pants fell off his waist, dropping his bottoms around his ankles.

It was the cutest thing I'd ever seen.

"Oh my god," I couldn't help but giggle coming to his aid. "Just release the harness."

"I don't want you to catch a chill." He wiggled out of his pant legs, kicking one side clean off like a wet dog after a bath.

"Just hold still."

Beck squirmed in all directions. Impossible to wrangle in. I pulled the final bit of fabric over his ears and suddenly, his head and shoulders popped free.

"Thanks." He lightly tossed his hair out of his eyes, happy to be released. Then he caught sight of his helper, me, in just my underwear. "Hey, wow. Look at you."

His eyes raked over my skin.

I flushed all at once. My hands covered my soft belly, protecting myself from his observation. I'd never been quite so on display. Since our status as a couple had become official we'd kissed and rubbed and touched and cuddled what felt like every inch of each other's bodies. We'd had some hot and heavy sessions in my dorm, in the library stacks, and of course, on that trusty elevator, but this time, there was no clothing or sheets or books to choicely hide any flaws. All my weaknesses were revealed.

"It's not a matching set," I admitted, embarrassed that his first glimpse of me in lingerie was un-matching and cotton.

This was not how the romance was supposed to unfold.

All at once.

In bright sunlight.

Nothing hidden.

"A matching set? Who freakin' cares." Beck stepped towards me. "You look incredible." His arm snaked around me, pulling me in.

Skin to skin.

We both vibrated with pleasure. His body was almost hot to the touch.

Even more impressive, he'd reeled me in with one palm. The other hand still maintained our perfect weather. I looked incredible? With that kind of praise, I could breathe free. Beck always knew just what to say. Happily, my arms floated around his neck. My covered breasts squished against his bare chest as he playfully bent down to be closer to my lips.

"Hi, parabond." His voice was sexy.

"Hi," I whispered back.

Then we kissed.

Deeply.

His tongue slipped into my mouth, searching, longing, caressing.

Lost in this moment. I didn't want it to end.

He tasted so sweet. I could have stayed there forever, the hot sun radiating on our bare shoulders, pressed skin-to-skin. Finally, Beck pulled back a little, but not to end things, to take another glance.

"You look amazing," he assured me. His tone made me believe him. His blue eyes fell to the curves of my breasts pushed up against his chest. He let out a small, contented sigh. "This is the best."

"I don't know. With all your flailing, I didn't really get my chance."

"To what?"

"To, you know, see what you're working with."

He gave his own shy grin, then stepped back.

It also exposed my body, but I ignored my insecurities, appreciating the moment to really take Beck in. What a perfect specimen. Beck had no reason to be shy. His body was strong and straight and lean. While he didn't have some crazy pecs or six-pack abs like a super-hero, his arms and shoulders and forearms were clearly defined. The muscles pulsed under his skin.

Ready.

Willing.

Able.

And that little trail of hair... the most delicious road map I'd ever seen. A trip I'd one day like to take.

Playfully, he spun around, slowly, showing off his strapping back and bum in his form fitting boxer briefs. He averted his eyes for a second as if he might be nervous, but really, he was gearing up to give me a playful side-eye, out from under tousled hair, my favorite of his many smiles.

Seeing him so confident and comfortable gave me the support I needed to finally relax. The twinkle in his eye told me he loved every curve that I offered. Finding new courage, I gave him a playful swivel as well. He let out a low whistle of appreciation, then I approached, ready to climb back into his arms.

"Are you ready?" Beck asked, closing the distance.

"I'm ready," I purred, expecting his kiss, but Beck had other plans. He dropped his shoulder and tossed me up, over his arm. My feet kicked up in the air.

"Oh my god! Beck! What are you doing?!" I squealed. I tried to squirm. But already, we were both headed for the water. Beck ran forward, plunging us head first into the lagoon. We both shrieked as he stumbled and fell. The water splashed up around us. Immediately, we were soaked to our skin. The water was deceptively cold.

"Beck!"

While his witch harness had raised the temperatures of the air, the *water* had had a month to grow cold. It was not a pleasant swim.

"It's freezing!"

"Come on!" He shouted, diving further into the pond. He was intent on seeing what was behind the secret waterfall. We'd come this far... I quickly followed. My heart beat wildly at the shock of the cold. I was a stronger swimmer than Beck, although he was taller, so we were a good aquatic match. In the end, I was first to arrive at the falls. The water splashed down, foaming up, surrounding us and we were lucky to discover the sting of the cold wasn't as bad here as when we'd first jumped in the pond. We looked up at the gushing water.

"Ready?" He asked.

I nodded.

"Here we go!"

We pushed through the falling water, Beck and I both blindly moving forward in tandem. In a moment, we were through. Beck was right. There was more behind the falls. We both looked around in surprise. It was a grotto cut into the rocks. A bigger cave on dry land too. Totally hidden from the outside world.

I swam the final few strokes from the lagoon to the bumpy ledge of the rock wall. There was so much more to explore. We both climbed out, dripping wet in our skimpy clothes. The undies were stretched and sopping, but luckily, they continued to hold. I smoothed back my wet hair and took in the sight.

A secret cave that had been here for thousands of years.

Were we the first people ever inside?

I looked to Beck, crazy impressed. He wrapped his arms around my waist and kissed my shoulder as we both took in details. Maybe he was thinking the same thing. We were the first. This was our magical kingdom. No one knew about this place except me and him.

"How big does it go?" He wondered, taking my hand. Together, we walked back to explore.

"Wow," I murmured. It was huge, and quite defined. The walls were smooth rock. Mighty sturdy.

"I hope there's nothing living in here." Beck playfully mimed taking a bite. I swatted him.

"Why'd you say that!" But we both giggled. Nothing moved, or came out of the shadows to greet us, so the joke was alright. Our exploring took us all the way to the back of the space. It was our own special, secret compartment. Closed off from the rest of the world.

"This part's almost like a bed," Beck noted of a flat area of rock.

I checked it out.

It just looked like every other stone to my eye. But I was game. "Let's see. Is it comfy?" I lay down on the surface.

"Let me try," Beck joined me. "It's hard," he complained.

"Rock hard," I laughed. "And there's only room for one!" I shoved his gut with surprising force. Caught off guard, he toppled to the ground. "Oh no!" I laughed and shook my head. "Beck, I'm sorry." I hadn't intended that he would actually fall. But now I'd thrown down the gauntlet. Beck's eyes lit up, and he leapt back over me. Like a cat, he landed on the far side of our little rock bed. Now I was the one facing out. "No, wait," I begged. "Wait, stop."

Beck wolfishly grinned, not waiting at all. He started pushing me straight off.

"Wait!" I battled helplessly against him, giggling and clawing away from the same fate as him. "That was for throwing me in the water!" I told him. We both knew he was too strong. "Truce! Truce!" I wailed.

Beck laughed and slid me further.

Dragging me inch by inch.

He could have easily shoved me to the ground, but we were both playing. He pushed me just enough to keep me guessing and I fought valiantly against the pressure to stay on our little rock mattress.

"You wouldn't push a girl!" I squealed. "We can both fit, we both fit fine!"

"Alright," he agreed, letting me live atop of the rock kingdom by his side. He shifted around, forgiving my transgression. "We both fit." He agreed.

"We fit," I repeated, puffing, cuddling together.

"You and me." We settled.

"You and me," I mirrored. I shivered. We cuddled closer, but our wet fabric and hair and skin brought a chill into our rock home.

"You're shaking."

"No, I'm good." I cuddled deeper, stealing his body heat. "Just a little."

"Guess my sun's not too effective in here." He let go of his harness. The sunlight streaming in through the falls disappeared.

We fell into darkness.

"No, that's much worse," I laughed. My teeth chattered quite loud.

"Let's get out of here." Beck helped me up and we went back to the way we'd come in.

"We'll come back here when it's warmer," he told me. "Next spring. Or maybe in summer."

I glanced at the back of his head, unbeknownst to him, a new warmth flooding in.

Next spring.

Beck was already considering what we'd do in the future.

In *our* future.

Months from now.

Spring and summer.

Like it was nothing.

Like it was a *given*. Of course we'd still be a couple at the start of next summer.

He looked back, slightly worried at my pause, but I grinned.

"I can't wait," I agreed.

"You okay to swim out?"

"I don't see another way..." I shrugged.

"Well, we could try to think of something, maybe there's another exit-"

My face broke into a smile and I shoved him off the rock shoulder into the pool below us. He hit the water mid-flail. Beck shot back to the surface in surprise.

"You said truce!"

"I did," I dove in right after, not giving him a chance to take retribution. I popped back to the surface beside him. "About the rock bed. *That* was for throwing me in the lake." I told him and he splashed me. Playfully, squealing, and laughing, we swam back to our clothes on the beach. Both the wardrobes were there, Beck's strewn about, mine piled neatly in one stack.

"You threw me in twice!" He complained again, as we climbed out of the lagoon.

"Yeah, well, you threw me in *first* and that's twice as bad!" My chattering teeth had returned, so I desperately pulled my jacket around my wet shoulders. He immediately reignited his weather harness. The hot sun flooded the forest. He grabbed his own sweat shirt and pulled it around me. He rubbed the fabric over my back to help dry and warm me. "No, you need that." I tried to give him his hoodie back, but he tucked it around my arms even more.

"I'm good," he said. "I'm great. We've gotta warm you. Are you okay?"

We could both see the goosebumps on my skin. I

nodded. "Whatever you do, don't drop the sun," I warned.

"I won't. Come here." He tucked my wet head under his chin. "Let me help." We swayed and rocked together.

Cuddled.

Warming.

The initial shock of the water temperature and cool cave had passed. We were calm and safe in the sun on the shore.

"I promise not to do it, again," I told him.

"Which part?"

"My rock bed is your bed. And I'll never throw you into a lake without checking in first."

"Good."

"What about you?"

"What about me?" He grinned. Seeing my mock-displeasure, he tucked me back into his arms. "*Okay*, I promise I won't throw you in any more lakes. I got a little excited," he confessed. His hands roamed over my back and shoulders. In the sun, I had almost warmed back up to room temperature. The shakes disappeared. Then, his voice thickened like honey as his fingers continued to search over my skin. "You're just so sexy."

I felt a different type of energy buzz between us. It started in my legs.

Beck's rubbing had shifted.

His touch took on a new, more romantic massaging. He fondled my back and shoulders, applying pressure through the fabrics wrapped around me. I quietly let him. We stood so close.

"Mae, I think you're amazing."

"Even now?" I murmured. "After I pushed you out of the bed?"

"Especially now. So warm and cozy."

"I've been pretty cold."

He let that comment go.

The jokes disappeared.

He was unwilling to let me derail him. Brought me along to where he was headed. Intent on taking me with him. I let his breathing take control.

He touched me gently.

Sometimes roughly.

Always watching for approval. I gave it handily.

"You make me so crazy," he murmured, his mouth brushing down to caress my neck. As his lips passed, his voice growled low in my ear.

I let out a low moan.

Right back at you.

I couldn't stand his teasing. I found his lips and I kissed him with intention, thrusting my body forward, desperate to close any space between our limbs.

Our arms embraced. Snaking up.

Caressing.

He felt so good as he tugged me and teased me. I kissed him deeply, feeling the strength in his limbs. Vibrations of pleasure soared over my skin.

Almost naked, we made out beside the water.

Then, Beck leaned down. Even with one hand still

gripped in the harness, he found my bottom. With precision, he cupped his hand under me, then bent over slightly. Suddenly, I found myself lifted in the air. He picked me up with one hand and one harness and I let him. Eagerly, I wrapped my legs around his torso. He raised me high, held my butt, carried me up to his height. Mouth to mouth. Face to face. Hip to hip.

Greedy, I giggled. I kissed him deeply.

Our bodies held in position, but only for a moment… it turned out, one handed, he couldn't hold me up in the sexy aerial pose.

"Oh no."

We collapsed, giggling. Falling on each other.

Messy.

Playful.

Scrambling.

But neither of us disengaged any parts of our bodies. We hit the sand. And instead, I crawled over on all fours. The rest of me found him. He sat up and then pulled me on top of him. Onto his lap. Once again, body parts all aligned in a row.

"Hi," I grinned.

My legs wrapped around him. This time, sitting on him, his arms didn't have to support me. I could feel him beneath me. Our torsos so close. Only the flimsiest of fabric between our parts down below.

The passion rose up to greet me.

I groaned, now feeling Beck deeply.

Breast to breast.

Lap to lap.

Soul to soul.

On my upper half, Beck fought through the sweatshirt and jacket to put his lips on my collarbone. His tongue raked across my wet skin. Every inch that he nibbled sweetly sang. Begging for more. He pulled back the clothing, revealing my wet bra and body. Kissing as he traveled across my trembling curves.

"Beck," I moaned, my head falling back, running my fingers through his hair.

I drew his face up to mine. His eyes were so beautiful, so deep and open.

"Hey," his grin undid me.

So attentive. So alluring.

We kissed again.

He held my butt and slid me up, pushing gently. I felt him there, as I moved. Strong beneath my legs.

"Beck-"

Gravity slid me down but he didn't let me go. His strong grasp pulled me higher. Grabbed and rocked me. Pushing me forward on him.

"Beck-"

Riding.

Grinding.

The tiny fabrics between our legs barely holding us contained.

"Oh god," he moaned as the rhythm rocked and rolled him. "Mae. *Oh*."

"Beck," suddenly I felt urgent. This was all happening so quickly. Too quickly. "Beck, wait..."

He dragged me forward. We were both riding on the wave.

"Beck, slow down." I slowed the friction. Delayed the action. "Just, wait a minute."

"What is it?" Beck finally realized what I'd been saying. He opened his eyes. "What's going on?" He dropped the rhythm. Attentive. Listening. Our bodies pulsed where we sat, entwined.

He was so close.

He was ready.

This was right. So hot.

So juicy.

I wasn't ready. He was ready.

But, I wasn't ready.

Wait.

Was I ready?

No... I wasn't. *Yes, I was.*

Well, I-

No.

Maybe soon, but... I wasn't ready.

Not now.

Not this second.

I had stopped us in our tracks.

I had no words to explain how I felt. I had no clue what I wanted. Everything felt good. Great. Amazing. I liked him so much. But I felt compelled to slow down.

It was all too much.

I just wasn't ready to ring the big bell.

"Let's -" I fumbled, embarrassed. "Sorry."

"Hey, it's okay."

As soon as I'd said it, I wished that I hadn't. I'd said both nothing and said everything. There was no taking it back. Tears of frustration leaked out of my eyes.

"What's going on?" Beck leaned in, trying to get me to open up.

I wanted every inch of him. Every thrust. I really wanted it. With every fiber of my being. He was exactly what I wanted. So why did I ask him to stop?

The vexation washed over me. I was awash in confusion. But Beck stayed motionless. He didn't recoil or frown. He didn't try to push things forward, my hips still straddling his hard body. He just waited for me to say more. To offer how I felt.

Except, I had no idea what I was doing.

There was nothing more to say. Or words to explain what I wanted.

Because I wanted everything.

And less.

And more.

All at once.

I dropped my head on his shoulder, silent, unsure how to approach this. Or where we might go from there.

"It's okay," he finally whispered. Which was true, even if we didn't want it to be. "We've got time. We can wait." Our lower halves remained frozen in space as I leaned on his hot skin. He was careful not to flinch.

"You must think I'm such a tease," I said, finally.

"I think you're special."

"God, why are you so nice?"

"That's what a boyfriend is."

I hugged him close as a thank you for understanding, but also, because I didn't want to release him. I didn't want things between us to stop for one second, even if I wasn't ready for us to go all-the-way. I wasn't sure *what* I was ready for.

The movement of his warm hands had gone from tender comfort to urgent desire and now back to tender comfort once more, rubbing my shoulders. I climbed off his lap and he lay out on the shore, pulling his jeans on, letting me tuck in beside him.

"We just got carried away," he told me.

"Yeah," I agreed, *we both did.* "I'm sorry, I..." I trailed off, knowing full well I was complicit in the terms. Our bodies throbbed with unrequited passion, but Beck didn't try to spur on another round.

I was thankful.

I guess the truth was, before I would go there, before *we* would go there, there were things I wanted to know. Things we had never spoken out loud. And I wanted to be more sure.

"Have you... did you and someone ever... I mean, are you... experienced?" The words tumbled out. What did I want to know? Was Beck a virgin? Had he had sex with Josie? He definitely had sex with Josie. Lots of sex with Josie? Had he had a bunch of romantic partners? Was I his only virgin girlfriend?

"I have experience," he agreed, nodding slightly,

smoothing my hair from my face. Looking in my eyes. "Is that okay?"

I nodded.

"But this is your first..?"

"You're my first serious boyfriend," I told him. We both nodded. "I'm on the pill," I blurted. "I've been on since I was like thirteen, for like, you know, period control. My cramps, and well... yeah... so that's taken care of. It's good for other reasons... but also good for that, good for pregnancy, for not getting pregnant... just so you know."

Why did I say that?

It felt icky and awkward to tell my birth control plan to my partner. But, if we were going to go there physically, it felt like something worth telling my guy. If we were going to get there, really get there, I should be able to say these things out loud.

"Good to know," Beck agreed.

"So I'm ready. I'm just... not... *there*... yet."

"But you will be. At some point."

I nodded. "Is that dumb? God, that sounds dumb to say."

I wasn't experienced.

Not like him.

Not like Josie.

That first green light... that was a big deal.

"Okay," he acknowledged. "We can wait. We'll wait it out," he assured me.

I nodded again, although I wasn't sure what '*it*' we were waiting for.

Just that it hadn't arrived.

We stared out over the sparkling water. The majestic waterfall pummeled down.

"We could live out here forever, as cave people. Forget the coven and the castle. Bathe in the falling water shower, forage around," he told me.

I smiled at the thought. "I'd grow us a garden," I offered. "Everyday could be bright and sunny. How's your hand?" I wondered, picking his still-harnessing palm up and examining the fingers he held tight in a ball. The harness he was creating was fairly low-grade, refracting a little extra sunlight was nothing, but every witch power required energy and that effort could exhaust you, and he'd been holding the warm sunny weather for a while. "You can release it."

"Get dressed and I will."

Our swimming wardrobes were mostly dry by now.

"We should probably go," I realized. As it was, we were already late for dinner with Aunt Abeline. I hadn't noticed the time when we were busy with... other suggestions. As we pulled on our clothes, I leaned over and kissed Beck's cheek.

"What was that for?"

"Nothing," I smiled. "I just like you."

"I like you, too." He grinned.

As we walked back to his truck together, I couldn't stop smiling. Things were good. We were a happy couple. In the search for information about my parents, we'd found some new answers. I knew my dad's name!

And Beck was waiting for me. He understood. He was looking forward to our future.

One day I'd be ready.

Our classes and our training at the High Council were barreling forward. Things weren't just good in my life, they were the best they'd ever been.

FOUR

TWO TEENAGERS IN LOVE

"AUNT ABELINE!" I called out ahead of us as Beck and I stomped up the stairs to her apartment over the Tartan Spice Shack. She had settled into the new digs pretty quickly, but one of the things I missed most about the lake house that had been destroyed in the earthquake was the swish of the kitchen curtains the moment your car crunched into the gravel driveway as you arrived. You never had to announce yourself there. Your presence was clear. But, while insurance paid for the cottage to be rebuilt (the hand-of-god clause covered it, no one mentioned to the insurance men that the house was destroyed by a bunch of witches), this small one-bedroom suited my aunt pretty well. We'd lived in a lot of rustic apartments just like this one. She'd been here for a little over two weeks.

"In here," Aunt Abeline called from her kitchen, as if there was any doubt. I grinned over my shoulder at Beck, then popped through her door.

"Hello!" We greeted the others, happily.

"About time," Aunt Abeline breezily complained.

"You didn't want to sit here, did you?" Lady Blue Moon worried, already staking her claim at the table.

"They did not," Aunt Abeline threatened, motioning the older witch right back on her hind quarters. "People who are late to the party get no dibs on the seating arrangements. Pizza's already been ordered. Hi, Beck."

"Hi Aunt Abeline," he grinned sheepishly. The boy was just as late as me, but of course *he* wasn't frowned at or blamed. He kissed my aunt's cheek.

"Thank you for dinner, and sorry." I snacked on a nearby bowl of carrots. We plopped down at the table, grabbing ringside seats to catch their Scrabble game mid-swing.

"Where were you?" Blue Moon wondered.

Beck and I glanced at each other.

Aunt Abeline *tsk-tsked*. "Bonnie, you should know better. You never ask two teenagers in love where they've been."

I shone bright red and looked down. Two teenagers in *love*.

Beck and I had never admitted such things.

I wanted to crawl under the table and die, but Beck just tossed his hair and grinned. "Very wise, Aunt Abeline," he winked. The ladies blushed in return.

The game was already two-thirds over. No surprise, Aunt Abeline would handily win.

"You know you don't have to always play scrabble,

Bonnie," In the presence of Aunt Abeline, I called Lady Blue Moon by her non-coven name. We weren't supposed to mention coven secrets around non-members. Names included. "Abeline does know other games."

Aunt Abeline looked up and frowned, but I shrugged and grinned. She'd fired shots first, teasing me and Beck.

"I know," Lady Blue Moon plunked her word onto the board.

Harried.

With the double word square and a cross-word addition, Blue Moon's effort tallied thirty-six points. Not bad. But no bingo. One of the letters in her word had already been in play.

"So why do it if you know you're gonna lose?" I wondered.

Aunt Abeline played next.

Atemoyas.

Triple word score.

And a bingo for using up all her letter squares.

Eighty-nine points added on to her score.

Lady Blue Moon shrugged. "One day, I'll win. And that will be oh-so satisfying. I'll know I stayed with it, I played the course, even if it was hard."

"Sounds delusional. Cut and run while you can." I laughed.

The tiles were getting low. We could all see, this wouldn't be her win.

"Oh, would you mind giving me a lift home

tonight? My car's in the repair shop," she added, rear-ranging her letters. Some lunatic drove it out of an exploding volcano, I thought to myself. Vince and I were responsible for the damage. But she wasn't looking for blame, just a ride, so I nodded to my friend. "At your Dad's," Blue Moon added to Beck.

"He'll take good care." He finished the bowl of carrots in one bite, crunching loudly. We all looked at him. "What?"

"We're about to have pizza."

"I'll eat that too. I worked up quite an appetite this afternoon." He shrugged.

I blushed.

"Young man," Abeline frowned. "That's TMI. Too much information," she clarified to me and Blue Moon.

"We know what TMI is, Aunt Abeline."

But Beck was undeterred. He looked over Blue Moon's shoulder, pointing at her scrabble rack. "You could do *plank*."

"*No helps*," Aunt Abeline and I said at once. Our rebuke was so uniform and absolute, Beck jumped back in surprise.

"Alright, alright." Instead of fighting, he retreated and dropped his head into the fridge looking for more munchies.

"The Kingsleys feel quite strongly that we should do it all ourselves," Blue Moon warned him.

Beck put up two innocent palms in surrender, one

of the hands already holding more baby carrots. "Just trying to help."

"Where are your keys?" I asked him. "If Blue- if Bonnie is coming back with us, I want to clean up the truck before she gets in it."

Beck dug into his pocket and tossed them across the room. In a smooth motion, I caught them midair.

"Don't do that on my account," Blue Moon said without looking up from the board.

The game was wrapping up. We could all feel the impending tension.

"It's fine. Be back in a jiffy."

"*Climate*. Final letters." Aunt Abeline announced. She put the tiles down on the board. They tallied the scores. Aunt Abeline had almost doubled Blue Moon's record.

Finished the calculations, the witch sat back with a sigh. "Maybe next time."

"I'm in on the next one." Beck immediately started flipping tiles back over. "You ladies are going down!" He tossed his hair.

Both women grinned.

"Mae, are you joining?" Aunt Abeline wondered.

"You go ahead," I told her, "I'll be back in a minute." I slipped back into the hallway and down to the street below.

"Aw man, I got the *Q*," I heard Beck moan.

All you need now is the U, I knew Aunt Abeline would reply. *Or possibly an I, for Qi, in a jam.* I could hold the entire imagined conversation. In her mind, all the tough letters meant good things. Higher scores. I wanted to hurry to get back.

I jogged down to street level. In the truck, I only needed to neaten one thing: our new pile of paperwork. Blue Moon couldn't know where we'd been. Currently, the printouts sat in a suspicious lump under the passenger seat floor mat. As a hiding spot, it wasn't exactly slick.

Where to relocate them?

I checked the truck bed and the glove box, but neither would work.

It wasn't a smart idea to keep it all in one stack. Instead, I divided the paper work up. I slid some files under my mat, more under Beck's. Even a fair share under the mats in the back seat. I bulked up the amount of papers at each location until even one more sheet would give away the bulge. But it wasn't enough. I still had more to hide. In fact, I still had the entire master list. The truck was already full. Where could I shove the rest? I looked at the stoop at my aunt's doorway. There on the ground was a welcome mat.

I grabbed an errant plastic bag from the cab and slipped the extra papers inside, spacing them evenly in two piles. Finally, I slid the entire package under the mat. It laid nice and flat. No one would know the list was there and Beck and I could come back and grab it easily, next time we were in town. Just as I finished admiring my handiwork, the pizza delivery person arrived.

"I'll take that." I paid and tipped the driver,

slammed the truck doors, and brought our dinner up to the rest of the clan.

"All set?" They asked as I returned. Quickly followed by "ooh, pizza!" And my task was forgotten.

I smiled. "Everything's perfect," I agreed.

And for the second time that evening, I really thought that it was.

FIVE

A + A IS TWO

AFTER SUCH A FULL DAY, I fell asleep the second my head hit the pillow.

In my dream, I entered a coven classroom. Several of my fellow classmates also studied at the desks. At the front of the room, Lady Blue Moon held the floor as she taught basic math.

First addition and subtraction, then multiplication.

She ran the drills. Trying to solidify our skills. But, instead of using chalk or whiteboard markers to draw out the equations, she glued Scrabble tiles on the board. And then pointed to their small etched numbers in the corner. They stuck to the wall.

Not with glue. There wasn't glue on the squares, per say.

She simply raised the tiles and they just stuck where they were without any noticeable adhesive. The little wooden squares held seamlessly, so the rest of us could work on the equations.

I typed all the answers into my phone.

Most of my classmates sat attentive. Hilde, Greg, Vince and Ferris. Beck and Ethan perched in the row behind us, sitting backwards over chairs. Everyone listened and discussed the answers. Nicolette passed the classroom door again and again, always hungrily looking in, but each time she passed us, over and over, she became less likely to come through the door. I could feel from my group, they didn't want her there.

I tried to be immersed like the others, but I'd hidden so many secret documents underneath my seat cushion that my chair soared up into the air. I was roosted an entire head taller than Beck, the tallest guy in the room, my butt firmly propped up on all my papers. Still, somehow no one seemed to notice this was weird.

Dream logic.

Everything was wrong and fine all at once.

Suddenly, a man stuck his head into our classroom. Although he looked in our direction, I couldn't see his face. Just as quickly, he popped back out.

"Did you see that?" I asked the others, but no one answered me.

"A + A is two. Can't you see?" Lady Blue Moon was pointing at the Scrabble tiles.

Silently, the faceless man walked away.

"No, wait."

I followed him out of the classroom into the hall, but the second I arrived in the corridor, I wasn't in a hallway. The whole room had morphed. It was just nothingness. Space and time. I was traveling through it. So had he, somewhere. I couldn't see him. Uncertain which direction to head in, I slowed.

I turned to my left.

Wrong way.

Over my right shoulder, there he was!

The man was departing, disappearing into the night. His back was to me. His face was blurry. He never looked in my direction, but I knew who it was, in the depths of my bones. And now, *I knew his name.*

"Wesson Zaid!"

The faceless man froze. He didn't turn. He didn't dare.

I was staring at the back of my murderous father.

"This is for Sierra!"

A shaft of lightning scalded through the air and struck where he was standing. At the point of impact, a huge explosion ripped through the empty space.

Ker-ploom!

I shot straight up in my bed.

"Mmm. What happened? Are you okay?" Beck wondered, sleepy. He was a common fixture now, sleeping beside me in my bed.

"Nothing. You're fine. It was nothing. Go back to sleep."

He nodded, turning over. Probably not even awake for this conversation.

But I didn't settle. It wasn't nothing.

It was a vision.

And I was a dreamcast.

I opened the notebook on my bedside table, as was my habit, and wrote down all that I'd seen. While it was still fresh and certain, I tried to record every tiny detail.

SIX
IS THAT WHAT YOU WANT?

BY THE TIME Beck awoke to his morning alarm, I had put almost a full hour of reading into the new files. The archives from the Konya Thomas Special Collection were fascinating. I had already learned a great deal.

Wesson Zaid was a lie-guard, for one.

His entire family was born and raised here in town. I might have a set of paternal grandparents somewhere in the vicinity. No aunts or uncles. My dad was an only child. At least, from what I could find. Either that, or his siblings weren't deemed fit for the High Council. Like Aunt Abeline, they might have been canceled out of the files.

I'd put his new details on the spread Beck lovingly called my 'murder wall', a visual collection of all of the information I'd been gathering about my family and my mother since we'd arrived at the witches' school. It was the kind of thing serial killers did in the movies we watched. All that was missing was the connective red yarn. But I didn't care. It was the easiest way to get all the information in the same spot. I didn't have a picture of his face yet, but the new name was a great place to start. Soon, the other parts of the story would resolve and I would learn all my father's details.

Then I'd see to it that justice prevailed.

Zaid should never have messed with a Kingsley.

I knew in my heart, he would pay.

I would make him.

"Hey, parabond," Beck murmured. His hand clamped down on the snooze button. The incessant bleating came to a halt. His voice was thick and sleepy, his bedhead running wild, but he dragged a finger across his sleepy eyes and smiled.

"Hey, yourself," I smiled.

"Come on in," he offered.

I climbed across the covers to wiggle back under his arm.

The High Council dorms only provided single occupancy beds, but Beck and I didn't mind the close quarters. We were happy to cuddle in. I had heard that Greg and Marcy actually carted his mattress down the hallway and then pushed the two single beds together to make it double-wide. That made the room wall-to-wall bed. It was a clever work-around to the solo accommodations, but for now Beck and I were happy to huddle up and be tight.

"How'd you sleep?" He sighed. "Did you dream? I kinda remember you waking."

I recounted last night's vision. As a dreamcast, it was important to focus on even the tiniest detail. We never knew when some specific moment might come into play in some future event. Other pieces of the vision were there purely for more dramatic license, or as an amplification of my fears or insecurities. I couldn't control all the things that came into my brain.

"Is that what you want?" Beck asked when I had finished my report of the vision. He sat up, more awake, taking me in. "To blow up your Dad?"

"No, of course not. I want him to pay for what he's done." I avoided eye contact. We could both hear my anger flicker, then hide behind acceptable terms. There was a violence behind those words. It was not an empty threat. The person who poisoned my mother would pay. Even if he was blood related.

"Mae, you don't even know it was him... *if* it's him." Beck frowned. "Wesson Zaid might not even be your dad."

"I *know*." I cut the conversation short. And with it, our cuddle. "Are you ready to get up?" It was way too early to disagree. I hadn't even read half the information I'd gathered. I'd reserve judgment until I did. But Beck should also refrain from defending him. He could be safeguarding the worst man in the world. I stood up, pulling away from him, more proof we were done with the conversation. "I could definitely eat breakfast."

Beck took the hint. Groggy, he shrugged and ambled out of bed towards the bathroom. "I just meant that we should know for sure... before we do something we'd regret." He chose the words carefully, as he opened the bathroom door.

"Hey! Someone's in here!" Nicolette threw her weight behind the door from the bathroom side. It smashed back in Beck's face. She was probably naked or in a skimpy towel or something.

"Sorry Nicolette!" I called out through the doorway and gave Beck a frown.

"But I have to go," he looked stricken. "My morning pee!"

"Guess it's back to your own dorm."

"You could have a bit of sympathy," Beck complained, wiggling into his bottoms.

"Well, it's her bathroom too, and you didn't think to knock. No one said she has to share with you."

The idea of Beck doing a morning walk of shame was pretty cute.

"I'll see you down at breakfast," I told him. I gave him a quick kiss, then he bolted for his room. I was actually a little grateful for the reprieve. Beck was a really awesome person in a million different ways, but we weren't on the same page about my dad.

Wesson Zaid.

The second I'd heard the name, something inside me switched gears.

I knew exactly who he was. He was definitely my father. Some time in our past he had loved and lost my mother. And he'd used a potion of lover's pall to take the most important woman in my life far away. He destroyed my mother. And I would make him pay. The when and the how of that justice were the only questions to debate.

"Sorry, Nicolette," I gently rapped on the shared doorway. No answer. "Beck's gone," I added, as if that should matter. I heard a shuffle inside. Nicolette was still in there.

"You know, the dorm rooms are only built for one person, and the bathroom's built for two. Not three." She complained through the wood without opening the door.

"I know," I conceded, trying to be sympathetic. She was correct, but only to a point. The High Council couldn't control who I put in my bed. Or who I cuddled with in the morning. Beck would be here if I wanted him. Still, I also wanted to make peace with my moody neighbor.

"I'm headed down to the cafeteria for some breakfast. Wanna meet me in the hall?"

For a moment, there was silence.

"I'm not hungry," she said.

Then, deep into the other bedroom, her footsteps disappeared.

SEVEN

THE COURT OF OYER AND TERMINER

"OKAY, that's it for today. Make sure you read through chapter seven for tomorrow," Lady Gray dismissed the group after lessons. I looked around at the other student witches. Sloane stacked her tablet and her textbooks neatly before she swooped them into her arms. Greg and Marcy elected to carry neither books, nor writing utensils. How they ever passed the quizzes having taken no notes or referred to any text books, I had no idea. And on the other side of the room, Nicolette was clearly still a little mad. She made a point to make zero eye contact with either Beck or me through the entire social justice seminar.

It wasn't as big a loss to either of us as she'd hoped.

Rick and Vince chatted amicably by the door. As the school year had progressed, they'd become pretty good mates. Little Hilde looked wistfully back and forth between them. Every now and then she let out a little song of her own.

Whew-whew.

A quiet whistle. Under her breath. As if only she could hear the tune.

We'd made it through to the end of the day, everyone was intent on leaving, the lesson over. Even Lady Gray was headed out, happy to be done, but, before she could check out completely, I headed her off at the pass. I'd developed some questions that needed answers, so I stopped her at the door.

"Lady Gray, do you have a minute? It's not... school related."

"Oh? Well, I... " She glanced at her watch then strove to give me her full attention. "Sure." She tucked her single streak of gray hair behind her ear. "What is it, Mae?"

"The Witch's Tribunal," I stuttered. "How do you get someone tried? Or arrested?"

"Do you have something you'd like to report?" My teacher frowned.

"No. I-" I flushed. "I read something. The Court of Oyer and Terminer..."

"To hear and determine, yes." Lady Gray nodded. "There are several layers to the High Council Judicial System. Of course there are societal laws outside our walls, secular matters – don't steal, don't murder, that sort of thing – with local, state and federal cops. But we also have coven laws for our particular magic: what can and can't be done, how we should act as a unit to keep everyone safe. The Oyer rules. How one must act according to changing coven requirements. The contracts you sign, for example. If you break them, what impacts you'll endure. They all layer on top of each other."

"So if you break one law, you probably broke another?"

"Most criminals do."

"And after a trial at the Court of Oyer and Terminer you're found guilty or not guilty?"

"No. Justified or improper. In witch law, you have to prove yourself against what you're accused of. Or, I should say, your magistrate will." She glanced at her watch again. "Perhaps I need to do a whole class on witch justice. It's a fascinating landscape. There's parallel due process, even jury selection."

I'd heard of that one. "The Coven Five."

"Very good. But, don't worry yourself. The use of the Terminer System is increasingly rare. Child runs a tight ship," she winked.

Cornelius Child.

The leader of the High Council.

Officially, his title was Headmaster of Judicial Studies at the High Council, but we'd learned in time that he ran the whole coven. Child and his group of wise elder witches, which included Lady Gray. Of course she'd sing his praises.

"And if someone doesn't like what we're doing, they're free to move on from this home. It's not like the coven will hunt you down or make you suffer. We're interested in keeping people happy and safe. You included, Mae." With that, she'd hoped to end things.

"But what if a witch did something especially heinous?" I dragged her back.

"What kind of heinous?"

"I don't know." I knew very well. "Murder, let's say."

For a moment I'd piqued her attention, but now she frowned. "What you're suggesting is very rare." Lady Gray ebbed herself out of our conversation. I had more questions, but we both knew she was ready to bail. "Tell you what, I'll put it on the curriculum," she told me.

I nodded. I could see trying to push it further today wouldn't serve me. I let it go and released her from conversation. "That sounds good. Thanks."

I wouldn't gain anymore today.

Gray nodded and headed down the hall. The others had already headed to dinner. She might have thought she was being comforting letting me know the Council wasn't in the habit of handing out drastic retributions, but she had misread the situation. I *wanted* Wesson Zaid to pay. By killing Sierra with a poison that was undetectable in the secular world, so far he'd all but escaped judgment for his actions. The doctors didn't know what had killed her. As a murderer, he couldn't be blamed.

But I knew what he'd done.

So would the witches of the High Council.

It was up to them to dole out the justice in this case. I sought vindication. I wouldn't rest until I got it. Round and round the same arguments marched in my head. I was so lost in thought I barely noticed my surroundings as I loaded up my plate with butter chicken, made my way through the cafeteria queues, and started looking for my friends.

Whew-whew.

Hilde gave a little whistle. I turned towards her melody.

"Thanks," I appreciated her calling.

The cafeteria had swelled with witches as everyone sat down to eat their meals.

"Why the frown?" Sloane asked as I plunked my tray down.

"Miss your biggest fans?" Vince laughed.

"My biggest.. what are you talking about? What frown? What fans?" I stuffed a forkful of the thick, warm tomato-y sauce into my mouth and looked around, first at my gathered classmates, then across the room at large.

"Your fans-" Vince gestured vaguely. "You didn't notice?"

"I guess I didn't." Surprised, I looked up. "Holy crap. You're right."

"Usually am." He grinned.

I glanced around the cafeteria and made eye contact with zero staff. No fellows, or ladies. Also, no nods from other students. That never happened. I was always able to catch somebody's eye. I couldn't stop them from looking. Someone was always staring my way. But today...?

"It's a freakin' miracle!" I broke into a smile.

For weeks, since the Battle, and then even more so with the confrontation with the Damocles coven, or one could argue even all the way back to our first introduction into the High Council, every witch in the castle had been watching my every move. I didn't want to sound too full of myself, but it was true. They hung on the words I said, and took note of every action. Random witches constantly said hello and goodbye as they passed in public spaces, they chimed in with little thoughts and suggestions when they'd see me, they tried their best to make us into friends. I had had a fan club since the first day I entered the High Council. Some days, I would be greeted by upwards of twenty or thirty witches. But today... they left me alone with my thoughts.

I'd been set free!

I was so lost in consideration over what to do next about Wesson Zaid, I hadn't even noticed the anonymous way I'd slipped into the cafeteria. No one had greeted me, or tried to save me a spot in the line. I was completely unacknowledged. It was great!

Maybe things were finally settling into another new normal. I was about to be just another random face in the crowd.

"About time!" I laughed, stuffing another spoonful in my mouth.

"Only you would be happy about waiting in line." Tej rolled his eyes.

Rick and Hilde finished up. They nodded farewell. We all shifted around the small table.

"What'd you ask Lady Gray about?" Sloane redirected the conversation and also snuck a piece of my naan.

Instinctively, my eyes flashed to Beck. I could tell he was on edge about how much of our clandestine activities I might reveal to the table, but I had been trying to go through school being both a little more open and truthful, and there was nothing about my conversation with Gray that I'd be worried about saying out loud.

"I just asked about Oyer and Terminer justice. Like if someone in the coven were to break a law or rule, what would happen?"

"We've signed so many contracts." Tej pushed his meal around on his plate.

"Are you worried about your actions?" Nicolette piped in. "Like you might be arrested?" Her big eyes blinked at me.

"No, I wasn't," I said, slowly. The question stung. Was there some truth to that accusation? Nicolette shrugged and sat back. I looked at the others gathered at the table. "Should I be?"

Sloane hedged, looking for a softer, more tactful truth telling. "You did break a few rules."

"With good reason-" Beck cut in to defend me.

"I wouldn't arrest you," Sloane raised her hands to reject his disdain. His tone wasn't called for.

Nicolette shrugged. "A rule is a rule." She organized her dishes.

"Meaning what?" Vince challenged his parabond.

She glared at him. "Meaning *nothing*. Just a *rule* is a *rule*. Our choices have consequences." She swept her belongings away from the table and strode away from us, leaving an angry pall in her wake. We each tried to make sense of it.

Was that a warning?

A threat?

Blowing off a little steam since this morning's indiscretion?

"I think she's still mad that when things went down, you didn't include her," Sloane warned me.

"In what? My aunt's life or death mission?"

When Aunt Abeline had been severely injured in an earthquake, my only thought had been to rush off to the rescue. I hadn't stopped to see if I'd been inclusive in my requests for help from my other classmates. *That* was Nicolette's problem with me?

I scoffed. "That's why she's pissed?"

"It was a little hurtful not to be needed," Sloane admitted.

"Yeah, Mae. I thought you were my girl. I could've hooked you up with all these crazy effective weapons - like, there's this explosive called the Udak. It's super powerful. Super deadly. Only problem is, it has a really short fuse," Tej told me. "I coulda made you one."

Vince laughed. "What good is a bomb with a super short fuse? A suicide option?"

"I said it was a problem," Tej shrugged. "But the bomb is super cool. The explosion is, like, huge! You could light it with burning arrows, maybe." Tej pulled his arm back and fired the imaginary weapon. "Pew!" He shot the imaginary arrow. "That would be cool. Point is, I would have come through."

Amazingly, Vince agreed. He also imagined the fiery arrow. "That *would* be cool."

I glanced between the other faces in the group. Sloane and Tej each wore similar expressions. I was surprised this was still an issue. Aunt Abeline was mostly healed. But it still rubbed them the wrong way. I guess I should have been more thoughtful in my calls for help in the midst of my panic.

I sat back. "Hey, no, you're right. I'm sorry. I didn't realize that would hurt. I was so wrapped up in my thing, it didn't cross my mind that you guys would be insulted, but of course, I would want all of your help on anything. Tej, you're my boy..."

"Nope. No slang." He shook his head. "It was cool when I said it, *you* can't pull that off." We both laughed. He was right.

"Fair enough." I glanced over at Sloane. I could see the damage wasn't permanent. But she was much more understanding than others. "I should probably apologize to Nicolette."

"She'd just find another reason to be pouty." Vince shrugged.

"Yeah." The others nodded. We all started to clear our plates.

"That's fine, but a new issue would be hers. This one was mine, I guess."

"I think she'd appreciate it," Sloane said.

"Your funeral," Vince added.

But I didn't like the idea of lasting conflict. I would pull Nicolette aside and properly apologize, first chance that we got. No need to let bad feelings fester. I was about to go looking for my dorm-room neighbor, but as we left the cafeteria, before I could even start to try and find her, we were practically side-swiped by a hurrying Greg.

"There you are!" He grabbed my arm and dragged me behind the protective shelter of one of the atrium's large columns. He seemed so insistent and weird, handling me by my forearm, that the others tagged along for the show. He ducked his head low and beckoned us to follow.

"What on earth are you doing?" Sloane frowned.

"Over here, over *here*." When we squished in together, hidden, he continued. "I got a text. From Marcy." He was sweaty and pale. He held up his phone.

Vince grabbed it. He read aloud.

I'm thinking of cutting my hair.

Greg looked at all of us as if the ground had shifted in place.

"So?" Beck asked.

"So! It's code. Marcy knows I freakin' love her hair.

Her carpet matches the drapes if you know what I'm sayin', she'd never touch it without my blessing. It's like she's firing a red flare. Something is seriously wrong."

We could see he truly believed what he was saying. He clearly thought his girlfriend was in danger. The words had so much meaning behind them, he sent a shiver through the group.

"What could it be?" Beck asked.

"I don't know!" Greg wailed.

My parabond and I exchanged glances.

"No offense, but that's not much of a signal," Tej frowned.

"It's more than you've got," Greg snapped.

But I totally understood.

The code was meant to sound innocuous so only her partner would get the meaning. That was its purpose. That way, no one could claim that Marcy tipped him off, or that she warned him of impending danger, because depending on what was actually happening, she might get in trouble for that too.

"Mae," he turned to me. "She wouldn't use it lightly." Greg's eyes searched mine.

I nodded. I turned to the others. "Guys, think. If everything were fine, she would be *here*."

This made the others pause.

Greg and Marcy were an inseparable couple. Even more so than me and Beck. Where there was one, you'd always find the other. Only... Greg was here, and so was this text.

Marcy was missing from the group.

"Maybe she wanted some space. Girls do that," Vince frowned. He wasn't ready to jump into believing she was in a dangerous scenario. But I could tell, even he wasn't sure.

"I can ask Sissy if she's heard anything," Beck offered.

That was his nickname for his older sister. Sloane and I involuntarily shuddered. The girl was a walking nightmare of a human. A person whom I disliked immensely. But Brandi Templeton did have her ear to the ground in the clan. As long as *I* didn't have to talk to her, Beck was welcome to ask what she thought.

"We should probably move out of the open." Vince noted. "If Tweedle-dee is right..."

I looked at him, surprised at the about-face in the most skeptical boy's opinion about the situation, but nodded. Smart idea. "We'll be in Stone's lab," I told Beck.

He headed one way while the rest of us moved towards the classroom down the hall. As we entered the education corridor with the science labs, we saw another entourage moving across the adjoining hall. Instinctively, my friends ducked into alcoves to avoid being discovered. The other assemblage marched on its way, crossing in front of us, but turning down another aisle without looking down our hall.

"Was that... who I think it was?" Tej whisper-asked.

We all saw her.

Clear as day.

Marcy.

Marching in sync.

Surrounded by Ladies and Fellows.

Lady Mauve at the company's helm.

The girl looked positively sick.

Greg collapsed against a closed doorway. "They got her."

"Now hold on," Sloane comforted him. "We don't know what this means-"

"Yeah, we do," Vince cut her short.

"Dumb-dumbs, what are you doing out here in the hallways?" Brandi hissed, coming up behind us. "Get in, get in. Do I have to do everything for you?" She shoved us all into the nearest lab room. We quickly followed, closing the door shut behind us. The room was unfamiliar, used only by upperclassmen, but it was quiet and empty and safe. "God, Mae. Try to *think*." She marched ahead, her black hair swishing behind her back. "Get away from the window," she added. "First years are so stupid. Get away from there."

We followed her command.

I wanted to snipe at her, she was so sharp in every instruction, but Beck was reaching out for help, and we'd literally called her to this gathering, and since we had no information about what was really happening, I had no choice but to bite my tongue. Something *was* going on. If Brandi could shed some sort of light on the situation, I could absorb her little rude jabs.

Luckily, even with his family, Beck still had my

back. He sighed at his impossible sister. "Just tell them what you told me."

"Fine." She leaned closer. "Rumor is, they have a witness. The elders are putting together an inquisition. A fact-finding for the Damocles protests. I hear it's getting pretty bad. Their star is naming details. Mae," her dark eyes sparkled in my direction. "For sure, you're getting kicked out of the clan."

"For stopping the fighting?" Sloane was surprised.

"No, babe. For *how* she stopped the fighting," Brandi corrected. "Apparently," she looked me up and down, not willing to crouch any words, talking like I wasn't even present, "our little default witch used some pretty shady methods. She broke the rules. The contracts meant nothing. She defied the coven orders. It's all over the school." She glared at me, no doubt disgusted by my existence in general, but also furious about how my choices might affect her baby brother. Behind the storm in her eyes, I also detected a sick little grin. There was a tiny hint of pleasure, like maybe she was happy about how this whole thing would land on my back.

"So that's why you lost all your fans," Vince noted. "They already know. You're dead man walking."

Greg and Tej involuntarily moved away from me.

"Not just her," Brandi corrected. "Anyone who helped. Anyone in her social circle could be on the chopping block. You need to get out while you can," she told Beck.

He rolled his eyes.

"Don't do that. You hitch your ride to that horse and you'll drown."

I flinched at the mixed metaphors, but Brandi wasn't finished.

Her dark eyes affixed on the rest of the group. "All of you will. Crash and burn. She's already gone."

Some of the others bristled, but Beck stood his ground.

"Listen to me, for once in your life." Brandi huffed at her baby brother.

"I'm not leaving Mae," Beck said.

"She'll tie to your waist like an anchor!"

Beck shook his head.

I came beside him. "Maybe we can-"

"Did I say you could talk?" She snapped. She gave one last glance to Beck, but he picked up my hand. "You'll regret the day you got in her pants. All of you. I've already said too much." She turned on her heels and stormed out of the class.

I looked at my classmates. My face felt hot and red, like I'd been whipped around by the wind Brandi could harness with her palm. The girl had been talking to Beck, but those last words were correct, her warning could be doled out to any of my friends. They were at risk. With my aunt and the Damocles coven, most of my group had defied the rules of the Council and broken their contracts with the clan.

Everyone except Tej and Sloane, Rick, and Nicolette.

"Never mind, Mae." After our verbal berating, Tej

was the first to breathe again. "Your apology's rescinded. I'm happy you left me out of your plans." His tone was aiming for lightness, but I could tell he was shaken.

We all were.

Sloane sighed. "I guess that means we're safe from coven vengeance."

"And so is Nicolette." Vince nodded. "But the others..."

"Poor Marcy," Greg moaned. "My pretty baby."

Not just Marcy.

Hilde, Ethan, Ferris...

"A storm is coming," Vince said ominously.

"We've got to warn them," I agreed with a frown.

EIGHT
A STORM IS COMING

QUICKLY, we decided Sloane and Tej should leave us and find Ferris, Ethan and Hilde. They'd ask them to come find me. Face to face, I'd deliver the news that we'd learned. They were, unfortunately, complicit in my actions. It was necessary, before any councilmen grabbed them, to regroup to discuss where to go from here. I didn't want any of them snatched unaware. If the elders were getting their stories straight, so would we. As the untouched first years headed out, the rest of us stayed hidden in the upper grade science class.

None of us risked using our phones.

It seemed crazy and paranoid to think the coven might have a way to tap into our digital conversations or messages, but at this point, we weren't willing to put the hypothesis to the test.

An inquisition was coming.

What that meant, I had no idea. But it sounded bleak. And scary.

Vince manned the door, watching for trouble, ready to pull in the others as they passed.

Greg just sat and stared at Marcy's last message. "I might never see her again."

"Don't be so dramatic," Vince snapped.

"Her last words," Greg whimpered. "Her *hair*. I don't want them to cut it. You don't think they will, will they?"

"That wasn't actually happening. That was code, remember?" Beck frowned.

Greg was losing it.

My parabond glanced my way, growing worried.

"Greg," I said softly, looking at his device. "They might have a geo-tracker on there or something. We should probably turn it right off," I admitted.

He stared at his phone with dawning horror. We all looked at our devices. Vince shut his down and tossed it on the table. So did Beck.

"But what if she messages again?"

"It's for everyone's safety," Beck said. "Yours included. Marce will understand."

The boy glanced at his girlfriend's loving sentiment one more time, as if he didn't already know it by heart. He hit his power button and gently put it down.

I was about to follow, when a message came through from Lady Blue Moon. I couldn't help but open it. "That's strange."

311151111011111241

. . .

"Mae, turn it off," Vince snapped.

I looked up, confused, but nodded. Lady Blue Moon had never sent me a text like that before. A complicated list of numbers? I grabbed an erasable marker and scribbled the digits on the whiteboard.

"What is it?" Beck wondered.

"No idea," I said.

"Come on, Sunshine." Vince was waiting for my device.

I made a big show of shutting it down. "Happy now?"

"When has Vince ever been happy?" Greg groused. "*I* was happy with Marcy. She's the best I ever had. Now that's gone. Who can say when we'll ever be happy."

Beck and I tried not to roll our eyes.

Vince reached out the door and snatched little Hilde as she passed. Tej or Sloane must have got to her first, before the elders. But she wasn't alone.

"Short stuff, inside." Vince dragged her forward, but he stopped Rick at the door. "Not you."

"Why not?" Rick frowned.

"Because I told you." The two boys squared off. "You're not welcome."

"What's going on?" Hilde looked between us, immediately feeling the tension. I didn't like the fear in her voice.

"Just a little precaution," I assured her.

"I mean it, Rick. We don't want you involved." Vince didn't back down from her tall partner.

"I can make my own decisions," he replied. Neither budged.

"There's trouble," I told him. "But, right now, it doesn't concern you. Vince is trying, somewhat bullishly, to stop you from getting involved. It's about that... thing... I did. For Aunt Abeline." I didn't know exactly how to phrase my Valdeez plant-finding arrangement. My aunt's life-saving task? The life or death magical mission?

It *had been* life or death at the time.

I had acted wildly to save my family. I wasn't thinking clearly at the time. In the moment, it seemed like no one was. The Damocles clan had invaded. Showed themselves all over Plumpkin. They caused a magical earthquake at my family's cabin, as a bit of payback for my part in the Battle of Four. It was supposed to be a warning message. A threat to force the High Council to give in to their demands, like they should hand over what the Damocles wanted or suffer the consequences. Only, it turned out, Aunt Abeline was inside the lake house hiding when the dangerous stunt went off. She was gravely injured. Crushed. Pinned and dying, I found her under a table. I had only moments to save her. But, even once we were free of the wreckage, her body couldn't be revived with modern, secular medicine. She would never have recovered. Not on her own. The Plumpkin doctors couldn't help her, but Dr. Winters in the Damocles coven knew of an enchanted answer. He had a magical solution. I needed the same spell-binding potion for her recovery as he required for his clan. Plus, if I delivered the necessary ingredients, he promised he'd also orchestrate the departure of his coven from the town. It was win-win in the moment. We decided to work together to get it. I said yes to save my aunt. Only, I didn't consider the greater repercussions. By then, there'd been too much damage between the enemy clan and the Council elders. The Damocles witches officially became enemies of our coven. The Elders forced all us students to read contracts specifically limiting our behavior around the rivals. Contracts we all signed.

It said we couldn't leave, but I left the castle.

It said we couldn't talk to the other coven, but I worked with them, and befriended them as well.

I had no choice.

No other options.

I had to do it to help my aunt.

In fact, I tried to get the magical branches on my own. Beck, Ferris, Greg, Marcy and I snuck out. They helped me find Ethan's secret emissary in the forest. He was going to give me the precious plant and blame the theft on the Damocles coven, but the foreign witches sabotaged the plan. They didn't believe I was secretly helping us both.

After that, what could I do? I broke the contract again.

To save Aunt Abeline, I had only one other option. Grow the magical thing from scratch.

By then, Aunt Abeline was hours from death. The Damocles had the seed, and working apart had caused us loads of trouble, so on my second attempt at the mission, I agreed to a double partnership. It was tenuous and strained.

I went to Rick for chemistry potions and he created all the spells that I asked for. But he refused to break any rules of the coven in order to help me. Rick was the only member of our group whose contract boundaries were never crossed. A distinction that mattered now.

He frowned, knowing full well what I was referring to. "They should have said no to your plan," he said to me, looking past Vince. "Like I did."

"Well, we didn't." Vince snapped.

Rick turned towards him. "Poor decision making."

"Gee, thanks," Vince snarled in return. The boys glowered at each other.

But even *that* wasn't the end of the task. After I was armed with Rick's spells, Vince came with me and two Damocles boys on the second plant-finding mission. Unbeknownst to us, Hilde snuck along for the ride. It wasn't easy. We killed a sea monster, blew up a lake, and raced out of an erupting volcano, but eventually, we got all the enchanted ingredients necessary to finish the magical job. We were successful on the impossible mission. We had what we needed to grow the magical plant.

But it was too little, too late.

By the time we returned to the castle, the covens' tenuous, peaceful agreements with the Damocles had all burned to ash. We arrived to find two warring factions. The grounds were fiery with extirpation. And the spell for the Valdeez plant growth didn't take hold. We couldn't grow the vital plant after all.

Aunt Abeline was on her last breath, so I just threw caution to the wind.

I stood up, and shouted for mercy. I asked if any among us had a Valdeez plant to offer... that's all it would take to save her life! To end the war!

At first, there was nothing.

No one said anything. No one came forward. Then something happened. Others started to seeI was right. It was possible. We could stop this unpleasant battle if the coven proved generous. Members of the High Council coven came to Abeline's rescue, and they came to the aid of the Damocles coven as well. They delivered the Valdeez potion so all the sick families could be saved. The red-wearing clan hurried home to their own land. And Aunt Abeline was cured and healed. Her recovery took a few weeks, but in an instant, the chaos and panic was over. The castle returned to life before. Everything went back the way it used to be. I saved the day and stopped the war.

But I did break several rules along the way.

Was it worth it?

To me? Hell, yes.

To the High Council? I wasn't so sure. Would they pick my choices apart? Would they put me on trial for the means, not the end? It seemed hypocritical and cruel.

But whatever it was, however this shook out, it didn't involve Rick.

"I'm alright," Hilde told her parabond. We glanced at her, surprised. "It was my choice to sneak away."

"This isn't your deal," Vince added. He was still standing tough, but his tone had softened a bit. After all, the boys were friends.

"Fine." Rick glanced between them, letting his displeasure hang a moment more, then he departed.

We all sighed.

"Can you give me your phone?" Beck asked the girl. Hilde handed it over. He turned it off and tossed it on the table with the others.

"Incoming. Two more," Vince told us, seeing the approach of Ferris and Ethan. "Psst." He signaled them into our hideout classroom.

"When Brandi said you were looking for us, I wasn't sure," Ethan said. "Kinda thought we were walking into a trap."

"I told you," Ferris told him then turned to me. "When your phone wasn't working, I figured it was the real deal."

"It's tough to think that girl could do good." Ethan

shrugged, still thinking of the messenger. I guess once someone had kidnapped you and locked you in a barn without clothing, it might be difficult to trust anything they'd say.

"No offense," Ferris added, seeing Beck waiting.

"None taken," he shrugged. By now he was well aware of his sister's charms.

"We've turned off our phones," Greg counseled the new pair.

"Why? What's happening?" Ferris shot a raised eyebrow my way, not willing to let Greg take the lead on any detail.

I nodded. "Just as precaution."

They looked down at the pile of electronics. She and Ethan pressed their power bars and tossed their phones in the mix. Seeing that we were all together and no one else was coming, Vince grabbed a nearby poster off the wall. He shoved it over the small glass window in the door, left the sight-line of his post, and joined us by the teacher desk.

"What's the deal?" Ferris asked again.

"There's a coming inquisition... into what happened with the Damocles coven. The Valdeez plant in the forest... there's some questioning..." I trailed off. On purpose, I didn't mention who had given us this tip.

"Damn it, Fair. I *told* you," Ethan snapped at his girl. Ferris held her ground. She narrowed her eyes and gave him a pointed frown, quite aware we were all watching this little interaction. Ethan bit his tongue for now.

"What's that got to do with us?" she asked me. Her tone was measured, sending more unspoken messages. She glanced at Vince and Hilde. Even Beck. Those three weren't with us on the mission. Should they be hearing details about this task?

Vince caught on to Ferris' meaning. "Kid, let's look at the code Blue Moon texted," he told Hilde, guiding the girl to the classroom's whiteboard.

"What are the numbers?" She wondered.

"You're so smart, I thought you'd figure it out."

We tuned them out.

I spoke a little quieter, leaning in. "We think that Marcy's their star witness," I admitted.

We all glanced at Greg, he put his head down in his hands.

"And she turned on the plan?" Ethan asked.

"We don't know," Beck admitted. "All we know is she's talking."

"We think she's talking," I hedged further.

"She wouldn't..." Greg shook his head. "She wouldn't say a word."

"Why did you have to get us involved?" Ethan was talking just to Ferris. His tone was angry, but she didn't back down.

"She needed help."

"And you had no choice but to save her?!"

"She needed *my* help!"

"*I* need you to *think* before you *act*!"

The harsh words hung in the air. The two faced off. I hated that I'd put them both in this situation. Awkwardly, Beck, Greg, and I looked anywhere but their mutual frowns. The stand-off was long-lasting and terrible. Finally, Ferris sighed.

"What do you want me to do about it now? What's done is done. Seriously, Ethan. What?" She glared.

"Just... let me think," he said. He stepped away from the group.

Ferris let him go.

He needed a moment. She probably needed one as well.

She looked in the other direction. "What's with the code on the board?"

We all glanced over. Vince and Hilde turned back to us. Obviously they'd been listening to every word of the interaction. They had yet to make heads or tails.

"Is it binary?" Beck asked.

Vince and Hilde shrugged.

"No idea," I admitted. "But Blue Moon sent it to me, so she must think I can get it. I don't know binary..."

"It's a language in zeros, ones, and twos," Greg told the group.

"Are there twos?" Ferris wondered.

"Well, there aren't *fives*," Vince said with certainty. "I think."

"What's going on?" Hilde asked, not for the first time. It was time to let her in on the truth.

"Marcy's been captured," Greg announced.

The girl gasped.

"Questioned," I tempered. "We *think*. The Valdeez plant retrieval is being examined to determine whether everything we did was... within coven rules."

We all knew that it would fail.

The rules had been smashed by each and every person in the classroom.

"How much do they know?" Ethan asked, coming back to the group. He and Ferris exchanged another glance. Out of all of us, he had the most to risk. Technically, he had stolen the High Council plant for the group. He'd snuck it out of the High Council tents and into our clutches. But in the moment, he successfully played the whole thing off as an attack by the Damocles clan (they did, after all, ambush us just minutes after.) But, everyone knew the whole story could collapse under stress. He could be found culpable for his actions.

That was a real possibility.

The other option was that the coven *wasn't* aware of his role. If they believed his story that he was an innocent guard who was attacked and failed to protect the Valdeez plant from outsiders, if *that* were the case, he really shouldn't be here. His very presence at this meeting would put his narrative at risk.

A sort of damned if you do, damned if you don't situation

It all depended on how much they actually got from the girl.

"We don't know what they know," I admitted. "Marcy *was* on the forest crew."

"Greg?" Ethan's eyebrow shot up.

"She won't squeal. I know my girl. She's not a rat."

"We shouldn't be here," Ethan said quietly to Ferris. "*I* shouldn't be here."

"And if they gave her truth serum?" Ferris asked.

Greg shook his head.

"She won't be able to help what she says," Beck admitted for him. We all remembered the embarrassing secrets Beck had confessed while under the influence.

"Is that a risk that you'd like to take?" Ferris asked.

"What I'd *like* is to not be in this *situation*."

"Who cares what you did!" Hilde complained. "Who snuck where, or what happened. Our actions saved the coven!"

"It's not that simple," Vince told her.

"Well, it should be."

"Yeah, it should be," Ethan agreed, sadly. Even Vince nodded. Having the two boys on her side, Hilde beamed. But the rest of us understood the finer detail of what they were saying. It *should* be that easy, *but it wasn't*.

"H, this stuff is rarely cut and dry," Vince said.

Ethan shifted, uncomfortable. He looked back towards the doorway. "I'm gonna go."

"Babe-"

"The longer I stay the worse it's gonna be. The Damocles stole the plant." He said with finality. He grabbed his phone and hers. "End of story."

Ferris shook her head. "I'm staying." They stared each other down. "You go," she told him.

"Fine. Try not to make any decisions that will change my whole life."

"I'll do my best," she snapped back.

He barely acknowledged the rest of us and left the classroom.

"No promises," Vince called behind his back.

I frowned. No need to pile on like that.

"What? The guy was a jerk."

"No, I was," Ferris frowned. "I got him involved without him having any choice."

"We'll do everything we can to protect him," I told her.

"How?" Ferris got right to the point. She crossed her arms. The frustration she'd felt with Ethan now shuddered in my direction. I looked at the others as well. They all wanted answers. Answers I didn't have.

But there was something I could do.

"There's no point in everyone being dragged out," I told them. "I'll confess and take the heat. If they kick me out, they kick me out. I'll be okay. You know, so be it. It was worth it. To me. It really was. Aunt Abeline's alright. I did what I had to do at the time."

"Mae, no-" Beck interrupted.

"It's alright." I shrugged. Rules or no rules. "I'd do it again."

"That makes one of us," Vince frowned.

"It *was* basically your fault," Greg agreed, as if I'd

dragged him and Marcy into my plan and they hadn't rushed out to join us just for the thrill of the chase.

"I'll take the banishment. You'll all be covered." I confirmed.

"What if they don't banish you, Mae? You'll be tried in the Judicial Council. The Court of Oyer and Terminer." Ferris warned me.

Vince's eyes widened.

"I think Oyer and Terminer courts are extremely rare," I said, taking note of her tone.

"Who told you that?" She asked me. "That's not how it is. Mae, you're not some graduating student who's decided the magical life at the castle will impede on your family's business. Ho hum, council life's not for you. That's not who you are. You've held the attention of the whole coven. *Twice.* You're a winner. You're a freakin' leader. You've developed a huge voice at the castle and that makes you a risky proposition. They won't just slink you out, thanks, no thanks, see you later. They'll make an example of you."

"Strip your magic away," Vince agreed.

"Fine. Let them take it." I shrugged.

"I don't think you know what that means," he warned. I glanced at him and Ferris. They both looked horrified.

"Think about where your magic comes from," she said.

"Where does it come from?" Hilde wondered.

Vince pointed to my head. It was in there. While I slept. Lodged in some unknowable part of my head.

"So? How will they remove it?" Beck asked.

There was that look, again. It seemed to me, they were negotiating who would explain it. This time, even Vince chickened out. Finally, Ferris crossed her arms across her chest. It was Beck's question, but she stared me right in the eyes as she spoke.

"If she's found guilty of betraying the High Council, they'll lobotomize her brain."

NINE

A NO BRAINER

"THE COUNCIL REMOVES YOUR MAGIC, by force," Ferris told us.

"What?!" Beck and I exchanged a glance.

"Our powers are found in two locations. For harnesses and lie-guards, it's in our hands. You cut one off and a witch can't perform," she said.

Harnesses, sometimes called empaths, could manipulate things, like the weather (Beck), birds (Marcy), water (Vince), rocks (Greg), and wind (Brandi and Hilde as well). These were real, tangible things that existed in the known universe that bent to the empath's will. Things science couldn't explain.

Lie-guards were even more powerful. They envisioned ideas, made them up out of nothing, and then through some sort of warped energy that could only be described as magic, their illusions became real. Need to trap someone in an imaginary hedge maze, a lie-guard could do that. Want to open a door with a key? A lie-guard could make the hardware real enough for the mechanism to be manipulated. The only way to stop a lie-guard illusion was to break through the person's perspective of the vision. This could be done by seeing it from a different angle or discovering a faulty detail... or a lie-guard illusion would collapse if the witch who was casting it could no longer hold it, usually because at the source of their power they felt too much pain. Since they were literally building something out of nothing, the exertion on those witches was fast to build. We classified such tension in the boundaries between a witch's enchanted abilities and the physicality of the natural world as extirpation; the uncontrolled energy build up created when witch powers were used. The tension of that power released through fire. And once it got started, anything it touched would start to burn. Including a witch's hands. They could light on fire. They had to deal with uncontrolled sparks and licks of flames. No matter the strength of one's power, when it was over-used, extirpation was inevitable. All magic required energy to sustain it, and if someone cast a vision too big, or for too long, or involving too many people, that energy would combust into flames. I had seen it.

"For dreamcasts and chemists, the powers come from up here," Ferris pointed to her temple, continuing, "it's your knowledge they have to slice and dice to remove."

Chemists knew a lot about the world. Expert researchers, engineers and scientific inventors, they could keep straight all the technical and chemical properties of plants, and had a sixth sense about how machines, energies and ingredients combined in the real world. Chemists remembered complicated spells and made effective potions. They could make bombs and elixirs, sometimes out of very little, going off the natural reactions of little known plants. They worked like giant, instinctive encyclopedias. They stored all the technical information in their brains and created magical things. After that, they made and distributed their potions to other witches. We all benefited from the spells they made.

The final type of witches, my type of witches, were the dreamcasts. Dreamcasts saw the potential future while they were sleeping, in complicated, sometimes misleading, dreams. A dreamcast needed to remember and interpret. Then, in real life, they could manipulate the visuals they'd seen. The visions gave witches ideas and solutions, and offered hidden details. They worked well if you could understand what you'd seen. Hence, I kept my handy bed-side notebook of dreams. Sloane had once admitted that she tried to capture the feelings and details through art, little drawings and temporal creations. I thought that was a cool expression, though not quite right for me. If I was honest, I still didn't have an awesome handle on how to use the visions, but at least I could remember what I had seen.

The idea that the Council would try to take those special powers away... for a while, our group fell silent, each in our own way exploring what that finality could mean.

They would cut off our hands or alter our brains?

Involuntarily, Beck and Greg flexed their casting muscles. No doubt they wondered what life would be like without the use of those hands.

What had I gotten them into?

If I had known the physical penalty for going against the High Council's wishes, I still would have done anything I could to save my aunt. That much was certain. But I would *not* have recruited my friends.

Especially not Hilde or Ethan.

Losing a hand was one thing. But as dreamcasts, they might lose their *heads*. As a two-fer who had both talents as a dreamcast and as a wind harness, Hilde might lose both her hand and her brain! I also touched my own temples. What would be left if the Council were to dig into there?

"So, I run," I told them.

"It's a no brainer," Beck agreed.

Greg burst into laughter. "Get it? A no *brainer?* Clever, buddy." But that wasn't a joke Beck intended. No one smiled. "Guys, you gotta laugh," Greg complained. "When something's so effed that it's funny? You laugh in its face. That's what my Marcy would say."

But Marcy wasn't there to back him.

"I don't know." Ferris ignored him, considering the options. "If they charge you, they'll hunt you. And if they hunt you, they *will* catch you. The leader of the coven doesn't like to look weak."

"Child holds the power close to his chest," Vince agreed.

"Exactly. So now's the time to skip town. Before they get to the point of ever claiming I did something wrong." It seemed obvious. "We could travel," I told Beck.

He nodded.

"All of us?" Little Hilde wondered. "What about our families? Or Rick?"

"He was too smart to get involved," Vince appreciated the choice in retrospect.

The rest of us exchanged a glance. Who would tell the young girl that running away meant leaving her family and parabond and everyone she'd ever known?

"I just meant me," I told her gently. "And maybe Beck, if he wants to." I chickened out of looking to see if he was still nodding.

"What are these numbers?" Ferris asked again, finally looking at the whiteboard.

"It looks like stupid math," Greg groaned. We all examined the numbers on the board.

It does look like math, I realized. There was math in my dream last night... *taught by Lady Blue Moon!*

This was her text. The others continued to discuss it, but I was now all in my head. More details of my dream made sense. We were all there for the lesson, I realized. These four. They were all present. And she definitely wrote math on the wall, only in my dream,

Blue Moon didn't write numbers, she used Scrabble pieces. I remembered distinctly writing that small detail in my journal. The game-board pieces had been stuck up on the wall.

"You even listening?" Vince snapped a finger in my face.

They all looked over. I blushed. I hadn't been, but that didn't matter. I was too geared up to backtrack now. If my dream was right, I'd cracked the code!

Sort of.

Maybe.

"What if the numbers are Scrabble values?" I asked them. "That's something I would know. That would make sense."

We read the numbers again.

3 1 1 1 5 1 1 1 0 1 1 1 1 2 4 1

"One is the most common value, so of course there'd be a lot of them." I continued the analysis. The others drew closer, following too. "It's like hangman." I drew blanks above each number. They each represented a letter. "A zero is a blank in Scrabble, it means nothing." I put a slash through that spot as a flat line.

"So... two words," Ferris caught on.

"Exactly."

"Scrabble letters have value?" Greg wondered.

"Sure." I drew a sample letter square, added the

letter (in this case, an E) and then drew in a small number one in the bottom corner, in typical wooden Scrabble tile design. "It's how you score the game, and how you win."

"But you just said it yourself, there's like a million one-point letters," Vince countered.

"Yeah, but for higher numbers there's only like one or two options. We start with those and-"

"Fill out from there." Ferris got it.

"I'm good at word puzzles!" Hilde said.

"Okay, we should write out the high value letters." Beck instructed. He grabbed a marker and went to the board.

I racked my brain. "G, X, Z, Q... J."

Beck wrote them all on the board. "Y, I think," he added.

"Um, M?" Ferris chimed in.

"H and D are higher," I tried to visualize, but it was harder than it looked. I'd never memorized the letters' exact values because the point system was always prevalent, written on the squares.

Aunt Abeline would know for sure.

I could call her. But we'd turned off our phones. Better to try and figure it out on our own.

"I've never played," Vince shrugged. Hilde gestured the same.

"What letter's worth nothing?" Greg wondered.

"*That one's blank,*" we all answered at once.

"I already said," Ferris added. "That's what the slash is for."

"Okay. Geez. I get it."

"Two words." Beck added that notation to the board with two lines.

"Two long words," Greg muttered.

I counted. An eight and a seven letter word. Pretty high value in a game of Scrabble, for sure.

"I think we're still missing some, write the whole alphabet on the board," I suggested. Beck did as I asked and I went behind him with a second marker, crossing out all the lowest value letters. Vowels were worth one. So were common word builders like R and T, S and N. I crossed them out too. In moments, I'd struck ten letters from the board. Also, since her highest code-number was five, the premium valued consonants were too high for Blue Moon's message. That took out Z, Q, X and J.

We were narrowing it down.

I circled the leftover letters that I felt pretty sure had higher values.

Eleven were still in the mix.

"Now what?" Vince asked.

"They could be twos, or threes, or fours," I murmured. I tried to assign a value to the letter B, the first unknown on my list. I chose a three. Three points. But immediately rubbed it out.

"No, that's good. Trust your instinct." Beck rewrote the number I'd assigned. "It's buried in your subconscious. You've played so many times."

"Which ones are fives?" Vince asked, as that was

the most important number since it was placed prominently in the word.

3 I I I 5 I I I

I stared at the remaining letters. They all started to
jumble in my mind.

"Guys, I'm really not sure. We're wasting time." I
glanced towards the door. Child's High Council
gestapo could bust through at any second.

Hilde hopped down from her chair. She wrote CH
on the board.

Then MP.

"Kid, what are you doing?" Vince frowned.

"No time for doodles," Greg added.

"You know what a doodle is, right?" Vince
snapped.

"I'm not drawing. I'm writing. You're worried
about the wrong number. Focus over here." She
pointed to the second coded word.

I I I I 2 4 I

"Two value letters are strung side-by-side together.
That's where to start. I do lots of word jumbles at
home." She shrugged. "This one's just extra hard."

"Right," Beck agreed. "So there's CH like church and MP like blimp,"

"Or palm, that has P and M," Greg added, still not getting what the others meant. "And-"

"Tonight!" I shouted. "It's GH!" I led my finger across the numbers on the board. T-O-N-I-G-H-T. "It fits." Then I pointed to the five. "And this is the highest letter left. It's got to be K, cuz the letter K is the toughest remaining consonant to place."

Beck wrote the letter K above the blank over the number five. Then added the letter B that I assigned a three.

We stared at the blanks for a moment, what word started with B and had K in the middle? Then Ferris had it. She took the marker and filled it in on the board. B-R-E-A-K-O-U-

"Breakout!" Greg shouted, convinced he'd solved it first.

"Thanks genius," Vince rolled his eyes.

And there it was.

We'd solved the message. It was written on the board:

BREAKOUT TONIGHT.

TEN

BREAKOUT TONIGHT

WE ALL STARED at the words scrawled on the board.

BREAKOUT TONIGHT

Vince gave a low whistle. "Well, this isn't good."

"You whistled!" Hilde perked up. "I whistle too."

"You're focused on the wrong thing, kid."

"No, I know. Of course." Hilde put her serious face back on, her cheeks red at the rebuke.

"Is it possible you decoded it wrong?" Greg asked.

"Anything's possible," I agreed. But no one tried to solve the riddle again. Deep down, we all believed what I knew in my heart. Blue Moon had risked all that she could to send me this message. The warning was clear. The Council was coming for me. Maybe for all of us. We had to get out while we still could.

"I don't wanna go," Hilde admitted.

"You don't have to," Ferris said.

"None of us do," Beck added. "It's totally your choice."

"But kid, it might not be safe to stay," Vince admitted. Hilde's eyes welled with tears. "Come here," he offered. She flung herself into his chest to hide her snotty nose. He rolled his eyes at us, but softly comforted her. "It's gonna be okay."

Ferris grabbed an eraser and cleared off all our work, eliminating any trace of the decoded message from the board. Smart idea. We didn't want to connect anything back to Blue Moon. No one could know that we'd been tipped off.

"The message might be for me alone," I told Hilde, rubbing her back, thinking of Ethan. "I'll go. But you should stay."

"That's not a risk she should take," Vince disagreed.

"Who asked you?" Ferris crossed her arms.

"Why don't you ask your man?" He didn't back down. "Now or *then*. Then you wouldn't be in this mess."

"If I could time-machine back, I *would*."

"Maybe take it a little farther back to improve your attitude," he muttered.

"How far do I have to go for you to mind your own business?" Ferris returned. "Mae, I'm in."

"And now you're deciding for him again," Vince laughed.

"He's not here!" Ferris shouted. "Vince, he left!"

"Don't fight, man. At least Ethan has a girlfriend." Greg interrupted the fight. "I'd give *anything* to have Marcy again."

"She's not dead," Vince stopped him. "She's just a snitch."

"You don't know what she said! She's not a rat! She's an angel-fish!"

"Alright. Just... everyone take a breath," I told them. This was all my fault. They were lashing out at each other, but they should be lashing out at me. "No one has to do anything. Go anywhere. This is *my* stuff. I'll take care of it."

The other teens frowned. No one jumped in to protect me, but at least they weren't fighting anymore.

"I'll fix it. *On my own.*" I stressed.

The tension broke.

"I won't leave you," Beck told me.

"We're all coming," Vince spoke for the rest. "At least 'til we know that it's safe."

Ferris agreed, although she still wasn't looking at Vince. Beck and Hilde nodded. We all looked at Greg.

"What about Marcy?" He asked, weakly.

"Greg, she's the High Council's key witness," Beck said. "She turned on us."

"So, she can't come."

It wasn't a question. It was a dawning realization.

"No," I agreed. "She can't."

"We should leave," Ferris interrupted. "Now. Every minute we stay is a minute more they're coming closer." She pulled the poster off the window and glanced out in the hallway, half expecting to see a witch army awaiting us there. Thankfully, there was no one gathered. Vince joined her by the door. At least he agreed with her on that.

"So, we're all in?" Beck asked.

The others nodded.

"Wait," I realized. There was another solution. "Marcy turned me in."

"You don't know that." Greg defended.

"No, I'm not blaming her. Don't you see? More of you could do it too. Turn me in. The contracts we signed have a clear clause. If you turn in another witch for their crimes, you won't be charged. Even if you were there. That's Marcy's play. But, it works for you too. *You should turn me in.*" The answer was obvious. "I'm already screwed either way."

For Beck, Ferris and Ethan, their level of culpability in our previous acts might preclude a path to freedom. But for Vince, Hilde and Greg, the option was very real. If they ratted me out, they'd be given a free pass.

"I'll understand." I added, softening the harsh edge. "It's no betrayal. You only broke the rules 'cuz I asked."

Vince stepped up. "Mae, everything I did was for the good of the coven. Same goes for you. I'm no snitch."

"Me neither," Hilde agreed, standing tall.

But the young girl's bravery made me sad. "Hilde," I knelt to her level. "I know you want to be heroic, but are you sure? You have the most to lose. Do you want to stop and talk to your parents? Or maybe Rick? If you leave with us now, you might never get back."

"Don't just follow me," Vince warned.

"I understand." She nodded. "I don't need to talk to them. I already know what they'd say. *When you stand, stand on the side of angels.* Always do your best. That's all you can do." Hilde recounted. "Mae, you're on the side of the angels."

I felt a knot tighten in my stomach.

On the side of the angels?

That's not how I'd describe myself. But at least she and Vince were right about one thing. Every choice so far, every dumb decision I'd made, was in service of a greater good – to help at least one person, and in lots of cases, I'd helped the whole coven. I *was* in the service of justice. For our coven, for the Damocles people, for my Aunt Abeline, and also for my dead mother.

"I'm coming." Greg surprised us. "I'm not a rat. And neither is Marcy. You'll see. Besides, immunity's not guaranteed. I can't risk my hand." He pulled his hands out of his pockets and showed them off. "I happen to use both of these on the regular." He made an obscene masturbation gesture. The rest of us groaned.

Hilde crinkled her eyebrows, uncertain. "What?"

"From time to time, we all enjoy a little tug. Fellas?" Greg grinned.

"If you're coming, you're not allowed to be gross," Ferris told him flatly. Greg dropped his grin. He was definitely coming.

So it was decided.

Our team of six would run as fast and as far as we could.

"Where will we go?" Hilde wondered.

"The important thing is to build some distance between us and the coven," Beck told her.

"There's an abandoned barn that we know," Ferris suggested. "That will work in the short term. If we can get there safely."

I agreed.

"I've got my Dad's truck," Beck offered.

"And my boat," Greg lovingly referred to his sedan.

"We'll take them both," Ferris agreed. "We can use one or the other later, if necessary, to shake off a tail."

How much chasing would the High Council do? We were just a bunch of dumb kids who'd decided to bail on witches' school. Surely once they realized we were no threat to the coven they'd let us simply disappear? That seemed reasonable, but it didn't quell my fear.

"Alright," I nodded. "Let's move."

We'd already been hemming and hawing too long. Vince checked out the exit route one more time and Ferris led us out into the hall. The group moved quickly, in dead silence. Even Greg knew better than to chat. Pausing before every corridor turn, peering for waiting enemies, Ferris snaked us through the building. We were almost to the back exit to the parking lot when she held up a hand to tell us to stop. She glanced around the coming corner.

"Mauve and Gray," she mouthed.

The two ladies were waiting in the final hallway, chatting and chuckling, not tense, or guarding the path. But that could have been a façade to lull us into safety. I wouldn't have put it past Lady Mauve. With her short hair, tattoo sleeves and her gritty little body, she was strong and tough in all the ways that Lady Gray was matronly and soft. She scared me more than any other person at the High Council. Even more than Cornelius Child. She was not someone I wanted to cross.

"Hide," I told them, trying all the doorknobs in the hallway surrounding. The nearest doors were locked. There was no room we could safely duck inside.

"Go back," Ferris motioned.

We turned to retreat, but Vince also came to a stop.

"Ferris, make us second years," he hissed back. "Now!"

Ferris took his serious command. Without hesitation, she balled up her palm. In a flash, I wasn't looking at my group of friends anymore. Ferris disguised each of us in a detailed illusion to make us look exactly like the second year students I recognized on the Council grounds. I appeared as a girl named Viola. Beck became Hendricks, and Hilde redressed into the older girl named Anne. The others took on new appearances as well. And it was lucky she had acted so quickly. As my hair magically turned from brown to blond, Cornelius Child rounded the corner walking directly towards us in the hall. He wasn't alone. There were two fellows also in his stead. They were talking heatedly.

"Someone's tipped them off," one of the men informed Cornelius.

"For sure," the other fellow agreed. "They're not up in the dormitories on fifth."

"Damn it. This place leaks like a sieve," the coven leader complained. "That's something to fix," he told his follower pointedly. The man nodded. Another problem for another day. "What are you doing here? Get to your dorms." Child barked at us. While our true identities were now obscured, that didn't mean he was happy to see a group of second years carousing his halls. Especially a hall *he* was marching through. "Go on. *Disperse!*"

"Sorry sir," one of the boys whispered. I thought it might have been Vince, but even our voices didn't sound like they should.

Quick as we could, we scurried past the coven leader and his two council members, heads low, our hearts beating wildly in our chests. We ran two, three corridors away, our speed getting faster, until finally, our new, chaotic route brought us to another external door. It wasn't near the back parking lot, but we didn't care.

"Go!" Beck-as-Hendricks shouted and we burst out of the castle.

Our sneaky-strategy collapsed in favor of pure speed as we stopped being mindful of who might see us and instead ran full tilt to Greg's car and Beck's truck. At least no one would know who we were, looking like a bunch of second years panicking on the lawn. But also, it wouldn't take much to figure out the lie-guard. Some of the older teens were faster than Hilde, so I slowed down to grab her hand.

"We got this," I told her.

The teens loaded into the two vehicles with Vince and Beck in the front truck. Me, Hilde and Ferris piled in the back car with Greg. I would have liked to ride with my parabond, but there was no time to fuss. Hilde and I tossed our bodies into Greg's backseat. We'd barely closed the door when he hit the gas. He rocketed out of the High Council castle parking lot only inches behind Beck's tail lights. Both boys drove for the exit at a speed that was perilously fast.

"Watch out!" Ferris shouted, dropping her lie-guard, as Greg swerved a touch too late on a turn.

"Greg! Watch the road," I piled on.

He rolled his eyes in the rear view, not braking. "Why'd I get stuck with all the girls!"

"Keep watching," Hilde chimed in next.

"I *am!* Sheesh. You're like five. How do you know how to drive?"

"I see how *you do it*, then do the opposite," she scolded. Hanging out with Vince had taught her a few tricks with her tone. I couldn't help but grin. Another woman capable of taking on the Gregs of the world and putting them in their place. Ferris also smiled. But, we didn't have much time to enjoy.

Suddenly, a lightning bolt screeched through the clouds.

It crashed to the earth ahead in the lane.

"Holy crap!" One of us screamed. It echoed how we all felt.

The lightning cratered the road in front of our convoy. Unable to stop, Beck drove right into the hole. He crashed. His front tires careened into the cavity, dropping down. His engine slammed to a stop. His back wheels spun helpless in the air above the road.

"Beck!" I watched in horror.

"Stop!" Ferris screamed at Greg.

He punched down on the brakes, but too late. There wasn't enough distance between the two vehicles to stop. Greg's sedan smacked into the truck's airborne chassis, giving our friends in the front vehicle a serious jolt. The truck bounced back down on top of its hood and at the impact in our car, the airbags burst out on Ferris and Greg.

For a moment, nobody moved.

"Is everyone alright?" I checked the others.

They fought them down, dazed, but safe.

"Yeah, I'm good," Ferris told me.

Hilde nodded. A goose egg had appeared on her

forehead, already starting to grow. A physical impression from where she'd hit her head on Greg's headrest. "I'm okay."

"Look at my car!" Greg moaned. "What was that?"

"A lightning strike from a harness," Ferris noted through gritted teeth. "A powerful one. The High Council is coming." She looked over her shoulder.

"What do we do?" Hilde asked.

We stared out the rear window of the car. One-by-one a group of ladies and fellows in their signature white tracksuits appeared over the horizon, marching towards us, coming up the road in a wide line. They looked angry and determined.

"What do we *do*?" Hilde repeated, since her first question hadn't elicited any answer.

Greg, Ferris and I stared out at the dire situation.

"Kid," in an effort to keep calm, I addressed the girl using Vince's friendly nickname. "We don't know."

ELEVEN
I'VE GOT SAND IN MY HAIR

WITH OUR HANDS held up to surrender, we exited the vehicle. The boys in Beck's truck did the same.

"Don't attack anyone," Ferris warned us. "They could add it as an extra charge against you."

"I won't do anything," Hilde agreed, barely moving her lips.

We stood beside the two broken-down cars in the lane. Waiting. The truck and car blocked any potential traffic in or out of the castle. But that was alright. We weren't going anywhere now.

"Are you okay?" Beck found his way in the group to stand beside me.

I nodded. "You?"

"I should have dodged the crater," he shook his head, mad at himself.

"It was magical lightning," I told him. "From the harness of an elder. I'm just glad we're all safe."

"Are we?" Vince muttered over my shoulder. He had a point.

There were five of them, goons from the High Council. Six of us. So the numbers were on our side. That made it seem like it was possible we could beat them in a hand-to-hand situation, but after years of practice and honing, the dynamics and skills of those five witches were likely far more powerful than ours. Even Ferris, the oldest among us, was only in her third year at the coven. None of our powers were yet fully formed. Not only that, but without a car to take us, even if we escaped a first confrontation, it would be difficult to get off castle land. At least for now, we could cling to the fact that our attempted exit had been an innocent departure. Since they hadn't caught us or charged us with anything, we couldn't be expected to know not to leave. But if anyone on our side started a fight with the coven, our innocence would break down.

The largest of the High Council guards walked towards us. He had an ugly red scar pushing into the hairline of his brow. His face was forced into an angry, unappealing glare.

"Mae, I've seen him..." Hilde whispered. "I've seen all this," she realized. "Quick, everyone, shield your eyes."

I clenched my lids closed. So did the others. Not a moment too soon.

A vicious wind whipped through the dirt road.

The gust sucked up all the loose gravel and dirt particles and spun them wildly in a dramatic circle.

An airborne whirlpool of detritus.

The surge stung our faces, our arms and our necks. Any exposed skin felt attacked by the grime. A thousand tiny pebbles and stones pelted us. Blindly, I shifted my hands to protect myself. I dragged the bottom of my t-shirt over my mouth and nose.

"Greg! Are you doing this?" I shouted, unable to see him, lost in the dirt cloud. He could harness small rocks, but I'd never seen him control near this much earth at once. The flurry of motion cut us off from the High Council members' sight.

"You think I know how to do *this*?!"

"Get back in the car!" Vince directed.

We raced back to Greg's vehicle and lunged into the cab for protection. This time, all six of us smushed in together, piling high in the rows. When everyone was in, we slammed out the storm.

The coughing and talking began in an instant.

"What was that?"

"What the hell?"

"What is happening?"

"What's going on?"

Everyone spoke at once.

"Hilde, are you okay?" I checked the girl's hands. She was a wind harness, but I knew it hadn't been her who created this powerful windstorm. She had seen it coming in a dream. I doubted she could pull off something that strong. Aside from wiping away stinging tears, her hands were limp. I was correct. The forceful winds hadn't been generated by her, or Greg, or any of us, yet still they trapped us. Round and round the car, the gale raged. Keeping us in and the High Council out.

"What now?" Vince asked.

"I've got sand in my hair," Greg complained. "It's in the gel. I'll never get it out."

"Look-" Beck's voice caused us all to follow his gaze.

Through the windstorm, a figure emerged. A man dressed in black clothing and a gas mask. The dirt storm whipped around him. Then two more gas-masked people appeared. Another man and a woman. Towards our car, they extended a hand and gestured for us to follow. One of the three, the shorter of the two men, had his hand balled up in a fist. He was the wind harness creating this windstorm. The shorter man and woman disappeared back into the haze, but the first man remained. Again, he gestured to the car.

Greg started to open his door.

"Wait!" I said, stopping him, slamming it shut again. We had no idea who these masked strangers were or what they wanted.

"Mae, no! When a sexy stranger comes dressed in full riot gear, offering to save you, you go!" Greg announced, flinging open the door. "God, I miss Marcy!" He added over his shoulder, as if she was the only one who would understand his pain.

"Greg!" Beck shouted, but he was already gone into the storm.

The man in the mask led him away.

Hilde looked back and forth between us, then ran out after Greg.

"Come on!" Ferris shouted. She raced into the storm next.

"What makes the riot gear sexy?" Vince groused, but he followed the girls.

Beck glanced at me, but I was already moving. Better to be wrong with our friends than left here alone. We raced after Vince's trail. The whirling gravel and dirt particles blinded our passage and caught in our throats, but the tornado was actually quite shallow, designed to be an optical hindrance more than an actual one. Running straight forward, we burst through to the fresh air on the other side of the storm in only a few strides. Two of the three riot-geared witches were waiting. The woman and the harness. Silently, they directed us into the forest. Beck and I, like the others, crashed wildly into the woods, following their guide.

Where were the Council guards?

And did following the directions of these unknown masked witches now count as an act against the coven? Like the winds they'd whipped up, the thoughts swirled in my mind. I was still choking on dust parti-cles as I ran.

These new three were most certainly witches. They came prepared. Each sourced with a gas mask. We, on the other hand, were running chaotic and blind. The tree roots underfoot came fast and loose. We raced through thick brush with no path. Beck's shoe caught on a root and he pitched forward, but I caught his hand before he crashed. We had to keep our heads up and our arms extended or risk being whipped in the face with a branch. Ahead, we could see Hilde had started slowing from the others. Her shorter legs were dropping her back in the pack.

"Come here, I got you," Beck swooped her up on his back, piggy-back style as we ran.

"You alright?" I asked. We could see she'd been crying. I checked her hands and face, but there were no injuries. She was just scared. I couldn't blame her for that. I was terrified too.

"You're safe," Beck comforted her. Hilde hugged tight to his neck.

"Move!" The two masked witches collapsed into our space, looking over their shoulders. We again picked up the pace.

How long could Beck run carrying her? How long could any of us keep this up? Racing into the unknown with random saviors and unseen captors was an awful endurance test. My breath heaved with panic, my blood pumped too loud in my chest. I sprinted over the ground, protecting my eyes and my face.

I thought we might run forever, but then the High Council stopped us in our tracks.

Vince, Ferris and the others were the first to stop running.

Then Beck, Hilde and I caught up.

Our final two masked saviors brought up the rear of the pack.

We were trapped.

There was no way forward.

Our entire group had raced right up to the side of a giant concrete wall. Twenty feet tall, unending before us. Cutting the forest in half.

TWELVE

COMMON ENEMIES DON'T MAKE
YOU FRIENDS

"THERE'S NO WAY," Vince muttered. Even he, our most skilled climber, couldn't find an edge to scale the gray concrete expanse. The entire structure was smooth and flat, designed with precision to thwart such a path. There was no way to climb up or over.

"It's a lie-guard," I said, although that must have been obvious to them all.

"If we don't believe, it's not real!" Greg told us. He ran at the barrier full tilt. I guess he hoped it would poof, disappear, or break or shatter. Instead, he smacked into the concrete wall.

Hard.

Greg fell to the ground in a heap. The rest of us sighed or ignored him.

"Where do we go from here?" Beck's question was directed at the witches in masks. Him asking them for guidance felt wrong, like we were just assuming they were allies. But that was foolish. We didn't know who the hell they were. Somehow, I didn't trust these new three. I'd been around long enough to realize just because you had a common enemy, that didn't make you friends.

The first man whipped off his helmet. He was gruff looking, and older. He wore a salt-and-pepper buzz cut with darting, crinkly brown eyes. "Fourteen, which way?"

Fourteen, apparently, was the woman.

She took her mask down next. A blonde. Older than us. Early thirties at least. Kind of attractive in a ragged, worn-out manner. "Go left," she said.

"Get down!" The third guy shouted.

We all fell to the ground as a huge light illuminated the forest. It searched over the place where moments ago we'd been standing. We hugged the earth, waiting.

"Who are you guys?" Vince asked.

"No, wait!" I stopped whatever might come next. "We don't know them," I whispered to the others. The mask-wearing witches were in ear-shot, but I didn't care.

"That's why he asked who they *are*." Greg rolled his eyes.

Ferris and Beck nodded. What was the big deal?

"I don't think we should align ourselves with every rando in the forest," I sniped back in Greg's direction.

"How about just every rando that saves our skin?" Greg replied.

"We're not aligning," Ferris said. "It's information."

"Information is power. The better to fight with," Beck agreed.

"But we don't want to fight," I countered. "We agreed to escape."

"Dude, they *saved* us." Greg complained.

"Or did they cause the lightning strike that caused us to crash?" Vince's skepticism also kicked in.

"Sorry. That wasn't us. None of us can harness the weather," the third masked witch pushed his helmet up off his eyes and shrugged. He was sweaty and tired. Clearly not a strong soldier. He had fallen to the earth near where I was positioned. He looked relieved to be removing the mask. "Sorry to eavesdrop on your not-so private conversation about whether or not you can trust us, but we did just save you and run with you into the forest, and now we're all lying on the same ground inches apart. It was kind of hard not to hear. But no, none of us are weather harnesses. Just to make that clear."

The taller man shimmied across the ground to his side and rapped an aggressive hand on the shorter man's shoulders. "What Twenty-Thom is trying to say-"

"It's Twenty. Just Twenty, Diego. You know that." He frowned as the bigger man jostled him around.

"-is you should be grateful we came and helped you at all. Now that you're on their radar as escapists, your relationship with the Council is toast."

"We could still rat out Mae," Greg defended.

I didn't realize he still held that as an option. But he was right, he still could throw me to the wolves.

The light shining overhead disappeared.

"Come on," Fourteen said.

We all rose, low to the ground, and moved forward. It was no longer a dead sprint through the trees, we were now skulking around.

"I wouldn't," Twenty-Thom shook his head at Greg. "Rat out the girl and escape? That's not how it works. There's no such thing as immunity in their world. If there was, you'd have to offer a pretty big thing. Like monumental information. No, you turn in someone that you *'helped'*," the unmasked witch air-quoted, "you're literally as guilty as them. Only now, the Court of Terminer and Oyer doesn't have to prove it. 'Cuz *you* already did."

"Basically, it's a shortcut to removing your hand," Diego nodded, "or your brain." He touched a bit of Ferris' red hair.

"Keep your hands to yourself," she snarled.

"Down!" Fourteen instructed.

We all dropped to the ground as the light searched the area again.

"Sorry, babe. Didn't mean to ruffle your feathers. I didn't mean anything by it. I'd have to be a lecherous oaf to try and flirt with a girl half my age. Especially with your he-man right here," he grinned into Beck's angry glare. We all knew Beck was *my* he-man, not Ferris', but no one corrected him here.

Diego didn't drop the smile. "I'm a good man, aren't I, Twenty-Thom. Nothing to fear."

"You're *something*," Twenty frowned.

"No harm. No offense," Diego put his hands up. The rest of us were not convinced.

The light flickered ahead in another part of the forest, so we all rose again, picking our way down the length of the wall.

"Who are you?" Greg asked the question again.

I didn't have the energy to fight a second round.

The two masked men glanced at each other. They hadn't come with an answer prepared.

"We're part of an anti-High Council," Fourteen told us. She seemed more in control of her emotions than either of the fellas. "It's a small group. We were part of the coven, now we're not. Like a place for former members to go when they want asylum."

"Like for crazies and weirdos?" Greg frowned.

"For those who want or need to escape from the clan."

"Why would someone need that? People can leave all they want," Hilde looked confused.

"Oh?" The salt-and-pepper man leered at the girl. "*You* left. How'd that work out?"

She shrunk back.

Ferris stepped between her and the man, but his point was made.

"Some people can go," Fourteen also intervened. "If their exit won't upset the balance of power in the coven. Those witches are free to leave and to return.

But a whole class of freshmen running amok of the rules then deciding they're better off without the clan?"

"With Cornelius Child at the helm?" Twenty-Thom shuddered. "Fat chance."

"Get down!" Vince warned.

We all dropped as the light smothered our part of the forest again.

"Trust us," Diego nodded, his face inches from the earth. "Getting out is a blessing."

Trust him? Unlikely.

His compatriots could also see he'd already burned that bridge.

Fourteen lowered her voice. "When we were like you, the Council wasn't like this," she said. "All power and silence and awful. It was a happy training ground when I was a student. Witches learned and got better. We met others like us in a safe environment. Fate bonded us together. But then the elder selections began. Class sizes got more selective. Cornelius grew in power. And a hierarchy emerged. You weren't an elder because of time or experience. You were selected. And what the chosen elders said, went. Then the punishments started."

"And the contracts," Twenty-Thom added.

"And the rules and the *justice*." She scoffed. "We don't want any more witches to lose their hands..."

"Or their heads," Diego chimed in.

I glared at him. But Fourteen brought me back.

"Including you, Mae."

"How'd you know who I am?" I sputtered.

They seemed surprised. "We know all of your names."

"That and you're a dead ringer for Sierra... oh, poor choice of words. Sorry," Twenty-Thom frowned.

Dead ringer. They also knew Sierra had passed.

"We're friends with your dad," he admitted. The others nodded.

My peers looked surprised, but generally pleased about this new revelation. I hadn't told them much about my estranged father. It seemed hearing these were his pals was received as good news to them. But Beck knew that wasn't the case.

Friends. With my *dad*.

I felt the earth spin out of control. Luckily, I was already lying down. They knew Sierra. They knew she was gone. They knew both her and my father? They must have known what he did to her. And still they were *friends? With the man who'd killed my mother?!*

I couldn't handle another word but the others' patience was also wearing thin.

"No offense," Vince groused. "But this isn't much of a rescue."

"Rescue... with the wind and the forest?" Diego chuckled. "That wasn't it. We intend to get caught."

"What?" Ferris snapped.

The other two nodded.

"We've just been waiting until they're close enough in range," Diego told us. "Gotta make it look good to the High Council."

"What?!"

Our mouths dropped open with more questions, but from there, things started happening very fast.

"We're good," Fourteen nodded.

"Come on!" Diego told us. "Let's go. Now! Stand!"

Greg started to follow their orders, but we pulled him back down. Fourteen, Twenty-Thom and Diego did it anyway.

"What are you doing? Stop," Ferris ordered them.

But they purposefully stood right into the source of light. Their bodies were illuminated against the wall in the forest. Their shadows shouted to the world where we had hidden.

"We couldn't control the time of your departures," Fourteen told us, "so we had to make an alternate plan. We'll get you out, I promise." Her voice was kind enough that I almost believed her. But these were my father's friends.

"Time to go!" Diego exclaimed.

"To the left!" Fourteen called new commands.

"Move," Twenty-Thom ordered. "Go, go, go!"

The rest of us had to choose between trying to hide in a forest location that had been tipped to the Council guards, or following the newer, messier plan. It felt like chaos. The light was so bright we were stumbling blindly. We couldn't hide if we wanted to. Ultimately, we had no choice but to follow what the three rescuers said. We ran wildly along the wall that had no beginning and no end. Until finally, we saw where the three deliverers were headed. There was a large hole dug in the ground. It went right under the wall. We could escape through their tunnel.

I glanced at the woman's hand and saw my suspicion was correct. Her fingers were curled into a ball. Another lie-guard. The tunnel was an illusion. The wall was created by the Council. The escape tunnel was created by these rebel fighters. None of what was happening in the forest was real.

Except maybe the danger.

"Get in!" Diego shouted, Twenty-Thom led the pack down. My friends jumped in, a herd of lemmings. We all followed his route. It was imperative we hide. We had to keep moving together. Escape while we still could.

"You first," I tucked Beck and Hilde in front of me.

"Can you climb?" He asked her.

Hilde nodded, feeling much stronger. Ducking down on the forest floor she'd recovered a second wind. There was no time to think, only do. Everyone moved at once. We were fleeing. She was small, but tough as nails like the rest of our crew. We scrambled down into the hole after the others. The escape route Fourteen had created was big. We had to duck low and crowd together to traverse through the tunnel, but we could all fit and move under the wall in a group. It was a simple solution to the High Council's complex lie-guard.

Sunlight filtered down from the other side of the tunnel. We headed for it. We were about to get out of the hole when suddenly, that light was blacked out.

Then the blinding light from the forest behind us disappeared as well.

Darkness overtook our small group.

The High Council had plugged both the holes from both sides.

We were trapped underground.

"Masks!" Fourteen ordered, but she was clearly only talking to her two other compatriots. The rest of us didn't have masks to hide us. We scuffled forward in darkness. Seeing nothing. Going nowhere. It was imperative to keep moving. Then, a pinpoint of light in the entrance re-appeared.

"Cover!" That was Fourteen's muffled cry.

I heard something clatter.

Ker-Poof.

I couldn't see it, but I felt a shockwave as a mix of chemicals exploded in the tunnel.

It was a potion. Or spell. It burst to life in the enclosed capsule. In seconds, the air grew thick with the cloud.

I coughed. "Beck." Instinctively, I reached out for him.

"I'm here."

In the pitch black, our hands connected and he pulled me to his side. I tried to wrap my arms around his chest, but, before we could come together, the whole world came crashing down.

The High Council's chemical warfare knocked me unconscious and sent me into a vivid dream. In my vision, Josie and Sloane faced off against one another in a boxing ring. Except, it didn't look like a boxing ring, and it also didn't really look like my two dear friends.

I just knew that's what it was.

And that's who they were.

And I was watching it go down.

They circled each other, both in fighting stance, ready for action when-

Ding, ding, ding.

A bell went off to signal the start of round one.

Josie made the first move by smashing a sachet containing a spell onto the ring's floor. As the packaging burst into pieces, snakes of vapor wafted up from the broken contents. They floated straight for Sloane.

The girl with the long blonde hair didn't flinch away. Instead, she spoke a rapid incantation, too quiet to really hear. But, the words out of her mouth protected her from the gasses as they rose, almost piling on top of them, weighing them down. Pushing them back towards the floor.

Sloane mastered the counter attack. She won the first round. Josie's spell had no power against her rapid conversation. A nattering of surprise and approval went up in the unseen crowd. I could feel them chattering around me.

Josie whipped her hands backwards to silence the audience behind her. Her black eyes seemed so sharp they could cut through Sloane's fleshy parts. Her movement was so acute it subdued the whole room. She wasn't one to be trifled with.

No one counted her out. They waited to see what she'd do next.

And the girl wasn't giving up.

Instead of smashing a potent spell again, this time, she held the little sachet up to Sloane's face and gently blew with the wind from her lungs.

But Sloane didn't fear.

"Past and present and future self." The girl told Josie. "I can use it all now. And your spells will run out." Then Sloane began to mutter another verbal chant. Rapid. Bewitching. It didn't matter what was said, it was the cadence that quelled the reach of Josie's spell. The miasma of the chemist's conjuring dissipated into smoke.

Ding, ding, ding.

The boxing ring bell rang out again.

Sloane's hands raised in victorious praise! She had put all of Josie's weapons in their place. The crowd started chanting her name.

Sloane! Sloane! Sloane!

Until, somehow, in the moment, I realized the voices had changed. Their voices chanted another name.

Mae! Mae! Mae!

They were cheering for me. Repeating my name.

Because now I was in the ring.

Who was my competitor? It wasn't Josie, was it? I didn't want to face my friend. But, I supposed I would.

It didn't matter who stepped in. I was ready. Ready to do battle. I wouldn't go down softly in the ring.

I steeled my resolve, beating my hands together like I'd seen boxers do with their gloves. I would take my competitor down quick and easy. Because I was ready to fight. I was ready to win!

Until I saw my opponent...

Lady Mauve stepped into the ring.

THIRTEEN

WAKE UP LITTLE MOPPET

"IS SHE READY?" A familiar voice roused me.

A teacher.

The toughest High Council instructor.

Lady Mauve.

But she wasn't talking to me.

I was barely conscious. In my muddied state, I didn't exactly hear the answer. More of a murmur.

"Let me see." Mauve peeled apart my sluggish eyelids and stared into my eyeball. My pupil retracted in the bright light. "There she is. She's good. Wake up little Moppet," she patted my cheek.

I struggled to sit up, coming around in the room.

"I have to say to her the-" I heard the other woman step forward, intent on some sort of routine of initiation towards me, but Mauve held up her hand. I tried to focus. Their hazy bodies came into view.

"In a minute," Lady Mauve stopped her companion, her tone making it apparent she was in charge of the proceedings in the room.

The walls of the cell became clear to my perceptions. The other woman backed down, dejected. In quiet objection, she leaned against the back wall. Mauve turned her attention back to me.

Full throttle.

It was unsettling.

"There you are. Welcome back." Her smile was cold.

I had stirred to fully awake in a dark, windowless room. I sat in a chair, my arms restrained with three straps. I was tied to the armrests. I flexed my hands. The first of my constraints held my elbow, the second gripped my wrists, and the third stretched my fingertips flat. I couldn't ball my hands. The bondage was specifically designed to keep witches' powers in check. I tugged against the fetters, but nothing moved.

"What did you do to me?" I asked. The inside of my head felt like it was covered in toffee. Sticky and slow. Dripping down my throat. My tongue was dry and large in my mouth. I still couldn't think clearly. "Why do I feel like this?"

"I gave you truth serum." Mauve sat opposite me now, like a therapist to client relationship, but we both knew she had no intention of nurturing me with this conversation. "Oh, and you likely inhaled some other sleeping agent down in the tunnel. They probably don't mix super well."

"Don't mix..." I rolled the words on my lips.

"Dry mouth is a side effect." She leaned forward, unsympathetic. "Now, let's get right to it. Who are they? The three in the forest?"

"I don't know," I admitted.

"They just showed up and started fighting for your escape?"

"Basically, yes. They had ulterior motives," I confessed. The extra words came tumbling out. I couldn't hold them back. I hadn't wanted to add that information. Her truth serum was working.

"What motives?" Lady Mauve sat back.

"I don't know. They didn't say."

True. Thank god for that.

"What are their names?" She narrowed her questions.

Crap.

I don't know. I wanted to answer, but more truthful words formed on my lips. "No names. Numbers. One was called Fourteen. The other Twenty-Thom. Oh, and one might be Diego, I think. We weren't properly introduced."

Mauve's eyes flashed at the name.

Diego.

Stop being so specific, I critiqued myself in my head. I didn't want to give Lady Mauve these details. But I couldn't seem to stop myself from saying any truth that popped into my brain.

"Twenty... Thom?" The other woman gasped. "Do you think there are more than *twenty*?" She asked Lady Mauve.

We'd both forgotten she was there. Now I glanced in her direction. I didn't know her. I was sure. I'd never seen her around the castle before today. Lady Mauve held up a hand in rebuke to stop the woman from speaking again. Sharp. Decisive. The woman fell back as if she'd been slapped.

More than twenty?

That was a detail Lady Mauve didn't want me to have. I filed it away for later use.

But that tiny info dump didn't really inspire me. Instead, I was struck by the movement. The little action Lady Mauve had just made. Her hand had sliced through the room. The motion she used to dismiss the other woman. There was something familiar about it. I had just seen it. I had *envisioned* it, I realized. In my dream. Only moments before Lady Mauve woke me up here.

In the vision, Josie had whipped her hands backwards to silence the audience behind her. Her black eyes seemed so sharp they could cut through Sloane's fleshy parts. Her movement was so acute it subdued the whole room. She wasn't one to be trifled with.

Just like Mauve.

And in my vision, I'd stepped up next to fight.

Sloane had fought back against Josie's sharp spells with a barrage of words. They leapt out of the blonde girl's mouth. All her talking collapsed Josie's spells. She battled back with her answers. Maybe I could do the same with Lady Mauve here and now.

What had Sloane said?

Past and present and future self. I can use it all now and your spells will run out.

A dose of truth serum didn't last forever.

I couldn't stop myself from spilling real answers to Lady Mauve's questions, but I could crowd the pertinent details out by filling the space and time between us with a barrage of my own stuff.

Harmless words that wouldn't help anybody.

Until I could regain more control.

Maybe.

It was worth a shot.

"Who's Fourteen?" Mauve refocused the conversation.

"I have no idea. I'd never seen her before today."

"Her?" The background woman uttered.

Damn. Had I given something else away? This time, Lady Mauve didn't flinch. Did the three gas mask wearing witches also get captured in the tunnel? I couldn't be sure. Mauve was fishing for details about them. It was possible they escaped.

Take control of the conversation.

"She seemed nice. Fourteen. I thought she was pretty. In a gritty sort of way. She wore her blonde hair in a low ponytail with a side part. I think she could also look good if she cut some bangs. Some people can just carry it off. You know? Bangs. Not me. Not at all. But some people can. Is it true that you lobotomize witches?" I asked. "Do you cut into their brains?"

It wasn't a perfect deflection, but a start.

"As a punishment, yes. We can." She answered my

question. Then had another of her own. "Mae, have you done something that needs to be punished?" Mauve knocked my volley right back in my lap.

"Yes. Lots."

Shoot. Why'd I say that?

"Like what?"

Don't try to lie, I reminded myself. Just start from the beginning. The way-back beginning. As far back as you can. *Fill the space.* I took a deep breath.

"When I was four, I said a curse word. Butt. Well, it's not really a curse word, but a curse word at age four, you know what I mean? I called Mrs. Langley the pre-school teacher Mrs. 'Long-butt' and I was reprimanded and put in a time-out. Not even Lang-butt. Nothing funny. I wasn't really clever as a kid. A little rowdy, maybe, but nothing clever. But the punishment worked. If you think about it, to this day, I still don't swear very much. Except in my head. Sometimes. When I'm angry. I think swearing's a little uncouth. It's definitely uneducated. A well-placed f-bomb now and then might be necessary, but when someone just rolls it off their tongue like with every other word... I guess I just think, read a book sometime, you know? They could have a better vocabulary if they wanted. *You* don't swear much and you're the scariest person I know." I approved of Lady Mauve, but then I stopped myself. *Keep it away from your opinion of your captor, I* warned my brain. *You wouldn't want to spill the true opinions that you hold of that elder.* In the conversation, I made an abrupt turn. "Aunt Abeline and I have really large vocabularies. She could put someone in their place with a thousand different selections. I love Aunt Abeline. I don't think she looks anything like Sierra, and they were sisters. But, back to punishment. Um, what else did I do? When I was twelve, I started to shoplift. Small stuff. I didn't even need it, but I liked the rush when I didn't get caught. It made me happy to spend time alone. Like, I can get by on my own. I was always alone growing up. Just me and my aunt. But, then they caught me. The rent-a-cop. In the drugstore. I had two lipsticks and an eyeliner in my sleeve. That was the trick, you just hovered with an armhole over whatever you desired and whoosh, sucked it up. Then just walk out, still in your hand. But it didn't work. The guard stood at the end of the aisle and frowned. It was so dumb. I don't even wear lipstick. Never have. Never will. But I thought maybe, to look older, I should. It was a nice color. It just didn't suit me. The manager called Aunt Abeline and she was super mad. We moved soon after that. Punishment of a different type, I guess. We moved around a lot. I didn't always want to, but sometimes picking up and leaving was easier than making friends..." the stories of more minor infractions in my past rolled out. As I spoke, I took note that my tongue was no longer feeling as large or as rough.

It was working. The drugs were starting to wear off.

Lady Mauve held up her palm. "How about today? Have you done something *today* that needs to be punished?"

"I did not attack the guards. I didn't use magic on anybody. I left with the others but I tried very hard to stay within the rules. We all did. We want to leave. I like my brain."

Suddenly, I caught sight of something. Or rather, the lack of the sight of something.

The other woman's arm.

My second interrogator's hand was amputated just above the wrist.

Mid-forearm, a prosthetic took hold.

"You were punished?" I asked her over Mauve's shoulder.

The truth serum had completely worn off.

The lady looked to Lady Mauve to see if she should answer. Mauve shrugged. Sure, why not. The woman could say what she pleased.

The guard nodded, self-consciously hugging the phantom limb to her chest. "I was an animal harness."

"And you work here?" I was incredulous. "For them? After they did that?" Why would she work for a Council that cut off her hand? The woman looked me dead in the eye.

"Where else would I go?"

"Literally *anywhere,*" I scoffed. That was ruder than I might have liked, but I couldn't blame the drugs. I was back to my usual, frustrated self.

Abruptly, Lady Mauve stood. "Mae, are there any more details you don't want me to know?"

"No." I said. "You know everything."

That wasn't true.

There was plenty I was hiding. The truth serum had worn off. I was free to lie once more.

Mauve realized it, too. "Can we give her another dose?"

"The reset for prime effectiveness is six hours," the woman told her.

"Bring her back in four," Mauve said to the guard. Then, she frowned in my direction. "Mae, if you're caught using magic while in the High Council's custody, you will be automatically found guilty of all charges."

"What charges?"

But Mauve ignored me. "Read her the rest," she said, already leaving.

Since the drugs had worn off, the interrogation was over.

"Lady Mauve, *wait.*"

But Lady Mauve didn't. She left, forcing the other woman to finish the job of reading me my rights. The one-armed guard stepped in. She knew the words by heart.

"You are being held in the High Council Judicial Chambers for the Court of Oyer and Terminer. Charges against you have already been filed. The nature and scope of your indiscretions are a matter for the Coven Five. Before these proceedings commence, you have a one-time offer for leniency if you confess to your actions and all previous crimes. While a lighter sentence cannot be guaranteed, every effort will be made to consider your change of heart. Do you want to confess?"

"What are the charges against me?"

"The nature and scope of your indiscretions are a matter for the Coven Five. You have a one-time offer for leniency. Do you want to confess?" She parroted a second time.

"Did you confess?" I asked.

She flinched.

For sure she did. She confessed to everything they were accusing and they *still* cut off her hand.

The woman cleared her throat and regained composure. "Do you want to confess?"

"There are other places you can go," I told her.

"Do you want to confess?"

"I can show you. I can help you."

"A fifth failure to answer the question will submit an answer in the negative. You have a one-time offer for leniency. Do you want to confess?"

"No." I told her firmly. "I do not. I've done nothing wrong."

"Very well." She adjusted the straps on the interrogation chair to loosely buckle my feet together and release my arms from the chair. I still couldn't move very well. Still a prisoner in shackles. "This way. I will lead you to your cell." Although she phrased it like an invitation, we both knew I didn't have any choice. She led me like a dog on a leash.

The one-armed guard unlocked the interrogation room we had been in and we traveled down a short hall and through a second set of double doors. They were electronically locked. Someone needed to buzz from somewhere else to let us through. All the locks were automated. The plain walls were dingy. While the castle above us was styled with beautiful modern and classical design features, the basement dungeon had no architectural flare.

That's where I assumed that I was.

I couldn't be sure that the window-less halls were running beneath the classrooms and accoutrement of the High Council castle, I had no proof. But that's how it felt.

Cold. And damp. Like a basement.

Unloved.

She walked us quickly through the labyrinth of small rooms and locked cells. The bindings from the chair had become a sort of harness. My arms and legs were still tied down, but moveable now, so she could lead me where she wanted. Obediently, I followed her path, trying to pick up information on our route. The rooms all looked the same. I tried to peek in doorways as we passed. Most entries had small viewing windows that, from the hallway, could be opened or shut closed.

In one such cell, I saw Ferris. Still buckled into her interrogation chair. Her questioning had yet to start, it seemed. Her head was flopped over, as yet unconscious and still.

In another portal, I thought I saw the top of Hilde's head.

As we marched forward, the one-armed woman didn't say anything. Just silently led me.

"How long have you worked here?" I tried to engage her.

But she knew better than to have a conversation with her charge. Instead, she picked up the pace. "Keep up," she complained. Easy to say. She wasn't the one still in shackles.

We turned a corner and I was surprised to see Diego being shoved into a cell. His gas mask was gone. He looked older here, and more tired. For a moment, we locked eyes. He flashed the same roguish smile he'd had in the forest, and I felt my skin crawl even as I was glad to see a familiar man. The smile reminded me that they'd said being caught was all part of their plan.

Some *plan*.

Immediately, my guard pulled me back. She dragged me into the previous hallway to wait. We weren't supposed to cross paths.

"Keep your head up, Mae! Keep watching! The moon will guide the direction!" Diego shouted as he was shoved into another small room. I could hear the forest-man scuffling at his entry. He was overpowered by High Council guards, shoved into his room.

Ker-plank.

The door to his cell slammed closed.

As soon as the hallway was clear, my guard marched us forward.

Next up, I glimpsed Vince and Greg. They were rounded up in a much larger room than the individual cells. The back wall of their space was lined with equipment and various prosthetic hands. I thought she would toss me in with the others, but she marched me right by, even as they ran to the window in their door as we passed.

"Mae! Where are you taking her? Come back! Damn it." I heard Vince yell. Frustrated, he slapped the metal door.

"Where are you taking me?" I repeated his question, trying to fall into step, but the woman was intent on marching alone.

And where was Beck?

These corridors were like a maze.

It seemed that everyone who'd been trapped in the tunnel in the forest was now locked in some small or medium sized room in the basement, all without injury, thank goodness. We were captured, but healthy. Unscathed. But, until I saw Beck's sweet face, I wouldn't be sure he was safe.

Was he being held for further questioning?

And if they put him under a truth serum like I'd been, could he keep all our secrets at bay?

The one-handed woman made another turn. We'd been marching forever. The place was terribly winding and confusing. It seemed inordinately large. A much bigger footprint than the castle floors above us. With each step I became more desperate to see my parabond's face. Instead, I saw Ferris.

Again.

The shock of her red hair was so unmistakable.

This time, she was conscious but still locked in her chair. She was face to face with Lady Mauve. Heated in conversation. Her face was twisted into a frown. They were hashing things out. I hoped she'd figured out her own way to beat the truth serum. But there was something else about this sighting.

I'd already walked once by her cell.

They were leading me in circles, I realized. To disorient me.

Well, it was working. I had no idea which way was out.

But, it also meant that the prison wasn't as large or dramatic as they made it out to be. If Beck had been caught in the same net as all the others, which I had to presume was true, he was probably locked in one of these nearby rooms.

My guard woman stopped. She nodded to a camera, hidden high up on the wall. Someone on the other side of the lens unlocked the door. It swung open to another larger room. She motioned for me to step in. End of the line.

"Beck! I'm here! I'm alright!" I shouted down the halls. "Beck! Where are you?!"

Mmph! Mmm Mmpheph! Someone's muffled cry shouted back.

"Beck!"

"Get in!" The woman stripped the shackles from my ankles and my wrists and shoved me inside the cell. The door slammed shut behind my back with a clang. Like Vince before me in his cage, I turned and raced back towards the door. I slammed my hand on the steel. The metal thudded from the inside out, but the window to the hallway stayed closed. The woman shut it when I started to shout. I was trapped in the room by myself. There was no one there to hear me. At least in Vince's case, he and Greg had been locked in the same room. But me, I'd been shoved here alone.

No.

Slowly, I turned.

Not... alone.

The room was stocked like a hospital ward. There were six single beds, made up in white linens, each large enough for one person to rest. The mattresses were on moveable platforms with handles and wheels. They were designed to move a person from one location to another. Like a patient might be shipped into a surgical ward at any moment. Beside each of the beds were sterile white tables, all tall enough to roll over the base of the patients' legs. Interspersed between each bed were floor-length curtains one could tug around a track.

The illusion of privacy in the hospital dormitory.

Machines and monitors lined the walls of the room. Most were off, pushed to the side. A few steadily beeped. Awful fluorescent lighting shone overhead.

But the beds weren't all empty.

Of the six white linen cots, four were taken with an occupant. The men and women resting recumbent didn't flinch at my messy entrance or my shouts or my door raps.

They were people I'd never met before today.

But they didn't sit up. They didn't look my way. They stared up into nothingness. Flat on their backs.

"Hello?"

No one answered.

My eyes flitted from the closest patients to the people further back into the space. Tentatively, I moved towards them. "My name is Mae Kingsley. Do you know where we are? Is this the High Council's prison?" I rounded the first bed and looked down at a bald man, in his early fifties with strands of gray hair interlaced in his beard. The tucked, white hospital blanket came up to his chest. Underneath the covers, he wore a white gown. His eyes looked glossed over and empty. A deep red scar was cut into his forehead. From temple to left eye. It wasn't like the guard's ugly gash in the forest. This laceration looked clean and finely sliced.

Surgical.

Exacting.

He didn't glance over as I spoke to him.

If it wasn't for the machine beside him softly bleating, recording his breathing, I wouldn't have believed he was alive.

"Hello?"

I moved to the next bed and the next body. A woman with gentle wrinkles around her eye lines, with a matching straight scar, same as the man. Her slice was bright red, probably fresher than the others. I judged her as being in her early forties. She also didn't register any response to my sounds.

I looked at the positions of all four people's bodies.

Their hands were tucked beneath the blanket folds. Were they also cut off? Fearfully, but also with morbid curiosity, I reached out to where her hand would be hidden under the comforter. Afraid to feel the firm, unforgiving nature of a prosthetic apparatus, or worse, to find nothing at all. But the woman's digits were all there. Her palms hadn't been cut off. Sadly, I held her hand through the blanket, looking down at the glassy eyes that couldn't seem to acknowledge I was there.

What had the High Council done to these four?

How had they created those red forehead scars?

The number of beds in the room wasn't lost on me. Still two empty, ready and waiting. Clearly, they were willing to do more.

I glanced at the other two patients. They were as dormant and unresponsive as the first pair. Their scars were paler than this woman's, so I concluded, this was the last person to go under the knife. Absently, I continued to pat the woman's hand.

"It's gonna be okay," I whispered. More for me than for her.

Ferris was right. The evidence was clear. When you were found guilty, they cut off a harnesser's hand. Or a lie guard's. And they sliced into dreamcast and chemist's brains. But it was far worse than that. Like any brain surgery risk, when the magic was removed, other parts of the person also seemed to disappear. Any sense of who the witch had been before the operation appeared to vanish. They were barely breathing. They couldn't move.

Would this be my fate very soon?

"Why?" I murmured.

It didn't seem fair.

True, I'd broken a contract that I'd signed.

Twice.

It said not to leave and I left. It said not to speak to the other coven, and I did.

If those were the charges, they were right, I was guilty. But was the Council really chasing, imprisoning, even torturing my friends over that?

I left my breaking and entering into the Konya Thomas Special Collection file room off my mental list of crimes. Yes, that *was* a serious transgression, but I felt sure no one knew about that.

"We're gonna get out of here," I told the woman. "Things will get better."

"Go."

Shocked, I looked down at the bed-ridden woman whose hand was still layered in mine. She hadn't moved. Hadn't blinked. Still stared up, glassy-eyed. Her conversation hadn't lingered, but her lips were now open a crack.

Were they always like that?

"Did you-" I bent closer, better to hear her.

"Go." The tiny voice wheezed the instruction.

Holy crap.

"Where are we? What's your name? I'm Mae Kingsley. Are you okay? What's happening?" I searched for every answer at once.

The woman couldn't move. She didn't budge. If I hadn't heard the whispered word with my own ears I never would have believed it was true.

"Is this the High Council castle basement?" I narrowed my questions down to just one.

But the woman didn't answer. It might have taken every ounce of energy for her to find the strength to utter the two words that she'd said.

"I hear you. I'm listening." I leaned in, waiting, encouraging. "Try to speak again."

The room grew so quiet you could hear a pin drop.

I remained frozen. Hoping she could gather more strength. The silence became an ocean between us.

Suddenly, the door crashed open again.

"Get in," an angry guard ordered. He pushed the entry to the cell open with such vehemence, it clanged against the wall. Shackles fell with a clatter as Ethan was thrust into my cell. The arrival was so loud and violent compared to the woman's breathy whispers, I jumped out of my skin. When he was shoved all the way in, the door slammed shut once more.

"Ethan!" The sheer relief to see someone I knew had me running to Ferris' boyfriend. He let me throw my hands around him in an embrace. While his hands didn't pull me in like Beck's greeting, it felt amazing to find comfort from a friend.

But, how had he gotten down here?

I drew back. "What are you doing here?"

This time I realized what his presence could mean. He hadn't come with us on our escape. He and Ferris had gone in separate directions. Ethan stayed at the castle to stay out of the realm of culpability. And yet, here he was. By my side. Down in jail.

"Hey." He glanced over his shoulder at the closed lock. I dropped the hug. The boy looked miserable. Who could blame him?

I searched his frown. "What's going on?"

"My parabond was caught running from the castle." His voice was pointed and cold. I immediately recoiled further. "They think I know more than I've said. They don't seem to realize that Ferris does all kinds of things without talking to me in advance."

The words cut hard. There was a lot left unsaid.

For a moment, we just paused. I felt the need to clear the air.

"I hope you know, I never wanted to involve you in a negative situation."

"You know what Mae, that's coming a little late. Love what you've done with the place." He moved past me to look around his new digs. Sheepish to have tossed myself into the arms of a guy who could barely look in my direction, I let him take in the new situation from several paces away.

"Sorry." I offered again. "I'll do what I can to get you out."

But we both knew that was a promise I couldn't fulfill. He waved it off.

Ethan seemed a bit disoriented. Prison would do that, I surmised. I knew I should give him plenty of room to digest the situation, but I just couldn't stop the question from pouring out of my mouth. "I don't suppose, I mean, when you were being questioned, did you see... Beck?"

"No."

I felt my heart drop.

Being reunited with another someone had temporarily reignited my hopes. And my fears.

I still hadn't seen that Beck was alright.

He was fine, I assured myself. In a room similar to this. Likely reconnected with others from our party. Maybe they were dividing us in pairs? They were probably keeping the bonds apart on purpose. Separate for our interrogations. So we couldn't get our stories straight. Police did stuff like that in the movies. This would all be sorted soon. Beck was alright. I insisted on my own encouragement. But, there were comatose patients all around where I stood.

Alternative endings to our situation had to be feared.

"I saw Ferris," I blathered, in case he was worried. "She was here. In another room, being questioned by Mauve."

"Fair can take care of herself," Ethan said.

I didn't doubt it.

"Ethan," I started.

The boy explored the room, just like I did. He

went to the bedside of each patient and checked on them, one-by-one.

"Ethan," I repeated, desperate for connection.

"*What*, Mae?"

"What do we do now?"

"I guess we sit and wait? I...huh. I know her," Ethan said. He'd stopped at the bedside of the woman whose hand I had held. "I mean, I remember. I saw her at the castle. When I was in first year. Or maybe second? She used to be a teacher at the school." He looked for a sign or a label or a chart at her bedside.

"Do you remember what she taught?" I flanked the other side of the cot.

There was no paperwork to be found.

"No. She taught the upper years. Lady Marshmallow? Ecru? Maybe Oatmeal?" He racked his memory. "Some sort of white... I remember white on white piping, I think."

The ladies and fellows had colored stitching on their tracksuits in the colors matching their namesakes.

"It's gonna be okay." I patted Lady Ecru's hand, the same gesture as before. But in front of Ethan, she didn't repeat her word. I was about to tell him about it, when a shiver tickled my spine. "Wait. You don't remember what year you saw her?" I asked, suspicious.

"What?" Ethan had been busy checking the wheels and gears underneath the bed, but looked up. "I think it was Ecru. That seems right."

"Just now. You said you didn't know? First year? Or maybe second?"

"Mae, what are you talking about?" He straightened, frowning again. But I didn't back down. My senses were heightened. I'd been fooled by lie-guard lookalikes before.

"You don't remember what year she taught you?"

"She didn't teach me. I said I saw her. It was a while ago. What's the big deal? It wasn't my class."

A lie-guard could take on another witches' perception and look and talk just like your friend. Most illusions fell away in seconds, but, if you didn't know the person that closely, it could feel very real for a time.

"Don't take this the wrong way, but I need you to prove that you're Ethan Grady." I crossed my arms. "Right now."

He frowned. "How do I know that you're Mae Kingsley?"

"You first, then feel free to test me. Where did we first meet? Where and when? Be specific."

Ethan frowned. "It was the night before the Battle. In the training room. We sat on the floor. I told you a story." He didn't break eye contact. "What was the story about?"

"Mauve." I told him. "Her origin story. How she joined the High Council. A bit of your kidnap as well." For a moment, we stared at the other, evaluating. But, eventually, I smiled. He'd passed the test. He nodded. As had I.

Identities verified.

"Alright. Before you got here," I started to spill the beans, but he held up a hand to stop.

"Mae, the room might be bugged..."

I hadn't considered that possibility. We started looking around, touching things with fresh eyes, searching for a listening device. I felt under ledges and around corners. So did Ethan. But, I remembered the way the guard had nodded to someone in a camera, watching. If he was right, if the room was bugged, it could be wired from anywhere. Be anything. It was probably everything and nothing. I was about to quit the search when the entry opened a second time.

Ethan and I spun.

Beck?

I stood in twisted shock, but Ethan had the presence of mind to run towards the door. He raced around the hospital equipment. But he didn't make it. Before he got to the closing exit, a new prisoner was shoved inside the cell.

The guards slammed the door. Now there were three of us caged together.

But it wasn't Beck who had joined me and Ethan in the hospital ward prison.

It was Rick.

FOURTEEN

CAN YOU DREAM OUR WAY OUT?

ETHAN and I ran right past our new prison mate and shoved up against the door, trying to pry it open. But it was no use. We heard the heavy, electronic lock shut us in.

"What are you doing here?" I spun to see Rick. I wasn't floored with relief like I'd been at Ethan's arrival. More filled with new surprise. He had specifically opted out of any and all questionable activities since our first day arriving here at the High Council. That should have saved him from our fate. We'd sent him away from our plans in the classroom with that express intention. What was he doing down here now?

There was no way they could punish him for anything.

He was as clean as they come.

"They said my parabond was caught escaping the castle," he told me quietly, rubbing his wrists where the cuffs had gone on. He was so large the restraints had bound tight. "I expressed that she was *leaving*, not escaping, which implied I was aware of her situation," he continued. "They asked me to say more. I declined."

So you're in jail because you didn't rat her out, I realized. They both were. But I didn't say it out loud. Instead, I told him another truth that might be more vital. "Ethan thinks the room might be bugged."

"A reasonable conclusion," Rick agreed. The two boys stood awkwardly, side by side.

"Rick, this is Ethan Grady, Ethan, meet Rick Lowe. He's bonded with Hilde. Ethan is Ferris' partner, you remember my battle-mate from the Battle of Four. The one with the bright red hair," I added as a helpful detail.

"I am familiar," Rick nodded. "Good to meet you." He offered a formal handshake.

"Yeah, you too." Ethan returned the gesture. A weird bit of normalcy on this wild and crazy day in jail.

"Where are you taking me?" Suddenly, a little voice floated in from the hallway.

Hilde!

My eyes flashed to the boys. She was coming, being escorted by someone. We quickly moved, all thinking the same thing. The upper window on the door's panel was closed, so the guards couldn't see in here. When the others were thrown in the cell, I'd been dazed on the other side of the room in shock. This time, we were all quite close to the exit to the hall. When it opened to bring Hilde in, perhaps we could overpower the guard?

The boys seemed to be on the same page.

We split up and tried to surround the entry location.

Waiting.

"Please, I wanna go home."

"Shut up, girl," a gruffer voice said.

"I keep telling you, I don't know anything," she whimpered. "Call Rick. Call my mom."

My eyes flashed to the bigger boy. Hearing that little voice invoke his name must have shot his heart. But Rick didn't flinch. Just stood his ground. Ethan nodded at us. We stuck to our positions. Three points of contact at the door. We all crouched. Coiling like cats. Ready to pounce.

As soon as the door was opened, I didn't know what we'd do for sure, but we all had one goal in our minds. To get out.

Instinct would take over.

Unbeknownst to me, I held my breath, listening hard.

Any second now.

"Just wait," Hilde cried. But this time, something was off. Her voice moved past the entry. They weren't bringing her to our cell. They moved further down the long corridor outside our room. Their group was headed further into the labyrinth of halls. "Please talk to me. Somebody. *Any*body."

Instinctively, I rushed towards the exit, out of my

hiding spot. "Hilde!" I banged on the thick metal door.

Not wanting to let her go.

"Hilde!" I wanted to reach her. Let her know she wasn't alone.

My hands made dull thumps on the door.

"Hilde!"

"Mae?"

"I'm here!" I shouted.

Things would be okay. We were close.

"Mae!" She shouted back. Her voice grew more insistent. "Mae! What do I do? *Mae, help!*" The squeak of panic filled the hall.

"I'm right here!" I thumped on the door. "You're alright!"

"We're here!" Ethan and Rick rapped the steel door as well.

"Mae! Ethan! Rick!" Hilde wailed in the distance. "No, no!" She let out a blood-curdling scream. It filled the whole room then was abruptly cut off.

We immediately dropped our hands.

Silence flooded the space.

I felt like I'd been punched in the gut.

She was there. So close. Fighting to reach us. I had called her. We all did. Then abruptly, she was gone.

Disappeared.

I looked at the boys. Their faces were stricken as well. White and ashen.

"We shouldn't have yelled," Ethan said.

I was already thinking the same thing.

But Rick disagreed. "She's not alone. Now she

knows."

Even after the girl's pitiful cry? Rick's calm demeanor gave me hope as well.

"What do we do now?" I wondered. "Keep looking for listening devices?"

"No, forget the bug. Just watch your tongue." Ethan said. There was no point in ripping the place apart, when every inch was under the Council's control. The listening device could be anything. Everything.

"Perhaps you can dream our way out?" Rick suggested.

Ethan and I looked at each other. We were both dreamcasts. I had already used a vision's details to avoid spilling my guts with the truth serum, but to manufacture a dream to help now? It was the first time I'd considered trying to capitalize on my witch powers in that manner. Dreams on command.

But why not?

If the Council was willing to go to such lengths as to lobotomize our brains just to mitigate our witch powers, they were clearly the strongest skills we possessed.

"Perhaps there is something you've already seen that will help?" Rick coaxed.

Of course. He was used to this. Pulling information out. Hilde was a dreamcaster too. She probably didn't know how to use the skill any better than I did.

"My vision was already spent," I admitted. "In interrogation. I'd need a new dream."

"I could do it," Ethan interrupted. "I just need to be unconscious."

"No." I shook him off. "It should be me. You're both innocent in all this, remember?" I told him. "Two innocent by-standers who had no clue what was going on. You can't go doing defiant things now." I said pointedly for the ears of any potential listening devices. Then added, "I'm sorry that you were brought into this at all."

Rick was already in agreement. Ethan stared at me for a moment, then nodded.

It was decided.

I would dream. They'd knock me out.

"Do either of you know the tension grip?" I wondered.

I'd had it done on my neck when I was training for the Battle of Four. It was a tense little squeeze on the right spot. On your shoulder, at just the right nerve. Hit that reflex and I'd go out like a light.

The boys shook their heads. Neither knew how it was done.

"Well, it can't be that hard," I offered. "Just, knock me out."

We walked over to one of the empty beds and I climbed on top. I kicked off my shoes. It seemed rude to put grubby sneakers up on the white linens. I laid back, flat on my spine like the other hospital patients, and stared straight up at the ceiling overhead. The white speckled acoustic tiles offered no new information, but they gave me a point to concentrate on. If the High

Council found me guilty of whatever charges they were planning, this would be my eternal vantage point. Like Lady Marshmallow or Ecru, or whatever. And all the others.

Flat on my back.

Staring at nothing.

Forever.

"Just... give it a try," I told them, motioning to my shoulder.

The boys had a silent game of 'no, you go first' above me, but finally, Rick stepped up to the bed.

"You are sure you're alright?"

"I trust you."

Grimly, he nodded and slid his fingers beside my collarbone. I lay still, doing my best to be a good patient. Gently, he pressed and tweaked in the right general area, but nothing happened. I didn't feel anything. Either the pressure or the positioning was off. Maybe both. Either way, nothing kicked in on my circulatory system.

"Anything?" Ethan asked.

Rick and I both shook our heads. He couldn't get the job done.

"You try." I offered Ethan.

The boys switched places. This time, I swooped my long brown hair clear out of the way. Clean access for man-handling. Ethan frowned.

"It's okay. Knock me out." I giggled. The request sounded absurd when said out loud. "I know you want to."

"It's something like this." Ethan pressed a little harder than Rick, but aside from the gentle relief of applied pressure on my shoulder, his squeeze didn't do much. He tried several other hand-holds. Still nothing. At best, a mild massage.

I couldn't enjoy it.

We were all stressed out of our heads.

"Get another pillow," I suggested.

"You think if your head's positioned a little higher?" Ethan grabbed my request from a nearby bed. I waited until he returned with the fluffy white cushion before admitting why I wanted it.

"You can smother me."

"What?"

"Cut off my air supply." I grabbed the pillow. "Just a little. Don't look at me like that. We need me to be unconscious."

Ethan frowned. "So you can dream, not be dead."

"A little choke. Then you bring me right back. I'll be alright."

"No."

"Don't be so stubborn."

"I'm not stubborn. I might *kill you*."

"You won't."

"How do you know?"

"I know."

"Mae, you'd be *dead*. That's what you're asking."

"I'll be *unconscious*. Dreaming, casting visions. Just what we're wanting. And you can revive me once I'm done. I trust you."

"I have zero experience in suffocating."

"It's okay I-"

"It's not okay! Are you mad? *I* don't trust me with that."

"Well, what do you wanna do? *Hit me with a bedpan?*"

"No!" He stepped back. "I don't want to hit you or choke you at all! A pressure pinch was one thing. What you're talking about is a whole 'nother level!"

I half sat up. "You have a better idea?"

"No!"

"Then, just do it! Knock me out."

"Mae."

"It'll be fine!"

"*Mae.*"

"You'd knock out Ferris if you thought it would help us."

"It's never come to-"

"*This will save her!*"

"You don't know that!"

"Yes, I do. Just do it now! Then bring me back. Ethan, I trust you."

"Mae-"

"If Ferris was here, you would totally smother her!"

"I wouldn't suffocate the girl that I love!"

"Of course you would! You'd kill her to save her!" I roared. Then, I heard what I was saying.

You'd kill her to save her!

That was what I was advocating he do? I burst into

an impish laugh. It was so insane. Ethan started laughing as well. Relieved. The wildness of our argument finally caught up with our brains. With our mouths. You'd kill her to save her, that was the solution we'd found? What the hell were we doing? I sat up all the way, still chuckling, making room for him to plop down beside me on the bed.

"Just a no-murdering policy," he said. "As much as possible."

"Well, I guess that's a good choice," I agreed. "I mean, Ferris will be glad."

"I do what I can."

Despite ourselves, we both grinned. He raised a hand and for a second, I thought he was going to rake it through his hair like I always saw from Beck. Instead, he just stretched.

I sighed.

I loved the way Beck did that little thing with his hand. Pulling his hair out of his eyes. Helping himself see more clearly. Physically, but also sometimes mentally. I hoped the strain of his confinement hadn't brought him to dumb ideas like mine. Ethan seemed just as lost in thought about his parabond as I was about mine.

"I don't like to fight," he admitted. "It's just-"

Somehow, I knew he wasn't talking about his and my little confrontation. That was over. He didn't really want to fight with *her*. With Ferris.

Especially now.

With all this scary stuff going on. Both of them, thrown in jail.

The last thing they'd shared was a disagreement. I could understand how Ethan might want to clear the air.

"You were put in an impossible situation," I admitted. "I get that. So does she. In her cell."

Ethan half-smiled.

I leaned towards him, dropping my voice. "When we get out of here, Beck and I are gonna run away. Far and fast. Maybe you two should come too."

"That's the first good idea you've had on this bed."

I shrugged. "If you talk long enough, you're bound to spit out something."

We chuckled. My demand for my murder and his refusal to kill me had opened us up. Fast friends. Ethan was strong in his convictions, and a little sardonic. I could see why Ferris liked him so much. Good or bad, he wouldn't back down from a fight.

Thank god for that.

"We still haven't figured out how to cast," I frowned.

"Well, perhaps-"

We spun around. Rick looked up from a medical cabinet he'd been exploring at the back of the room. He'd already jimmied it open and rifled through the contents during my spat with Ethan. He'd organized the containers on the shelves and now held two bottles in his hands. He looked up at us and nodded.

"I can help us with that."

FIFTEEN

EVERYTHING COLLAPSED INTO BLACK

"AMABLE CIEL AND FIXED BORNA." He brought us the two small bottles. "Alcohol-based and a binding agent. Mixed together, they're very noxious to humans. One whiff and you'll be knocked out," he told me. "But, it could get us as well." He nodded to Ethan. "If we're going to use it, we have to be very gentle with exposure."

"Will it hurt?"

"Says the woman who suggested being hit with a bedpan?" Ethan laughed.

I nodded. Well yes, that was me earlier, but now I was back in my right mind.

"No, but it smells." Rick shook his head. "Like rotten quail eggs. And vinegar. And old cheese steaks."

"That's not so bad," Ethan shrugged.

"Yes," Rick disagreed. "It is."

I knew to trust the large boy. If he said the stuff was powerful, it would knock me on my butt. If he said it smelled bad, it was about to stink to high hell. But we were desperate. I was ready for anything.

"Let's do it." I hopped down off the bed. The stone tiles were cold on my toes.

"You sure you want to be the one unconscious?" Ethan checked.

I nodded. That hadn't changed.

"You stay back," Rick directed. "Ethan and I need a moment to prepare. Protective clothing," he told him. They grabbed more supplies off the shelf. They slid on hospital gowns backwards, like aprons, over their clothing. They donned protective goggles and plastic gloves. "And here." He even found clothes pegs for each to clamp over their nose.

"Ah, feels terrible," Ethan moaned as he pinched shut his nostrils.

"Bet you wish you'd choked me out now," I joked, trying to ease the tension that was growing in the room. Ethan was too serious now to fully laugh, but he gave me a grin. He and Rick both held an individual bottle, ready to go.

"I'm going to count us down. You ready?" Rick checked in with me.

I sat back on the bed. "Ready. Sitting up or lying down?"

"Sitting up, this way, so when you pass out you'll fall back, away from the fumes," Rick decided. He turned to Ethan. "I'll count us down like this." He folded back fingers. Three, two, one and go. "You count one second, then close it back tight again. We cannot open our mouths."

For fear they'd inhale it, we got it.

"Alright?"

"Three, two, one, open, then immediately close it back up." Ethan repeated.

We both nodded, super serious, even though none of those instructions were for me.

"We'll bring you back in five minutes," Rick told me.

I blew out some of the apprehension I felt inside. I shouldn't be worried. For me, this was just like taking a nap. The boys would take care of me. So why was my heart beating so fast?

The guys readied on either side of me, their horrible gear all intact.

"Ready?" Rick asked.

We all nodded.

He counted us down.

Three.

Two.

One.

Rick and Ethan both opened their vials.

The pungent odors hit me in rapid succession. Rotten quail eggs. And vinegar. And old cheese steaks. A million stinky socks. The spray of a skunk. The world's hottest, most disgustingest outhouse. The smells all attacked me at once. Involuntarily, I recoiled. They sealed the containers up quickly. But the tiniest moment of aromas was more than enough. Immediately, I felt my head swimming. Then everything collapsed into black.

In my dream, I awoke on a bed of asphalt.

No, not a bed.

A road.

My body felt tingly. Wobbly. I stood up. I dusted the dirt and pebbles from my butt and shins. I had grass in my hair. The night was dark. It was quiet. I was cold.

Blaaare!

A horn angrily sounded. Suddenly, bright headlights flooded over me.

A spotlight cutting out through the nighttime.

I threw up a hand to shield the blinding lights from my vision.

A garbage truck came barreling down the street.

It was headed right for me.

On a collision course with where I stood.

I squinted. Trying to get my bearings.

Faster and brighter it drove towards me, until the white of the lights was all I could see up ahead.

It was coming right at me.

Gonna hit me.

Roll right over.

The driver laid on the horn again, but he didn't slow. I had to do something to avoid the collision.

Something *fast*.

What to do? I only had a split second.

I couldn't move. My feet didn't want me to go.

I shielded my eyes from the bright lights of impact. Preparing.

Would it hurt when I was pulverized into the road?

Would my life flash before my eyes as my face hit the gravel?

As my body crunched under wheels, where would my soul go?

It was coming.

There was nothing I could do to stop it. To protect myself. All I had was my small body.

At the last second, I wrenched both my arms to the right, as if to avoid it. As if in dream logic, I could swerve the whole world. And-

Crash!

"Oh my god!" I flailed, shooting up from the bed, but strong arms held me down.

"It's okay," Ethan soothed.

I couldn't move. But quickly, I figured out why. Rick and Ethan were holding me in place. Safe on the small bed. When I stopped struggling, they let me up. I was still on the hospital cot, lying down. Ethan hovered over my location while Rick, still in goggles and gloves, put whatever he'd just used to awaken me safely to the side.

"Smelling salts," he told us.

Groggily, I sat up on the cot.

"Did you cast?" Ethan asked, hopeful.

"A little bit. I did. I was on a road. A dump truck was bearing down."

"Well that's good. A road's outside," Ethan interpreted.

"No. Sorry. Not a dump, a garbage truck. You know with those big double prongs?" I motioned like the front of the truck would, attaching to a dumpster. "It was coming right for me. I tried to stop the crash."

"Did it work?" Rick asked.

"I'm not sure." I admitted. "I don't think so." The last thing I'd heard was a loud smash.

"But you were on the road. You were out. You were successful. So maybe our escape has something to do with the trash? A garbage truck. We should look there?" Ethan wondered. He grabbed the garbage pail from beside the jimmied shelves.

Rick and I glanced at each other. My dream was about the *truck*, not the garbage itself, but I didn't shut it down. I didn't have a better idea. There were no trucks in this cell.

Ethan tilted the canister over, spilling it out, but only a clear plastic bag was inside. He pulled it out of the can.

"A plastic bag," he offered.

Again, I didn't think that had anything to do with my dream. But, I didn't want to be hurtful. "Now you could choke a person out," I told him.

"Or tie a person up?" Ethan wondered. He twisted the bag in his hand. It became taut and strong like a rope. The closest thing to a weapon we had. Dream or not, it might actually have some value and it was worth keeping handy. I was glad.

But what was the vision about?

Suddenly, we heard a small, metallic scraping. Ethan immediately hid the new bag behind his back. All three of us turned as the small porthole in the door was opened from the external corridor.

"Hello?" I called.

A face appeared. The one-handed guard who'd delivered me to this room. "You have a visitor," she said.

Ethan, Rick and I looked at each other, uncertain which 'you' she had meant.

"Her," the woman clarified.

I glanced at the others, but hurried over to the door in my stocking feet as quickly as I could.

A familiar face entered the small window pane. Lady Blue Moon!

"Hey, hi!" I raced in. "What are you doing here? Are you alright? Are you good?"

"I should be asking you those questions," she said, sadly. "I'm on this side, fine, over here."

But that was a relief. Blue Moon wasn't under arrest. She was just fine.

"What's going on?"

She frowned. "They didn't tell you? Of course not." Her eyes flashed in disapproval to someone in the hall. The woman with one hand must be standing right there, I realized. I'd be extra careful about what I said. "There's an inquisition. It's formal. It's already started. To look into the actions of coven members during the Damocles occupation." Blue Moon raised her eyes to the ceiling, then looked back at me. *'They're recording'* she mouthed.

I gave a tiny nod.

"What's that have to do with me? With us?" I asked, for the benefit of the High Council listeners, playing dumb.

Blue Moon sighed. "Hopefully, nothing. But it might take a day or two or more to sort it out. Until then, you need to sit tight."

I nodded. When I'd seen her face pop up in the window, I'd hoped for a little more guidance than *'cross your fingers and wait'*.

"You have my number? In case you need to ask my opinion?" She asked, her eyes slightly narrowing.

Yes, of course I have your number, I thought. It was a text from Blue Moon's phone that sent me the coded message: BREAKOUT TONIGHT... unless, was *that* the number that she meant?

"It hasn't changed," she said. "The number's the same."

The message was still on point?

We should breakout tonight?

But how could we breakout from prison?

I knew she was doing her best to speak in code in case anyone was listening, but I feared I wasn't getting the whole message. I wished she could say more.

"I'm not sure I understand. You want me to use the same number as before?"

She nodded. "The same number still applies. Even while you're here. The number hasn't changed." Her eyes widened, hoping I was getting her message. I hoped I was too. "There are lots of people with my number." She added. "You're not alone."

There were more of us breaking out. Tonight.

"Okay."

"Also, and this is totally separate," she went on, "If you're charged, you'll have the opportunity to hire a magistrate, it's like a lawyer, for the coven. At that time, if it happens, we'll brainstorm who'd be the best representative for your defense. For now, there's nothing to do but wait." She shrugged. She looked at me secretly, again. "Things will happen. In their right time. Come here."

I stepped forward.

Kindly, through the small window, Blue Moon patted my cheek. That was unusual, we weren't especially physically touchy women in that way. But she patted it in a very specific manner. I took special note.

With one finger twice.

Then with three.

Finally with all five.

"In time. Everything will be fine. I promise." She gave me a serious look. "You can do it. I have faith. Things will be okay."

"Moon," the one-armed woman looked over her shoulder. "Wrap it up."

"Is it eleven o'clock already? Alright." Lady Blue Moon stepped back. "Thanks Steel. We're both Blues," she told me. "Blue Moon and Blue Steel." She gestured to the woman in the hall. The other guard simply grunted. I realized, this visit to me in the prison was a personal favor. Lady Blue Moon and the one-handed guard had some previous rapport. My friend stood back from the window in the door and crossed her arms. On her own arm, I saw she patted the sequence again.

One finger twice.

Then a three.

Then a five.

I didn't want her to go.

"I'm scared," I admitted.

"A very natural reaction," Blue Moon nodded. "Just wait for your time. We'll play Scrabble again soon, before you know it. Maybe this time I'll beat Aunt Abeline." She gave me one last reassuring smile. Then, the door's window panel was closed.

"Well, that wasn't helpful," Ethan frowned. Immediately, he pulled back out the hidden garbage bag.

I'd actually forgotten they were there.

"Did you learn any new information?" Rick asked.

"No," I shook my head. "I think it was a warning shot," I told him. "A heads up. Something's coming." I made a bee-line for my shoes, thinking of all the coded messages she'd just sent. I couldn't say them out loud to the others. Blue Moon was right. The Council might be watching, or listening, or something. I couldn't threaten Blue Moon's standing and reveal them to my friends.

Use the same number again. She had told me.

And the purposeful pats on my face and her arm.

The references to time.

One, one, three, five.

Blue Moon did it all with a purpose.

She had risked coming here to try to help me. She was giving me a message. A real instruction. We would break out tonight.

At 11:35.

I COULDN'T TELL them out loud what I thought, in case there were listening or recording devices hidden around the cell, so instead, I passed the information off to the boys' ears in whispers. One at a time, I told them my best guesses. They nodded and said nothing. None of us in the room had a watch, so Blue Moon telling us to wait and be patient was a bit like being tortured in the jail. How long was an hour? How long was a minute? There was no light from the outside world. We had no clue. But Lady Blue Moon had hinted it was evening. The minutes ticked by, slow as molasses.

Still, we waited. Hopeful. Uncertain.

None of us said much, for fear of the listeners, but as time marched on, our emboldened daydreams started to leak in the room.

"If there *was* an escape, I mean, hypothetically, at some distant point in the future, if we could make that happen, what do you think we should do?" I wondered.

"We should run. The second the door's unlocked. Run hard and don't look back," Ethan said. "Find Ferris and the others and," he clapped his hands together, "run for the hills."

"I meant more specific, like left or right to leave the dungeon?" The one-armed guard had twisted me up in knots before throwing me in this cell. I had no idea which way was the actual exit.

"Oh. *Right.* Right, for sure."

"How do you know?"

Ethan shrugged. "I don't. But there's an old saying, *'He who hesitates loses'.* Mae, if we ever do have a hypothetical escape plan you just pick a lane and go." He hopped up, and for the thousandth time went wandering by the door. Tried to see out the cracks around the portal window.

"I wish I had your confidence," I muttered. I also wished he'd just sit down. As he helplessly fidgeted, checking and rechecking the walls for imaginary glimpses into the outer halls, I realized he was just as scared and nervous as I was, he just expressed it in different ways. Rick and I just watched him pace from afar.

"What about you, Rick?" I asked the quiet chemist. For him, the stakes were different. He hadn't even been a part of our initial discussion about the original escape into the forest, he was at a disadvantage. We hadn't let him in the door. Fat lot of good it did. He was here now because he wouldn't rat on his partner. Or his friends. "If there was an... opportunity... would you go?"

"I am punished not for actions but for silence. I have no choice." He nodded.

I sighed. "I'm sorry you got wrapped up in this. You and Ethan both."

"Mae, it is time to stop apologizing for things outside your control." Rick's eyes bore into me, until he felt he had made his point. "To me, to the boy, and to others. This is not your battle alone. It never was."

I looked around. I'd made plenty of mistakes, of that I was certain, but Rick was right. I didn't have to apologize to him for his imprisonment today. It hadn't been my choices that had brought him here. Locked him in a prison. Sat him amongst lobotomized witches. Forced to wait his turn to go under the knife or a trial. At least, it hadn't been my choices *alone*. The High Council had to take credit for some things. Rick would take credit for others. And he was right. Ethan and Ferris had made their own choices as well.

"Sorry," I apologized again, nodding. Then I realized I was still doing exactly what I had been before. "I will," I agreed, trying to be more firm. "Starting now."

I turned and looked at the other lifeless witches, still in their beds.

"Are we just going to leave them?" I wondered out loud.

Go.

The woman had whispered the word in my ear. She was at least partially aware of what was going on. They weren't just human potatoes. I stood up to look over her bedside.

"Do you want to go with us?" I asked.

"We can't take 'em," Ethan looked up from his plastic analysis. He'd vacillated from the door to the precious trash bag several times. "They're too far gone."

I leaned in close to her. "Are you in there?"

"*Go.*"

My eyes grew wide. I definitely heard her again. "Lady Ecru's still here," I told them. "She just told me to go."

"Great. She's encouraging us to escape," Ethan said.

"I don't think so. I think she wants to come. She wants to *go.*" I turned back to her, gesturing to her bedding. "Is it alright if I check?" Lady Ecru could not acquiesce, but I felt alright about moving forward with my observations, because she would know I was trying to help. In as noninvasive a manner as possible, I started looking around at the medical devices where she lay. Could we take her with us? Under the blankets, she was hooked up to a catheter bag. It rested in two sling holders attached to her leg. There was a valve at the bottom. Every so often, it would need to be changed. I could do that. Likely, she was eating through some sort of funnel or tube. I didn't see an IV, or special feeding system, so yes, we would have to figure out how to get the nutrients in her, but from everything I could see here, she was mobile enough to leave.

"It may be some gas in the fundus region, or something settling in the pylorus. Unconscious patients can murmur, even moan," Rick warned.

"It's probably gas," Ethan agreed.

"No, I definitely heard her." I looked back at our patient in her bed. Lady Ecru couldn't move, but she was definitely in there. "She's talking to me. Sending us a message. Probably using every ounce of strength that she has."

Both boys frowned.

BANG!

"What was that?" Ethan spun.

We looked up, frantic. The sound was too insistent to be ignored. We all turned and checked the cell, although instinct alone told me the noise hadn't happened inside our small prison. The hospital quarters remained untouched. Something had exploded or shattered somewhere else in the halls. Probably still on this floor. A little further out.

"It must be 11:35," Ethan said, glancing at his arm. He didn't have a watch. Excited, he ran towards the door. Rick and I followed. For a moment, I forgot all about my bedside patient. Ethan grabbed the handle and pulled.

Nothing happened.

"No."

He yanked again.

"Let me try," Rick stepped in. He grabbed it tight with his giant hands, but still, the door didn't open. It didn't budge. The mechanical locks stayed in place.

"Hey!"

We banged on the door, although, except for the loud noise, nothing about the prison appeared to be different.

"Let us out of here!"

Suddenly, we heard a large, metallic shudder.

It was like a magnet shot through the door. The lock to our cell clicked open. We looked at each other. This time, Ethan easily pulled open the door. We stared out. In the halls, we heard others start to talk and shout from inside their prisons. We were free to escape. All the doors had opened at once.

Little Hilde's voice was closest. "Hello?"

"Holy crap," Ethan muttered. "It really worked."

Lady Blue Moon's messages were correct. There really was a breakout.

"Now's our chance!" He pushed the door wide open. "Hilde, where are you? We're coming. Come on. Let's go!" He ran straight out the door, and true to his word, he did break right.

"Wait!" I shouted, but Ethan was already long gone. "Shoot."

Rick ran back to the shelves. I looked at the exit, then back at my bed-ridden friend.

"Here." Rick had grabbed several supplies, including the Amable Ciel and Fixed Borna. He gave one of the bottles to me. "For defense."

I nodded, also pocketing the gloves, nose plugs, and goggles. Next, I went to her bed. "Rick, I can't leave her," I told him. "She's not brain dead."

"You don't know that she's still living."

"Yes I do. She *is* living. She's not like the others, Rick. I heard her. I can hear her. I could *be* her... so could you." I looked him right in the eye. "Wouldn't you want someone's help if you were her?"

He hesitated for a moment, then nodded. We would free her as well.

In a flurry, I looked around for things to help me transport Lady Ecru. Rick sat her up in the bed, talking softly to her, warning her before every move that he made.

"Careful of the catheter," I told him. Near the wall was an old fashioned wheelchair. I grabbed it from its resting spot in the corner and brought it around.

"Come on!" We heard Ethan shouting to others somewhere down the hallway. "Mae, Rick, we gotta go! Get out of there! Now!"

"We're right behind you!" I shouted, as we lifted her motionless body into the wheelchair.

Where were the guards? Where was the High Council?

I didn't know and I didn't care.

We worked as fast as we could.

Rick tried to use smelling salts to revive her, and shone a bright light in her pupils. "I'm not convinced that she's here. Without an MRI, there's no way to judge actual brain function. She may never move or stand."

"I don't care! She said 'go'. Not once, but *three times*. She wants to leave. I know it. I'm not leaving her behind."

"Alright." He agreed. "I am with you."

"Don't worry, Ecru. We're taking you too," I told the woman.

"Grab the sheet." He tied her into a pocket, then we lifted her down into the chair. After all her time in the bed, she didn't weigh too much. Like a small child. If it had come down to it, I might have even been able to lift her myself. We used the linens pulled tight to secure her upper body to the chair. "There. We got her."

"We got you," I repeated to Lady Ecru.

Rick pushed the chair and she rolled forward. We were about to follow Ethan's route. He guessed right, I could hear that more teens seemed to have gathered. Maybe even Beck? I couldn't wait to be reunited with him. But, when I glanced out into the hallway, I immediately fell back. I thrust a finger to my lips. Shushing my partners. Freezing in place. Rick collapsed against the wall beside me, instinctually following my moves.

Two High Council guards turned the corner and ran by our doorway. They were headed Ethan's way.

We froze in place. But they didn't even glance through the open doorway. They already assumed the ward was empty and headed towards the voices in the hallway that were moving away. In a flash, they passed our room and turned the corner in the corridor. When they were gone, we started our journey again.

"This way," I pointed in the other direction. We went left. It was too risky to follow. I hoped Ethan and the others would still be okay.

Out of our room, the hall continued on in several directions. There was an immediate corridor to the right, and a set of closed doors to the left. If I had to guess, the guards had come from there. More of the High Council ladies and fellows were likely on their way.

"Let's go straight," Rick took the new lead.

We wheeled Lady Ecru down the hallway. When that corridor ended, we were forced to turn again.

More cells.

More directions.

It was a maze. Designed with purpose. The halls led in circles to stop prisoners from escaping. There was no way to discern which direction to head in. We would have to start opening random doors. I grabbed the first handle. We pushed it in.

Nothing.

A single occupant cell.

We ran ahead. I put my hand on the next doorway and shoved it open.

Another empty bay.

"We're in the wrong area," I realized, sensing a pattern. "It's a dead end."

Rick was getting the same impression as well. It seemed we'd found our way into the bowels of the basement. "At the next hallway, we turn left," he announced. That decision was good as any. Together, we raced ahead.

But then, I heard a magical sound.

A sweet voice I had hoped to hear since we'd arrived in this place.

Low and resonant and sturdy and seductive.

It was echoing down a corridor very close to where we stood.

The voice was moving.

Coming towards us.

He was yelling.

"Go, go! Move!"

It was Beck.

SEVENTEEN

FRIENDS OF MY FATHER

"COME ON!" Beck was yelling.

Racing with someone.

"Beck!" I shouted ahead.

Rick and I stopped. We could hear them coming. On our left. Coming up fast.

"Mae?"

"Beck!" I hurried forward.

"Mae, look out!" He and the other woman, Fourteen, rounded the corner, running full tilt in our stead. It should have been a joyous reunion, but I could see that Beck was overcome with panic and anticipation. On their harnessing hands, they each had some sort of oven mitts.

"They're right behind us!" Fourteen shouted. She ran right by us. "Move!" She tried to grab my arm and pull me or Rick into action behind her, but she missed. She didn't slow down.

"Mae, come on." Beck's free arm cupped me towards him and I fell into stride, grabbing his hand on the fly. Rick immediately turned with our charge.

"How many of them?" He asked, powering Lady Ecru forward in her chair with valiant effort. We picked up the pace.

I glanced over my shoulder, as we rounded the corner from whence we just came. I saw the peek of a signature white sweat suit coming up behind us. The guards of the High Council were in hot pursuit of the pair.

And now us.

"Two? I don't know. Maybe more," Fourteen told us.

Rick and I looked at each other. "We don't have to outrun them," he said.

I nodded.

"Come on!" Beck insisted, but past the next corner, Rick and I put on the brakes.

"What are you doing?" Fourteen and Beck careened to a halt.

"Just - hold your breath," I warned. We grabbed our nose plugs and held out the bottles like guns before us, aimed against the coming witches.

"Ready?" Rick asked me.

"Ready," I told him.

I didn't take my eyes off the turn. The second the witches rounded the corner, Rick and I opened our bottles in tandem. The Amable and Borna let off a terrible stench.

We held the bottles open in their direction for only a second.

"Oh! My god," the others stumbled.

"What is that?" Beck complained, his fingers flailing to his face.

"Don't inhale," Fourteen warned. She must have recognized the smell.

But the caution was already too late. If she smelled the first waft, it was already in her head. The fumes infiltrated their senses. Rick and I resealed the containers. The High Council guards fell to the ground in an unconscious heap. But so did Fourteen and Beck. Rick and I sealed the bottles and ran in opposite directions. He checked the pulse of the High Council members. I went towards our friends.

"They're alright," he said, looking up, letting the guards fall back to the floor, limp without his care. "What about them?"

Beck, Fourteen and Lady Ecru had also fallen senseless. I gently tapped Beck's face, trying to revive him. "Totally out."

"I still have the smelling salts," Rick dug them out as we removed our nose plugs. The stench wasn't nearly as potent as before, but we sniffed them first. He knelt and waved the reviver gently under Fourteen's face. He waited until she started to rouse before he passed them over to me. I did the same motion for Beck.

"Oh." Fourteen moaned, sitting up.

The aromatic spirits caused Beck's lungs to

expand. His body took a big, involuntary gasp. The oxygen flooded his brain and he shot awake again.

"What is that?" He asked again, coming back to his senses. "That smell..."

"Smelling salts or knockout gas?" I asked. I passed the ammonia compound over to Rick so he could wave the salts under Lady Ecru's nose too, although, conscious or not, with her we couldn't see any change.

"All of the above. Gross." Beck grinned at me. Happy to see me kneeling by him, he dragged his hair out of his face. How I'd missed that little tousle move.

And that smile.

And that face.

"I'm so glad you're alright," I told him, lunging into his arms. The oven mitt felt awkward over my back, but I'd take a weird hug from him over no hug, any day.

"I'm alright. You're alright?"

"I'm good."

He briefly kissed me.

"Have you seen the others?" Rick wondered as we broke apart.

"Hilde's with the group," Beck told him, knowing Rick's actual first priority was his parabond partner. "She got to us. I was in a room with Vince and Greg and Ferris. Last I saw, they'd reunited with Ethan. Then, these guards came running. Twenty-Thom said he'd lead them out of there, I was still looking for you guys. And before I knew it, the same guards were chasing my tail. The others must have got by them, so I think they're good. Twenty-Thom really saved the day."

"It's just Twenty," Fourteen said. "Thom is Craig's last name. It's just Twenty, or Craig, not *Twenty-Thom*. That was just Diego being a fool. I'm Gennady. Well, Gen for short."

"Mae, Beck and Rick," I offered, although I felt sure she already knew. Gen nodded. Quickly, we got back to our feet.

"This way," she motioned back the way we'd come.

"We've already been there," I warned her.

"It's okay, I have a map," she pointed to her head. "And Wes should meet us any minute, over here."

"Good," Rick said.

Beck grabbed my hand and dragged me forward. Behind her we all started to jog down the halls, following her trail. Rick pushed Lady Ecru in the wheelchair. I ran in step, but alarm bells had started ringing in my head.

Wes should meet us any minute?

As in *Wesson Zaid*? The name I would never forget?

These rebel fighters had said they were friends with my father.

He was the one who was breaking me out of jail?

Suddenly, we saw another guy running towards us from the opposite direction. He wasn't dressed in an all-white tracksuit, so I felt pretty certain that he had to be with Gen.

"Wes!" she shouted.

"Everyone alright?" He asked, coming up fast to our route. "We gotta keep moving. The whole Council's coming. Before we could stop him, the first guard triggered a full castle alarm."

So these first few henchmen were only the prison guards on duty for the evening. More were coming.

"Here they come." Rick said. He'd stopped in the crossroads of the hallway, looking in both directions, right and left. We arrived only moments behind him. Both routes I now realized were double-locked entrances fed by the upper floors and stairwells. Through their vertical windows, we could see a league of High Council witches were now making their way down the stairs towards us. It was a wave of white tracksuits. From both directions. They were marching right for us.

Rick, Beck and I froze in fear, but the older witches didn't stop.

"Come on!" Wes shouted. Spurring us to action. "Gen, do what you can. Try to hold them back!" We all ran.

"Wes, I've been capped." Gennady told him.

"Cloth, metal or plastic?"

She held up her oven-mitted hand. "Plastic!"

Wes balled up his fist, and suddenly the mitts melted off both her and Beck. They were both freed. Gennady balled her own palm and in one motion, the stairway double-lock doors slammed shut in both ends of the hall.

Thwack!

Through the windows we could see the surprised witches race towards the shut doors.

"Diego, now!" Wes instructed into a cell phone.

Suddenly, we heard the metallic shudder for the second time that evening. The locking machinery inside the doors sprung back to life. The guard witches were trapped outside of the jail, shut out in the stairways. For a moment, we'd locked ourselves safe inside the prison walls.

"We gotta keep moving," Wes warned. "That won't hold them for long."

Beck grabbed my hand, I looked to Rick, and he started wheeling. Gennady and Wes led the way. We raced back down the hall, in the direction that Ethan had headed when the madness had first started earlier that evening. Though he was now safe, long gone.

"Diego, the cell block entrance," Wes continued barking. The cell door to an individual enclosure popped open. Second from the left on the back wall.

Diego must have escaped from his cell and gone to a communications hub or central work area. Like a guard at the controls, he seemed to have access to every door.

"Let's go, let's go!" His crackling voice instructed through the phone speaker.

"We're on the move." Wes agreed. He creaked open the new door and at the back of the cell, behind the toilet, where the wall should have been, a hole had been blasted into the façade.

A hole *out* of the High Council castle.

That first blast that we'd heard.

This must have also been where Twenty-Thom had helped the others disappear ten or twenty minutes earlier.

We quickly ran in.

Gennady first, Rick, Lady Ecru and the wheelchair, me and Beck to follow, and then Wes at the rear. The cell was so small you couldn't even fit two across in the room.

"Here." I helped Rick lift the wheelchair over the destroyed plumbing apparatus into the tunnel. Beck didn't question who she was or what we were doing, he just boosted the back wheels. Lady Ecru traveled over our heads and into the shaft that was blown open behind the High Council. I climbed right after.

"Are you alright?" I checked in with her, but of course Lady Ecru didn't speak. She still couldn't move. I gave her an encouraging smile. She was getting her wish. We were escaping.

"We're good. Lock it down," Wes told Diego on the phone. "See you on the other side." He dragged the cell door closed behind us, and slid his communication device back into his pocket, now turned off. He climbed over the same apparatus that we did, until everyone was safe and enclosed in the tunnel behind. Wes pulsed his hand into a ball and collapsed the castle wall, sealing us in. "We gotta move. I don't know how long those magnetic locks will take to open again."

Already, in the prison we could hear destructive forms of magic trying to break down the door. In that interior corridor, there was a lot of collective magical power working in tandem. We needed to get more distance between us and the castle. And quickly. Our group ran forward with Gennady at the helm.

Somehow in the transfer into the tunnel, I had started pushing Lady Ecru's wheelchair. She wasn't heavy, but it was awkward because the tunnel wasn't flat. Blindly, we hurried in semi-darkness, putting as much space between ourselves and the High Council dungeon as we could. Until someone crashed in from another dugout hallway beside us to the left.

"*Ahh!*" Gennady screamed, but then laughed.

It was only Diego, the other salt and pepper haired man from the forest, racing down a perpendicular shaft.

"We did it!"

"You scared me!" She swatted.

"I know, was I trying!" He admitted, laughing and playful. Nobody slowed. He fell into step, racing forward. We ran until we arrived at a fork in the tunnel. It was more than a fork. It had too many options. It was a fiver. There was the path we had taken and four new, separate, different roads. Which way led back out?

"We need to split," Wes told us.

His partners nodded. I could see from their demeanor, this was always part of their plan.

"I'll go with Beck," I told them. Effusive, my parabond nodded.

But the rebels shook their heads.

"No," Wes said. "You can't."

EIGHTEEN

EVERY REBEL TAKES A KID

"EVERY REBEL TAKES A KID," Diego told us. "You with him, you and her, me and you." He tried to push each of us towards an adult. He indicated the guys go with the others and urged me into his route.

"She's not with you," Beck told him flat out, remembering his weird vibes with Ferris.

"Fine, whatever. I'll take you, he-man. She can ride with Pops."

Both Wes and I shot the other an uneasy look.

Pops. A nickname for father.

Confirmation.

Wes was exactly who I feared he'd be. Wesson Zaid. My estranged dad.

"I wanna go with Beck," I said.

"Well, too bad," Diego snapped. "That ain't happening. You don't even know where the safe house is."

"I don't care." Beck and I held hands, our bodies

stiff. We had only just been reunited. Neither one of us wanted to split.

Suddenly, closer to the prison, we heard a loud fracas.

The guards were making their way into our tunnel shaft.

"Damn it, we don't have time!" Diego said. "They're coming. This ain't some drill."

"I'll take Hot Wheels," Wesson said, grabbing her chair from my hands.

"Her name is Lady Ecru," I told him.

"Her name is Lauren Bixby," Wesson corrected.

My eyes widened in surprise. He knew her? Diego and Gennady nodded. They both knew Lauren as well. So they were intimately familiar with the coven and with this woman. That answered the first of my many questions, like who our lobotomy patient was. But there wasn't the opportunity to pepper them for more info, we could all hear the danger approaching. The guards of the High Council were coming. We needed somewhere safe to hide. The commotion in the tunnel grew louder in warning. There was no more time to discuss.

"We can each take one of you," Gennady said. "At the sub, you'll reconnect, I promise."

Beck and I looked at each other, uncertain.

BANG!

Something smashed into the tunnel, this time breaking through the foundation.

"I'll go with you," Rick offered to ride with my dad

and with Lauren, but I shook my head, grabbing the chair back from Wesson's hands.

"No, I got this. She asked for my help. I've got Lady Ecru, er, I've got Lauren. You go with him." I pointed to Diego. I didn't even trust the shifty guy with Beck. But we all knew Rick could handle any situation.

The two men nodded at each other.

"I'll go with Zaid," I agreed to the partnership, but felt unable to casually throw out my father's first name. And I certainly wouldn't call him dad.

It was too close.

Far too personal.

I looked at Beck with purpose. "I'll see you at the rebel camp."

"You sure?"

"Kids, we ain't got time for goodbyes," Diego told us.

But we ignored him. I nodded. Lauren was my responsibility, I would see to her safe escape.

Beck kissed me, quickly. "I'll see you there."

I offered a sweet smile. "Yes, you will."

"Let's go," my estranged dad encouraged us. "You'll see him soon enough."

I glared at the man, but we nodded and split in opposite directions, following the instructions of the rebel witches, ducking into dichotomous tunnel holes. Our group was now racing in multiple directions, I realized. Under the High Council grounds. They'd split up our exits on purpose. We'd be harder to catch or follow in little units. I pushed Lauren on the bumpy passage, moving as fast as I could considering all the weight on her wheels.

"Wes! Be careful!" Gennady called as we parted.

He nodded, but didn't shout in return. Instead, he paused and used his powers to fill all the tunnel exits. First Gennady's, then Diego's, next the empty one, then the one we'd come from, and lastly our route after we'd passed. When he was finished, he quickly caught up with me and Lauren in her chair.

"We've got to keep moving."

"I'm going," I frowned. "But the path isn't easy on wheels."

Wesson balled his fist again and the base of the tunnel suddenly altered. All the bumps flattened out, smooth and slick. "Better?"

"Yes." I was reluctant to give him even the slightest compliment, but it *was* better.

Silently, we ascended the shaft.

The path through the earth was long and winding. It was clear, someone or some*ones* had been digging under the property for years. While the flat bottom to our route wasn't real, this entire hole wasn't a lie-guard. It was the real thing, painstakingly and mechanically dug in the earth. Someone had done a lot of strenuous, incredible work to build infrastructure under the castle. And then they used it to break me and my friends out of jail. Why?

"Here, let me push."

"No, I got it." Stubbornly, I wouldn't let him take over the wheels. It was hard work. The initial rush of adrenaline I'd felt as we were escaping was over. Pushing Lauren, or Lady Ecru or whatever you wanted to call her, wasn't easy, but I refused to let Wesson know that small truth. I didn't want him to know anything about me. The desire to follow him and the other rebels blindly away from the castle had seriously waned. I didn't know them, and I didn't know their motives. "Where are we going?"

"Back to the sub. To the safe house."

I nodded.

"Don't worry. You'll meet back with your boyfriend there."

I wanted to snap at this man, at this *stranger*, that he had no right to talk about me or my boyfriend at all, but even saying those words out loud to rebuff him was more acknowledgment than I wanted to give. I kept it all locked in my throat.

"I'm glad you're alright," he stiffly added.

"Let's not." I gave a small head shake.

We weren't doing this now.

Not here.

Not in this tunnel.

Not *ever*.

I'd learned his name. Seen his face. Met this stranger. Yes, he was being nice, but I wanted him to pay for what he'd done, how he'd hurt my mom. There were things he had to answer for.

Not only that, he'd basically abandoned me as a child.

Of course now, it was more complicated. He and

his allies had come out of their way to save us. They'd put up a rescue. For that, I did have to give him some merit. But just some. He hadn't earned the right to know me. To say 'nice to meet you'. To have some play-time as my dad. Father/daughter moments? No. We'd never have that. Or even be as cordial as two acquaintances. We wouldn't be coming together. Better to nip that in the bud.

Wesson seemed to understand.

Neither of us said much after that. I concentrated on the path. Pushing Lauren's wheelchair was quite physical, even with the lie-guard flooring. As we made it around another gentle curve in the tunnel, finally, I saw the way out. The sweet silver glow of natural light up ahead.

The exit.

At the far end of the passage, we emerged into the forest under the cover of nightfall and tree limbs. The stars were out in full force. I was pleased to see there wasn't a coven ambush waiting in the wings. We'd gotten out cleanly. There had been an entire tunnel system under the castle all this time and the elder witches hadn't known it was there. We came out under leafy cover only steps from the township's main road.

Wesson released the lie-guard tunnel floor. Again, behind our tracks, he crumbled the tunnel walls. That would slow any followers down. And there was more to his plan. In the trees, he worked fast, lifting a chicken wire fence off the nearby shrubs.

I was surprised.

The man-made barricade had been so tied up with branches and leaves in homemade camouflage, I hadn't even noticed it was there. Not until he lifted it up. Underneath, he revealed a black, shiny motorcycle. All the tunnel exits must have external bikes, I realized. That's why each rebel could only pair off.

Wesson flexed his hand again and he created a magical side-car for Lauren.

I realized now, in the eerie blue-silver glow of night, what I guess I'd taken for granted at first. My estranged dad was a talented lie-guard. Anything we might want, he could make appear. It didn't even seem to tax him like I'd see it pain some others. The witch was so strong, the expenditure of energy was nothing more than a flick of the wrist.

Fast as I could, I loaded Lauren and her wheelchair inside the small sidecar. Wesson would only be able to drive with one hand on the motorbike, the other holding the illusion firm. With his unused hand, Wesson gave me my helmet.

"Ready?"

I nodded. And before I could second guess my options, I was up on the back of the bike, threading my arms around the waist of my estranged dad. The man I had never met in the past seventeen years. What the hell was I doing?

But Wesson didn't wait, he took off. He drove the country roads without his lights on. The moon was bright and he knew the hilly routes seemingly by heart. I guess he wanted to limit the presence of our travels on the roads. Keep us as incognito as possible, so no one would see our headlights coming, although our presence wasn't a total secret – as we drove, the engine still roared.

I didn't try to speak over the wind.

I'm not sure what I would have said without the noise. We were headed away from the castle and for now, that was enough.

"You're free," Wesson told me. "You and Lauren." He sounded a little giddy.

But I saw it ahead in the road before he did. "No," I sighed. "We're not."

"What the hell?"

NINETEEN

THIS WASN'T JUST A WALL

AHEAD, in the road, there was a wall made of jelly.

No, not jelly, exactly.

Some gooey, viscous substance.

It was enormous.

My eyes followed its rubbery boundary skyward and I realized this wasn't just a wall. It was an entire jelly dome. A High Council lie-guard, or several lie-guards, had created an enormous bubble over the entire castle vicinity. All of the trees, the full road, everything on the nearby grounds was under the overarching slope. Including us.

The Council guards didn't have to follow us blindly as we split up in the tunnels. They put the whole property under a net. They had us caught.

We were helpless.

Futilely, I looked around. I couldn't help but worry Beck and the others had been captured as well.

Wesson revved the gas and we drove up to see the

material up close. The wall was at least three feet thick of clear, glutinous material. He parked and hopped off the bike. I quickly followed. We each reached out to touch it. Though the bubble looked almost opaque, the feel of the material was fairly tense and kind of tough. There was no give or weakness in the rubber. It wasn't something we could cut through. And even if it was, I'd left my three-foot knife at home.

"Come on," he muttered, getting back on the wheels.

I followed. "What should we do now?"

I thought maybe we'd just go in the opposite direction, but Wesson drove a little ways back, thirty feet or so, then stopped the bike.

"It's a lie-guard. We're gonna go through it." He revved his engine.

But he hadn't turned around the bike. We weren't facing the wall.

"Wait, what?"

"In reverse," Wesson said. Then he slammed on the gas.

Our bike and sidecar shot backward.

"It's too big," he yelled over his shoulder as we flew backwards. "There's no way they thought of every perception! I'm a lie-guard. There's no way they prepared for someone to ride through it full speed in reverse. We'll break right through it!"

"Are you crazy?!"

"Exactly! You'd have to be crazy to try it like that!" He yelled. But that didn't deter him. He didn't stop.

The insanity of his action was why he believed it would work. On his hunch, he was risking our lives. He watched behind me as he gunned the bike backwards towards the very thick, very permanent rubber barrier.

I stared in disbelief.

He *was* crazy. That much was accurate.

In my head, I remembered Greg running and crashing into the wall in the forest. Full blast. On impact, he had splattered to the ground. That had been a lie-guard too. Greg ran at it with full force and he was tossed like a salad. He couldn't break it. It knocked him dramatically on his butt. At that speed, he hadn't been injured. But at our speed...

Wesson cranked the gas even higher as we approached.

"Zaid! Stop!"

"Just hold on!"

"No, wait. Stop!"

There was no time for braking. I ducked my head on his back and braced for collision.

Full impact in three...

Two.

"Hold on!"

"Oh my god..." I clenched shut my eyes.

One.

TWENTY

FREE AS THREE BIRDS

ZOOM!

Wesson, Lauren and I burst through the bubble like there was nothing to it. The material disappeared into the ether. Wesson was right! The strength of his weird perspective and dare-devil driving had freed us from the lie-guard. The spell dispersed. The bubble disappeared.

"Woohoo!" Wesson pumped his lie-guard fist in the air. He slammed on the brakes and I couldn't help but laugh in my own relief as he braked to a dramatic stop in the middle of the road. The adrenaline rush I felt was insane. Wesson was also piqued! We were so pumped neither of us could see straight. He had just performed the craziest bike move I had ever seen and we were liberated! It was crazy! The entire bubble structure no longer existed. Wesson had disintegrated the entire illusion the moment he burst through.

We were back on the main road.

Free as three birds.

Liberated on the paved highway.

I regained my bearings.

On the wrong side of the highway.

Blarrrre!

Suddenly, a horn blasted down on us. Only forty feet away in the opposite direction.

Our heads spun.

Straight ahead in the laneway, a garbage truck was coming right for us. It crested the hill. Driving fast. Only to discover our little trio parked directly in its route. There was no time to swerve. The driver couldn't turn. He slammed on the horn and punched down on his brake.

But the oversized vehicle couldn't slow fast enough, traveling at the highway's high velocity pace. It would mow us down in its path. What could we do?

Blarrrre!

"Zaid, go!" I urged my dad, but the man had become frozen in fear.

The truck's lights got larger and brighter.

"Come on. Move."

But Wesson couldn't seem to hear.

"Where's the gas?! We've got to do something!" I demanded over his shoulder. I knew enough about bikes to know the accelerator was in the hand grips, not the foot pedals, but I still needed more information. I needed Wesson to move.

But he couldn't answer.

The man was petrified in fear.

Our faces were illuminated in the headlights. The giant truck would hit at any moment. I could see the panic in the driver's eyes as he came barreling down the hill.

Suddenly, I remembered my dream. "Come on!"

The garbage truck.

The lights.

I had seen this scene in a vision. What did I do in that interaction? I reached through Wesson's arms and toggled the throttle in his right hand. The motorcycle roared to life. But we still didn't move.

Blarrrre! Blarrrre!

The truck was almost on top of us.

Blarrrre! Blarrrre!

Only seconds left.

The impact grew near.

I yanked the handlebar towards me, blindly moving my palms in the way my dream-hands had rotated in the vision. The engine gunned to life and the bike shot out of the way.

Blarrrre!

The truck raced by. Only missing us by inches.

The wind whipped around our helmets. We escaped by the tiniest shred.

The motorbike shot onto the shoulder as the truck roared by in the right lane. But, from behind Wesson's arms, I couldn't hold us. I couldn't control how we moved. We hit the rough edge between the gravel shoulder and pavement at top speed and the wheels kicked and frayed beneath us.

"Zaid!" I screamed, but there was nothing he could do. The bike careened into the ditch on the highway's side. In a violent dust bowl, we crashed.

On impact all three of us were thrown into the ditch. The bike smashed hard into the earth. It ricocheted and skittered. The engine roared, then choked and died. For a moment, there was quiet all around.

"Ohhh." I let out a moan.

Wesson, regaining his senses, picked himself up as well. He was scratched and the sleeve of his left arm was ripped.

Every muscle in my body hurt. But, at least I wasn't in pieces.

The bike on the other hand...

"Are you alright?" I asked, turning to the unmoving woman.

"I'm okay," Wesson murmured. He didn't know I was actually checking on Lauren.

In the chaos of the impact, Wesson had released his hand and completely dropped the illusion of a side car. She had smashed to the ground with both him and I, and she had pitched across the wild turf as well. But Lauren seemed to be okay. She was still wrapped in most of the blankets, and her catheter hadn't released from its holder on her calf. Out of the three of us, she had actually fallen the most safely in the tallest grasses in the gutter. I checked her over. She'd be bruised for sure, but there was no blood or open wounds on her skin. We were all a bit tattered, but not broken. I climbed up the embankment to pick up the remains of our things.

Turning back, I realized Wesson was on his feet, but not back at the helm of the machine. "How's the bike?"

He shook his head. "Toast."

I came to look over his shoulder. I didn't know anything about motorcycles or trucks or any other vehicles. That was in Beck's wheelhouse, not mine. But I agreed with Wesson's assessment. The bike looked smashed up pretty good.

"You can't fix it?" I wondered, already knowing the answer.

He shook his head.

"Well, can you at least fix it magically? You know, like you did with the side car?"

Wesson frowned. "Well, sure. But if I use that much magic, we can't head to the sub. It'll leave too large an energy trail. The Council could follow. It was already a risk with the lie-guard sidecar, but that was when the bike worked."

"So what, we're stuck here in the forest? If they can follow the energy of your lie-guards then they'll know that we broke through the bubble right there," I gestured back to the now non-existent barrier. "We have to keep moving."

Wesson nodded. "We need a safe place 'til morning. With the right tools, maybe I can fix the bike? I dunno. We'll figure out something from there."

"Do you have another safe house?"

Wesson frowned. "We can camp out in the forest."

Hunkered down in the woods, jumping at every sound, flinching at any action? That sounded pretty terrible, but at this point, I was accustomed to terrible things. Luckily, it didn't have to go in that direction. I had an idea.

"I know a place," I said. "Where we could be safe. For one night."

"Not your Aunt's."

"No, of course." That was a lesson I'd already learned.

Zero involvement from family or friends. I had learned it so thoroughly that with our broken bike, I didn't even mention Beck's mechanic dad. I wouldn't have him involved.

But hearing Wesson mention Aunt Abeline brought chills to my skin.

How much did he know about Sierra's sister?

Her only other living relative.

Other than me.

"It's somewhere they won't think to look," I said. "At least not for a while, I think. Bad karma abounds in the building."

Wesson seemed skeptical, but nodded.

We couldn't stay where we were. We couldn't go to his base. What else could we do? My suggestion was the best choice in a sea of limited options.

"You ready to ride?" He asked Lauren, re-balling his hand. He picked up the bike and the motorcycle and sidecar reappeared, good as new. Shiny and fresh.

He helped me get Lauren back into the bike-chair. "Where to?" He asked, handing me my helmet.

I told him the address.

He nodded. "Yeah, that's a pretty good suggestion. I wouldn't think to look for you there. You sure?"

"I'm sure," I agreed stupidly, not really thinking it through.

TWENTY-ONE
WE'LL STAY HERE TONIGHT

WESSON DROVE us to safety in silence.

Maybe *safety* was an overstatement.

He drove us to the quiet spot I'd offered, where we could regroup out of reach of the High Council.

Well, not out of reach.

They could still get to us here. Wesson was worried they might track the trail of his magic. But at least it wasn't in the forest or right beside the halls of the castle. Any distance we could build between ourselves and the coven had to be beneficial.

As we drove over the hill into Plumpkin, things started to look more familiar. Even in the dark, I felt it in my bones; this was a better place to wait out the storm. I hadn't suggested the home of a friend or family member, I'd learned that lesson with the Damocles coven. Instead, I'd proposed a property I'd only been to one time before in my life. But I knew it was deserted. There wouldn't be a soul on the grounds.

It was Kate Hucklebee's farm.

Young. Dead. Teenage. Kate.

After her ghastly fall from the loft in their barn, the Hucklebees had left town. They barely packed. They just escaped and never looked back. I couldn't blame them. After such a tragic passing... I wasn't sure if the property would ever sell, what with the girl's blood still leaching into the ground. But as far as I knew her parents weren't even trying to take it to market. They just left. Never to return.

An instinct I now understood.

Coming here tonight felt eerily similar to the night of her death. That had been a midnight visit as well. The last time I'd approached these structures, Josie and I had parked out on the road and snuck ourselves in. But tonight, Wesson drove his bike and the sidecar all the way over the grounds. The house and barn were both dark.

I was right.

There was no one to fear at the farm.

We stopped just before the barn door. Wesson held the bike still as I climbed off and swung open the outbuilding doors. He rolled the bike the final few feet in, dropped the kickstand on the concrete pad and released the illusion of the side-car chair that held Lauren. Quickly, I closed the barn doors, sealing us in.

I checked on Lauren, and emptied her catheter before I put back in her wheelchair. It must be hard to be so powerless in such an unusual situation, I realized. But Lauren was alright. In that immovable body I imagined someone fierce. She'd be strong. She'd get by. I did the best I could to help her. The bedsheet and the wheelchair held her upright, nice and tall.

"Are you alright?" I asked, bent down to her level.

No response.

At this point, I wasn't expecting it.

"We'll stay here tonight," Wesson told me. Firm. "Tomorrow, I'll get something else to drive. Another vehicle. Then we'll make our way back to the safe house."

I nodded towards Lauren, then pointed to the rooster perch. "I'm gonna make her more comfortable. But there's a lookout up there. If you're worried about the Council following us, you could watch for movement from that viewpoint." It was the same place that Kate had stashed my necklace and Josie's watch. Our High Council offerings. She had tried so hard to stop us from joining the coven, she had wanted us to join her instead. At the time it had seemed so subversive, but had she known from the start what a life of witchcraft at the High Council would entail? Was she right in her goals? Now here I was, months later, back in the comfort of her barn, running away from the very same clan I'd been so desperate to join.

Wesson found a ladder, leaned it against the perch and climbed his way up to the lookout. From there, he could definitely see any High Council witches coming. On the ground, I searched for a warm blanket for my new friend. Without the movement of her arms and legs, Lauren would be more susceptible to cold than Wesson or I.

I averted my eyes from the ruddy brown spot where Kate's life had come to an end. It was still there. The pints of her blood were still seeped into the concrete pad. They would never come out. The machinery that impaled her was gone. Locked in police evidence? Maybe. I wasn't sure. Still, a lot of the barn's old accouterments were here.

Including two horse blankets.

Scratchy and dirty and warm.

I shook out any hay and brought them back to Lauren in her chair.

"We'll stay here for the night," I told her, tucking the blanket over her legs and chest. "I hope you're alright in the chair."

Lauren said nothing.

"At the safe house, Wesson and the others can give you a proper bed, or a chair, or some medical attention. Whatever you need," I told her. I had no clue if that was true. All I could say was, if given the choice between lying on one's back locked away in a prison or sitting free in a cold, uncomfortable chair, my prefer-ence was clear. "I emptied your catheter bag. You should be good for the evening. I'm sorry I can't offer you any food. Not sure how you'd eat it. That's another thing we'll work out when you get to the safe house, I swear." I sighed. I wished Lauren could talk to me. I worried I'd made the wrong choice. She wanted to be free, we both knew that, but could I really tend to her?

She would definitely need more care. "I'll be back in a little while," I told her. I looked up at the rooster perch. "I'm going to try to get some answers." I glanced at my dad, the total stranger, staring out over the farmer's fields. I had waited this long to get to know the truth about my family. I wouldn't let this opportunity slip away in silence. "Wish me luck."

Lauren, of course, said nothing.

I patted her knee, grabbed the second blanket and started climbing up to the perch. I'd thought about staying with her, but the wood and hay would be softer and warmer to sleep on, and, much as I didn't want to admit it, I was drawn to spend time with this strange man.

Wesson Zaid.

My estranged father.

So far, we hadn't said too many words.

The ladder shifted and shuddered as I climbed upstairs to greet him. At the top of the ladder, I swung my leg off the rungs and joined him on the rooster perch, careful to bring with me the second horse blanket, strewn over my neck. He hunched down at the window. Waiting. Watching. At my arrival, he didn't look up. I peeked out behind him. Acres of untouched farmland shimmered in the glow of the stars. There was no light pollution in Plumpkin.

"Looks like we'll be safe for the night," he approved, finally looking back at me. "You good? Are you cold?"

Until now, my adrenaline had been pumping,

keeping me warm, but the night air was crisp and chilly and I was tired to my bones.

"I brought up a blanket. It's not large." I started to unfold it, but the man's watchful eye stopped me cold. His gaze had landed on my neck. My fingers self-consciously fluttered to the circle moon charm I always wore.

"Sierra used to wear that," he said.

"I know."

I watched him.

He shifted uncomfortably and broke our gaze. "Right. Of course. Well," he said finally, glancing at his own wringing hands. "I suppose introductions need to be made. Mae, my name is Wesson Zaid." His tone was formal and strained. "I am your father."

"I know," was all I could say.

TWENTY-TWO
PROVE IT

"I'M SURE YOU HAVE QUESTIONS…"

I did.

But suddenly, I didn't want to ask them. Almost on purpose, I ignored the monumentality of his introduction. Why should I care about this strange man? Because the word *father* was his? He'd never acted like one. I stiffened. Instead, I'd ask about the people who truly carried weight in my world.

"When can I be reunited with my friends?"

It hit as I intended.

I wouldn't give him the satisfaction of digging in. In my life, my father-figure was nothing more than a shadow of unanswered questions. I wouldn't beg for answers. For now, he could just sit on his hands.

"Your friends?" he asked, surprised. Saddened.

I nodded, hanging tough.

Specifically I would have liked to know more about when I could reunite with Beck at the safe house, but I didn't say his name. I actually didn't want my dad to talk about my boyfriend. It seemed too personal for him to acknowledge the details of my love life. It wasn't his information to state. He didn't know a damn thing about me. He'd never bothered to learn. I wouldn't let him claim even a small piece as if he had.

"At first light, I'll secure a truck and take you both to the sub." He nodded down to Lauren as well.

Okay, fine. So tomorrow Zaid and I would part ways forever and I'd be back where I belonged in my makeshift, found-family unit. On my own. With my friends. The people that truly cared about me. Good enough.

For a while, we both sat in silence.

I'd thought, coming face to face, I'd be flooded with questions for Wesson – or maybe a thousand accusing statements –but I didn't want to give any of that acknowledgement to him. Not even the gift of my pain or my anger.

He didn't deserve it.

He hadn't earned it.

He didn't warrant the right to feel my rage.

This man didn't feel like a relative. He didn't seem like a friend. He was just some random person who happened to have my father's name and appearance. A name and appearance I'd never even known before these last few days. My mom had kept them from me. And he had killed her. Here we both were, and I could confront him, but it wasn't what I had expected. I wanted to scream and shout, but he was being so cordial and sad. I didn't know how to talk to him. Even though I wanted answers. I sighed. Beck would have known what to say.

Give him the benefit of the doubt, he'd tell me.

Hear him out. Maybe offer him another chance in my world.

That wasn't something I was prepared to do.

Man, Beck was so great. I would have loved to see him now, to have proof that he'd escaped. And also to have someone safe to talk with about how I truly felt... but we'd be reunited soon. I could wait one night. I kept repeating the timeline in my head. One more night. Until then, the conversation was with myself. How did I feel...?

Disappointed.

Self-protective.

Numb.

Wesson was totally willing to let me lead our discussion. Or say nothing at all. We might have sat all night in total silence if a question didn't finally come to my lips.

"Why... are you here?" It tumbled out slowly.

Why dramatically risk yourself and all your relationships and touchpoints at the coven to save a girl you've basically pretended didn't exist? The second question was more on point with how I was really feeling, but they were specifics that I didn't verbalize.

"You want the short answer? Or the long one?" He kind of chuckled, but we both knew he hadn't earned my goodwill.

"Forget it." I pulled the blanket around myself, not offering him any.

"No, hey," he weakened. "God, you're so much like Sierra." He looked away, suddenly making like he needed to check our exterior surroundings, but we could both see, there was no one closing in on the horizon. For now it was safe to converse. "Why am I here?" He repeated the question, thinking it over.

This time, I waited.

I sort of enjoyed watching him squirm. He seemed to wrestle with what to tell me. But, if he'd come this far, done this much, he must have had a reason or two.

"I loved your mom. Very much," he started.

"Prove it."

He could see, as an audience, I was going to be tough. I didn't care. He could take it.

"You're a dreamcast," he tried to lead in again.

I nodded.

"Sierra was too. But, not in the same way as you are. I hope." He shifted, getting more comfortable. Finding an entry point that didn't feel too strained or weird. Sinking into the memories of his story.

I waited again.

"All her visions, at night, were about Cornelius Child and the elders, not her own personal situations, or things that would happen to her. Unless she crossed paths with some of them. Then her dreams would kick into high gear." He smiled, wistful for a moment. "I should say, they weren't really *leaders* at that point. Back then, the High Council was mostly just a bunch of fun contests. They didn't let everyone in, mind you, fate still made the decisions and the bonds, but it was relaxed and cool. You know?"

I didn't know.

He went on. "We'd exercise our powers. Have a little fun around like-minded witches. It was essentially playtime. It didn't matter. But it was also everything, 'cuz it was our whole world."

He checked in for understanding.

I did understand *that*. Since I'd joined the coven it had been all-consuming.

"She realized pretty quick, she could win the challenges and get away with it because her dreams would reveal the details she shouldn't know as a contestant. But at that time, she never took it seriously, even as she won. She used the power loosely, you know, to blow off steam or have some fun. Sierra was a blast."

I thought of all the contests in the archive newsletters. All the photos of Mom celebrating her wins. Receiving accolades. She wasn't some challenge monster, perfect contender. She'd had the inside track.

"It was... great." He thought back. "I was her date to all the celebratory dinners, but I warned her to be careful, win too much and the elders would start to catch on. They did anyway. At first it was who cares, no big deal, it didn't matter. We were just a couple of young witches having the time of our lives. It was different then. Not so regimented. Not like it is now. No power. No hierarchy. No weird, white wardrobes." He rolled his eyes. "But Child wanted a different sort of organization. And the higher he rose in power, the more he aligned himself with the persuasive people in the coven, the more, bit by bit, he took over control. They implemented more guides. And then the guidelines became rules. And the rules became law. And the punishments began. The High Council opened an official school. Training. Law and order. Fate still found your parabond at the fall reapings, but that was just for show. It was the elders who really decided who got into the coven. They'd choose the students in votes. Some say they'd sabotage the partnerships they didn't want to let enter. Soon, the whole clan was divided. The old faction against the new rule. And they forced people out of the coven. First a few, then lots of others. Bending the witches' will. The more they'd take, the more we'd have to give." He swallowed. "Sierra could see it all. Front seat. She managed to thwart some of what was happening, but, eventually, they did catch on to her gift. Child gave her a choice: stay and face sanctions, or be kicked out of the coven forever. For her, it was an easy pick. But for me..." A dark memory twisted his face. "I wasn't ready to leave. I wanted to stay. Fight. Take back our perfect High Council. I didn't like him. Didn't like what was happening. I couldn't just walk away, I couldn't let Cornelius win. I thought we could rebuild from within. But Sierra... didn't. She left us. Left me. She was protecting you, our daughter. But I didn't know that. I didn't know you existed then."

I tensed. It felt weird for me to come into his tale.

"For years, I thought she turned her back on our clan, on me, on the life we wanted, exactly when we needed her most. The Council just got worse. Slowly at first, then very quickly. Codified. Regimented. There was so much you could no longer do. I fought for six long years. I fought and I failed and I struggled. I was his biggest threat and Cornelius knew it. Me and some of the others. We were in danger, staying back at the castle, but at that point, I didn't care. I stopped caring about anything 'til Sierra returned."

In spite of myself, I leaned forward.

He took a deep breath. "She'd been gone six long years. But then one night, your mom had a vision. I think she'd had lots of them since she'd left us, but this was one she couldn't ignore. In the dream, Child was framing me for murder. She came back to warn me. To warn us. And the second she did, it all came washing back over. Our past. The life we'd said goodbye to. How we were. How we made each other better. I couldn't live without her. And I know she felt it as well. We had this beautiful night together. Holed up and secret from the world. One perfect night of the life we should have always been living." He chuckled to himself. "Older. Wiser. Dimpled. Exhausted. I begged her to come back home. But she couldn't. She'd made another place her world." He looked up, his eyes searching for mine. "With you."

For a moment, I was sucked into his gaze, then we both dropped it. His love for her, for Mom, was palpable in his voice. How could he have killed her? But Wesson wasn't done with his tale.

"Mae, she told me about you. For the first time. A daughter. Our daughter. Showed me pictures of the most beautiful baby girl. But you were no longer a baby. You were like six by that point. Six long years we had never met, I didn't know you existed. And I knew immediately that staying and fighting the Council was wrong. I was packing. I was leaving. Coming home. To the family I should have always belonged to. I should have been there. From the first moment. To meet you. To love her. All I'd missed. All I'd known." His eyes clouded over. "I made a new commitment. We were so happy." His voice caught in his throat. "There was this old bottle of champagne. From years ago. A prize from one of the many silly contests she had won. We uncorked the top in celebration. I was finally coming home! We couldn't wait to start the rest of our lives, away from the High Council. To finally leave this dark world behind us. I wanted to celebrate the crazy moment. It was so huge. I only had these awful plastic cups. We toasted to past victories and new beginnings. A toast to a deep rekindling. Reigniting the love that we'd lost. Drinks were poured. When we clinked the cups together, mine burst open, cracked in pieces, flooding champagne all over the floor. She took her first sip, laughing while I was pouring a replacement, cleaning the mess, teasing that she couldn't wait another moment to have her bubbly. As she drank it back, her lips made a weird frown. The alcohol tasted strange, old and metallic, she said, which made sense because the bottle wasn't new. The bubbles did a crazy dance in her throat. I was so busy pouring my drink. I didn't listen. I wanted to 'cheers' properly, you know. Wanted to celebrate my homecoming. But suddenly, she realized what the drink was doing. She swatted the champagne from my hands. She saw it. The scene. The moments. The little motions. She recognized the tiny happenings. From the vision. Her nightmarish vision. She started feeling it inside her belly. The symptoms came on fast. The poison coursed through her bones. And she knew it. This was the exact vision. It was her. Cornelius set me up and now it was happening to her. Poisoned. Dead by my supposed hand. Framed for murder. With lover's pall." He clenched his palms. He couldn't look at me now. "It was with love he lured her to be with me. With our love, he had us destroyed. Somehow Cornelius manipulated that dream. I tried to save her. We tried everything. My god. Everything we could think of. But it didn't matter. The die was cast. The future was already told." Tears welled in his lashes. He blinked them away. "We knew then, with Cornelius Child at the helm, you would never be safe. She made me promise not to go near you. She trusted Abeline to keep you company. While you grew up, I was supposed to fix the coven. Return the Council to its previous glory. But as you can see, I failed.

"And then I joined the place you hate."

He nodded, sadly. "Abeline assumed Sierra would

want you to join the coven. To follow in her mother's footsteps."

"She doesn't know Sierra was murdered," I realized.

"But you already knew," he said with surprise.

I hadn't flinched throughout his entire tale. "I knew she was killed," I agreed. "By you."

"By me." For a moment, we both sat with the story.

He had poisoned her, and it was a murder. But he wasn't the killer. Finally, I shifted. "But that doesn't answer my initial question. Why are you here? Why now?"

"You can't keep crossing Child's path."

"I didn't mean to. I never meant to. It's just what happened."

"He's not going to risk keeping you around."

"You think he'll lobotomize me, like the others." I glanced down to Lauren, who had yet to blink in her chair.

"I think he'll do whatever's necessary to ensure the safety of his coven. And you and the other first years have become a serious risk to his plans."

TWENTY-THREE

THE PAIN SNUCK BACK IN

IN THE ROOSTER PERCH, I slept in fits and starts. I meant to go down to check on Lauren at least once more in the night, but my exhaustion took me by surprise. I closed my eyes and Wesson's story played out over and over like a movie in my head.

Mom. Before she got sick. Beautiful. Smart. Playful.

Wesson. Smiling at her.

I aged him back. Stripped off ten years of pain and hiding and hurt. He would have been handsome and strapping back then. Cocky as well. Devoted like Beck. The pair were happy, and playful, and young. But it didn't last.

The pain snuck back in. It always did.

Next, my imagined movie took them back to the accusation of murder, to the act of him physically doing it, handing her the poison, to them falling for it, the happy moment scorched with fear. My mother, come to warn him, to the two landing in the Council's trap. Forever altered. The begging she did to keep her daughter from their terrible world. His daughter as well. And he agreed to leave me, to never reconcile. I imagined the anguish he might have felt. The fear and suffering as she became ill. As they said their last goodbyes.

When I tried to picture them again, young and in love with the world, the image faded to black. She was gone. Only he was left. And this was his sad tale.

Should I trust this stranger in my midst?

He'd had ten years to come up with a story to make himself sound like the perfect victim. That was true. In this version of the story, he was basically blameless. But also, the other thing niggled at me. After all this time, he didn't have to come back.

Ever.

He didn't need to intercede in my life. Or do these things.

He was free of me and free of the High Council. I might never have found him.

So why did he come back now? Risk everything he had going? Why did he risk his life entirely, to save me from their jail?

I slipped into a fitful slumber, tossing and turning with these thoughts.

Could I trust him?

Did I even want to try?

I sort of had to. At least for now.

True to his word, at first light, Wesson drove off on

the broken motorcycle and an hour or so later, he returned in a blue pick-up truck. By then, Lauren and I had relocated from the barn floor to the front porch of the Hucklebee house. She, in her chair, me sitting on the steps half-way down. It was harder than I'd thought to stay near the spot where Kate had died. I thanked her spirit for guidance through the night, then I moved on. I was ready to get home to Beck. I looked forward to the safe-house now.

I didn't ask where he'd gotten the truck. I decided to assume Wesson made a legal barter or maybe a sale. Perhaps he'd borrowed it from an old friend with the promise of bringing it right back? Any legal possibility was alright. Illegal ones I refused to consider. I just couldn't let my mind go down another dark path. I already had too much on my plate to consider that my estranged, murderous dad might also be a thief. I was okay without asking him to explain.

At first, we tried to prop Lauren up in the truck. Using the sheet and the seat belt, we could position her, tied into a seated position, but I worried all the knots and tension might be uncomfortable or cut her catheter off. It was empty now. None of us had eaten or drank anything in many hours, but I didn't want to risk pulling it out. So ultimately, we decided to lie her down on the truck bed in the back. Though I didn't say it out loud, I was starting to worry that perhaps freeing her from the medical prison was more complicated than I'd first hoped. I didn't know how to feed her or help her with aches or with sores. But until we figured those other issues out, the only real question was this: *was her current situation better than an eternity flat on her back?* The answer seemed a resounding yes.

"Are you okay?" I asked her over and over.

'*Go.*' She had said in the jail. We were going. I just hoped she was alright as we went. We laid the horse blankets down, then lay Lauren on top of the gentle cushion. I used the sheet that had tied her upright in the wheelchair as a makeshift pillow under her head. It was hard knowing she couldn't advocate for how she felt.

"Maybe we should go straight to the hospital," I feared.

"They know you took her. That's the first place they'll look."

"I know, but she needs proper care."

"We'll have the chemists look her over at the safe house, *then* decide what to do."

I glanced at Lauren, uncertain.

"Go," the woman murmured. Like a tuft of smoke, it was there on her lips, then disappeared. This time, I wasn't the only one who heard her. Wesson and I glanced at each other.

"You heard the lady."

"Alright. Of course. We're going. We'll make it work." I patted her hand. "I'm gonna ride in the back," I told him. Wesson nodded. I played it off like it was safer for her, or more helpful, but really, I didn't want to be alone with the man in the cab. I climbed in beside

Lauren. "You're safe now," I told her, cuddled beside her arm.

I had no idea if that was true for her.

Or for me.

But together, we were along for the ride.

Wesson started the motor and the truck bed vibrated. He shifted into gear and we started the drive. I sat up to watch the Hucklebee barn and the farmhouse disappear from sight.

"Thank you, Kate," I told her, leaving her property. It seemed like a lifetime ago when we first had that fight. And it was *someone's* lifetime. Only, not mine. Kate was gone, but her memory always lived bright. I should have been a better friend when she was alive. For safety, I lay down at Lauren's side. I couldn't risk that anyone I knew in town might see me. Who knew where the reach of the High Council really stopped.

Even with two blankets down, the truck bed was cold and hard. How much of this was Lauren experiencing? Could she feel the uncomfortable shudders as the vehicle lurched? Hear the engine gunning? See the clouds as they passed overhead? The limits of her experience would be mine too, if Cornelius finished his inquisition. If he passed awful judgment and I let him, I would be lying here, like Lauren, with just one desperate thought in my head.

Go.

That could happen.

It might still happen.

That's why Wesson Zaid and the others planned this awful raid.

To break us out.

To save our skin.

To come and rescue the new batch of students before harsh judgments could be made.

It was a herculean effort. And I was grateful.

No, really. I was.

I just hoped he didn't expect me to be bowled over with thanks. Or to stay.

I wouldn't stay with this man. My supposed dad. Not now. Not ever. Wherever he had made his rebel base, I didn't care if the walls were studded with diamonds. The moment I was reunited with Beck and made sure that Lauren and my other friends were safe, I would get the hell out of Plumpkin. I wouldn't stop at a town nearby. The others could come if they wanted. There was nothing here for me now. When it was safe, I would send for Aunt Abeline. Reunite with her, and we would be disparate, free-flowing nomads, moving wherever, whenever we wanted. And we would be happy, magic-free, and safe.

Seeing his parental neglect dressed up as some sort of loving act of service did nothing to endear me to the man who was driving. If his story were true, *and that was a big if*, he wasn't the vicious murderer that I feared, but he still wasn't really my dad. Not *really*. Not in anything more than a name. He abandoned me in some kind of misguided service to Sierra, but also in fear and self-serving. Beck would understand.

I sighed.

How I missed Beck. At least, we'd be reunited soon.

I felt the truck careen right and left. We'd already been driving for what felt like a while. Twenty-minutes? Maybe more. We had to be getting close to their hideout.

"I'm gonna look around," I told Lauren.

She didn't nod in return.

I sat up in the truck bed, my hair whipping about in a frenzy as the truck drove quickly down the rural highway. I grabbed the mop of fly-aways and dragged them into a rough ponytail I held in place. There were still a few stragglers, but I could see, and I started to describe for her all the sights as we passed them.

"Over here there are horses, six, no seven, brown ones, one little gray guy. He's so sweet, eating hay. We just passed an abandoned gas station... A billboard for slip and fall lawyers... Sheep!" On and on, my play-by-play went. It felt good to chatter to Lauren. When we drove through small towns, I slunk low in the bed, but mostly, our journey led us farther away from people, and deeper into the forest and untouched land. The variety of sights and wildlife slowed. Overtaken by unending trees, rock faces and shrubs.

I lay down beside her again.

The gentle rumble of the truck lulled us off. I sank into a visionless sleep. When I woke up, I checked on Lauren. She was motionless, just as before. The vehicle seemed to be making a lot of gentle swerves. I pulled myself up to a seated position to check out the new surroundings.

Whoa.

The two-lane road we were on was wide open on the right side, winding and turning its way around an enormous body of water. It seemed there was barely a shoulder for safety between us and the plunge down to the shore. Our road rose thirty feet above the water. All that stood between us and a long drop to the bottom was two feet of gravel and a metal guardrail. It was dangerous. But wildly beautiful. I wasn't scared. The road gave an epic view of the surrounding nature. Beautiful rolling hills, crystal blue waters, trees on all sides.

"You should see this," I murmured, in spite of who I was talking to. The expansive lake went on and on as the road wrapped around it. I was mesmerized.

Until suddenly, the trunk's turning signal light started to blink. Wesson was slowing.

"Lauren, I think this is it."

He pulled over on the shoulder in front of a grown-over rustic laneway. It was sealed with a large metal gate. He got out of the truck and pushed it open. He flashed a small smile back to me, but neither of us said a word. He drove us in and pushed the gate closed again.

"We're here," he rapped the side of the truck as he passed us.

I just nodded.

No clue where 'here' was.

He started to drive again. Trees closed in on the path overhead. We moved slower, careful over bumps and rocks. The road progressed steadily down towards the lake. To the waters I'd just seen from the highway. I gripped the side of the bed, the car lurching. Wesson stopped at the bottom of the hill and I looked around us and frowned.

There was nothing there.

No house. No safe-house building.

But quickly, I realized that was an inaccurate first impression. I was wrong. Wesson put the truck in park and I climbed down from the back, to see for myself. There wasn't *nothing*. Ours wasn't the only car parked off this lane. There were about twenty vehicles of various sizes to the left and right of us, tucked between the trees and stumps. They were all concealed with camouflage shields like the motorcycle at the High Council. Pallets and sheaths of chicken-wire fencing were obscured with sticks and leaves to cover the machinery. Once you saw them, you couldn't miss them, but I had to admit, it took me a moment to notice they were there. Wesson was already fussing with a camouflage tarp for this newly arrived truck.

"Let me help."

Together we silently worked to create the visual cloak. When we had the sheet of branches in place, it really worked. The blue truck blended right in. If I didn't know better, I wouldn't know it was there.

I got out Lauren's wheelchair and we adjusted her back to a seated position in her chair. I was happy to see, throughout her entire journey thus far, she seemed no worse for wear. But, Wesson had said there'd be chemists who could help Lauren, medical supplies, and better equipment. I didn't see any of that. In fact, other than the hidden vehicles, I actually didn't see signs of a rebel base. Where was the camp?

As if he was reading my mind, Wesson pointed to the lake. "It's over there. Come on."

"Across the lake?"

"Inside the lake. Let's go." He wheeled Lauren down to the water. Tentatively, I followed. We made our way out onto an aged dock with a rusty boat still tied up and attached. No oars or motors, just an empty hull. "Help me get her in," he said.

I held her handlebars as Wesson took the weight of the wheels. We lowered Lauren into the boat beside the dock, then he and I scrambled in. Wesson untied the weathered rope tying us to the dock, slid his hand under the rickety seat, and a small motor clicked in. But, my first impression wasn't wrong. The engine wasn't actually in the boat, it was on the dock. Or... under the dock, it seemed.

Suddenly, the little boat started moving.

We floated out. I looked out behind us. The small hull had two pieces of metal attached on either side under the keel. They were connected to a motor and a pulley that, once the engine engaged, pushed us out on its track away from shore. When it was protracted, the system was completely hidden beneath the dock. As we rolled out into the water, I wasn't sure what was coming, but so far, I had to admit, there was incredible thought into each step of the path.

As we were fleeing, someone called their safe house the *sub*. Maybe Gennady? It could have been Diego? At the time, I'd assumed it was a nickname. But was it possible that their safe house was a submarine? Was an actual underwater vessel the location of their house? It sure looked that way.

The motor on land slowed and stopped. On the two metal rails, we were an extra twenty feet from the shore. The water here was darker.

Deeper.

Foreboding.

"Here it comes," Wesson said, looking down.

I couldn't see anything. Nothing but blue water extending forever.

Then suddenly, there was a shift.

A lighter blue outline emerged from the depths.

It appeared, growing brighter. Rising to greet us.

Larger and larger beneath our little boat.

Inch by inch, the vessel came higher.

Until with very little splashing, it actually emerged.

Periscope first. An upper hatch next. Then all at once, the large sleek body of the ship pushed into the air. Water slipped off from all sides, making a ring of waves around where it had appeared. Suddenly, we weren't alone. We never had been. The secretive boat had always been there.

"Why are you living underwater?" I asked, almost

mesmerized as the waters settled and the submarine came to a rest beside our little boat's bow.

"We've had all sorts of set ups, but we found an underwater location is a spot the dreamers can't find. The liquid above us clouds their visions and down below we can use our gifts and magic as much as we want. The energy can't be tracked. Underwater, we can't be traced. It takes a little effort and planning to sustain it," he added, modestly, "but we've had almost ten years to engineer the thing. For the first two years, it was much more of a lie-guard. But now the boat's fully built." He hopped out of our little vessel and up onto the sleek submarine body. In a friendly manner, he double tapped the periscope valve, then bent low to undo the hatch.

"Come on in."

TWENTY-FOUR
HE'S ALSO... MY DAD

"MAE! OH MY GOD!"

"Wesson!"

"Is that Lauren Bixby?"

"Holy cow."

"Holy crap!"

"Welcome home."

"What took you so long to get here!?"

We were flooded with greetings the second we got down through the hatch. Several witches rose to help carry Lauren. Hilde and Greg practically jumped on me, and other rebel members rushed to welcome my dad.

People who I assumed were nurses or doctors went straight to Lauren's paralyzed aid and whisked her to the side to sort things out. I tried to follow what they were doing, but it was hard to see much of anything. There was a swarm of people around us in the small submarine hall. As we'd loaded onto the submerged vessel, Wesson had pressed the same under-seat button and the above-water boat had reset itself back to its dock. Behind us, the surface hatch was sealed and without fanfare, we were encased in the submarine world. The ship shuddered and sank once more. As a slew of voices chattered at once, I could feel the vessel moving – although it wasn't much more than a vibration – but I couldn't focus on that. I was distracted by a million other things in the hall.

Like where was Beck?

Wesson made a point of introducing me to everyone gathered. I was led in circles, taking names and shaking hands, trying to remember everyone but the greetings escaped me the second they were made. There was too much at once.

Where was Beck?

I was happy to see everyone. Excited to be reunited. As the final arrivals from the shocking, successful breakout from the High Council prison, we were greeted as minor celebrities. I hugged back all the outstretched arms, but there was only one face I was desperate to find on board.

Where was Beck?

Suddenly, the crowds cleared. I looked up. Saw that face. Found that smile. He stood back from the mob, waiting for me to make my way through the chaotic ballyhoo. As we finally locked eyes, the whole world seemed to slow down.

Beck raked a hand through his beautiful brown hair. His soft, pink lips opened in a smile. His blue eyes watched me coming, full of sparkle. Magically, in my eyes, he was the only one there in the crowd.

"Hey parabond," he grinned, all smooth and casual.

But I couldn't play it chill. "Oh my god!" I jumped myself into his arms.

Beck caught me and held me high on his waist, my legs straddled around him. Our faces nuzzled side by side, every inch of him pulling me in.

"You're alright!" I exclaimed, full of relief.

"I'm alright," he nodded, pulling me tighter into his arms. I felt him and smelled him and closed my eyes, lost in his arms. I pulled back to really see him and he searched my face, saw my lips and kissed me so passionately, I thought I would melt.

I wanted him.

Every inch of him.

And I could feel how he wanted me as well.

"We're alright," he whispered in my ear.

"We're alright," I whispered back.

"*This* is why I miss Marcy," Greg moaned.

Someone else cleared their throat.

Embarrassed and humbled, Beck lowered me back to the ground. Both of us blushed. The urgency of our passion was diluted by the crowd. So many faces watching. We stood apart, but I didn't lose touch with his skin. I kept my arm wrapped around his waist. He did the same for me. It felt so good to be back in his arms.

"Everybody," I said to the gathering – if they were

watching, I might as well make use of their attention —
"this is Lauren Bixby." I touched the paralyzed
woman's shoulder lightly, by way of introduction.

"Mae, they know," Wesson said kindly. "This is
Aine Chrisianne, the chemist I told you about.
Lauren's best friend.

I looked at one of the two witches who'd been
helping her. "You know her?" She nodded. "Is she
alright?"

"She will be." Aine put a familiar hand on her
shoulder. Was it in my mind? Or did Lauren slightly
lean into that hand? Just a hair? No, probably not. I
knelt to the woman's side. We hadn't known each other
long, but it had been a tumultuous ride. "Lauren, we
made it. You did it. You escaped!"

"Thank."

For a second, I blinked. Did her word just change?

I looked at Aine in shock. "Before, she could only
say 'go'. But she just said 'thank.' As in, thank you," I
told her, wide-eyed. "Lauren, you're welcome, I'm so
glad you're alright." Perhaps there was more to her
recovery, yet! "Aine's going to help you. I promise.
She'll get you all set."

Aine swept right back in. "To start off, let's get you
out of this chair." The woman nodded at me, then
rolled Lauren away, talking her through each step as
they left. At the High Council, Lauren had been left to
rot in the bed. But maybe with personal care and physical therapy, her condition would start to improve? I
looked over to Wesson. He raised an eyebrow,

surprised. I could tell he was thinking similar things. I was so glad we hadn't left her alone in that cell.

"And, guys, I'd like you to meet someone else," I added, straightening to address just my friends. They were all there, I was thankful to see the prison breakout had a one hundred percent success rate. We all made it out safely after the raid. I smiled at Ferris, who was holding Ethan's hand, little Hilde, so casually close to Vince who ignored her, and Rick standing stoic behind the two friends. Last but not least, there was Greg, picking something out of his teeth. Finally, my eyes settled on Beck. I nodded at him, and turned to Wesson. "*This* is Wesson Zaid."

He gave a curt, introductory wave.

"He's the one who saved me and Lauren from the High Council prison. He's the witch who started the whole raid. He's kind of the leader of the rebels. He's also... my dad."

I could see the shock in the group. Beck tried to read my face.

Wesson waved again, this time, to acknowledge the awkward energy. "Please... call me Wes."

I had hoped, after our dramatic welcome, the crowd might disperse and Beck and I could have a moment alone. I was desperate to reconnect. But, there was a push to take me everywhere, show me everything, and it felt like everyone wanted to be part of the tour. Or maybe the overwhelming, claustrophobic feeling was just elevated by the small, enclosed spaces in the boat. I held tight to Beck's hand, reassured to have his fingers entwined in mine.

The underwater lair was an impressive sight.

Some areas had halls with small rooms on either side, while others were a thick chain of larger spaces where everyone could sit and work, or play, or relax. There was a kitchen and a pantry and a mess hall dining room. At the start of the submarine was the control room. The engineers went into great detail about how the whole ship worked. Something about ballasts and air pressure and water levels. The thing I recognized most was the periscope. That was the same device Wesson had tapped on our way into the sub.

The bedrooms were small with four, sometimes six, bunks to a dorm room, and the washrooms were communal down the hall. Some poor witch tried to explain the difference between black and gray water tanks, but I didn't take the specifics down. It was all too much to learn at once.

The infirmary was large, laid out like an army base, almost like the rebels expected to take on heavy casualties. With an angry coven of witches now fighting against them, maybe that was good planning, I supposed. But I hoped we'd never have to spend time there except to be reunited with Lauren, or get well. She was there now, sat up, in a clean, proper hospital bed, tucked in fresh blankets, being talked to in a circle with excited coven members. I hoped she was happy where the rescue ended up. Aine saw to her every requirement. Wesson was right, they'd take good care of her here. I waved, but didn't expect anything in return.

Beside the infirmary was a room built for chemistry exploration. It had sinks and bare counters, elements and beakers, heating plates, the whole thing. There was a pantry of full chemicals and even an underwater greenhouse from which to pick plant clippings.

"How does the light enter in?" I asked.

"We have circadian optic lights to mimic sunlight. It's not as good as the real thing, but it does the trick," Gennady told me. She looked less stressed today than she had at the raid. I noted they had their own clipping of the cherished Valdeez branch. I could have saved myself and the others a lot of trouble if I had just come *here* for the plant. I reached out and grazed my finger on the leaf of the nearest foliage, but Rick gently interceded.

"These plants are very delicate."

I snapped my fingers back. He would know, as the most talented chemist in our clan.

Everywhere we went, there were airlocks. The doors were smaller than the hallways, you had to step up and over a foot-tall steel lip as we passed into each space. That way, any of the rooms could be isolated and sealed very quickly. There were also sump pumps, should a leak ever happen. They were prepared for the occasion of water getting in. If a hole in the hull could be fixed, they'd seal it off, apply the fix and push the water back out of the vicinity. If not, the room could be permanently sealed. On top of that, there were hatches on every external surface. Every room had at least one emergency exit on a wall. An underwater egress to escape in a rush.

The last stop on the tour was the artillery. In rows and rows, the ingredients for bombs, potions and explosives stood labelled and ready to be grabbed.

"No guns?" I murmured, surprised. This was all witchcraft.

"Wes doesn't believe in them," Gennady told me, with what I read as admiration. "Isn't that right, Craig?"

"Any good witch could disarm you in seconds," Twenty-Thom agreed. I barely recognized him without the gas mask and the forest, but now that we were safe, I guessed I should call him by his first name.

"Like you would know," Diego teased. He poked the chunkier witch in his belly.

"Cut it out, D," Craig frowned. "I mean, we have a flare gun in the pantry, I've touched *that*."

"Why would you have a flare gun in the pantry?" Greg wondered. But no one bothered to answer the boy.

"All of these different bombs and knock out gas." I read the labels.

"Serums and salves, ready made and good to go." Diego told us. "We could take an army out in one swoop." He was proud of his group and their stash.

"You should add the combo of Amable Ciel and

Fixed Borna. It'll knock you out real well," I told the others. I glanced at Rick. The tall boy actually cracked a small grin.

"Only if you add nose plugs with soft covered prongs," Ethan complained.

I continued to read all the potion and spell names until my eye landed square on the last one. The Udak bomb. "The one with a notorious short fuse..."

"Longer fuses are here," Diego shrugged. He dug a hand into a box of candle wicks.

"Different bombs have different purposes," Craig told me. I didn't mention I'd already made use of quite a few. Blown a sea monster to bits, in fact. He seemed pleased to play the role of knowledgeable guide.

"Enough show and tell. I'm starving," Greg butted in. "Now they're here, can we eat? We should eat!"

My stomach growled. With all the excitement and the travel and the escape, I realized Lauren, Wesson and I hadn't eaten all day. I was totally famished. No one objected, so we headed back to the kitchen to prepare. Or almost everyone did. As the entourage filed out, Beck slowed down. So I also held back. When we were the only two left in the room, he quietly closed the artillery door. My stomach fluttered with butter-flies and anticipation and I felt I could breathe a little easier, knowing it was just him and I in the room.

"You're really alright," he checked, looking me over.

"I'm alright," I agreed.

"They didn't hurt you."

"Just made me wait. I mean, they questioned me with truth serum, but I don't think I said anything they didn't already know."

Beck nodded. He'd had a similar experience. "They wrapped my hand in this malleable plastic so I couldn't harness anything, but then your dad melted it off. Is that alright..? To call him your dad?"

"Did it hurt?" I checked his fingertips. They still looked perfect and rustic and strong. Purposefully, I ignored the Wesson question. This moment was a chance for our reconnection. I wouldn't let my estranged dad in the room or my thoughts. Instead, I scrutinized every inch of Beck's palm. Beck watched me examine his skin. He took my details in with the same level of care as I offered to his hand. It felt good to have his eyes on me. I felt excitement smolder at the act of being watched.

Keenly seen.

Truly desired.

I had missed Beck's devoted care so much. We couldn't really express the extent of feelings earlier, with the attention of all the others in the crowd, but now, quietly alone in the artillery, it was just me and him. I brought his hand to my lips and slowly, staring deep into his eyes, I kissed the index finger. Willing and docile, Beck simply watched.

"I couldn't stand-"

I kissed the middle one.

"If something were to happen."

Ring finger nibble.

"To even the smallest-"

I kissed his pinky finger.

"Precious part of you."

I finished with the fingers and went back for his thumb. He didn't flinch, totally entranced. Waiting for another kiss. But instead of gently pecking his thumb like I did the others, I rubbed it on my lips, then slid it into my mouth. I embedded his thumb in my soft, wet grip, caressing with my tongue. I dropped my teeth down in a playful little bite.

"Oh," Beck moaned in pleasure at the simple, little suck.

I took his thumb again and this time, went a little deeper, sliding it in and out of my mouth. Still damp with my saliva, he took over and gently traced the plump outline of my lips. "God, I missed you so much."

"I missed you too," I agreed, but he was already coming in. I squeaked out the words just before his lips closed on my mouth. He kissed me passionately, drinking me in, his tongue sliding between my lips. Massaging me inside out.

Our bodies collided, our hands searching wildly.

With forceful desire, his palms cupped my butt. He raised me up. My body pushed forward to greet him, as his kisses covered my cheeks, my ears, my neck.

He pushed me up against the shelves, and I let him. He raised my right arm above me, controlling my being. I quickly gave in.

"Beck," I murmured his name, wanting to tell him I

was ready for anything, but suddenly, we weren't alone anymore. The door to the artillery room flew open.

"They're over here!" Hilde called.

Beck and I jumped back, pulling away from one another.

"Aw, come on!" Greg complained, poking his head back in. He watched us fall back, red-faced and heavy-breathed, as more of our friends returned to the room.

"Maybe don't make out around the dangerous equipment?" Vince complained.

"Dinner is ready," Rick told us.

Ferris made a playful face. *Sorry,* she mouthed a silent apology.

"I mean, not at dinner. People are hungry. We were waiting for you." Greg grumped. "Have some courtesy to the other stomachs of the group."

Ethan just grinned and mussed up Greg's hair as they left again. This time, Beck and I sheepishly followed.

"I tried to stop them," Ferris whispered to me, as Beck and I fell into step. "But, they didn't want to wait. You heard Greg. He's hungry."

"It's okay. I'm hungry too," I agreed. Hungry for what, I didn't mention. I tried my best not to blush. They led the way to the mess hall and we entered.

Greg took one last look at our crumpled wardrobes and flushed cheeks and sighed. "I miss Marcy."

"What do you think she's doing right now?" Greg wondered.

"Who?" Hilde wondered.

"Who do you think?" Vince rolled his eyes.

"Marcy?" Hilde asked.

Greg sighed.

I ended up at the dinner table between little Hilde and Greg. The others had joked that Beck and I couldn't be trusted to sit side-by-side. But across the table, I still didn't take my eyes off my guy, anyhow.

Whether on purpose or not, I sat as far as possible from Wesson.

Still, out of the four full tables of witches, and two empty options, he chose to sit at the helm of ours. But we didn't speak. There was nothing more to say. The meal was served family style. As the dishes went round, we all dug in.

"She's the best," Greg sighed, still thinking about his girl.

"You really miss her?" I asked him. "Even after she turned you in?" I bit deep into a thick, buttery roll. The nerve endings under my tongue tingled with pleasure, reigniting my salivary glands. The flavors exploded on my taste buds. I was far hungrier than I thought from the last two days.

"She didn't do that."

"Uh, yeah. She did." Vince cut in.

"You don't know that. You don't know what she said." Greg sputtered, his mouth wide open with food.

"Well, we know Rick's here," I gently countered.

"He's the best," Hilde added, mimicking Greg's compliment, nodding at her partner.

"And Ethan," Beck added.

"*He's* the best," Ferris grinned. Ethan gave her a tough smile. They were still working their issues through.

"So?" Greg took another heaping helping of beans.

"So, they're here 'cuz they wouldn't rat their parabonds out," Vince said. "Or me. Or you. None of them snitched."

Greg looked up, surprised.

Rick and Ethan nodded.

"And for *that*, they were arrested and jailed," Ferris said. The rest of us waited for the rest of the realization to set in. The boys were here, Marcy wasn't. From that, one could infer what the contents of her communication with the Council might have been.

But Greg didn't care. "That doesn't prove anything. I know my girl. She'll protect me, however possible." He shoveled in another mouthful. "And when we're reunited, look out! Make-out city! Unlike these two," Greg pointed in our direction. "*We'll* be hot and heavy." He waggled his tongue in the air. Bits of salad stuck to his lips.

"Gross," Hilde scrunched up her nose.

"Forget PG-13," he told her. "R-rated." He flexed his tongue again, just to prove his point.

Beck grinned, locking eyes with me. "I don't know, I thought our reunion was pretty good."

I smiled. "Two thumbs up," I winked, giving a

double entendre. Beck choked on his food in surprise. We both grinned. He even blushed. Vince dropped his fork.

"Some of us are trying to eat."

Under the table, I playfully touched Beck's leg with my foot.

"That's not Beck," Ethan said.

"Oh, sorry. Crap."

"I can't wait for my first kiss," Hilde mooned. Her eyes furtively floated in Vince's direction. The older boy stabbed a hunk of meat on his plate, and shoved it in his mouth. Ferris tried to grin at Ethan about these little things, but he still looked away from her. She sighed. There were more reparations needed between them.

"How many people live on the sub?" Ferris turned away and asked our hosts.

Craig, Diego, Gennady and Wesson all sat down at her end of the table.

"Thirty-two now?" Gennady did the math in her head.

"We've had as many as forty," Diego told her. "Until the dumb-dumbs get bored and decide to head for greener pastures. Isn't that right?" He slapped Craig's shoulder.

"Underwater living is tough," Craig agreed.

"It's not easy," the others nodded.

"And everyone here is a refugee of the Council?" Ferris asked.

The other four nodded. I looked around. Logistically, that was a lot of escapees from one place.

"Why not just go? Move far away. Like super far." Beck wondered. "Start again?"

"Others have tried," Gennady admitted.

"Like Lauren," Diego offered. We looked over at her table. Aine had brought her to join at their dinner table. Although she still couldn't eat outside of a tube, she was situated in a much better chair, and she was propped up with a seat at the table, just another one of the witches gathered for the meal. She looked happy to be a part of the group. To this clan, they weren't just being kind to a patient, Lauren was their friend. She was used to living in their ranks. I was glad to see her included, welcomed at the table, even if her medical situation hadn't magically improved.

Gennady watched all our stares. "Two years ago, she left with several others."

"There were more patients in the medical ward," Ethan admitted. Now I felt bad we hadn't got everyone out of the jail. The rebels exchanged glances. They weren't surprised. More rebels were missing.

"Cornelius eventually finds you. Hunts them down. Puts 'em on trial, removes the threat of magic at the source," Wesson said.

"Or worse," Gennady added quietly.

A twang of pain hit me. My mom had left the coven. It was rare. But she had gotten out, safely. Why didn't she just stay away?

"People leave, and never come back. Maybe some

even successfully escape. But the odds aren't good." Diego shrugged. "Down here, you're safe."

"The waters block their visions," Gennady nodded, reflecting a similar understanding as to what Wesson had earlier said.

"So our choice is to be hunted down and captured, lose our hands or our heads, *or* spend the rest of our existence in an underwater prison calling it freedom," Vince summed up.

The others frowned, but Craig sadly nodded his head. Vince wasn't that far off.

"At least we'll be together," Hilde offered.

But that didn't bring comfort to Vince.

"You get used to it," Wesson told him, he told all of us.

"And lie-guards can offer all sorts of temporary comforts," Diego added.

"But we haven't even been tried," Ferris pointed out. "Technically, we've done nothing wrong... we only left without notice and escaped the jail. Would Cornelius really still hunt us down in the streets for that?"

"*Yes.*" The four voices answered in tandem.

"I hope Marcy's alright," Greg piped in.

Almost everyone ignored him.

"You're in grave danger. You can't leave, it's far too dangerous," Wesson told us.

I realized he had started by talking to Ferris, but now was looking straight at me.

"What if we join another coven?" I wondered.

The others stirred.

The Damocles coven.

That could be a possible solution. Vince, Hilde and I had left their group on good terms. Perhaps we could leave the High Council and join their numbers. Like Lady Mauve had years ago left her own group and in effect joined the High Council. Wouldn't that offer protection?

"You know another coven?" Diego scoffed.

I nodded. "We've worked with them."

"To retrieve Valdeez plants," Hilde added.

"Basically, it's the thing that made Cornelius pissed," Vince said.

The older witches were surprised.

"No wonder he was coming in guns blazing," Gennady said, sitting back. "The thing Child wants more than anything is control. You befriending another clan of witches without him..." She tried to imagine.

"No one has ever defected," Craig mused. "Do you think it can be done?" He looked to Wesson. We all did.

"No."

"But Wes-" Craig countered.

"I said no!"

"You can't keep us here," I told him, evenly. "That would be as bad as them. An underwater prison." My eyes narrowed.

Wesson glared back. "We just saved you. I would think you could be grateful."

"We just want to keep you safe," Gennady diffused.

"You only just got here," Craig added.

"Thank you for helping us get away," Ethan said from our side.

"Yes, thank you," added several others.

Grudgingly, even I said it. Not wanting to start a fight, I now let the topic rest. But, I meant what I'd said. Whether we had their blessing to depart here or not, my dad and the others could not force me to stay.

TWENTY-FIVE

OUR FIRST IN-LOVE KISS

THE REST of dinner went back to normal chatter. Neither Wesson nor I uttered another phrase. But the day had been long, full of stress and surprises. When the last of the dishes were washed up, I was happy to call it a night. We all nodded and parted ways.

"Good night, everybody. Good night."

"I've got a surprise for you," Beck's eyes twinkled as we stepped through one of the many airlocks into the hallway with all the bunk-rooms.

"What?"

"Our own separate room for tonight." He stopped in front of an open airlock, swung open the door and showed it off. I looked in. "It's all ours."

It was a tiny rectangle with four bunk beds built into the walls, two on each side with a narrow laneway between the small shelves.

"Wow." I stepped through the capsule door.

The beds were slimmer than traditional single

mattresses and the headspace was tight. I wanted to sound enthused, but the room wasn't much to observe. "So, this is where people sleep?"

"The girls' bunk. I know. It's not awesome," he admitted. "But for tonight, Ferris and Hilde said they'll find another spot. We can have this all to ourselves." He wrapped his arms around me. I leaned back into his chest. While the reality of the gesture wasn't much, it meant a lot. Beck did it for me. For us.

"After our little interruption in the war room, they must have thought we could use some time to ourselves."

"Someone may have strongly hinted," Beck wriggled his eyebrows suggestively.

I laughed. Ferris and Hilde were sweet for going along. I'd have to thank them in the morning. "A thoughtful gesture, even if *this* is the room," I teased, going behind him to close the door.

"It's not so bad. Come on," he climbed into the first lower bunk and tugged me in after. We landed softly together. The mattress was flat. The pillow was thin. The bed was terrible. It was a squish to be holed up together on the uncomfortable cot, but with my guy, all those details disappeared. I was back at his side, so everything was right with the world. "I slept in the guys' dorm last night. The hum of the sub will knock you right out."

"I don't want to knock right out," I giggled.

"I didn't get much sleep," he admitted. "When you three didn't come right to the sub with the rest,

Gennady and Diego were sure you'd be safe, but I couldn't stop worrying about stuff." He wiggled onto his side to see my face. "You and your dad. Everything was alright..?"

I sighed, appreciative he was trying again. I kept blowing the subject off, but now that we were alone for a while, I opened the conversation's door. "We spent the night in Kate's barn as a safe house. Kate Hucklebee?"

Beck nodded, although we both knew the two of them had never been friends.

"Zaid said we couldn't risk bringing his magic around the safe-house. I guess the Council has a way of tracking energy like a beacon? I'm not really sure."

"Did you two talk?" Beck asked, lightly picking a fuzz from my shirt. He watched me closely.

"We did." I gave a deep sigh and unfolded the whole story as I knew it. "He and mom were, I guess, parabonds. He says he loved her and Cornelius threatened them at the castle, a lot. Zaid wanted to stay and fight, but Mom wanted to go. She was pregnant at the time. With me. But he says she didn't tell him. And then, they went their separate ways. Separate journeys. Him in the coven. Her outside it. Six years later, she had a vision and she had to warn him. I guess he'd become quite a thorn of opposition in the High Council's side. In her dream, she saw Cornelius and the others frame him for murder, so she came back to tell him, and encourage him to leave the High Council and start a new life." I looked down at my hands.

"When they reunited, he said it all returned. Their love. Their happy life together. Zaid realized he was wrong, had chosen wrong, and said that he would leave. With her. To start a new life together. So, that's when she told him about me." I bit my lip. "He says they opened a bottle of champagne to celebrate his new family. He poured her a glass, and she drank it down before he took a sip from his own. He didn't know it was spiked with lover's pall 'til too late." I shrugged. Beck knew the story from there. "Zaid said he stayed away 'cuz that's what she wanted. Sierra thought, if Abeline raised me, I'd be safe. And that's that."

"Do you believe him?"

That was the question.

"Yes," I started. "Well... no. Maybe? Or not. I don't know." I turned to face Beck, lying on my side as well. "Beck, I don't know what to think." I met his eye line. "It does answer the questions. But maybe a little too neatly? I'm not... sure."

Beck nodded. That was fine. I didn't need to decide things tonight. My indecision was safe with him. He bopped the tip of my nose. "Well, I'm glad that you're back."

I laughed and scrunched up my face. His finger lingered just above me. "Why'd you do that?"

He shrugged. "Just proof you're really here." His finger touched down softly on my bottom lip.

"I'm here," I agreed.

His digit re-traced my pink curves. I watched him

rubbing my mouth gently, mesmerized by its soft, pursed shape.

"You liked it when I sucked on your finger," I realized with a giggle.

"So much," Beck admitted, his whole body opening in my direction. Obliging, I nipped down, gripping his finger with my teeth. He groaned. I sucked the tip, just a nibble.

Playful.

Lingering.

"My god." Beck was like putty. "Mae, I'm so crazy about you." His head rolled around in pleasure.

Suddenly, I pulled back. The realization hit me hard. I was crazy about him, too. The chemistry and sexy banter was awesome. But it was so much more than that. Beck was a huge part of my life. He was the one person in the world who didn't judge me. Around whom I was totally myself. One day apart and I was already lost without him. I wanted him to hold me and touch me and make me feel safe, but our connection was so much deeper. I shared all my secrets with him. I always wanted to tell him how I felt. Really felt. And to check in on how he was feeling. And I knew he felt the same way as well.

"Beck," these new feelings filled me so deeply, with so much joy, I stared at him in shock. "I love you."

The words tumbled out.

Once I realized it was true, I couldn't keep them in. Not for one second. I just wanted him to know so much. My heart burst with love for this boy.

A huge smile spread across his face. "I love you, too," he said.

For a moment, we just smiled. Staring dumbly at each other. I memorized each line on his beautiful face. He was so good.

So strong.

So loving.

We'd been through so much. I really meant what I said. I truly loved him. And to know he felt the same way about me... my cheeks hurt from joy.

"What do we do now?" I whispered.

"We could kiss?"

"Oh, yeah. That'd be good."

He leaned across the small bed to peck me chastely on the mouth. Our first in-love kiss.

"I love you," he reaffirmed, kissing gently. He did some sweet pecks on my lips in a row.

"I love you, too." I let him kiss me, sweetly, softly. But then I smiled wickedly. When he next came to brush our lips together, I didn't let him go. I pulled him down, allowing our mouths to open much more.

Beck was so game.

"Come here," he drew me to him, as the yearning built for us both. He came across me to kiss my neck and face. He tasted like honey and fresh cut apples. His tongue slid so perfectly between my lips and filled my mouth.

We couldn't stop kissing.

We couldn't stop necking.

I wanted him to be all over me. Touching me.

Bringing new life to my body. I wanted to touch all of him and light him up just the same.

My hips rose up to greet him.

His hand slid away from my face to cup my shoulder, squeezing my skin, hugging me to him. Searching the bends and curves while we necked. He worked his way down my arm. But his fingers slid off at my elbow. Instead, he clasped my waist. His thumb traced the crack in my clothing's defenses, the tender bit of exposed skin between my shirt and my pants.

He lit a fire of longing inside me, but his hands didn't force their way into my clothes.

I rubbed my lower body against him. Suggestively rhythmic.

As we rocked and rolled, the narrow gap of skin between my fabrics started to widen. The shirt rose higher up around my body. Smoothly, he slid his hand in any place that felt safe and pre-exposed. He roamed the soft skin of my back. The deep curve of my hip. Up and down I let him touch me.

Safe and warm.

Hot on my skin.

Craving for more, I let him in.

His motions grew bigger, riskier, pushing the limits of what was uncovered. With a flick of a wrist, all my secrets would be exposed. But I trusted Beck so completely. Our desires cresting in perfect rhythm. Skin to skin. Never farther than I wanted to go. I felt a new sort of excitement. One I hadn't felt before. A new trajectory in our attraction. Like together, we might climb that mountain. Then his fingers fell back. He released me. Respectful. A gentle distance growing between us once more. Beck was being true to my boundaries. Remembering past conversations. Like a gentleman, he slowed.

No.

I wanted more. I wanted everything that was happening.

To slide deeper.

To go further.

To find a new and exciting open door.

"Beck." More intensely I rubbed us together. Wordlessly encouraging.

"It's okay, we'll take our time." He slowed things down. Kissing, smiling. Still playfully nipping. He felt so good.

But that wasn't what I wanted.

I didn't want us to slow.

Not this time.

"Beck," I pulled him up to look in my eyes. My mouth on his. Breathing heavy. I kissed him. "I think... I mean, I know... I'm ready."

I was *so* ready.

I saw a tiny flicker of excitement, but Beck didn't push for more. "Are you sure?"

"Mm hmm," I sucked his bottom lip. I was *so* sure.

"Oh my god," Beck moaned.

"Beck, I'm sure." One more night or day without him was one too many. I had never been so sure of anything in my life. "Take off your clothes." I assured him with my smile, this was really happening.

Beck grinned. If I was ready, he was good to go.

He raised up to an almost seated position. Watching me closely as I observed him, he took both hands to the neck and pulled up on his shirt. The fabric hitched over his head, exposing his lower abs, then he smoothly grabbed the shoulder stitch and pulled the shirt off to the floor. His hair got a little mussed in the transfer, so he raked his fingers through to straighten everything.

He was exposed. Half-stripped.

I could feel the heat of his body.

He smelled delicious. Woodsy and heavy.

I reached up for his unclad shoulders, now lying almost beneath him. He lowered his chest. He felt so good. At first, I made contact with his bare skin with reverence, then the excitement took over and I grabbed hold.

We were really doing this.

His mouth found my lips as his fingers located my waist. This time, his hand slipped right under my shirt.

"Oh," I moaned.

Beck grinned, watching my arousal. The skin under there was so tender. My nerve endings tingled as he made his way into my clothing. The inaugural mission to explore me. Every inch, an adventure of its own. His fingers stroked my skin, enjoying every place that he paused, caressing. He roamed forward, until at last he found what he came for and enthusiastically, he embraced both my breasts. I gasped as he took hold.

Beck kissed down my neck, then dropped to my stomach. He slid up my t-shirt. Licking. Hunting. He found his path. My bra and then my nipples. He pushed up the fabric sheath then filled his mouth. Eager for more.

"Oh, god." My back arched, and our hips pushed together. I rose to greet him.

And I could feel him. Every inch of space between our legs now collapsed.

He was excited. And I was ready to let him into the depths of my body.

"Get on top," he whispered.

"Alright." I nodded.

We shifted around on the tiny bunk. Beck lay prone as I straddled him, feeling his firmness rest just below my butt. I rubbed against him. Beck murmured, appreciative. It was everything that I wanted. He felt so good. Between my legs. Secure in my heart.

I leaned down, kissed him hard and wanting, deeply. His hands flew up my back, dragging my shirt with him, above him, until I pulled it off over my head. Carelessly, I tossed it aside.

We dove in.

Our skin, so hot. So slick. So sweaty.

This was further than we'd ever been before.

But I loved him and Beck loved me back. We weren't slowing down. All the build up, mixed with trust, and sweet cuddles had laid the groundwork. This time, I was ready.

Desire raging. The pining was over.

Beck had waited so patiently 'til I was prepared to be his parabond... to be his girlfriend... his loving partner... but, the waiting was over. I was ready.

Really ready to be his girl.

And I couldn't wait to show him.

In a thousand different positions.

Tonight. Tomorrow. Forever. Always.

Beck was mine. And I was his. Forever more.

TWENTY-SIX
THE MOST PERFECT NIGHT

IN MY DREAMS, I heard the familiar sound of the Damocles children singing their sea monster refrain. Little children's voices. A haunting melody. Down the halls it came.

In and out, around the forest,

Tick, tick, boom.

"Beck, do you hear that?" I asked my parabond, but when I looked in the bed, he wasn't there. "Beck?" My dream-self turned to find him. In the vision, the bedroom magically changed. I walked through a maze of white gauzy sheets, pushing them aside as I traveled, searching for the source of the song. The lyrics echoed through the chambers. They spurred me on.

"Beck?"

My cheeks were still pink from our newly minted union, but in dreamland, Beck didn't answer. I kept looking for where he went. Somehow, I made my way back to the mess hall. All the swaying fabric disappeared as I put my hand on the door. But when I opened the airlock, Beck wasn't there. Present, was only one man.

Sitting tall.

Waiting for me.

Sick and ugly and benevolent.

Cornelius Child.

He was relaxed over a piano, playing the same dissonant key over and over. His plunking the keyboard overtook the children in song. I was filled with rage at the sight.

Full of belligerence, I marched over. "Hey!" I poked a finger at him. "Let my friends go."

"Would I do that?" He asked. With his index fingers, he smoothed both the eyebrows on his face and smiled. As he did, his eyes turned red and a crazed look developed. He stuck out his tongue and it was forked, like a devil's. Maniacally, he started to laugh. "Come, little Mae Kingsley. Come into the pot." He opened a cooking dish on the bench beside him and as I looked inside I could see Beck and several others trapped as well.

Tap, tap, tap.

Cornelius wrapped the side of the container and the others tried to hide from him.

"Beck! Get out!" I tried to reach him, but he was too far from my grasp. I pushed to reach further, but something held me back. Fearfully, I looked up from the pot.

Suddenly, we weren't in the mess hall anymore.

Instead, there were trees all around. Cornelius held up a gun. Pointed straight at my head. Still, I couldn't do anything. My arms wouldn't move. And in dream logic, Beck was no longer in the pot, the pot didn't even exist now. Instead, he was behind me, shirtless, hugging my arms, holding me back. I wanted to lunge, but we saw the cold barrel of the weapon.

We stared right down the cylinder as the trigger started to click back.

A truck engine roared.

The trigger tick-ticked further.

"No," I whimpered.

The engine grew louder.

"I got you," shirtless Beck told me. But it was him I was protecting.

The barrel of the gun was certain.

"No," I murmured, worried. "That's not what I want."

The forest filled with a flash.

Boom!

"No!" My voice went hoarse. "Please stop." I tried to get up, "Somebody help!" But someone still held down my arms.

My *real* arms.

"No. Stop!" I sat straight up in the bed.

"Mae, shhhh. It's alright. Just a dream, you're alright." Beck held me. "You're okay."

I stopped thrashing, fully waking. "I'm alright." I agreed, now settling. "I'm okay."

"Are you sure?" He soothed.

"I'm alright." I repeated the mantra once more. I felt my heart beating hard in my chest. The images seemed so real. Cornelius Child was so awful. "Are *you* alright?" I asked, realizing I might have punched him. I patted his stomach and chest, looking for wounds. "Did he hurt you?" I asked, then realized how silly that sounded. I recovered quickly. "I mean, did *I* hurt you... with my hands?"

"I can take it," he winked. He released me and we both collapsed back on the bed. "Scary dream?"

"The worst," I agreed. "Cornelius Child was basically the devil. We can't trust a thing that he says."

"I already didn't," Beck shrugged. Then he let out a little harumph.

"What?"

"I'm just bummed. Here we were, having like the most perfect night, then you cast and yours is spoiled."

"Mine wasn't spoiled."

"By some awful dream." He looked so cute, all put out at the thought.

"Before my vision, you thought things were perfect?" I purred.

"Well, not everything," he conceded. "In a perfect world we might not have to sleep on a tiny cot sharing a pancake of a pillow. But other than that, yeah. It was pretty darn good." Beck grinned.

"Damn good." I smiled back. "Don't worry, my vision didn't ruin it," I told him, gently sloughing his hair off his forehead. "I'm getting used to them. And before that, I thought it was kind of near perfect too... although..."

"What?"

I playfully bit my bottom lip, then released it, tantalizing. "It's not morning yet."

"Oh?"

"Not quite." I shrugged, being coy. "I mean, there's no windows in here, but I'm pretty sure we've got a couple hours to kill. There's plenty of time to regain that perfection. Who knows when we'll have the luxury of another private bedroom."

Enticed, he mimed biting my shoulder. "I like you," he told me.

"You better," I nodded, pretending like I was going to put his finger in my mouth. Instead, I nipped at the air.

"Ohhh." He groaned, excited. "What are you doing to me, Mae Kingsley." He adjusted on the bed, then dramatically flopped back. "If we're going to... go... again... I need a glass of water. I am seriously dehydrated. Wouldn't want to get a cramp."

"A cramp? Down there?" Was that even possible?

"In my leg," he laughed. "I'll just pop down to the mess hall. Be back in a jiff." He swung himself out of our little love nest. "Then you better be ready for round two." He told me, hopping up. He leaned back in, mischievous. "And three... and four."

I giggled.

He kissed my lips. "You wanna come?"

"Um..." I pretended to weigh the pros and cons of

getting dressed and going with him or staying warm and snuggled in our bed, but I couldn't sell it.

"Alright, alright." He nodded. "Be right back." He tugged on his pants. "I'll bring you one too. Gotta replenish your fluids."

I raised an eyebrow, surprised.

He turned bright red. "Ugh. That sounded sexier in my brain."

We both laughed.

I glanced at his bare-chested body. For a second, the end of my vision flashed in my mind. "Take your shirt," I told him.

"Okay, weirdo." He grabbed the t-shirt off the bedside. "Be right back." He ducked out of our airlock and scampered down the hall. The door was still slightly propped open, but I didn't mind. At this time of night, there was no-one around in the halls. I flopped back on the bed, grinning, unable to wipe the smile from my lips. What a night. What an adventure.

I blushed, thinking of Beck's body.

The strength and rhythm of his hips.

The slow way he'd opened my world.

At first it hurt. A lot. And I was scared. Even though I wanted to do it. I wanted to do it *right*, and I wanted him to enjoy it, but I didn't want it to hurt. But, I didn't need to worry. He showed me. Slowly. Took his time. He was tender. And he waited 'til I opened. 'Til I could manage the pressure between my thighs. 'Til I relaxed. 'Til my body let him in.

After that, it felt good. Great. So full. And deeply connected.

We were entwined in every inch.

So this was sex.

I just wanted to do it again.

My mind continued to replay the evening's highlights while I waited for his quick return. There were things that I liked, that turned me on, that I wanted more of, and then there were moves that I thought felt kinda weird. We would teach each other, I giggled to myself. Both teacher and student. As many lessons as it took.

I glanced at the doorway.

I wanted to look as appealing as possible when Beck crossed back into the room. I hopped out of the bed and went quickly to look in the small wall mirror. My cheeks were rosy and plumped, my lips berry-red and moist. I tousled my hair around, trying to find the best I-just-woke-up-and-aren't-I-adorable option. I decided on a half-toss to one side. A little messy. A little buoyant. It was big, unkempt bedroom hair. I didn't want Beck to have any doubt.

Green light.

All systems go.

I heard him coming, so quickly as I could, I popped back onto our cot. I fluffed and folded the blankets around me, strategic in making sure both a long, sexy leg was available, with easy access, and the round shape of my breasts could be seen from the door. I decided to look away, and playfully turn my head to greet him as he arrived. But he didn't push through the doorway.

Whoever I'd heard passing in the hallway, it wasn't him.

False alarm.

In my perfect pose, I had to wait longer.

I adjusted again. That was alright. More time to find the perfect way to prop up. I rearranged for more leg. More boob outline. I fluffed up my hair even bigger.

But still, he hadn't returned.

Actually, he was taking quite a while. It wasn't that far from the mess hall to our room. I could have gotten our waters three times and been back by now.

"Beck?" I called out in a whisper, sitting up tall. I tugged the blankets around me. If he was waiting in the hallway to surprise me, that would be weird. "Beck?"

Still no answer.

I grabbed my discarded clothes off the next bed and slipped back into my things. "Beck?" I whisper-called as I walked forward, mindful that the ship wasn't that big. There were lots of people sleeping in the bunk-room hallway. I wouldn't want to wake any of them. He didn't answer, so I moved forward, quietly making my way through the belly of the ship.

The submarine looked different at night, with lower lighting. No other person was around. Suddenly, I felt my skin goosebump. It was kind of eerie. I couldn't explain why, but it felt too much like my most recent dream. Only there weren't any white gauzy sheets to push aside. Still, I couldn't shake the feeling.

Just then, the ship let out a groan.

"Beck, did you hear that?" I automatically wondered, but as the words came out, I clamped my hand over my mouth and closed my lips.

That was the exact sentence I'd uttered in my vision.

I took the elastic off my wrist and pulled my hair back. Still walking forward, now at half of the speed. The strange groan that I'd heard continued to gently shudder through the hallways. The ship was moving. I wanted to call out to Beck again, but I held back. That's what I did in my dream.

A vision with a terrible ending. So I kept silent as I moved down the halls.

There's nothing to fear, I told myself. Everyone's safe and asleep. But repeating reassuring words to my inner voice didn't help my goosebumps to abate. I came to the mess hall door.

Why were there no windows in this place?

If I ever designed a submarine layout, I would put windows in the airlocks to clearly see in and out. For public quarters it just made sense!

Beck's inside, I told myself. He's getting our waters.

But I knew in my heart he'd already taken too much time. Something else was going on. Was it possible my dream had come to life? Could Cornelius Child be waiting on the other side of this door? With red, glowing eyes and forked demon tongue? Ready to take me to jail?

No. Of course not.

How would he even find us here? We were underwater in a freakin' lake.

You're fine. Go in and find your guy.

I put my hand on the handle.

Mae, you're being silly.

I pressed down on the metal latch.

Click.

The tiny adjustment to the airlock echoed in the empty hallway.

Here goes nothing.

I opened the mess hall door and went inside.

TWENTY-SEVEN
THE MESS HALL AFTER MIDNIGHT

THE DOOR to the mess hall swung open with an awful, scratchy creak. I held my breath as the room came into view. But immediately, I let it out in a puff. There sat a shirtless Beck, halfway through eating a sandwich. His t-shirt was tossed on the table beside him. At my arrival, his mouth dropped open in surprise.

"Did I take too long?" He swallowed his mouthful. The two waters he'd said he'd fetch us stood untouched on the table. I couldn't help but laugh.

"Yes! You took forever!" I told him. But, I wasn't mad. He looked too cute, sitting shirtless, scarfing down his snack. I came towards him. "I just missed you." I draped my arms around his shoulders. It was so proper, how he was sitting. He'd made his sandwich, even got himself a napkin and a plate for crumbs.

"Wanna bite?" He offered, bringing the snack towards me. I let him feed me. The mix of bread, cheese and mayo tasted delicious. "My own secret recipe."

"Of cheese sandwich?"

He winked. "Want me to make you one?" He went back to eating his.

I licked the remaining grease off my lips. "No thanks, I'm good."

"You're great!" Beck said then took a playful, generous bite. He smiled in a sloppy grin.

The submarine groaned and shuddered. We looked around, but it quickly settled.

I laughed. "In comparison to a sandwich, I'm great. What a compliment."

Like little kids, we couldn't stop smiling.

"Hey man, that's praise of the highest order. This sandwich is pretty good."

"Is it?" I teased. I waited for him to finish.

Beck stuffed the rest of the snack in his cheek, chewed it up quickly like a chipmunk and swallowed it whole. "*That* hit the spot."

I found it so sweet to watch him, my cheeks hurt. I loved this man. And Beck loved me back. We would have a whole life of adorable moments like this one where we loved each other and life would be perfect and silly and wild.

"Now that that's settled," I pretended to be tough. "Can we go back to bed?"

"Just a sec." He hopped up from his chair and diligently cleaned the place where he'd been eating, sweeping any errant crumbs off the table and onto the plate. He fussed with his dish in the dish rack and dropped the soiled napkin into the garbage. "There. Like we were never here."

"Oh yeah. What are the rules about the mess hall after midnight?" I wondered. It only just occurred to me, we might have been breaking some sort of norm.

"Anything goes," Beck's smile shifted suggestively. "There's nobody here."

"Oh?" I played along, leaning towards him. "I'm here."

"Yeah, you are." In one motion, he reached out and grabbed the drawstring on my pants and tugged me in his direction. The fabric drew tight around my hips, pulling me to him. Waist first. The confident command lit me up. The air between us collapsed. Like I was helpless, he towed me into his personal space. Breathless, I waited.

Willing.

Aching.

Shirtless, Beck's woodsy musk aroused my senses, filling my head.

For a moment, he did nothing, just looked me over. His eyes absorbed every inch. A new kind of hunger on his lips.

For him, I was starving.

But he was patient. Letting the boundaries of desire between us build.

How he wanted me.

How I wanted him too.

He let it linger.

"Hi parabond," he said, softly and slowly.

"Hi," I repeated back to him.

Then he moved in for the kill.

I was begging for it. Totally ready.

Beck kissed me deeply. The desire between us already raging over my skin. The craving and passion thudded wildly in my chest.

I had no choice but to fully give in.

My hands searched his bare shoulders and his neck as his strong arms now embraced me. His hands grabbed every shape on my body while his tongue slid between my open lips.

Neck.

Waist.

Hair.

Beck touched every inch of me.

Finally, his palms cupped my bum. Pulled me towards him. Lustfully, I moaned.

We were rested, rejuvenated and feeling risqué. Was it possible we'd make love right here in this room?

He pulled me with him, moving backwards as one entwined unit, until we clattered into the wall. It gave him the leverage he needed to drag me even closer. Our bodies arching, any space between our extremities completely disappeared.

"Beck," I whispered throatily, coming up for air. "Someone might see."

In answer, he spun me around, put on display, and tugged me tight to his body, my bum crashing into his thighs.

I could feel the full extent of his excitement again. He pushed against the curves of my body, pulling me to him. His mouth kissed my neck and ear. I faced outward. Defenseless. Absorbing.

Seeing little.

I was blinded with passion. Letting Beck's foreplay wash over me. He was blowing my mind with his sexy intentions. Fully submissive, I let him take the lead.

"There's no one here," he whispered, so close it was like a sexy growl.

His hands went in my hair, knotting it there. He pulled my head back to him.

Over my shoulder, I kissed his lips. Let his tongue explore my gums.

This was wrong, I knew.

Too exposed.

Too exotic.

It was clearly too public.

We had a perfectly adequate bedroom. A safe space all to ourselves.

But here, in the mess hall someone might see us, and that too was exciting. We had room to play. It was hot. And oh so sexy. Oh my god.

Every moment we drove forward. I thought he might take me, right there, on the table. I should have objected, but I didn't. I let him build us further entranced. We'd done it once to full completion, and how I longed to come together again.

His fingers slid under my shirt. Across my bare stomach and up the tender route to my chest. My back arched. I rubbed my hips back in appreciation, feeling him taut against my bum. His bare chest was so hot. He radiated with energy.

"Beck," I breathed his name.

"Mae," he whispered back.

My arms floated up to clench him behind me. My body opened as I received him. His fingers fondled both my breasts.

In syncopation, our bodies started to roll. I felt scared but excited at what was coming, he would bend me over the table next and-

Bam!

The airlock from the pantry to the mess hall flew open. The door ricocheted on the back wall and Craig hurried into the cafeteria. I gasped, immediately collapsing my open stance, pushing Beck outside of my clothes. He quickly hid both his erection and his shirt-less body behind me. At the sight of us shambling to put ourselves back together, Craig stopped where he was. He looked just as surprised as us.

"Uh, hi!" I squirmed. "Good morning."

"Good morning," he averted his eyes.

"What are you doing?" I wondered, trying and failing to feel more presentable in the presence of this new man.

"We didn't think anyone was around," Beck piped up. That wasn't helping. I wanted to die a thousand deaths of dignity. On a submarine underwater, was it possible to sink into the ground?

The older witch refused to look up, as embarrassed

as we were. "I was just in the comms room," he nodded.

Suddenly, the submarine let out a shudder.

We pitched slightly apart.

"What was that?" I blurted, catching myself from falling, but then I looked for a real answer from the more knowledgeable man. Craig was familiar with the sub. He would actually know what was going on. But he had already started hurrying away. "Craig, are we good? Is that normal?"

"It was nothing. Just total fluctuations. Go back to what you were... doing. I didn't see anything. I was never even here." He didn't wait for our confirmation, instead just hurried out the other door.

"No. Hey, wait. We're sorry." I tried to stop him. "Craig, wait!" But the rebel harness had bailed to the hall, quick to go. Beck and I looked at each other. "Well, that was awful," I moaned.

"So mortifying," Beck agreed, already smiling. As if it had never happened, he reached for my hips again.

"Beck! That was a serious disaster. What if it had been Wesson?"

"But it wasn't."

"Still, it was kinda gross and weird."

"He said go back to what we were doing... he's not coming back." Beck tried again, but I pulled away. Playtime was over. We weren't making that mistake again. Beck gave up. He could see, for me, the moment had passed.

I went back to the table with our waters and Beck's

t-shirt. I picked it up and handed it back to him. Beck followed a little slower, but he didn't put it back on. He was still trying to figure out a way to put us back on the rails.

"We didn't do anything wrong," he said.

"It felt *wrong*," I complained.

"He just didn't want an eye full. I don't blame him. I've walked in on Brandi and Clint before, doing more. And trust me, seeing your sister like that? All you want is to disappear. I mean good for her, go and get it if you want it, but I don't want to see how the getting happened... neither did Craig." He shrugged. He had made his best play to coax me back into his sexual proximity, but I barely heard Beck's last few words. My eyes were focused on the two glasses of water on the table instead. They were shuddering.

"Beck, look."

The liquid was vibrating.

"What does that mean?"

"I dunno."

We glanced around.

"I think..." I looked up. "Is the whole ship moving?"

Beck frowned. "Why do I have the feeling that isn't good?"

TWENTY-EIGHT

THE CONTROL ROOM

"MAYBE A LITTLE MOVEMENT IS NORMAL? Like an overnight repositioning," Beck offered.

"You think?"

But he was already tugging back on his shirt. We were on the same page. "I don't know what to think."

Craig's sketchy behavior plus the sudden equipment groans and now the boat vibrations raised several red flags. Goosebumps formed on my skin. My inner warning system. Something was definitely off.

"Where does that airlock go?" I wondered. "He said the comms room?"

"Well, first it's the pantry, then the kitchen," Beck shrugged. Only moments ago, he'd made his sandwich in there. "Then maybe the communication room?"

I should have paid better attention on the tour.

We went through the airlock, exploring. Beck only one step behind. He was right, adjacent, it was the pantry, but it was also like a chain of rooms developing. We walked through the next door too. Next up was the kitchen. But beside it stood another door. The prep stations and dish pit all appeared undisturbed, but something in my bones told me we were on the right path. The next airlock was closed.

"What comes next?"

"The control room?" Beck asked.

"The comms room?" I nodded, as Craig had called it. "Communication?" Beck opened the next air lock. And it looked a little familiar. It *was* the comms room. We'd briefly been here before. The ballasts and the periscopes or the somethings. I had a vague recollection. It was indeed a busy communications center with a million mechanical devices for controlling the ship. I hadn't paid attention earlier, as I didn't plan to spend much time onboard the vessel. But now I could see, it took a lot of know-how to man the sub. It was weird the technical port was empty. Even in the middle of the night. So many things here could go wrong. There must have been a hundred dials and instruments all with readings lit up and functioning. I had no idea what we were looking at or how to tell if something was wrong.

Everything seemed to be running just fine.

Maybe Beck was right. Perhaps nighttime shudders were totally normal.

But Gennady had said something about rotating night shifts. And after taking it in, in person, I felt confident a submarine like this couldn't run on its own.

Craig?

Had he left his post?

It seemed the best bet that he was the witch still on duty. So why wasn't he here? In this room? Watching his command on the dials that we saw? Could it be we misread his awkward departure as a simple bathroom break?

I was about to shrug things off when Beck picked up a discarded gas mask from the ground.

Strange.

That didn't belong in a communications mainframe.

I went to the front of the boat and looked out the periscope. On the bottom of the lake, it should have been looking out at nothing but blue waters, but I was surprised to see that I could see land. The periscope was actually half out of the water.

"Beck, I think I know what the shudders are. We're rising," I murmured. "Out of the water." I spun the scope around. I could see the shore where we'd come out from the roadway, and the old dock and the mechanical boat still attached. It was all there, on the shore. For a second, I squinted. What was that?

I thought I saw something out in the forest.

Something moving.

With all the droplets of water on the sight glass, I couldn't be sure.

"Beck, I'm not too sure, but I think someone out there," I told him, squinting harder.

"Mae," he interrupted. His voice grew worried. "There's someone here as well."

TWENTY-NINE

A SIREN IN THE HALLWAYS

I WHIRLED AROUND. Beck had opened the door to a closet directly behind the gas mask and a man's body had tumbled out, slumped to the floor.

"Diego!" We dropped to his side.

"Hey, wake up," Beck gently shook him. I could see he was breathing.

"You're alright." We jostled him. "Come on."

"Where is he?" Diego suddenly shot to full consciousness

"Who?" I sat back.

"That little bitch." He growled, clawing to his feet. "Craig-gy ambushed me in a gas mask. Stupid coward must've shoved me in the closet." Diego went rushing towards the circuitry. "What did he do?" He started checking everything at once.

"We don't know," Beck admitted.

"There was a shake and lots of shuddering. I think we might be resurfacing?" I guessed.

"Check the ballast," Diego told me, but only he knew where that was. Beck and I helplessly glanced at each other. "Damn it." He pushed in front of us to do it. "He opened the air vent," he reported. "We're already at seventy-six percent." Diego flung himself into his work.

"Like seventy-six percent out of the water?" I feared.

"The ballast is seventy-six percent full of air."

"Why would he do that?" Beck asked.

I went back to the periscope and re-examined the shoreline. This time, I definitely saw movement in the forest. Even without a clear visual I realized exactly who would be moving out there, in the middle of nowhere, at this time of morning.

It was an ambush.

"To let the High Council come aboard," I told the other two.

"Son-of-a-bitch!" Diego slammed a hand down on the counter.

I stared out to shore.

They were there.

On the edge of the lake, waiting for the submarine to resurface. The gathered ladies and fellows had forgone their white sweatsuits of the castle and instead, today dressed totally in army fatigues. The greens and browns did their jobs, blending the witches into the forest. But they couldn't hide their leader's fiery orange hair.

Cornelius Child was waiting.

With the guards from his High Council.

Watching for the submarine's final surface.

Expecting to come on board.

There were at least twenty of them, coven members, watching and waiting. Maybe in the shadows stood a legion more. I couldn't tell, but it wouldn't have surprised me if Child had come with an entire army to take out this troublesome clan.

Diego didn't stop working. "Damn it! Somehow he's locked the ballast down! I can't seem to reverse it. We're gonna breach. There's no stopping. There's nothing I can do. We have to warn them."

"Who?"

"*Everybody.*"

"Zaid!" I yelled for my dad.

Diego dove forward and flipped another switch on the deck of instruments. Warning lights flashed and a public alarm started to blare. It wailed like a siren in the hallways.

"Are there escape tunnels or something?" I asked Diego.

We had to shout to be heard over the alarm.

"Just the pressurized hatches." Seeing our blank looks, he grew exasperated. He ran over to a sample hatch in the command room. "You tie yourself in, launch the door, the hatch shoots off, dragging you with it, before the water has a chance to flood in the room."

"Like an ejection seat," Beck followed.

"Yes. Like I was trying to tell you." He was harried.

The hatch looked like the exit of an airplane with a spinning valve to seal it and a handle to pull to release it. Two canvas loops were there, to strap yourself in. We'd seen the small doorways all over the rooms. There was one in almost every cabin. Little escape pods all over the ship.

"If we blow them, we'll sink," Diego admitted. "We have to find a better option."

Beck and I glanced at each other. No time to waste.

"You fix in here! We'll tell the others!" I told him, already half out the door.

"I don't know if I can!"

"Try your best!"

The airlock clanged behind us.

"Zaid!" I shouted, running forward. "Zaid!" I had to scream to be heard over the siren but I was no longer worried about who I might wake. If they were still sleeping through this, they would have to be unconscious.

"Rick! Gennady!" Beck was right behind me.

As we made it through the mess hall back into the bunk area, plenty of witches were already stumbling out of their dorm rooms.

"What's happening?" Hilde wondered, wiping the sleep from her eyes.

"What's going on?" Ferris and Ethan were smart enough to be far more worried.

"Can't a guy get eight hours?" Greg mumbled as he stifled a yawn.

But we rushed right through their crowd, looking for Gennady or Wesson or anybody who was in charge or who might know what was going on.

The two rebel leaders stumbled out of the same bunk room.

That was weird.

Beck had specified, none of the bedroom quarters were co-ed. I filed it away in my brain, but there was no time to question it. They saw the panic in our eyes.

"What's going on?" Wesson demanded.

"Diego pulled the alarm. Craig messed everything up. He drugged him. The submarine is surfacing." I told them. "We gotta move."

"What?"

"We do something!" Beck cried. "Now!"

"Slow down," Gennady told us.

"We saw him," I said

"Who, Diego?" Wesson tried to follow.

I shook my head. "No, Craig."

"And Diego!" Beck agreed. All of our words came crashing out. "We were in the mess hall, and-"

"Why were you in the mess hall?" Someone interrupted. Quite a group had gathered.

"We were getting a cup of water-" I said.

"Got some snacks-" Beck added.

"Oh, god. They were humping. That should have been me and Marcy."

"We were getting a drink and a snack," I snapped,

frowning at Greg. "A sandwich." There was no need to talk of sex. Wesson Zaid might have been an absolute stranger, but he was still my *dad*. "Then the submarine kind of shifted and Craig came by acting all weird."

"So weird," Beck echoed. "We retraced his steps to see where he'd come from-"

"And found Diego stuffed in a closet."

"He was knocked out."

"Then I looked out the periscope and saw Cornelius Child was waiting, right now, I just saw him. He's on the shore. We're almost breaching. Him and a bunch of High Council guards. That's when Diego pulled the alarm."

"It was Craig," Beck finished. "He set up an ambush."

The rebels exchanged a look of horror.

Child and the others were waiting on land?

We had only minutes.

"Get to the artillery!" Wesson ordered.

The herd of us raced down the narrow halls. Forced into a single-like file by the constraints of our geography.

"Everyone, load up your pockets. You'll need all the spells you can carry!" Gennady shouted instructions over her shoulder, but when she opened the airlock to the artillery, she smashed to a halt.

"Craig!" She stared, shocked. Several more of us fed into the small room, all crashing to a stop behind her. It took her a moment to regain her command. "What are you doing?!"

I could hear the mix of hurt and anger in her voice. This was her close friend. He'd been caught red-handed trashing the artillery spell room. Almost all the potions were crushed or mixed up or spilt and broken in front of us. They lay in shards on the counters and floor. The shelving units were destroyed. In our presence, he smashed a final bottle to bits.

"No!" Gennady yelped. "What are you doing?" She asked, again.

Craig looped one arm into the canvas buckle of the pressurized escape hatch. One second longer and he might have escaped unscathed.

"Don't come any closer." He held up a final potion as a threat.

"It's a Udak," Rick immediately recognized. My hair stood on end. I remembered that bomb. The name raised a red flag: the explosive with a super short fuse. Good for only one thing; a suicide mission.

"Craig-gy. Don't," Gennady whimpered.

"Why don't we talk about it?" I tried to get his attention.

"Got your pants on, I see," he snarled in my direction, although he was wrong about our previous wardrobes. Beck had been shirtless but I was always fully clothed. Not that it currently mattered. "I knew when I saw you two lovebirds my time started ticking," he shook his head. Probably thinking he should have just knocked us out too. I was super glad that he didn't.

"Craig-gy," Gennady tried to bring him back around.

"Craig, Gen. Just Craig."

"Craig. We love you. Don't do this."

"You don't love me," Craig scoffed. "You love him." He spit in Wesson's direction.

So I wasn't the only one who'd noticed their night-time arrangement.

Gennady flinched. Wesson didn't.

But Craig was dismayed. "You like me like a *buddy*. A little younger brother. That's all I am. All I am to you. All I am to anybody. I want *more,* Gen. I deserve more. What sort of life is this?" He gestured around.

I had only been here for one night and already I could see it was an untenable place. I couldn't imagine a permanent underwater existence... but these people had all been doing it for eight years. For Craig to betray them now, after all that they'd been through together... Gennady was holding back silent tears.

"So you'll turn against your friends?" Wesson asked.

Craig turned with vehemence. "You're not my *friend*. None of you. This is just some hideout. I built this place, so you kept me around. For what? We're not freedom fighters. We're not out to change the Council. We're just a bunch of rejects. Hiding. Claiming rebellion. Living underwater. Eight long years. Eight long *nothing*. We didn't do *anything*. Reformation? It doesn't exist. Nothing changes. Nothing ever did. We're down here. Worried. Too scared to do anything." Again, he glared at Wesson. "But when something matters to Wes, now suddenly it's time to make your move. You put us all at risk. Blew up our entire battle. And for what? To get your kid out of a jam? Another woman for Wesson. Another memory charm for the books. Wesson saved his lovely daughter. Hip-hip-hooray for everyone! What about me, Wes?" He asked him. "What about her?" He pointed at Gennady. "When do *our* lives get to begin?"

"You're right. And I can help you," Wesson told him.

"I've helped myself."

"Craig," Gennady whimpered. "What did you do?"

"I'm sick of this. Sick of all the *hiding*. The Council offered me an exit. Lead them here, they'll drop all the charges I face. I can go home, Gen. What do you know, after eight years of hiding, I'm a free man!"

"At what cost?" She asked. "Who will pay it?"

"You know, I'm sorry about that, Gen," he admitted. "Honestly, I am. I didn't want to... you shouldn't be in the midst of this. But you tied your yoke to the wrong man." Then he turned to Wesson, ice cold. "I'm not sorry, Wes."

"Where is he? I'll kill him!" Diego came running through the crowd, shoving forward. But the final witch was too late. With ferocity, Craig cranked open the escape hatch. The pressurized valve released in a flashing explosion. We shielded our eyes and Craig was sucked right out the door. The hatch blew clean off, while the lake water gushed into its vacated place. The Udak bomb dropped untampered with to the floor. Water flooded into the artillery.

"Vince!" I shouted, but my water harnessing friend was already fully engaged. His powerful hands immediately balled into a fist. With his magic strength, he held the waters back in an imaginary wall which he temporarily held at bay. But it wasn't an easy task. The pressure slammed against his will.

"I can't hold it," Vince warned us, his voice already becoming strained.

"Quick! Grab everything you can!" Wesson instructed. We splashed into the small puddle of water. I picked up Craig's Udak bomb off the floor while others lunged for the cupboards and shelves.

"The area needs to be sealed off!" Gennady shouted above our heads. She pushed the others back. It was hard for the collective to retreat. She forced them backwards towards the last airlock. In the artillery scramble, there weren't very many potions still intact, but we grabbed what we could. Vince held strong, keeping the water pushed back behind his wall.

Argh. He groaned.

"This is beyond his skill level," Rick warned.

"Speak for yourself," Vince tried to snark back, but Rick was correct, holding the pressure was getting the better of the boy. His seal was failing quickly. "Get them out."

"Out! Everyone get back!" I shouted.

We pushed more of the witches back, out of the

artillery, retreating into the adjoining hallway, until it was just the last few in the room.

"That's it," Wesson told us. We had grabbed everything of value.

"I can't hold it," Vince threatened.

"Come on, come on!" Ferris ordered our final steps from the pantry.

"A sleeping potion!" Hilde noticed under the lip of the shelving unit.

"Hilde, no!" I tried to reach her, but the girl was too quick. She ducked under the shelf.

"Mae, I can't-!" Vince doubled over.

"Get her out of there, now!" Rick commanded.

"Hilde!" We all shouted.

"I can't hold it-"

"I almost got it." She stretched a little more. It was almost in her grasp.

"Hilde!"

But it was too late.

"Argh!"

Vince let out a terrible wail. He collapsed into the hallway and the powerful surge of water he had been protecting blasted into the artillery room. The unstoppable wave smashed Hilde against the back wall.

"Seal the door!" Wesson shouted. "Seal the door!"

"Close it!" Gennady ordered.

"She's still in there!" I raced forward, but the other rebels did what they were instructing. They slammed shut the airlock. "What are you doing? Wait! No!

Hilde's still there!" I battered the doorway, trying to get it open.

Gennady pulled me off it. She put her body between me and the airlock. "Mae, we couldn't wait. Any more pressure and we'd never get the water stopped from flowing. It would crash from one room to another. We had to close the door."

"But she's still in there!" We were both sopping.

"She'll drown," Greg backed me up.

"Either that or we all will!" Wesson snapped. "We had to seal off the hole. It's the curse of this type of ship."

But that didn't quell the horror we felt in our bones.

"You can't just leave her," I told them, shocked at what they considered reasonable.

"When the water and air pressures stabilize, she can swim out to the surface." Gennady assured us. "She just needs to take a deep breath. Your friend can be alright."

"She doesn't know how to do that," I worried.

"How would she know what to do?" Beck echoed.

Rick tended to Vince on the floor, who looked positively gray.

"I couldn't hold it," he told his larger friend, weakly. "I had to let it go."

"You did what you could," Rick said. "I know... I know."

Vince wept. "She'll never make it." He voiced what we all were thinking.

Hilde was a scared little girl. She was tough. But she wasn't experienced. She'd never been anywhere like a sinking room in a submarine before. She would panic for sure. We were already panicked for her. Beck and I exchanged a glance.

"Rick, she'll never make it," Vince repeated just to Rick. "I couldn't hold it. What do we do?"

The large boy looked up. "I will help her. Get everyone out of here. I will flood the second compartment. I am a strong swimmer. Hilde can make it if I help her."

"No," I stood in dawning horror. What he was suggesting would put them both in grave danger. "Rick-"

"You can't make it," Greg sputtered.

"I can. Move now. Take him out. Go. Get moving. I will make it. Hilde and I will be alright." Rick rose. His formidable presence filled the room. We all fell back. No one was willing to tell the large teen what he could and couldn't do. Beck and I helped Vince out of the secondary room and into the hallway.

"Go!" Ferris herded the crowd through the doorway. "Back up. Everybody." Again, the rebels shifted backwards to make room for another airlock. Our friends were the last through the door.

"You try to hold your breath without a big pocket of air," Ethan suggested.

"Rick, you shouldn't have to do this," Vince said. He beat himself up for his error, even as he was so spent he couldn't stand of his own volition.

"What you did was amazing," I tried to comfort him, but Vince wouldn't listen.

"He's cleaning up my mistake."

"You did what you could." Rick came towards us, as we held Vince up between us. Gently, Rick cupped the side of Vince's face. In surprise, I glanced at Beck. "Now I will do the rest," Rick told him. He leaned in. Vince quietly nodded. "Please do not worry. My grumpy, angry friend."

Rick kissed Vince on the mouth.

He kissed him deeply.

My mouth fell open.

For a moment, they didn't pull away.

Then, just as suddenly, Rick pulled back. "See you soon."

Vince nodded.

Rick straightened. "Get him out of here," he quietly ordered.

"Come on, lover," Greg said.

"Shut yer yaps, chaps," Vince sniped in our direction. "You better get her. Come back kickin'."

Beck and I clamped our open mouths closed.

I had no idea that Rick and Vince were an item. I hadn't even known that either boy liked other boys. It wasn't any of my business who they were or weren't kissing, but that didn't mean it didn't surprise me. But there was no time to ponder any of this new information. Rick stepped back from the group.

Ferris and Ethan shut the second door.

At the last moment, the boys shared a tight smile.

Then Rick locked eyes with me as the door was shutting. He gave a curt nod. Awaiting his fate with pride.

He would risk his life to save Hilde.

And then he disappeared into the closed room. Ferris and Ethan twisted the airlock tight. He was gone. We listened to the silence in the second chamber, it was eerie quiet for a moment, then all at once, there came a huge, gushing roar. The pressure of the water from the artillery locker flooded Rick's compartment room. He had purposefully opened the second airlock. He and Hilde were in it now, together. Their fates entwined. There was nothing more for us to do but hope.

"They'll be alright," I felt compelled to say.

"You don't know that," Vince admitted.

"But I'm sure they will," Beck added.

"Rick's a strong boy," Ferris said.

Everyone was silent for a moment. All thinking different but similar things. Would they survive this fate? Would we see them once more?

"So you and Rick?" Greg broke the stillness.

"None of your business." Vince's surly manner had returned.

"I miss Marcy," Greg frowned.

We all looked at him.

"What?" He shrugged. "Love is love. The kiss was hot. I miss my girl."

Love is love.

I loved Beck.

Beck loved me.

Were Vince and Rick in love, too?

I would have liked to learn more about this new romantic couple, but I knew Vince would sooner carve me up with a stick than divulge the romantic notions of his heart. "You *will* have to tell Hilde at some point," I noted, knowing full well the extent of her infatuation.

Vince rolled his eyes, but gave a small nod. He knew the bounds of her adoration as well.

"*If* they make it," Greg shrugged.

"Greg!" Beck tried to stop him. But Vince jumped right into action. That wasn't a joke that Greg could make. At least not now. It wasn't funny, it wasn't honest. It was cruel. For Vince, it was like a knifing. There was too much on the line. He leapt up and slugged him, punching Greg right in the cheek.

"Vince!" We pulled him off as Greg yelped in pain.

"What was that for?"

"They're going to make it," Vince shouted, grimacing. He shook out his hand. "You got it?" I thought he might try to hit him again, but Greg didn't engage.

"Okay," he whimpered. "I got it."

"Are you alright?" Ferris asked him.

"No!" Greg snapped. "I want Marcy!"

"He's okay," Ethan told us, helping Greg regain his composure. "It was a poor joke. That's all. He didn't mean it. You're alright. He's okay."

Greg nodded. He was indeed okay. We glanced back at the door.

They will make it, I told myself.

Rick would come through.

Like Vince, I had to believe it. The alternative was simply too awful to comprehend.

"What now?" Beck asked.

We turned towards the rebels. Everything was happening so quickly.

"We have to get out," Ethan said. "We're sitting ducks."

"What do we do?" I wondered.

Wesson and Gennady exchanged looks.

"Everyone, listen up!" He gathered the attention of the growing chaos in the hallways. "We're gonna-" but before he could dispense the new plan, the submarine shuddered to a halt.

"No!" Someone wailed inside the crowd.

We'd stopped moving.

The ballast pump had finished filling the hulls with air.

We were back on the surface.

The witches of the High Council were coming aboard.

TOTAL CHAOS

FOR A MOMENT, we listened to the footsteps above us.

Several feet climbed aboard. The tinny echoes of boots on the metal body of the submarine struck fear in our bones.

How many witches were out there?

We had to run. Again.

Escape. *Again.*

But this was the only rebel base. Where would we go from here? As fast and as far as we could, we had to keep moving. I looked over to Beck. I could tell, like me, he didn't have any answers, but I slid my hand in his. This time, no matter what happened, we would not get separated. He gripped my palm. We were a unit. Together, we were whole.

"Wes," Gennady prompted him.

"Take the evac hatches like Craig did," someone suggested.

"That'll sink the ship," Diego blustered.

"What choice do we have?" Wesson asked. The other two had no thoughts. "We split up! Get to an evac! Lock the airlocks behind you. Get out, get safe, and then meet up at... Hucklebee farm!"

My eyes flashed to Wesson. That was *my* safe house. He hadn't asked to use it. But, I supposed, if they had nowhere else to go...

"No, wait. Go to Craig's," Gennady corrected. She shouted overtop of the chaos. "The Thom's farm," she told everybody. "Go to the Thom's farm!"

"Thom-thom the traitor?" Diego said. "You wanna go to his *home*?"

"They'll never think to look for us there." She shrugged.

"He's a traitor!"

"Yes, exactly. So, we can hide in relative safety. From there, we'll figure it out. For one night, we'll be safe for sure." The rationale actually made some sense. The house of the man who betrayed them was the last place I'd look for them. Diego shrugged. He agreed. Reconvene at Thom's farm.

"Move!" Wesson shouted.

The rebel witches jumped into action.

"Hey," I called my friends back. "Forget what he said. We go to Kate's." I told them. "You know it?" There was no longer any point in tying our fates to the rebels. They were just as lost as us. The larger group was clearly drawing the ire of the High Council. We should split up.

"Hucklebee farm," Ferris nodded. "We know it." From the determined looks on their faces, I could tell, I wasn't the only one ready to break away from the rebels' rushed plans.

We ran down the narrow halls, ducking corners.

"Tell Rick and Hilde first chance when we see them!" I added. The others nodded, already running, but I caught Vince's eye. He gave a stiff acknowledgment. I specifically used the word *when* and not *if*. In a time like this, word choices mattered. And I knew from past experience, hearing someone else use a *when* gave fresh hope to an *if*.

Vince needed that hope.

We all did.

At this point, Rick and Hilde were a pretty big *if*.

I had no idea if the big and little parabonds would survive, or best case scenario, how we'd find them even if they did. But if a choice that I made with my words could give some small hope to my friend, that in itself was worth the thought.

The halls were total chaos. Rebel witches raced in every direction.

"Incoming!" Someone shouted.

"Get down!"

We heard a metallic clatter.

Ker-pow!

Something exploded.

Then another bump and rattle in another part of the sub. The High Council coven was throwing exploding potions through a hatch above.

"Knock out spells!" Someone yelled.

"Run for cover!"

And just like that, the hallway exploded into a new level of madness. The mass movement in every direction was total pandemonium. There was gas. Everyone started running. Unfortunately for us, we were at the back of the pack. All around us, dorm room airlocks slammed shut. The bunks were already taken. Beck and I pushed further down the hall, covering our faces and mouths from incoming chemicals and spells. Our only choice was to keep moving to the mess hall and beyond. We ducked and covered, running forward. When Greg stumbled, Vince picked him up. The blood from where Vince punched him still wet on his face. It didn't matter now. All personal hurt was forgotten as we tried to escape from the other coven's grasp.

Ferris, Ethan, Vince, Greg, Beck, Gennady, Wesson and I all piled into the dining room. It was the last open door in the hallway. We slammed the airlock shut behind us and Vince and Greg made sure that it was closed. For a moment, we huffed and puffed in the cafeteria.

"Sorry I hit you," Vince told him. "And sorry you deserved it."

"Chicks dig scars." Greg shrugged.

"Marcy's gonna love it," Ferris agreed.

"I know. Sympathy lay." He grinned, nodding emphatically.

We rolled our eyes.

"You had to make it gross?" Beck frowned.

Greg shrugged again.

"What now?" I moved past the others' frowns. Our water glasses still stood lonely on the table. Ethan used one to wash out his eyes and to combat the effects of any gas. He'd been sprayed pretty good. "We should move on." I looked forward to the next doorway with realization. I did the math.

"There are only three more pods," Beck said. We were familiar because we'd only recently re-toured them.

Wesson and Gennady glanced at each other.

Next there were the pantry and the kitchen prep spaces, after that, was the control room. That was all. Three emergency exits for eight people. We had backed ourselves into a dead end.

"When we built this place there weren't nearly as many High Council escapists as there are now," Gennady shuffled. "We never thought..."

"You'd have to deal with as many evacuations?" I finished her thought. Then, a cold question hit me. "What about Lauren? Did anyone see if she got out?"

The woman was helpless. In the submarine in her wheelchair. How could she escape from here if she didn't have help?

"Someone would've gotten her out," Wesson said.

"Aine, maybe?" Gennady added.

But those were empty words. Did anyone see how they'd exit? And how would they have gotten to her? Could she seriously blast out of a side pod with the others? She couldn't move herself. Did someone properly hold on to her to help her eject the vessel? I didn't know, but the odds were not good.

"We've got to go find her."

Wesson got in my way. "You can't go back through those doors. The chemicals will destroy the whole room, we can't escape it. And what would you do if you got to her, Mae? You can't help her out of the door."

"I thought you said Aine did!"

We glared at each other. He knew full well that what he'd just said directly contradicted his previous statement. But before Wesson and I could further duke it out, behind the closed doorway we heard the *rat-a-tat-tat* of more explosions. Instinctually, we all ducked down. Although the fixtures in the room seemed to shake, the mess hall didn't explode. The High Council was decimating the submarine inch-by-inch. But so were the rebels, as smaller, secondary explosions launched left and right from the ship. Rebel witches launched their escape pods. Around the boat, the small hatches blew rough holes in the hull. All that would be left was a ship of Swiss cheese. The submarine would sink. It was only a matter of time. We were going down. As more air locks filled with water, the ballast tanks would be over-matched. With too many holes in its body, the vessel would have no choice but to drown. It would take to the bottom of the lake. With or without us inside.

"Look, it's fine," Ferris broke us up. "Two escape here, and two there, and the rest of us go to the controls. We blast out that door, the water fills the room, then, like Rick and Hilde, the remaining two in the room hold their breath and swim out."

"Or Vince controls the water with his mind," Beck added.

"I could try," he agreed.

"Who are our strongest swimmers?" Ethan started organizing.

"I'm good," I said.

"So am I," Beck agreed.

"Alright, so Beck and Mae."

"I think I could," Ferris counted.

"And me. I'm good to try," Vince added. That was four strong and willing swimmers. We'd simply enact Rick and Hilde's plan, again.

Gennady and Wesson shared a dismayed look.

"Why do you keep doing that?" I snapped. "Just tell us what's going on. What's the truth?"

"It's not that simple," Gennady admitted. She looked embarrassed.

"What isn't?" Beck asked.

She fought back a frown. "No one should volunteer to be left. When the pressures between the water and airspace equalize, the effects on a human body would be super intense. A lot of people pass out... and then..."

"Drown," Wesson finished.

"*Drown?*" I repeated. A lot of people? We'd all seen Rick and Hilde commit to that exact plan. They'd had no choice. These two leaders shut her in and forced her to swim. They gave her zero options.

"It's extremely dangerous," Gennady admitted.

"Deadly," Wesson added.

"But they..." I was dismayed. How could they do that to them? My stomach tied in knots. I wasn't the only one.

"You closed her in!" Vince lunged right for Wesson, Gennady jumped back, but the older man was ready to fight. He'd already seen Vince's physical attack on Greg. Ethan and Beck tried to grab the boy back. But Vince was too strong. He was raging with anger. "You killed her! You let Rick follow! And you knew what it meant!" He burst through the others' arms and smashed into my dad. As the two men collided, the tables screeched across the floor. Everyone was moving. The other guys tried to pull Vince off him, but Wesson was just as entwined. "You killed them both!"

"I had no choice!" Wesson raged.

"Argh!" Vince wailed. Coming again.

Wesson body-slammed Vince to the ground, but the boy wouldn't stay down. He was out for blood. He punched into Wesson's face and body as well. The men fought dirty and hard.

"Stop! Enough!" Ferris shouted. "Just stop it!"

"This doesn't help anything!" Greg tried to pull them apart.

"Wesson, please stop," Gennady implored him. "The High Council is coming!"

"Zaid!" I dragged him off. So did the others. We physically intervened, forcing the two men to opposite sides. Our group huffed and puffed in between. Beck, Gennady and I took away Wesson, Ferris, Ethan and Greg held back Vince on the other side.

Wesson was bruised and bloody. Vince had the start of a shiny black eye.

Both men were pacing. Still staring the other guy down.

"We had no choice!" The rebel leader spit out blood. He rubbed his eyebrow, smearing the cut above his eye. "If we didn't seal it off when we did, everyone would've drowned. You *know* that! You know how powerful the gushing water was. You *felt* it. We *told* you. If the water grew too high, we wouldn't be strong enough to close the door."

"She was a *child*." Vince's voice broke. The word caught in his throat. We could see, the fight had gone from his eyes. All that was left was his hurt.

"I know. I'm sorry. I know."

The somber truth sunk into the room.

"And Rick?" I asked, frowning.

"That was his choice."

Since Vince was no longer at blows with the rebel leader, the others in the room had also cooled, but I refused to let my dad off the hook. "His choice?" I scoffed. "You could have given him the truth." I growled. "You should've told him what you knew. That it was a terrible risk, a probable death sentence. That's what *you* knew. He didn't, but you knew it. You should've been upfront and honest with him. With all of us. You could've said to the guy 'hey Rick, I know you want to save the girl, but here's the news. Your odds of surviving aren't great. See there's an issue with the water pressure, and you'll most likely both drown.' Is that so hard? You should have told him the *truth*. Instead, you let him run in there, unarmed, knowing full well-"

"He still would have gone-" Vince admitted.

"-*A choice isn't a choice without the truth!*" The second the words were out of my mouth, I knew they weren't just for Rick. Wesson did to him what he'd done to me my whole life. Let him make a trove of decisions without the real facts.

Facts Wesson *knew*.

Facts he *withheld*.

Before I'd ever joined this place, Wesson knew a thousand details about the terrible truths of the values of the coven. He and my mother hated the High Council, and *still* he kept me in the dark. He'd let me join and pledge to the clan. I had to *fight* to be accepted. To join the group that *killed Sierra*?! My *mother*!

He knew!

And he never said a damn word. Just went along keeping himself protected in secret. Avoided all awkward conversations.

That was the choice he made.

The others just stared.

He was supposed to make a change, make the coven better, but he failed.

He'd watched me walk into the tutelage of Child without so much as a whisper.

Watched me battle the Damocles coven as their High Council victor, all without knowing who I was. But *he knew*. He knew for years and did nothing. For *years*. And it wasn't just me. This wasn't just some personal dilemma. We were now all complicit in his silence. The blood of every new recruit was on their hands. Wesson and Gennady had watched as Cornelius and the others brought in season after season of unsuspecting new witches into the coven. Knowing full well what they might be subjected to if they crossed the wrong man.

They knew and still they did nothing.

Beck, Hilde, Vince, Ferris... every one of us.

If they had been braver about what was happening, we all could have been spared. If Wesson and the other so-called rebels had stood up and told the truth...

But they didn't.

They hid out.

Huddled underwater. Kept all these terrible facts quiet. And now Rick and Hilde had run into a death sentence. Now we were trapped. There was no way out. I stared at him. My eyes blazing in anger.

Tap. Tap. Tap.

Our heads whipped towards the door.

Like the tapping Cornelius did on the pot. I recognized it immediately. In my dream. In my vision. He was right there.

"What was that?" Ethan asked.

"They're testing the sound," Gennady said. "To see if the room's full of water. A full room wouldn't echo when they tap."

"What happens if they know it isn't full?" Beck asked.

The High Council answered the question.

Boom!

A bomb blasted the airlock right off its hinge.

"Lie-guards, hide!" Wesson shouted. He balled his own fist. And in seconds, our whole group disappeared.

THIRTY-ONE

IT ALL HAPPENED SO FAST

I RECOGNIZED one of the first three witches through the door. He was a guard in the forest when we first ran from the castle. The man with the red scar above his eye. It was still noticeable even in the window of his gas mask. The High Council witches all wore them. I couldn't make out much more of their features to separate who they were. Their army fatigue greens and gas masks looked too uniform. The group matched perfectly. An impeccable set. They were ready to attack.

Not just ready, I realized. Organized.

The High Council had matching outfits and equipment.

It was bought.

It was distributed.

It was planned.

Their matching wardrobes and gas masks might have been a lie-guard, but I didn't think so. The

Council had already gathered their supplies. They'd been ready for this invasion. They knew all along the rebels were out there somewhere, they had just been waiting on the exact details. The location of the spot. Once Craig supplied the position of their rebel base, the trap was set.

Three more masked witches entered the mess hall, followed by the man with fiery orange hair. The terrible figure I'd seen on the shore. And in my dreams.

Cornelius Child.

I felt the others around me stiffen.

I was cloaked in some sort of invisibility blanket made by Wesson. I hunched with him and Beck. He hid us from the eyes of the High Council. And other lie-guards hid the rest of my friends. Under magical covers. Wesson had blanketed himself, Beck, and me in his plan. Gennady grabbed Vince, and Ferris swooped her vision over Ethan and Greg. In tandem, we'd all disappeared where we'd stood.

Looking out from where we crouched amidst the tables, even I couldn't see where they were. There was no longer any sign of the others. But I knew they were there.

Crouched.

Silent.

Like we were.

Desperately hoping the High Council coven might be fooled.

They weren't.

The leader took off his gas mask.

"Uh oh," Cornelius frowned, his voice thick and slow. "Run out of escape pods?" He wondered. "There's one in here..." he pointed. It was closest to our small huddled group. He signaled to his men and they fanned out to flank the room. "But that won't do. Will it? How many of you are there? In here? Three or four..? Seven..? Twelve?" Cornelius stayed in the center, pretending to guess and sympathize with our group. "Well, don't feel too bad about it. You should know, an escape from the sub doesn't actually mean very much. Craig told us all about the evac pods too. So we've got the lake surrounded. All your friends who blasted away have had a nice swim. A dip in the pool. Kinda chilly, but okay. They'll all be rounded up and carted off by now. Too bad about the sub, though. Those holes won't fill. Bye, bye rebel community housing." Cornelius shook his head.

I glanced at Wesson.

The man didn't flinch. I guess he was already expecting something like that might be true. Still, the attempted escape pod departure was the right call. The rebels had a better chance of fighting or escaping in the forest than they did head-to-head in a sinking can.

"First years," Cornelius changed his tone. "You can come out now. Our fight isn't with you. We know you were tricked into coming. You had no choice, blah, blah, blah." He cut himself off. Then returned his tone to soft. "We want you back in our homestead. Somehow, somewhere, something here became a little misguided. Miscommunicated." He chose his words carefully. Like we were neutral and innocent charges, like no one could possibly be blamed.

His soldiers stood glaring.

"Come on back." Cornelius instructed. "Your training and studies await you. It's time to come home. Have no fear. You're all safe."

No one moved.

I didn't believe him. None of us did.

Our time as innocent students was over.

Wesson motioned to Beck and I. He pointed two fingers left, then gestured forward like cops in the movies might do. But his gestures made sense. If we were slow and careful, maybe we could slip to the side of the mess hall and get around the High Council goons without their noticing. Slip out the damaged door without being seen.

Beck and I nodded.

Crouching low, staying as quiet as possible, we inched towards the far wall.

"Ferris? Ethan?" Cornelius wasn't done with his address. "The power couple. My two trusted allies. Our beautiful battalion victor, our cherished horseback emissary, what's done is done. What's past is past. You're not the ones. You did nothing wrong. Did you? Either of you? I wouldn't want you to become a casualty in this war." Cornelius' sugary tone had no effect. The third years' didn't dare reveal themselves in the room.

I hoped the others were also on the move while his monologue rambled on.

Beck, Wesson and I made it to the far wall. There was almost three feet between the escape hatch door and the nearest Council guard, so it actually seemed possible we might slip by and get loose if we kept this pace. We kept the momentum going, inching forward. If Child pontificated for long enough, we'd get out of the room unscathed.

"Mae Kinglsey," Cornelius addressed me.

Said my full name.

Straight laced.

With zero feigned kindness.

I wanted him to keep talking, but not about me.

My hair stood on end.

"Our little default witch," he taunted. "The girl willing to break all the rules just to get in. A friend even died," he shook his head, as if Kate's death were my fault. "Sacrificed or murdered in her barn."

That's not how it went down, I wanted to shout. But I wouldn't rise to the taunt.

"Lady Mauve warned me," he said. "She's so wise. Told me I should leave you on the curb. You just can't be reined. Too much like Mommy." Child shook his head. "Just like her Daddy."

I felt Wesson steel at his mention.

I refused to look in my father's direction.

"I think you have the wrong idea about them." Our captor appeared thoughtful. "See, your mom did escape... she left the coven to escape *him*. She lied. Hid her pregnancy and ran. She did whatever she could do because she knew who he was. She knew he was a bad man. No... not just bad... she knew he was *evil*." He took a moment to smooth out his eyebrows. The same ugly motion I'd seen in my dream. "Did you know that he murdered your mom?"

It was sick, but I couldn't stop listening.

"Zaid holds a dark form of magic, Mae. One that cannot be altered. It cannot be swayed. It can't be controlled. He's a dangerous man. It's selfish and it's ugly. And she tried to *save you from him*... so he killed her." He let the word hang. "Poisoned to death. But you already knew. You already knew. That's why you cared. Your father murdered your mother. A lover's pall murder. It wasn't easy. I hear that poison's a painful way to go to your death. The lover's poison only works with two people who are loving partners-"

Scree-

Cornelius stopped.

We all heard it. The tiniest creak of a hinge.

The door at the back of the room.

One of the High Council guards burst into action. A wind harness. He balled up his fist sending a huge gust of wind. It slammed the airlock shut at the back of the room.

It also shook the invisibility illusions loose.

None of our lie-guards had thought to secure their illusions against a powerful harness. In an instant, we were all revealed where we stood. I could see the other groups had had the same idea that we did. While

Cornelius was cajoling us, taunting us, trying to lure us out of hiding with his words, all three of our smaller groups had been moving around the room. Trying to escape him. While we had gone towards the left, Ferris, Ethan and Greg had moved right, and Gennady and Vince had slunk their way directly back to the pantry door airlock at the back of the room. But, the gig was up. With the last exit sealed and our hidden locations revealed to the Council members, escape was impossible. We had no choice but to fight where we stood.

It was eight versus seven.

The numbers were actually in our favor, but I knew Cornelius' guards had been chosen for their skills. Whoever he had brought along to flank him in battle would be a powerful group.

The first guard balled his hand. He let out a loud, sonic boom.

Ferris let out a wild cry and balled her hand up to stop him. His aural weapon bounced off the protective bubble she built. Vince and Ethan burst through her balloon, running right at the guards of the Council.

"There aren't any rocks on a sub!" Greg complained. His power was untouched, but he ran at the hubbub anyway. A witch who created lightning bolts hurled one at his face.

"No!" Ethan yelled.

"Ethan, stop!" Ferris screamed after.

Ethan grabbed Greg from the back and together they hit the deck.

An extremely narrow miss.

I dug in my pockets for the dribbles of spells that I'd grabbed in the artillery. I had to have something I could use as a weapon. Beck tried to call the sun, maybe to flash or blind the others. But, like Greg, as a weather harness, there wasn't actually much he could do in a tin can. At the very least, we could fight with our bodies. Stop the guards from using their powers. If we all fought at once, maybe we could stop them where they stood. The victory could be ours. But Wesson had other plans.

He grabbed my shirt, pulling me back, then, before I could stop him, with his other hand, he spun the escape hatch. He yanked me tight as the mechanism kicked in. It all happened so fast.

"Hold on," he said.

"No, stop!" I shouted. "Don't do this!"

Beck spun at my exclamation. The others turned. But it was too late.

Wesson pulled his other arm through a loop and released the hatch.

"Hold your breath!"

"No! Beck!"

In slow motion, I could see my parabond turn away from the High Council guards to come to save me. He reached out for my hand.

Our eyes locked in fear.

The second his back was turned, he was struck by a witch from the High Council. Some sort of a blow to his torso. As the hatch released, I saw him fall to his knees.

"No, Beck!"

Boom!

The hatch blew off. I screamed. My mouth filled with water.

In an instant, the world I'd known disappeared.

IMMEDIATELY, my lungs filled with water.

As Wesson blew out the hatch, I hadn't held my breath like he had warned. I'd been mid-scream. The last thing I'd seen was Beck falling, collapsing, the surprise on everyone's faces, the High Council guards taking control of the situation. The others had turned to fight and our supposed leader had completely bailed. He'd saved himself. And taken me with him.

Together, we shot through the water.

Wesson's grip around my waist, even through all the pressure, didn't fail.

We blasted away from the vessel, the pressurized thrust of the hatch shooting us out of the submarine's hull like an errant firework left over from a Fourth of July celebration. In mere seconds, the tank depleted and the trajectory came to a stall. That was the end of the path.

It was time to sink or swim.

My survival instincts kicked in. There was no time to process what had happened. I swatted Wesson's arm and he released my waist. He turned and dragged his other arm from the strap outside the handle. The heavy metal hatch was already sinking away. Soon it would be in the depths of the lake. My sodden clothes were heavy. Cumbersome. The water was cold on my body. My shirt ballooned out and dragged as I flailed. The pressure inside my lungs felt like panic. With every inch that I faltered, the desire to emerge from the water and take a breath started to build more intensely. It burned in my throat.

I needed oxygen.

The surface.

Some safety.

My priorities came crashing in.

First things first.

Air.

I kicked in the direction of the purple clouds above my head. The awful night of betrayal was over. In the heavens, morning had made herself present. She'd awakened a purple sky. I burst into it, gasping for air. Wesson emerged beside me, his hand shooting up in a fist.

"Invisibility illusion," he told me between burbles.

I nodded. We headed for shore, heads bobbing as we swam.

But the beach scene in the morning was drastically different from the nighttime shoreline. It was no longer a peaceful pond of lush greenery, untouched (or so it seemed) by human hand. In the purple-bruise of sunrise, the beach was now covered in red.

Red of battles.

Red of fighting.

And red of fires.

Cornelius wasn't kidding. His High Council members had been waiting on the beaches, ready to pick off any survivors from the sub. To stop any escapees as they fled from the watery cage. But the rebels of the submarine hadn't just given up.

All across the beach there was proof of strife and witch warfare.

There were bent trees, gashes in the ground, ugly black char from fires that burned. The banks had reached the point of extirpation. Too many witches had attacked or magically defended their positions, and now the unseen world was worn too thin. Nature could no longer hold the excess use of powers. As the witches battled with their gifts, fires marred the shores. Nature gave in.

In some places, the shrubs still burned.

"Damn," even Wesson's fingers throbbed from the heat. He plunged his hand into cold relief, releasing the lie-guard camouflage when we felt safe. The act of using his magic was too hot to hold for long. Luckily, we were too far upstream for any of the High Council members to come looking. They had enough to handle farther down the shore. We dragged our haggard bodies onto dry land.

"Into the forest," Wesson instructed, but I didn't need to be told where to go.

We needed cover.

Like drowned rats, we scampered into the overhang of our surroundings. We snuck into the darkness where the light of morning wouldn't illuminate our forms.

But it also wouldn't warm us.

Sopping wet, I shivered.

My teeth chattered.

My fears were for the others. Still in the boat.

Beck.

Where was he? Had he and the others given up the fight in a debilitating choice? I looked across the bay to the gray and white metal ship that we'd come from. It bulged in the water, slightly tilting. It looked rough. The body of the ship was held at bay by a makeshift gangplank. The witches of High Council had built their own tenuous entrance, not knowing about the secret to the old dock and boat. Even from here, it was clear, the submarine was going to permanently sink underwater, lilting and tipping under the hull's extra load.

How many rooms were now filled to the brink?

At what point would the ship just explode?

Beck.

Where are you?

The High Council had begun an impromptu round up. Herding the witch rebels into groups on the shore. Anyone they captured, they stuffed in black hoods. They forced them to wear a type of black oven mitt. Like the kind I'd seen before, in the prison. These mind and hand-cages were to keep the witches' powers controlled. The coven didn't bother trying to isolate who had what of the different abilities, or how an individual might hurt them if left alone, they simply forced everyone into wearing the same limiting head and hand contraptions. Once they were decked out in the binding ornaments, the sopping wet rebels were controlled. They were rounded up and herded into waiting cargo vans. Either that, or they were lined into rows on the shore. No doubt, the plan was to ship us back to the prison incognito, underneath the castle, their holes and escape routes in the tunnels all plugged.

Security in the prison was likely tightened too.

There, we'd await our fates at the High Council.

Live out our judgments.

Like Lauren Bixby had existed. Flat on her back. Staring at nothing.

I looked on shore and tried to find her.

A wheelchair or hospital bed should be easy to spot, I thought. But, I didn't see her there. Another dark thought. It was possible she was already loaded into a truck, but it was equally likely she was still trapped in the boat. That was a fate that I feared. After all, I hadn't broken her out of her jail just to drown her on this boat.

We had to do something.

I was about to implore Wesson into action, but

suddenly, I saw Beck, and for a moment, all my worries disappeared. He was already gloved and hooded by the High Council, but I would recognize that tall body anywhere. I knew the expanse of each muscle by heart. He and the others were being shepherded off the ship. The Council made them walk the gang-plank blinded by the hoods, a dangerous proposition. My friends were all there. Dejected, their heads hung low. Even Gennady's body signaled defeat as she moved.

When Wesson and I had escaped from the mess hall, it was clear Cornelius' witches had captured control. They had prevailed. From the selfish use of the escape hatch, only Wesson and I had gotten clear.

"Damn," he muttered. He'd seen what I did.

I was surprised to learn he'd held out hope that the others might have escaped after his selfish move. "We have to help them!" I started moving toward the beach.

Wesson grabbed me. "No, we don't. What could we do? Their fates have been sealed."

"My friends have powers. If we free them, they can fight back against the coven."

"Against the coven?! They're a bunch of untested kids. And the grounds are already steeped in the heat. Extirpation," he told me. "How do I explain it, it's like when the air gets so hot that it-"

"I know what it is!" I cut him off. "So what's your idea? Too bad, so sad. We just leave?"

"We regroup when the time's right."

"In another eight years?"

Wesson flinched.

"I'm going to help them."

This time, Wesson didn't physically hold me back. Instead, he marched beside me. "Doing what? How will you stop it? Mae, what's your plan?"

"I don't know." I tried to brush him away like a bug around my ear.

"How? Mae? What will you do?"

"I don't know!" I picked up the pace.

"There's a hundred witches there, every one much more powerful than you are."

"I know. I don't care." I ran forward blindly. "They're gonna chop off his hand!"

"And they'll drill straight in your brain!" He pushed a finger to the side of my head. I swerved.

"No!" I didn't see the stump protruding from tree roots as I ran. I tripped and fell, skidding in the dirt. My hands dug into the soil, scraped and raw. "We have to save him!" I cried as the helplessness kicked in.

Wesson was right.

There was no way to fight a whole witch army.

I was just one witch. A default, at that. What the hell could I do?

In frustration, I slapped the earth. The tears streamed down my cheeks.

"I know." He knelt and pulled me to his chest to comfort me. "I understand. Mae, I get it. I get it."

I snuffled and pulled together my emotions again. "We have to save him."

"We will. Now's not the time." He rocked me,

gently. "You can't. But, we will. Everything will be fine. You'll see. Everything will be good."

For a moment, it felt nice to be comforted. But at these last words from my dad, anger flooded back in. Everything would be *good*?! Was he seriously kidding?! They were taking Beck back to prison. Wesson had forced me to leave him behind. I didn't want to go. None of this was what I wanted. Now he was trying to say things would be fine?

For who?

For *him*?

Not for me.

Not for Beck!

I shoved Wesson away. "Don't try to parent me now! You're not my dad! You never were! You're just some stranger. Some murdering man!"

Wesson pulled back, totally surprised.

I was done running wildly across the forest to reach him, but my eyes never left Beck's hooded face. Across the water, I watched his every move. He was dejected. Probably scared. They'd forced him and some of the others to kneel on the shore, their heads aimed towards the lake. The cargo trucks the High Council had brought to cart off the prisoners seemed already full. I guess there were more rebel captives than they realized would be here. They needed another truck to haul everybody off.

"I should be there with him."

"What good is that? Another body on the beach?" Wesson asked. His tone flattened. "You don't have to think of me as your father, Mae. I accept that. But, I made a promise to Sierra to put you first. To keep you safe. However I could. And I have. I've done everything in my power. But, I guess that's over. If you want to be a dumb girl, risking your life for nothing, there's not much I can do about that." He stood and walked deeper into the forest. Didn't even ask me to come with him as he left. At first, I ignored him, but the crunching leaves beneath his feet grew more distant.

"Where are you going?" I asked without turning.

Wesson didn't answer. Just followed his own path.

"Zaid?" Even now, I couldn't call him by his first name. I certainly wouldn't call him my dad. I turned. I could barely see him as he departed through the foliage. He was making his way out of the forest, until he came to a clearing near a large stump. "Zaid?"

In the small opening, he pulled a sheath off a motorbike. Covered. Hidden. Just like the bike we'd used to escape the High Council.

"What are you doing?" I demanded, moving closer, although the picture was starting to come clear. He hadn't traded or sold the bike yesterday morning. He'd had it fixed and then come back and stashed it in the trees. Out here. Hidden it from the others, in the forest.

A secret get-away vehicle, just for him.

Then he'd borrowed one of the rebel trucks to get me and Lauren back to the hideout. In that way, he'd brought both vehicles home.

"I told you, it's over. I'm going. There's nothing

more for us here. We bide our time. We start over. Come if you want. Or stay here." He prepped the bike to take off.

"What about the others? Beck?... Gennady?" I'd seen the looks that they'd shared. They were a good match. She was back on the beach. Was he really willing to just leave? "She would want you to go back."

"She would want us to be free," he countered. "To make smart choices." As if to emphasize his point, he put his helmet over his ears.

"She would want us to fight. To fight with them. To stand beside them. That's where I should have been," I said. "You took that from me."

"I saved you from a lobotomy." He was done with discussion. "We'll go to Kate's farm. Craig's too. See who's left. Then regroup however we can."

"While they rot in jail?"

"Mae! I'm not the bad guy here. God. You're so stubborn. Just like Sier."

He cut her name short.

A cute nickname.

It stung my heart to hear her mentioned so casually here.

Wesson seemed to realize bringing her up was a bad choice. He pulled back his emotions. His voice grew very quiet and still. "There's nothing more we can do. Here. Now. Today. Beck and Gennady and the others would want you to be smart. To be safe. We escaped from the High Council to help them and all the others. But every second we stay, we're putting our own victory at risk. I'm done discussing, Mae. Put on the helmet, get on the bike. Hold on to my waist." He swung his leg over the bike's body and slid into the saddle position.

"No."

"No?"

"I'm not going with you. We're not together. You don't know me. You never loved me. But Beck does. I won't leave him here."

"You'll get caught."

"Maybe," I admitted. "Probably. At least I'll have tried."

"Fine." Wesson kicked up his bike stand. He revved the engine. "Good luck with your attempt." He picked up his foot and drove out into the forest, careful not to hit the larger vegetation as he left. His engine gunned. A dead giveaway. I glanced back towards the beach. Again, Wesson Zaid had made things easier on himself and harder on me. There was no way the High Council didn't hear the engine running. It was a clear tip-off to our current location. They would undoubtedly come back to check the area. I had to get out of these trees.

Helmet still in hand, I raced away from the sound of the motor. I hurried towards the patch of bullrushes at the edge of the beach. The reeds were tall enough to hide in. Without thinking, I waded into the mucky water. I ducked down, my clothing becoming inundated, reclaimed by the lake. This time I had enough sense to realize I needed to be hidden really well. I slid down in the muck, separated from the forest, still able to see my man on the beach.

Beck, what do I do?

It wasn't enough to object to Wesson's plan, I had to actually do something to effect any real change. The submarine was sinking. It was now partially submerged. There was no stopping that. It was filling up through the hundred portholes punched in its hull. It all started with Craig's departure. I looked around. But in the crowds of High Council witches, I couldn't see the betrayer standing on the shore. Probably didn't stay around and witness the carnage of his actions.

Coward.

My eyes drifted downwards. Found my person.

Beck, like the others, lay motionless on the sand.

Dejected.

Awaiting instructions.

I could see Cornelius and another elder casually chatting. They had the scene well in hand. There was nothing to fear. All the rebels were captured.

Well, not all the rebels.

Wesson and I had escaped their clutches.

I was still here. But I didn't know what to do.

They'd likely already dispatched someone or even a group of someones to try to retrieve any escapees or stragglers in the forest. Would they catch me? I wasn't certain. But, Wesson was right about one thing. I really was helpless. I was only a dreamcast. I hadn't even seen this in my visions. There was little else I could do to help my friends.

This was so much worse than what had happened to Aunt Abeline. At least when she was injured and struggling medically I'd been able to come up with a mission and a plan. I'd blown up a whole sea creature to save her!

The children's chorus returned to me. *In and out, around the forest.*

I'd heard that same song earlier today. In my vision. It had come to me while I slept early this morning. It was a pretty heroic act of bravery I had accomplished in the Pokna Mountains. I knew for a fact, it had shaken the whole lake when the bombs exploded... Was it possible to do something similar here?

Splish, splash.

Behind me, someone sloshed into the water. They were so close, I could hear them breathing, but I didn't dare flinch. I didn't move. Submerged as I was, if they didn't know I was there, any movement now would give me away.

Splish, splash, splish.

But there was no hiding.

The person came right up beside me.

"Alright, Mae." Wesson slopped down in the weeds at my hip. He stared forward, like I did, at the others waiting and helpless. We both looked out at their beach of broken bodies. "We'll do it your way."

THIRTY-THREE

I HAVE A PLAN

"HOW DID YOU FIND ME?" I stared incredulously at the estranged father who I thought had abandoned me in the forest only moments ago.

"You left your helmet in the trees," he told me. He'd carried it with him. Now he sunk it deep into the weeds.

"So it was you and not the High Council coming after me."

"Nah, they'll be looking for a biker in the forest," he nodded.

"So you never meant to leave us? The bike was just a ploy?"

"No, I wanted to leave. But Mae, I meant what I told you. My promise to your mother is eternal. I will keep you safe. Do whatever I can do. For however long I can stay. Even if that means a death wish, running straight at our enemies."

"Not straight at them," I countered. "But I do have a plan."

THIRTY-FOUR

HILDE AND RICK

WHEW-WHEW.

I softly whistled into the forest. Wesson and I had made our way around the lakeside woods, under the cover of trees, as quietly as we could. As we traveled I let out the familiar, airy tune.

Whew-whew.

It was little Hilde's whistle. Her soft, personal music. I was searching for her and Rick. It was imperative to my plan that we find them.

Alive.

Safe.

Okay.

"How do you know they'd wash up in this part of the forest?" Wesson wondered.

"I don't," I admitted. "I just hope that they did. Plus, this is the side of the beach that the artillery was facing at the time of the first explosion."

Wesson quickly checked the logistics. I was correct about the boat's position.

Again, I whistled quietly to the trees.

To the wrong ears, the tune might be mistaken for a song-bird. But I felt confident, if Hilde or Rick or both of them had escaped into this forest, if they'd swam to safety, they would recognize the tune. As they heard our boots crunching beneath us, I didn't want them to fear. We were friends, not foes, marching through. It was a signal. It was safe to come out here.

Neither Wesson or I discussed the likelihood that they'd drowned.

I simply clung to hope.

Blind faith.

An optimistic viewpoint.

It was all or nothing. If they hadn't escaped or we couldn't find them, there was no way that my plan would succeed. I needed Hilde and Rick. Simple as that.

Whew-whew.

I sent out the message again.

Whew-whew. The whistle returned!

My dad and I both stopped where we stood.

"Did you hear that?" Wesson whispered. But he knew that I did.

Confirmation.

We stood still, listening and watching for the pair to appear, then suddenly, we heard a rustle above us. I looked up. Hidden high up in the trees were my two friends.

Hilde waved. Rick merely nodded.

My heart flooded with joy. Both witches appeared to be okay. They had climbed out of the water and scaled a tree to wait 'til it was over. The High Council hadn't spotted their risky escape from the submarine.

"Come down," Wesson hissed, but the pair didn't move.

I stepped back, as if they needed the extra room. They didn't.

Hilde glanced at Rick, but he wasn't budging.

"We should stay spread out," the chemist told us, eyeing Wesson. "Not all clumped in the trees."

I shook my head. "I don't want to hide," I said. "Or run."

"See, I told you," Hilde nodded to her parabond. "I had a dream you'd help me down," she said to me. "I told you Mae would come." The young girl beamed.

But Rick was still thinking about things.

If we weren't running, or hiding, there was only one thing left to do.

He frowned. "You have a plan to attack?"

"I do."

"Did you dream it?" Rick put great value in my sleep sight. He didn't know how bumpy the visions could be. But this time, I thought he might be pleased.

"Sort of," I admitted.

He hesitated. Once again, his eyes sized up Wesson from afar. Perhaps he'd figured out for himself that the rebel leader wasn't a reliable source of information. That the man should have warned the boy how risky his rescue mission would really be. Perhaps he just hated that he'd shut Hilde out of the cabin. Put them both in that dangerous situation. The fact that he and his parabond both survived didn't make my dad less of a jerk.

"It's my plan, not his," I reaffirmed. "Rick, they have Beck... and Vince," I admitted. "All the others."

Rick's brow furrowed. Hilde's mouth dropped open in shock. They'd been so busy hiding themselves in the bushes they must not have seen much of the fight.

"We can save them," I added. "But I need your help... Even then," I decided to be honest, "it might not work. It's a long shot." I wanted to be as transparent as I could. I owed them that.

Hilde squirmed. She was desperate to jump down. She looked at Rick. Finally, he nodded. Quickly, she scampered out of the tree. I helped her find her footing as she climbed down from the limb. She slipped in a little squeeze around me.

"I knew you'd come."

Rick used his long arms to quietly swing his strong body back to the ground. His feet touched down with barely a rustle. I had no doubt that on his own, the boy would disappear into the forest, never to be heard from or seen.

But that's not what he wanted.

He clearly felt the same as me. No escape would taste sweet at the others' expense.

We had to save our friends... our sweet *lovers*.

Were Rick and Vince lovers? Maybe. Honestly, it was kind of a perfect partnership. Both boys were strong, smart, and capable men. I liked them both equally, in very different respects. How they felt about one another was none of my business, it was enough to know that Rick cared about his friends and about their justice. His convictions were strong enough that he was willing to stand. And even fight. He'd see it through.

"Here it is," as they leaned in closely, I laid things out for the other two. "On my last mission you made me a bunch of spells; sleeping potion, snap ribbons-"

"Truth serum, I remember."

"Good. 'Cuz whatever it was, we need it again. Exactly the same."

He nodded. He could do that. Maybe. He glanced around for supplies, but I barreled ahead.

"Hilde, you remember the sea monster at the Pokna volcano?"

She squirmed, eyes wide, wondering where this was going. Yes, she did.

"You're going to describe the sea monster to Zaid in every detail. An exact replica. He's a lie-guard. When the timing is right, he's gonna re-create the monster. But you have to be exact. We need to build the same mythological beast. Small details will matter. You think you can do that?"

"I can do that." Hilde grinned. She'd seen the squid-monster up close, just like I had. Every scary, tiny detail was still lodged deep in her brain.

"When the squid-monster ate the spell combination, it resulted in a huge, violent explosion. It rocked the whole beach," I told Rick and Wesson. "We're going to recreate that. Once you've made the spells," I gestured to Rick, "and Zaid makes the creature," Wesson nodded along, "I'll shove the packages in."

"In what?" Hilde asked.

"Down his throat. Force the monster to eat it."

Hilde scrunched up her nose. That was a part of the story she didn't like.

"The animal isn't real," I reminded her. Although it was real in the last battle. At that time, it was me or the thing, so I couldn't feel bad about who won the contest. "It takes a second or two for him to metabolize all the powders, then we count down. In three, two, one..."

"Huge explosion," Hilde threw her arms in the air. All three of us shushed her and looked around. But we were deep enough in the forest that no one overheard.

"Huge explosion," I agreed, this time much quieter. "Only this time, we're prepared. We know it's coming. We'll be ready. The impact and reverberation will be huge on the beach. When it hits, that's our chance to free the others. To get the upper hand."

"A blind-side rebellion," Wesson caught the picture.

"And in your mind's eye," Rick asked, bringing it back to my powers. "This was successful?"

I hesitated. "In my dream... I saw some of what's already happened. I saw Cornelius in the mess hall and

I heard the children singing in the dream. It was the folk song I learned to use to defeat the sea-monster the previous time we faced it. I last heard the tune when Vince and Hil and the Damocles boys and I were at the Pokna Mountains. I defeated the monster then. The song was there, tonight, back in my dream. It's not a coincidence. We could do it again." I took a breath. "I believe that we can."

"So do I," Hilde agreed.

"So do I," Wesson said.

Rick wasn't convinced. Maybe in his shoes, I wouldn't be either. But, I didn't have the luxury of doubt about the plan. "Rick," I locked eyes with my friend. "We don't have another option," I admitted. "If you wanna wait and see what happens..."

We looked down the beach towards the others. Beck, Vince and all the other rebels. Their body language told the tale.

They were dejected.

Destroyed.

Captured and crumpled.

A new cargo truck had arrived. The High Council witches were backing it down to the lakeside. Any minute they'd load the others in, and take the captured rebels to their jail. This was it.

Our time was running out.

"The plan is not good," Rick admitted. "I see many faults."

Hilde, Wesson and I looked at each other.

He was our only chemist. We couldn't complete

the task without his help. We needed his expertise. Moreover, we needed the specific list of the spells that Rick created on the previous mission. In order to get the explosion potion for the monster just right.

"I am not confident in this undertaking," Rick said. His frown etched deep into his forehead. He looked right in my eyes. "But I am in."

Hilde cheered. "Let's save the world!"

FIRST, Rick foraged in the forest.

We emptied our pockets so he could pick and choose from whatever ingredients we still had. It was up to him alone to recreate the combination of spells and potions from that previous mission exactly. Hilde handed over her sleep elixir, the one from the artillery she'd almost died while trying to retrieve. Since it wasn't on our grocery list from the spells of the previous mission, I gave the Udak bomb to Wesson to safely keep.

"It could help create a bigger explosion," he suggested. But I shook my head. It wasn't worth the risk.

"We go with what we know," I said. And you might need it to blow yourself out of trouble if my plan doesn't work, I added, unspoken.

Rick worked quickly, snapping branches, extracting pollen, testing chemical compounds, trying to build the spells we'd need from scratch with what we had. Sometimes he seemed able to identify complex ingredients on sight. Others he identified by taste, or composition or smell. His High Council instructors would be so proud. Soon, he had a few of the necessary spells together.

"We'll find the other ingredients back onboard." Rick said, tying the planting spell for snap ribbons closed in a small bag.

I nodded. I'd already come to the same conclusion.

"But the artillery was destroyed by Twenty-Thom," Hilde worried.

"Craig," Wesson corrected, sadly.

"Yes, but the pantry's still intact," I glanced back towards the water. "At least, it was when we left." The ship heaved and lurched to one side. "Rick and I will go back in, get what we need, shoot off the flare, then you do your part."

The others nodded.

Wesson insisted there'd be a flare gun in the pantry.

The plan seemed pretty clear... as long as you didn't focus on the details, we were all set. Details like the fact that Wesson's job was to create a sea monster from scratch based on the imagery that Hilde would describe to him from memory... or the fact that said monster, if created correctly, would definitely want to eat me alive while I stuck a bomb in its teeth... not to mention that, to work correctly, the device I was to feed to the monster would have to be made up of potions and spells in the exact same format that Rick had made for me on a previous mission... only, he didn't have any of the same building blocks or recipes to work with... and, lastly, to find the missing ingredients, we needed to swim back into a broken submarine and rifle in a decrepit pantry that may or may not be flooded... all before the broken vessel sunk to the bottom of the lake. Oh, and we needed to do it all perfectly while operating at an arm's length from a deadly group of witches, who had already captured all of our friends, and, most certainly, at the first opportunity, wanted to chop off our hands and lobotomize our heads.

So, yeah.

It was a great plan.

A super mission.

But, there was no other way.

"It's what we can do," Rick told me, told all of us, without flinching.

Without hope.

Without fear.

Without inflection.

It was what we could do.

It was up to us to see it through to the end.

"Ready?" He asked.

I nodded. I was ready. Ready as we'd ever be.

"Good luck," Wesson said. He offered Rick a hand-shake. The two men clasped palms formally while Hilde rushed to hug my hips. I held her small embrace, cherishing her goodness, breathing in as much of her blind faith as I could.

"I know you'll do great," she whispered, then ran to hug Rick with the same forcefulness. I wished for more of her generous grace. I nodded to Rick. Only one more person to see me off... Wesson and I looked at each other for a moment. This was it.

Each of us was heading into a different part of the battle.

"Good luck," he offered. Awkwardly, he again thrust out his hand. I looked at the gesture of good will and paused.

Did I want to touch this man?

He was no longer just the estranged father who had poisoned my mother. He wasn't even just the rebel leader out to save his own skin. He had come back. He had stood by me, side-by-side, now in our trenches, willing to risk his own neck on the line to save the members of our clan.

"Thank you for coming back," I said, making the choice to acknowledge him properly. I clasped our hands together. "We couldn't do this without you here," I admitted. We shook. Formally, he reached out with his other hand to pat my arm. I accepted that as well. "Watch your hands. The extirpation can be vicious. Don't cast the lie-guard until you absolutely have to," I micromanaged his part of the task.

"I got it."

"No, really. I saw how hot your hand was in the water, earlier."

"Mae, I got it."

"We don't need any heroes." It was a funny thing to say out loud because our friends clearly needed saving. Hilde, Rick and Wesson just nodded. We'd do our best to stay safe. "Okay," I said. Then I looked at all the others.

We were ready.

We were willing.

We had our mission.

"Let's go to work."

THIRTY-SIX
CAREFUL TO MIND THE SHARP CORNERS

WITH OUR FOREST ingredients and potions all safely bundled, Rick and I swam from the shore over to the metal submarine. The giant tub had achieved a sort of uneasy equilibrium with the weight of the water and the buoyancy of the air around it. Submerged in places, the fact that the large metal tube wasn't already on the bottom of the lake told us, inside the large drum, there had to be more submerged air pockets. Whether the oxygen bubbles would be close to the pantry or far from it, we'd only find out once we got back inside the submarine.

Rick and I kept our heads low and our splashes at a minimum, traversing the distance underwater as much as we could. Neither one had over-spoken it, we were both, in fact, pretty strong swimmers. We quickly found ourselves treading water beside the slick side of the vessel, steeling our bodies to take a final breath and dive into the hull. The gash in the side was several feet underwater. We kept ourselves protected from sight on the shoreline by keeping the submarine hull between us and the beach. We took two breaths beside the boat. I raised an eyebrow at Rick. He gestured. He was ready. It was time. I took a final great gulp of oxygen and dove.

In my wake, I could feel Rick was following, swimming close behind. We kicked along the structure, looking for the blown open gash in the mess hall, made by Wesson launching our escape hatch. That was our point of entry. In our theory, it was closest to the actual pantry, and most likely to still have an air pocket located within it, because of its shape and its size.

I would have classified myself as a fairly expert breast-stroke swimmer, having taken lessons all of my life, but pulling my body aggressively deeper underwater wasn't something I was used to. Fighting against my lungs' natural buoyancy was hard. From the outside, the submarine was much bigger than we'd remembered. With each stroke down, the pressure in my ears and nose started to build.

The air burned in my throat.

The gash on the ship's side was deeper in the lake than either Rick or I had hoped. We'd underestimated the sheer size of the hull. But, finally, as my air ran down to a minimum, the twisted hole in the metal came into sight. It was still another six or seven feet straight below me. With this breath, I couldn't reach it. My lungs felt like they were about to explode.

I peeled off and kicked back up to the surface once

more. As I neared the shallower water, my head pounded. I pushed up to the air. I surfaced and fought the natural instinct to sputter or flail. As I tread water, fresh oxygen flooded my lungs. Calmly. Gently.

Rick reappeared at my right. He looked more determined than I felt. I hoped I was also projecting certainty for him. We were swimming directly above the opening. When I caught my breath, I'd be ready to go again.

"Ready?" He whispered.

I nodded.

For the second time together, the two of us dove.

This time, I was more ready for the pressure and discomfort. Almost immediately, the air in my head felt like it was starting to expand. But I fought through it, ignoring the throbbing, cutting cleanly through the water, following the sleek metal curve of the hull. This time, as we knew where we were going, we easily reached the battered opening.

I grabbed the edge of the metal to help pull my body inside. I was careful to mind the sharp corners, but used the material to push indoors. The natural desire was to float back to the surface, and to air, and to safety, but instead, I dragged myself deeper inside the boat.

Our eyes adjusted to the haze.

The lights were still on, shining down, causing reflections and ripples through the liquid. Rick and I gazed up, inside the metal tub. The water's density made everything look a little blurry. The whole room was upside down and displaced from before. The mess hall tables were floating up above us, blocking the view of the surface. The chairs had all sunk near the bottom, and some seemed to have fallen out of the gash in the floor. The chairs were heavy, with legs of twisted metal, but the tables were floating, made of beautiful wood.

Floating.

In a pocket of air!

Rick was the first to push his body all the way through the ragged entrance. Quickly, I followed. We had to weave through the table legs and other detritus, but our analysis was correct, there was indeed an air pocket at the top of the room. Rick and I burst to that surface like two popping balloons.

"Oh my god!" The words rushed out in a flurry, releasing all of my fear. I panted, treading water. Rick huffed and puffed quietly beside me. He leaned on a table for support. The structure held him. "Holy crap that was rough," I moaned.

Rick nodded. But he was already looking forward. "Time is short."

The second truck of prisoners would be loaded quite soon. If the other coven wasn't still on the beach at the time of our explosion, nothing about our plan would work as we'd hoped. We had to keep moving. Quick.

"There," he pointed.

We were relieved to see the door of the pantry remained dry and sealed, hanging in part of the air pocket we had discovered. Rick and I kicked around the floating tables to get closer, then climbed on the furniture to reach the door. The floating wood held our bodies, the sturdy tables were large enough to carry both our weight without fail.

Because of the lurch of the ship, the pantry airlock floated above us and slightly to the side, but Rick was tall enough to reach it. Even from the floating table he could quickly spin it open. Rick pushed the unlocked door into the pantry wide open. To stop it from falling back into the mess hall, he forced it up with a heave. The handle banged on the inner wall.

"Whoops," I said.

"Come on." He held out a hand to help me, and I climbed into the room above us. The shelves of the pantry were a mess, but it was still dry and untouched by the lake. The ingredients were mostly still lodged on their shelves. We could work with this, I felt certain. As I entered, the room teetered, but held.

"What do we need?"

"Tea leaves, baking soda, laundry detergent if they have it. Mercury. A little yeast could go a long way." Rick braced himself on the doorway and readied to haul himself into the smaller room.

Dumbly, I nodded. I wanted desperately to appear cool under pressure, but I could feel that some panic was starting to set in. What if they didn't have what we wanted? I wished Beck were here. But of course he wasn't. That was why I was doing all this. To get him back by my side.

I blocked the pantry door so it didn't swing down on Rick's fingers. He used his upper body strength to pull himself up where I was.

The second he did, the submarine lurched to the side.

"Whoa," I stumbled forward. Gravity crashed me into Rick's body. He tried to catch me, but we collapsed to the ground.

Our weight was too much.

The whole room started to shift. The equilibrium couldn't hold on.

"Quick!"

Rick and I raced to the shelves looking for the final ingredients we needed as the battered ship let out a groan. Whatever peaceful balance between air and water had settled in the space before us, with the addition of our presence, the moment of equanimity had been completely thrown off. The boat continued to lurch. As the room dramatically tilted, more and more dry good items tumbled off the shelves. We did our best to keep our focus on digging into the wayward pantry.

"No loose tea, only tea bags," I reported.

"Cut them open!"

I ripped the packages apart with my bare hands. "Here." I made a big mess, but sprinkled the leaves into a pile in my palm. Rick and I each took a step nearer to each other to pass off the new material, but the second we did, the whole room violently lurched.

"No, no, no."

We realized our mistake immediately and Rick and I tried to separate like a teeter-totter but it was too late, the damage couldn't be reversed. The whole room had lowered.

Cantilevered.

While for one moment we had been safely in the air pocket, now the door to the pantry stayed open and a rush of incoming lake water found a new home.

The liquid gushed in.

Crashing over the boundaries of the airlock.

The room had sunk below the waterline. The opening filled forever with more water. Our bubble was bursting.

"Shut the door!" Rick yelled.

We both leapt on the back of the door's metal hinge, trying to reseal it. But, our body weight alone wasn't enough to force it closed. The pressure of the incoming water was too strong. Even against all our effort, it forced its way in.

"We're not enough!" I shouted.

Wesson and Gennady had been right in their fear. It was just like they'd described it. The more water there was, the more impossible it would be to get the door closed. We were already too late. The water kept flooding in.

"I will hold it." Rick pushed back against the doorway, using the shelving unit as a brace. "Slow it down." He couldn't shut the valve completely but he could keep the pressure at bay. "You find the ingredients while we can. Hurry!"

Dumbly, I nodded. Racing back to where we'd been.

I'd totally forgotten the whole list again.

"Thermometer-" Rick instructed, grunting.

Wild, my eyes searched the shelves.

Meat drawer? No.

Health and safety kit?

I lunged at the plastic box with the red cross. "Yes!" Victorious, I pulled out the thin glass instrument.

"Smash it. I need the mercury," he told me. Rick was struggling between applying pressure to the door-yard and instructing me with his unfinished spells. He opened a sachet. "Put it in there. No! Not that one. The third one!"

To me, all the sachets looked the same. I followed his directions exactly, smashing the glass pipe against a wall. Tiny shards flew all around. I fed the droplets into their new home.

"Seal it," Rick grunted. "We've got the tea in that one. The truth serum is complete."

We sealed the second package. Finished.

"We need the detergent. I saw it over there!"

I dove to where he was pointing.

"It's in pods!" Without really thinking, I just grabbed one and stabbed it with the jagged remains of the thermometer that was still in my fingertips. The thrust pierced the plastic and I dragged it open. "Got it. Where does it go."

Rick groaned. His biceps bulged under the strain. "The left one. Your other left!" He shouted before I could make the simple mistake. "Mae, I cannot hold it."

"You can do it," I moved in to help him, but instinctively, I knew what he meant. All my weight pushed against the door didn't even cause a dent in the incoming water. Pushing back against this deluge was like holding up a car with our bare palms. Not even Rick could do it for long.

I dove back to the shelves. "Where's the baking soda?" I wondered. Scouring the contents. "I see the baking powder. Why don't they have any baking soda!"

Argh!

Rick collapsed, tossed off his post, unable to hold on against the inevitable any more.

"No!"

In a much larger gush, a huge wave flooded the room. The influx knocked us both down. I grabbed all but one of the potions before they went under the water. I clamped the sachets closed in my hands.

"Rick!" I shouted, swimming towards him. The boy heaved and panted, shaking with effort. He was barely staying upright as the water gushed in. I swam to him and propped his head up on my shoulder. I held him upright, treading water for both of us while he gathered strength. We could no longer safely stand in the room. More water was coming. The pantry was going under. Our air pocket was shrinking. Fast. Rick had expended all his might trying to seal up the doorway, but now that we'd failed we weren't safe where we were. The oxygen was quickly depleting.

"There wasn't baking powder."

"Soda," he corrected. "It doesn't matter. I lost the package anyway," he said. "The salve is gone. We did not finish," he admitted. "Do you think it will still work?"

"The bomb?" I had no clue. "Wait. The burn salve?"

Rick nodded.

Relief flooded my voice. "Dude, I didn't shove the salve in the monster's mouth. I left it in the car on the mission. I offered it to the Damocles witches, but they turned it down, so I tossed it aside. It wasn't one of the spells in the monster's mouth! So we have them... we have them all!" Luckily, the other potions were safe. Sealed in my pocket, just like they'd been on the earlier mission as well.

Our air bubble shrunk down to a size of just a few feet between us and the ceiling.

"All we need is the flare. Hold on." I dove down.

Rick grabbed onto the top of a shelf. With wild eyes, I searched through the floating bits and boxes of food until I saw the red flare gun to signal the others. I grabbed it and tried to swim towards the exit, out the mess hall, the way we'd come in, but the current of flowing water pushed me backwards. It was too diffi-cult to hold our breath and swim upstream. Instead, I surfaced next to Rick. He was minding his strength, holding onto the top of a shelving unit, his head tilted back to get air.

I showed Rick the prize in my hand. We had

everything we came for, but there was a problem. "We can't get out the way we came. The current's too strong," I warned him, sucking back fresh oxygen as well. The three foot air pocket had shrunk down to one.

"You have to blast out in the hatch." Rick said.

I'd considered that too.

"We both will. It can work for two people. I already did it once with Zaid."

"Mae, I'm in no shape to fight a sea monster," Rick admitted.

"But the pressure of launching... if I leave you..."

"I'll be okay."

"Rick, the fact that you made it out the first time was a freakin' miracle, there's no way we can risk it again. Right now, you can barely swim."

"I'll be alright. So will you. Go," he said. "Finish what we started. Go save the world." He gave a wry smile. Maybe the first wry smile I'd ever seen from Rick. "Or at least, go save Vince."

I knew what he was doing.

He was giving me permission.

Telling me to leave him.

It was the only way we could successfully complete the mission.

We both knew it had to be done.

I forced a smile in return.

"I can save him." I agreed. "I'll save everybody. And I'll see you on the other side."

"You will."

Our tiny pocket of oxygen had all but drained. It was now or never.

"See you soon." I grabbed a final breath and dove. I shoved soggy cereal boxes and pasta noodles out of the way and grabbed the security strap on the emergency hatch. I managed to wiggle one arm inside it, but I didn't twist it tightly because I wanted to release the strap again as soon as I was on the other side of the door.

I lodged the flare gun in my waistband. Would it even work now that it was water-logged? There was no way of knowing. I wrenched the hatch doorway. The heavy wheel didn't budge.

Come on.

I put my feet against the door frame for leverage. This time, with all my strength, I was able to shuffle it a tiny fraction. But I'd run out of air. My lungs felt like they might burst. I thought about going back to Rick and trying to pillage the tiny air opening, but now I wasn't even sure if the fresh oxygen was still present. There might not be any more air. The pantry was filling with water, more liquid by the moment. I had to get out of there. But I couldn't get the hatch to move.

I panicked and lurched.

My arm was tangled now, all twisted up inside the strap. I'd have to unwind it to get myself back to the air pocket.

Would there still be an air pocket?

I wrangled with the material. I couldn't get it to

unwind. It snaked around my hand. My arm was trapped inside.

I couldn't open it.

I couldn't loosen it.

I couldn't do anything. I was trapped under the water, tied to it. About to drown.

No.

I wrenched my torso against the handle, my lungs shuddering.

I needed oxygen.

I needed out.

I needed someone… I needed my partner.

Beck.

In my mind, I tried to call out.

Please. Help.

But Beck couldn't save me. And I was helpless.

You're going to have to go on without me.

The bubbles drained from my mouth.

Beck.

Save yourself.

My head spoke his name, so sweetly. I wanted to implore him.

You're my parabond. My person. I love you.

Beck. I'm sorry.

I've done all I can.

Please, don't wait for me.

You have to save yourself.

The world started to black out.

THIRTY-SEVEN

ZAID! DO IT! NOW!

A DARK CAST came over me. Filled my head. Covered my torso. But it wasn't impending uncon-sciousness. It was a shadow.

The shadow of Rick.

The large boy closed in on top of me, trapped where I was. He smashed his lips onto mine and puffed out forcefully, giving me a mouthful of oxygen.

My eyes shot open.

He grabbed the handle of the hatch and wrenched it to the side.

Loosened.

Finally opened.

Then, he pushed off and swam for safety. In only seconds, he was gone.

For a moment, I was stunned. But then I realized what he'd done. He had given me his air and loosened the wheel of the emergency hatch. I was still tied into the straps. But the door would now work. I was free to go. All I had to do was pull the hatch.

I spun the wheel to the left. The mechanism clicked in.

Boom!

It sprung to life. Launching me from the sub.

As I shot through the water, the flare gun ripped away from my waist.

No!

But there was no way to slow my trajectory. I held on for dear life as the door ran its course and shot across the water. When the ejection part was over, I loosened my binds and swam hard for the shore.

Even with Rick's extra breath, my body was totally on empty. I needed oxygen now, more than ever, but more than that, the second half of the plan needed to start. We had all the spells that were necessary. Now I had to shove them down the sea monster's throat.

Without the flare gun, I'd have to use my voice to signal the others.

That would clearly tip the High Council witches to where I was in the lake, but I didn't care.

The second I breached the surface I didn't hesitate. "Zaid! Do it! Now!"

The whole beach echoed with my voice.

From the forest, Hilde pointed in my direction and Wesson appeared. He balled his hand into a fist. His powers started working. Beneath me, the water churned. From the depths, Wesson envisioned his squid monster. He brought the creature to life. Bit by bit. More and more. A new enemy that could either save or destroy me. Birthed beneath my kicking limbs.

But that wasn't all.

My shout hadn't gone unnoticed on the shore.

The other coven had pinpointed where I was. There was movement and gesturing on the shore. Other witches were gathering power. No doubt coming to strike me.

I narrowed my gaze, ready for war.

But they weren't the only ones stirring. As a surprising addition, the captured rebels, once dejected and broken, heard my triumphant shout and also sensed that something was going down.

The battle wasn't over.

We weren't defeated… and the rebel witches were awakening once more! Heads began to raise. Bodies sat up.

The only person I didn't catch sight of was Rick. Had he gotten clear of the boat as he'd hoped?

No time to watch on the surface. I kicked into action with the final part of the mission. Wesson's lie guard had developed, it was time to come face to face with the beast he controlled. We all knew the lie-guard wouldn't hold long. With the ravaged energy field on the beach, Wesson's fight against extirpation would be both painful and short.

I took a deep breath and dove, again forcing my poor body down to the depths of the lagoon. Below me, the water was colder, darker, and as I descended deeper and further, a new, horrible realization started to hit me too.

Wesson and Hilde had both done their jobs. But maybe *too* well.

Here in the weeds and bedrock there was a sea-monster.

A *giant* sea-monster.

Far bigger than I remembered.

Somehow, in Hilde's memories or Wesson's translations they'd made the beasty-squid-thingy staggeringly large. Its tentacles loomed huge, undulating in the waves. I must have counted thirty legs. At least, it felt that way, swimming between the indiscernible arms.

There was no way this creature would ever naturally exist. It was far too huge.

A legitimate monster.

Think of all the food it would need! At the very least, I told myself, it could consume a fist full of potions. I would force feed the spells in with one hand.

It would all be over soon.

I looked for the monster's mouth and teeth. I remembered the way at the Pokna Mountains, the squid's thorny bite had stripped back my skin. It was a pain I was willing to take on again. Totally worth it to set the captives free.

But, before I could enact the plan, I decided I needed another breath of air.

Swoosh!

As I surfaced, a diving hawk singed past my ear. Another angry bird dove down.

I had to fling up my hands to protect my face. The fowl attacked from all sides. Their beaks penetrated the water. Their feathered bodies bombarded me. I swatted the animals away as showers of flames and sparks spawned from their beaks and tails. In a panic, I looked towards the shore. I could see them. Scores of witches, staring out. Balling up their fists, looking to strike.

"Zaid!" I shouted. I needed help. I couldn't take a deep breath. I had no choice but to dodge the beasts of the skies. But Wesson was already holding together the lie-guard monster with his powers. For our plan to work, he couldn't let it go.

"Gen!" Wesson called out. "We need you. We need everybody." He shouted across the waterway, also exposing his location. The water echoed his request on the shore. He didn't add any details, and she was hooded, blind to the situation, but his imploring voice told her all that she'd need to know. To win, Wesson and I needed her help. All of their help.

Right.

Now.

"Beck!" I followed suit. Shouting for salvation as another eagle bombed. I dove to the side, but I still couldn't take a big enough breath to go down.

"I'm here, Wes. I got you!" Gennady returned. She stood her still hooded body up on the beach and jumped into action.

Beck's covered face also raised up.

"Vince!" Hilde followed our screams.

"Everyone. Move!" Gennady yelled at her hooded compatriots, rushing to her feet. Immediately she fell over some other unsuspecting rebel's legs. But that didn't matter. "Fight! Come on. Make noise. Whatever you can."

"Don't go easy!" Some other hooded voice shouted.

Ethan and Ferris and others stirred where they were.

More rebels joined.

They couldn't see, they didn't know where they were, or exactly how to help, but our partners on the shore didn't care. They got up and got crazy. Inconvenience would at least alter the other witches' hands.

Suddenly, the sky above me cackled and buzzed.

Something far more dangerous loomed.

More deadly than talons.

Electricity gathered in the clouds.

Lightning.

"Come on!" Beck yelled.

I had to go.

"Let's move!" Diego bellowed commands.

I dove again, as the others erupted on the shoreline. The lightning scorched the waves where I'd been only moments ago. This time, I swam deeper, knowing what monster I was approaching. The beast's beady eyes.

And its face.

And its mouth.

And its throat.

But the creature had also gathered some momentum. It was waiting for me. As I'd been finding my breath up above, it had been clocking me from below. The second I swam towards the squid-monster, a tentacled arm snatched around my waist and gripped me, rendering me immobile. The feeler slid around me like a boa constrictor. Choking me out. Amazingly, I wasn't scared.

In fact, the grip actually felt good.

Come on, Octo-beast. Reel me in. I waited for the monster to drag me to its toothy receptacle. But, the giant squid-type animal just held me firm in its grasp.

Come on.

I shoved the tentacled arm. Trying to get it to move. But the suction cups failed to release me.

Come on.

It was just holding me down, waiting me out. Patient for dinner to drown.

The beast wouldn't eat a wriggling meal, I realized. It would wait 'til I was gone. I tried to make my body relaxed and flat. But the monster wasn't fooled. Its instincts were correct. The squid was right to keep me at arm's length. I was a threat to its survival. But, soon, if the creature was patient, I would run out of my required air. The monster only had to wait me out for a short while.

My throat and chest cavity burned.

I was drowning.

Again.

One thing for sure, I realized grimly. If Beck, and I and all the others made it out of this predicament, it would be a cold day in hell before I took another swim.

Eat me! You're hungry! I willed the giant thing into action. But the monster didn't care. Its tentacles just hugged me, helpless where I was.

I was stranded. There was nothing more I could do to prevail.

I gave up on playing dead and banged my fists on its leathery feelers. I'd been underwater for too long now. I needed to take in another gulp of air. But, we both knew that wasn't happening. The squid-monster's grip only grew more patient and stronger.

Beck! What should I do?

Argh!

I punched and wrenched at the arm of the sea monster. The beast didn't even shudder. Wesson and Hilde had made it too big. This magical animal was far too awesome for me to handle. There was no contest between us. It easily overpowered me in its grasp.

Damn it! We were so close to fulfilling my plan.

One last step and this whole thing might be done.

Beck.

No. Please.

I'm coming.

I'll never give up!

I told him, as the darkness crept in.

For the second time this afternoon, I was drowning.

Only this time, there was no way for Rick to save me again.

No one was coming.

My body convulsed and shuddered one last time as the last of my oxygen faded away.

THIRTY-EIGHT
SOMETHING DEEPER IN THE WITCHES

GOODBYE, *Beck.*

Bye, Aunt Abeline.

My friends.

My enemies.

Goodbye terrible sea creature I asked my estranged dad to create.

Goodbye everyone. Mom... you know I'm coming.

The last words in my head floated away from my brain.

I couldn't function. I couldn't-

Whoosh!

The water around me spun backwards in a turbine, flinging itself up in the air. All the contents of the lake drained into the sky. The huge gust took me and the giant sea monster with it. Like little rag-dolls. we were hurled up in the air. Tossed all around. In shock, I gasped and greedily sucked back a fresh breath of air. As quickly as I could, I filled my lungs and my brain.

What the hell was happening now?!

My first thought was of Vince. Had he somehow harnessed the water? Suspended me up in the sunshine? But, this wasn't a water wall, it was a cyclone with me, the beast and all the lake water in it, spinning quickly, tossing and turning me around. As I spun, still in the monster's grip, I tried to glance towards the beach.

The shore had broken out into wild chaos.

Most of the rebels were still hooded and tied. But they were using their bodies as weapons and shields. They raced as headless torsos, knocking into the High Council members and taking out other rebel members. Their weapon was that they no longer cared. They couldn't use their magic. They couldn't even see where they were going. But maybe that had become an advantage out here. The energy fields flash-fired with extirpation. Any witch who tried to use their magic dealt with spontaneous burns. The energy disruption was rampant with infernos. Some prisoners' hoods had started to partially burn, others simply fought blind, no longer willing to give in to weakness. They hadn't reclaimed their eyesight from the hoods, but they had regained their will.

Our earlier shouts from the shoreline had awakened something deeper in the witches.

Hope.

Renewed vigor.

The desire to fight back and to win!

The rebels were no longer interested in escaping

from the High Council's clutches. The rebels were now fighting where they stood. It was a battle to be free, not contained by anybody. It wasn't enough not to give in, they wanted to win!

I spun wildly around in the cyclone above the water. I was still trapped inside the tentacle that gripped me strongly even now. The impressiveness of the windstorm caught the attention of some of the witches on the beach. They'd never seen such a feat. They'd never seen such a beast. If it wasn't Vince harnessing this twister, then who?

"Ahh!" Little Hilde screamed.

I felt the windstorm falter then disappear. The cyclone dispersed. The giant creature and I fell back down. We hit the lake with a huge splash.

Of course!

Hilde was a dreamcast, but she also harnessed wind power. She was a two-fer, or at least she had the powers to try it. Her training was only starting, but the natural ability was there. It was Hilde who had swept me up. Me and the squid-monster. Then the blazing energy in her hand had proven too much. She couldn't hold it, but she'd done her part.

It was exactly the amount of fresh breath that I'd needed.

I was revived.

Ready once more.

To finish the job.

The sea-monster hit the water first, making a giant

wave. The brunt force of the crash freed me up from its grasp.

I dove directly to the squid-creature's mouth.

There was no holding back. I shoved the combo of spells into its lips just as the monster's horrible teeth bit down.

Ow!

The fangs scraped my arm, dredging loose my skin, but I managed to wrench free of its bite. The beast's tentacles tried to re-ensnare me, but this time, I moved too quickly. I dodged within an inch of its grasp. I swam towards the submarine as fast and free as I could manage. When I re-emerged from the depths I tried to keep my head low for fear of another magic attack, but immediately, I could see the High Council no longer cared about one lowly swimmer.

The beach was in frenzied madness.

The forest was on fire.

The High Council witches had lost their advantage. They'd lost use of their magic. Every time they tried to harness a spell, they burst into flames. I could actually see Beck on the beaches fighting back. He was free. Helping others out of hoods and chains. But though the battle was turning, it still wasn't over. There was only one way it could end.

My eyes found Wesson on the shoreline.

He had run into the lake. No longer hiding in the bushes. He had his hands submerged beneath the water and even then, I could see his fist was smoking with steam. His face was torn in agony. But he had to hold the lie-guard.

I'd fed the beast. When would the chemicals kick in?

Just a little more. I willed him.

How Wesson was still holding the lie-guard under such intense pain and pressure was truly incredible. Little Hilde was slumped in the sand. She was totally spent.

You've done all you could do, I told her.

Hold on. Just another second, I willed Wesson. *Any second... any second...*

Unless my plan didn't work.

Unless the explosion couldn't be duplicated.

Unless we'd screwed something up in the-

No.

This time, I believed.

BOOM!

THIRTY-NINE

TWO PARABONDS ON THE BEACH

"RETREAT!"

From the water, I wasn't sure who started shouting.

The sea monster explosion assailed the beach with water, fire, squid guts and heat. Mighty waves crashed in on the shores. My exhausted body was tossed onto the beach. White-cap waves ravaged what remained of the boats. The energy of the bomb ripped the monster apart and dispersed its innards like a tidal wave in every direction, aggressively covering everything. Crashing on the shore. Waves doused the burning forest. Dampened the chaos. Smothered the High Council's plan once and for all. The will of the rebels burned brightly in the madness.

"Retreat!"

Others shouted.

I climbed out of the shallows, watching the human tidal shift as it happened. The High Council witches dropped all involvement in battle. Most of the camou-flage-wearing soldiers turned and fled. Their orange-haired leader was nowhere to be found. The coven master had run from the war to save himself. We did it. The war was over.

My arm throbbed.

With whatever energy I had left, I braced my raw hand to my chest and made my way back to the main shore. Beck saw me coming and raced over the dune. The canvas hood that had caged him was burnt down and ripped. It hung in ribbons around his neck. I was so glad to see him.

"Mae, my God!" He wrapped me in his arms.

I fell into his depths.

"You saved me."

"We saved each other," I murmured.

His arms around me had never felt so good in all my life.

"Did they make it?" I asked.

There were plenty of witches around us, helping one another, putting out fires, chasing the stragglers of the High Council, setting each other free and becoming unfettered once again. Beck couldn't possibly have known exactly which 'they' I was talking about, but I hadn't battled alone. I had to see that the others were safe.

"Come on." He took my good hand. We walked the beach.

Rick was with Vince, their loving reunion re-ignited. Already, they'd gotten comfortable together.

Now they worked to pick up overturned motorbikes and other detritus, cleaning the sand. Little Hilde was also there, nipping at their heels.

"Mae," Rick straightened as we approached. "Well done, my friend."

"I couldn't have done it without you," I admitted. I let Beck go, to fall into Rick's embrace. "Either of you," I said to Hilde, adding her to the cuddle.

She beamed. "I made a cyclone, like your water typhoon," she told a clueless Vince as we left off the long hug.

"I'll have you cited for plagiarism, young lady," he warned her.

Hilde laughed and laughed. At me, Vince smiled. I nodded, too.

Ferris, I found talking with Gennady.

"I can't believe he just rushed at the witches trying to save him. *Greg* of all people," Ferris was telling the older woman.

"Sounds like you and Ethan need a bit more communication. To take each other into consideration at the tough choices in real time," Gennady agreed.

I gave the girls a small wave but didn't stop to chime in on the conversation. Ferris was already nodding. Whatever Gennady said had struck a chord to the issue at hand. For her and Ethan to work things out. I hoped they would. It was what they both wanted.

Ethan, for his part, sat quietly on the beach. He was completely unentangled from the High Council vestiges. He stared out at the world. Greg sat beside him on the shore.

Contemplative.

For Ethan, I figured this type of consideration, even a meditation, was kind of normal. He was a thoughtful guy. There was a lot to unpack. But for Greg? The introspective silence was shocking to behold. No doubt he was wondering again about the fate of his girl. Where was Marcy? How should he feel about all that had happened to them and to her? Would they ever be reunited again?

Wesson was still knee-deep in the water.

He was treating his hands, letting the cool water wash over the raw, boiled wounds. His skin was savagely burned from the fires. Diego was trying to help him. I'd get Rick to make a burn salve as soon as I could. I turned to go find the chemist and nearly crashed right into Beck, I made such an abrupt turn.

His comfort was so at hand, I'd almost forgotten he was there. "You're bound," I realized.

Beck was still trapped by the High Council oven mitts. I quickly untied the magic-impeding bindings. Lovingly, he watched me work.

"I was just going to find Rick. We need a salve. Zaid looks burned, pretty bad," I said as I flinched. I'd overexerted my hand. The wound on my forearm was pretty raw.

"Your arm," Beck realized it as well. The squid-monster's teeth had dragged through my body tissue, it looked bad, but it was only a flesh-level wound.

That hurt a lot.

"I'll be alright," I tried to hide it.

The arm was bloody and distressed.

Beck stripped off his shirt and soaked it in lake water. "We have to protect your exposed bone." He wrung the t-shirt out in his hands. Gently, he took the ravaged limb off the protection of my chest. It hurt to move. I didn't want it in his hands, but I knew that it was best. He watched my face, carefully rotating the appendage until I acquiesced.

Finally, I gave in.

Beck gently wrapped his shirt around my jagged openings, a makeshift bandage until we had the supplies for a sterile, proper set. I winced a bit at the pain, but he was right. It felt better tucked away, safe and sound, from the air.

I looked at him.

We were free.

We were safe.

I embraced his bare chest. The heat from Beck's body vibrated on my cheek. I breathed him in. Together, all the world disappeared. For a moment, it was just me and Beck.

Two parabonds on the beach.

All the chaos and destruction wasn't ours.

"Everybody's safe," Beck murmured, lost in his own reverie too.

Exhausted, I nodded. Everybody's safe. Everybody...

"Have you seen Lauren?"

"No. But I'm sure she got out."

I'd heard that line before. I looked at the sunken submarine. Without use of her arms or her legs? He was sure she got out? In the chaotic mess of forced evacuation and all out war?

"Has anyone seen Lauren?" I asked around. The more we considered it, the more he realized it too. Lauren's magical exodus couldn't just happen. Someone had to help her. We became concerned. We broke apart to survey the beach. Lauren wasn't anywhere on the sand. Nor was Aine.

"Check the trucks," he called out. We headed in that direction. The High Council had just turned and fled. All their trucks were still here in the forest. Ready to load up and be gone. We ran to the closest vehicle.

"Lauren?!" I shouted. Even though I knew she couldn't reply.

"Lauren," Beck echoed.

But there was nobody there. The cargo hold had all emptied out.

We double checked the container and the cab, but she wasn't inside.

Was everyone wrong?

Did she never escape?

Was she still on the submarine?

Had I broken her out of prison only to let her suffer and drown?

"Lauren!" We raced to the second truck. "Laur-"

I crashed to a halt.

At the backside of the second truck, Lauren was

there, propped up in her wheelchair, beside a sniffling Aine, who from her body language I could see, was trying hard not to cry. High Council hoods still covered both their faces and shoulders. It was a cruel trick of the Council to have hooded the woman who couldn't move, considering they'd already performed a lobotomy on her mind, but that wasn't the worst of what I'd just found.

The women weren't alone beside the truck.

They were accompanied by one man.

Cornelius Child.

He stood at their sides. Eyes cold and wild.

"Child, what are you still doing here?" I asked as we approached. Soon as we fully rounded the corner, Beck and I both froze.

In his hand, he held a gun. The only man-made weapon on the shore.

"I was waiting for you, my girl. I knew you'd come. Rescued her once. You couldn't resist. That's a real savior complex you've got. Had to save her again from my world."

"Your *world*? She was locked in a prison."

"A medical facility!" He sputtered. He slammed the barrel of the pistol into Lauren's unmoving shoulder with every word. "At least we could properly care for her there!"

"We have help too. Aine was giving her care," I said. "Look, she's still here. At her side. So Lauren is fine."

For her part, at her name, Aine shrunk in size. She

wanted nothing to do with the vicious leader of the High Council. I couldn't blame her. Beck and I remained still, trying not to provoke Cornelius Child. The man was obviously unhinged. I'd have to be careful with my words.

"The High Council guards have gone..." I started.

"What do you want?" Beck asked.

Child could have turned and fled with the others, but he didn't. He stayed.

Waiting.

Hoping.

For what purpose?

Did he think that he'd be the only one here in confrontation with a weapon? That he'd come out on top? Well, he'd won. Beck and I were unarmed.

The High Council leader smiled.

It was ugly. Cold and victorious.

"I'm not returning to the castle empty handed. I stayed behind to make a deal. You wanted Lady Ecru, well here she is, you can take her and the nurse. But in her place, I take you back to the castle with me."

Aine started crying. She could no longer hold it in.

Beck bristled.

But I didn't budge. "Put down the gun. You don't need it."

"Uh, with raging extirpation all around, I absolutely do." Cornelius ran his other hand over his eyebrows in a raking motion, similar to how Beck always played with his hair. A nervous tick he couldn't help. An action I'd seen before... in my dream.

It was one of the images from my vision right before... Beck was shot in the gut.

His naked chest.

Damn it.

Why wasn't Beck wearing his shirt?

The clothing he'd been wearing was now wrapped around my arm. Beck was shirtless. This scene had appeared to me exactly like this, I realized. Fear ran coldly through my veins. Could I stop it from occurring now?

"I think it's more than a fair trade," Child grinned. "One for one. Everyone in the group's a happy camper. The rebels escape the wrath of the High Council and I put on trial the girl who started this whole charade. What do you say?"

"No," Beck said.

But I stopped him. I held up my clothed arm. "I'll do it." I told Child. "Beck," I turned to my man. "It's okay..." I called over my shoulder, but didn't break my gaze with my love. "I'll go with you."

Anything to keep that gun from firing.

"That's the spirit." Cornelius laughed. He roughly shook Lauren's shoulders around. Aine tried her best not to move. Under the hood, I hoped she'd regained some strength.

"Mae, no." The look in Beck's eyes hurt my heart.

"I know. I know. It's fine." I put my good hand directly on his chest. His heart was beating wild and fast. "I've always said, I'd go on trial. I'm not ashamed of what I've done. I can stand up and be counted. It's alright."

"But what if they decide to-"

"They won't. They won't get to. Don't think like that. I'm not guilty. I didn't do anything that wasn't necessary. We'll get through this. Like we always do." My un-bandaged fingers floated to his face. His eyes were so sad. Though he didn't know the reason why, it was clear, I'd already made my choice and I would go. "It'll be alright. I promise. Give me a kiss."

Beck didn't argue more.

By now he knew how stubborn I could be when I'd made up my mind. His eyes searched mine for a secret signal, like maybe I was disingenuous in my surrender, but I shook him off. I meant what I said. The idea of him shot, bleeding from his naked chest, was too strong for me to shake. I couldn't risk it. I pulled his face to mine and kissed him gently on the lips.

"Bye, parabond," I whispered.

He nodded. Tears welling under his lashes.

I held both hands up in the defensive position and approached. I walked to Aine and Lauren, keeping my eyes on the gun with every step. Cornelius watched, but he didn't interrupt me. I moved very slowly, ensuring that he wouldn't get spooked. When I was near, I put one hand on Lauren and the other on Aine's frame.

"Ladies, it's me, Mae. I'm going to take off your hoods." I undid the fabric and removed them first from

Aine, then from Lauren's face. "This is Beck, he's my boyfriend. You remember?"

Aine nodded, snuffling. Lauren didn't move or say anything.

"He's gonna take you two somewhere safe." I smiled at them. They could do nothing but simply stare back. But at least with this act, they were free. Aine only ever wanted to help her friend.

I glanced at Cornelius. He nodded. Permission granted. I encouraged them. Aine rolled Lauren to the other side of the circle and stood behind Beck. When they were clear, I stepped in line to become Cornelius' prisoner. Good to my word.

"Mae," Beck choked out. He looked so miserable.

Sadly, I smiled. "I love you, too."

"Let's get this over with." Cornelius nodded towards the truck. I moved to the passenger entrance, Child with his gun poked into my back. We were shuffling forward, when suddenly someone burst through the trees.

"Wait! Take me instead!" Wesson said. "I'll be your prisoner." He held out both hands to prove he meant what he was offering. He was humbled in the act of surrender. As he groveled, we could see the horrible burns on both his hands.

The war wounds he'd sustained enacting my plan.

A plan that had worked.

Until now.

"No, Zaid. Stop." I frowned. "I'm okay."

"I wasn't talking to you. Child, I'm the leader of the

rebels. That's got to be a better trophy than some dumb first year kid, take me instead," Wesson offered.

"Zaid, don't do this," I quietly countered, careful not to agitate Child with my voice.

"Some first year kid? You mean your *daughter?*" Cornelius bit the word in half in his mouth. He was so full of spite. But we could all see, he was intrigued by the new carrot dangling.

"Yeah, she's my daughter. So what?" Wesson said. "We both know I couldn't save her mother. Let me do it for the girl."

"No," I intervened.

"Mae," Beck frowned.

"She doesn't have Sierra's powers?" Cornelius mused.

"She's as weak as they come," Wesson agreed.

"We had a deal," I said to Child. Trying to interrupt them.

"And now I have a better offer." Cornelius smiled. "The leader of the rebel party. Brought in by me, single-handedly." He was delighted at the thought. He'd gone from capturing a crippled prisoner, to a first year trouble-maker, to the captain of the rebel army. In fact, he couldn't be more pleased. Child's pomposity returned. "Switch with the girl."

Cornelius shoved me away as Wesson stepped near. We passed shoulders in the midst of the group.

"What are you doing, I might get off as an innocent in trial. They'll find you guilty for sure," I hissed.

"Just one last moment of father-daughter bonding,"

Wesson told Cornelius and he hugged me. It felt stiff and weird. We'd never hugged before. Still, I let him pull me in. He whispered in my ear. "Mae, I failed you. I failed your mother. Christ, I failed our whole army. I didn't do enough to stop them. But *you* have a chance to effect real change. Look what you did on this sand. You're more of a leader than I'll ever be."

"But the trial-"

"There won't be a trial. Don't worry. I've got this. I've got one more trick up my sleeve." He winked, about to release our embrace, but something caught me. I threw my arms around his neck. Plan or no plan, I didn't want him to go. I gripped my father in my hands. It was Wesson's turn to stiffen, but then he re-engaged with me, and felt my fear and worry. He tried to really comfort me. He hugged his daughter to his chest.

"It'll be okay," he murmured. "I can handle this. *You* can handle this. My plan will work. We'll be free of Child by day's end."

I wiped my face, nodding. He grinned at me and stepped away. I couldn't help but smile. Only just a flicker, then I controlled all my emotions again.

So it was a ruse.

In a second, he'd be free.

Wesson nodded to Cornelius and moved up into the truck cab.

"I'll fight for you," I called after him to make it look good. "I'll fight for *justice*."

He stopped in the doorway.

"We can beat them," I said.

He smiled sadly. "I'll be proud either way." Then he looked at Beck. "Take care of my kid. She's a pretty special person. Sierra'd want to know that our daughter is okay."

Beck nodded sternly. He wrapped his warm arms around my shoulders. And even though I knew something was still coming and this whole maudlin father-daughter goodbye thing was a trick, I couldn't stop the tears from tumbling down my cheeks. I waved with sadness.

"I'm glad I met you," Wesson told me. "You remind me so much of your mother, it's uncanny." Her reference caught in his throat. Then he nodded and hopped up in the cab and disappeared. Cornelius and his gun followed him in. They slammed the door shut and Wesson started the engine. We watched the truck pull away and bump up the road. It rumbled into the forest, bending wayward branches out of its path.

Any second now, Wesson would use his final twist.

Whatever potion he still had.

He would outsmart Child one more time and save the day.

That was the plan.

Any moment.

It was coming.

Any second.

But then I realized what spell was still in his pockets.

The only thing that Wesson had in his grasp.

A potion I had passed to him. Given over for safe-keeping. Before I swam.

There was only one thing.

The Udak bomb.

The suicide explosive with a dangerously short fuse.

The truck rumbled forward.

"Wait..." I stumbled after it. "Zaid, no!" I pulled away from Beck, Aine and Lauren. I ran to stop it. Beck tried to grab me but I was too quick out of his hands. "Wesson! Don't do this!" I shouted. "This is not what I wanted!"

Flailing.

Racing forward.

Trying anything to get the attention of the two passengers in the cab.

"Wait!" I screamed.

But the truck barreled forward.

My dad couldn't hear me.

Or didn't want to.

"Wait! Please! Wes! Don't do this."

BOOM!

The truck exploded. Fire bolts shot out through the air. Twisted metal leapt into the forest in all directions. The cab of the truck incinerated in ugly orange flames.

"No!" I still raced forward, but this time, Beck

caught me as I stumbled to the ground. He bear-hugged me to his bare chest.

Held me.

Protected me.

I wanted to burst through the fires to save my father, but we both knew that Wesson Zaid was now dead. I wept uncontrollably in Beck's arms.

"No... Dad... don't go..."

FORTY

NOT FOR NOTHING

FOR THE REMAINDER of the day, we helped the other rebel witches cleaning the beach. They put out any lasting fires, removed the guts of the sea monster from the water, and gathered the errant debris on the shores. Rescue teams dove under the wreckage to salvage what they could from the submarine. Without their leader to mount another attack, we all felt safe on the sand. The High Council coven had returned to their castle. We didn't have to hide or escape from their wrath anymore.

At least not for now.

There was a lot of work to be done to return the lake to the untouched nature it once was, and at first, I threw myself into the labor. Even with only one good arm ,it felt good to dig in and be part of the task. But soon Gennady came and found me. She touched me lightly on the shoulder and signaled for me to join her. We stepped to the side.

"I have news."

The look on her face told me the information wasn't good.

I crossed my arms as if that might protect me. My eyes flashed to Beck. Instinctively, he knew I wanted him to be there. Beck came over and took my good hand. When I was ready, Gennady continued.

"We received word, Child didn't die in the explosion."

"It can't be," Beck blurted, while I audibly groaned.

Several others clocked our reactions and started to gather around our little huddle.

"How?" I asked.

"I don't know. He suffered burns, severe burns, but he got out." She frowned.

"That guy has some teleporting power or something," Greg blurted. "Remember at the Battle of Four? He could jump all over."

Vince and Hilde nodded. Even Beck remembered.

"You were busy running in a cornfield," Greg shrugged in my direction.

"It had to be a lie-guard," Ferris told us.

"Definitely magic," Hilde whispered.

"Some people say he was never there. At the truck. It might have been staged," Gennady admitted. "Some witches can use lie-guards to double their presence to make themselves look like they're there, when they aren't really *present*..."

"So his burns might have come from performing

the magic and the extirpation, not from the truck explosion," Diego said.

There was nodding and consensus among the others.

But they hadn't been there.

I was.

It seemed so real.

I was sure he'd been standing beside me. If he wasn't... "Then my dad died for nothing." I looked out across the lake.

"Not for nothing," Gennady pulled me back, locked our eyes. I tried to glance away, but she wouldn't let me. "Please don't say that. Wes died in the act of avenging your mother. Of saving his daughter. Those were the only two things that he cared about in this world." She let the words hang, until finally, I was forced to accept them.

It wasn't nothing.

Dad died trying to save me.

It didn't matter if the danger was real or imagined.

He'd fulfilled his promise to Sierra.

At last, he'd tried to enact real, lasting change in the High Council.

Dad.

That's what I'd just called him. All along, I'd called him Zaid to his face. In my head, he was Wesson. He didn't feel like either name anymore. Sometime in our final day here together, something changed. He'd tried to help me, to save me, over and over. At some point, I realized he stopped being some stranger and started becoming my friend. When it mattered most, he was actually my dad.

Diego squeezed Gennady's shoulders. "There were more than just two women in his heart."

Gennady smiled. She looked so sad. I nodded as well.

I had barely spent any time with these rebels, but even I knew without a doubt, that was true. She was a big part of his life. Gennady leaned back into Diego's hand, grateful and heavy-hearted. She wiped an errant tear from her cheek.

Wesson Zaid was gone.

There was no proper time or respectable space for a funeral.

We didn't have a body to bury or mourn. No ashes to spread on the lake or the sand. It didn't seem right to make a bunch of speeches about a man I'd barely known, but still, I wanted to give his spirit a proper send off. I could tell that others did as well.

"Ex-ladies and ex-fellows," Diego addressed the other witches who were still gathered. Some gave measured smiles. "First years and third years," he made eye contact and offered nods to the friends and rebels who'd recently joined them. "We lost a good man today. A mighty lie-guard. He sacrificed in order that we might have a better life. Let's say goodbye to Wesson Zaid."

The group nodded. Diego offered the floor to Gennady.

Vince and Rick leaned together, listening.

Hilde squinted, looking out over the water, considering the words.

"We lost a good man," Gennady started. "Someone we trusted. I trusted him so completely. He never asked to take the lead, but still he led. Without complaint. He carried our clan. I, for one, am glad I met him. I'm so glad that I loved him." Her voice broke. "I'm so glad he was my friend. I'm thankful for every day that we spent, most of them together." Some of the others in the crowd nodded her way. "Every night. A light in troubled times. I'll miss you Wes." She crumbled into tears.

Diego looked at me. He raised an eyebrow.

Did I want to say a few words about my father?

"Oh." I looked at all the gathered friends. "You all knew him better than I did," I admitted. But still, I tried to go forward. I took a deep breath. "I spent my whole life looking for my dad. And then I found him. Or, I guess he found me? We found each other. If it wasn't for him, we'd still be in jail." I glanced at my friends, then at Lauren. We chuckled at that. "I guess you could say that Wesson Zaid saved me. Saved all of us from that trouble. He made some choices that I didn't agree with, still don't agree with, but now I'm starting to understand. He tried his best. He was my dad. We were only just starting to get to know each other. I'm glad we met... I wish I'd gotten to know him a bit more. Now, I can't." The emotion started to choke in my voice as well. "But, I take comfort that somewhere out there, Sierra and Wesson are now reunited. Cornelius Child cannot hurt them any more."

The others murmured.

Sierra and Wesson were reunited.

The High Council could no longer hurt them.

I looked back to Diego. "That's it."

The older witch gave a stiff smile.

"He saved us all with his strength and his bravery. We don't have much, but we have our hearts and our minds. A wish and prayer for our dear departed friend. So please, join me in an imaginary toast." Diego held up his hand, miming holding a glass of champagne. All around me on the beach, the others did the same.

Tears streamed down my face.

My Mom had died with a champagne cheers. Now, Wesson was gone and we toasted his name. It felt so wrong and so right all at once. But, I suppose that was my entire experience with this man. My dad was flawed. But he was a good guy. Mostly. When it counted. It was complicated. A work in progress. I might never get a handle on how I really felt about him now.

For a moment, the crowd stood silent, reflecting on the leader that had left our midst in battle and all the choices that he'd made. Large or small. Right or wrong. Then, suddenly, real glasses of champagne appeared in our grasps. Raised high by everyone. The sparkling drinks twinkled in the glow of the setting sunlight.

My eyes flashed to Ferris, who had her hand balled by her side.

She winked.

Grateful, I smiled in return.

"To Wesson Zaid!" Diego told them.

"To Wes!" Gennady said.

"To Dad!"

We raised our glasses in appreciation of the man, then took sweet celebratory sips to drink all the memories down. Everyone took their own time. All around us, I heard vague conversations about the bits and pieces of the man my father had been. How he'd touched their hearts. How he'd be missed. Even by myself. When the moment was over, Ferris released her lie-guard illusion and the glasses and toasts disappeared.

I was still chatting with Ferris, Ethan, Gennady, Beck and some of the others when Rick and Vince and Hilde came over. I noted, stifling a smile to myself, that the boys weren't engaged in any public display of affection, although their dangling hands did sway very near to each other's hips.

"Where do we go from here?" Rick asked Gennady.

She seemed surprised the question was directed at her, but it seemed only natural to us that she'd take up the lead. She'd always been Wesson's partner. His second in command. With him gone, that placed her front and center of the troupe.

"I'm not sure," she admitted. "Split up? Find new places to hide?"

"But they'll track your magic," Ferris said.

"We should stick together," Vince nodded.

"There is safety in numbers," Rick added.

"I miss Marcy," Greg sighed, taking note of all the various couples, mostly ignoring our conversation.

"We miss her too," Ethan tossed his arm around his buddy's shoulder. I wasn't sure he'd ever even met Marcy, but Greg had been suffering since the start of the inquisition. It was the right thing to say. It was the right thing to do. Beck squeezed his shoulder as well. Perhaps they both knew in their own hearts how hard it would have been to go through all this turmoil without their loving partners. I offered Greg a supportive smile.

"But where should we go?" Diego wondered. "We can't stay here."

That was plain as day.

Not only did the High Council now know about this location, through the mess of destruction there was nothing here to stay for.

"The water messes with their tracking abilities?" Beck asked.

Gennady and Diego nodded.

"They only found us here because of Craig-gy the Rat." Diego glowered at his name.

"But we can't stay in the sub," Hilde worried. "It's too damaged."

Our eyes trailed to the sunken, broken vessel. At least, we took in the parts that still floated, the bits above water that we could see.

"Yes," Gennady agreed. "We can't stay there."

"Maybe in time, we might repair it," Diego wondered.

"Maybe..." she wasn't convinced.

"I know of a place," Beck offered. He glanced in my direction. "If that's okay with you." He asked.

I raised an eyebrow. Please continue.

"Mae and I found it. A river waterfall with a large cave hidden behind. The movement of the waters would mask the energy disruptions, I think."

The waterfall we'd discovered in the forest behind the Konya Thomas Special Collections property. Of course. "I think it's big enough to fit the whole group," I added.

Diego and Gennady exchanged a glance.

"A waterfall? I guess we could try it out while we figure out our next steps," Gennady said. There was no better suggestion. The others nodded, slowly at first, and then more certain. A cave underground might not have the infrastructure to be a permanent location, but it did offer cover and safety. It was a place to start.

"So that's it. We'll relocate to the Beck Waterfall and create a new existence," Diego announced.

"The Mae Waterfall," Beck deflected.

"The Zaid Waterfall," I offered.

"The Zaid Waterfall," Gennady nodded, liking the name. "We'll go and plan from there," she said wisely, not willing to put all their hopes into one basket.

The other rebel witches nodded and began to take preparations to shift the whole coven. We would create a new hideout under the splendor of nature. Everyone was on board. But, I didn't agree one hundred percent with this move.

I didn't need to plan. Or reassess. I already knew what would come next.

I was done running.

I was done hiding.

It was time to stand up and fight for the freedoms I wanted.

To leave.

To live.

Without looking over my shoulder.

Without the Council controlling what I did or who I loved or the choices I made in the moment.

I would be brave like my mom.

I would be bold like my dad.

The final battle was coming. I was ready. I would face Cornelius Child and the rest of the High Council once and for all.

And I wouldn't take no for an answer.

Ready for more? Find out how the story ends in the final book of the High Council chronicles: Powerful Bonds.

JULIE CATHERINE
POWERFUL
BONDS
THE HIGH COUNCIL WITCH CHRONICLES
6

WHAT NOW?

Want to dig into sneak peeks, learn about the next releases and find all the other freebies and literary goodies? Join my newsletter at www.juliecatherineau thor.com.

Xo
　Julie

ACKNOWLEDGMENTS

Thank you for spending time with me, Mae, Vince, Beck, Blue Moon, Wesson and all the other witches.

Thank you to my editor, Allana Stuart. When I opened the doc and saw a notation saying I had 400 edits to consider I thought *what have I got myself into*, but it was quick and painless and the story's so much better for it as well!

Thank you to Allana Giesbrecht, Erin Hempel, David Wong and David Guthrie. I appreciate all the check-ins and supportive conversations.

My goal writing this series was to create a world where someone might like to live for a while or at least happily visit, taking the time to peep into the trials and tribulations of other people's fantastical lives, living with their successes and their troubles and of course exploring a few potential romantic entanglements too.

This is my sexiest book to date (with the consummation of Mae and Beck's romantic relationship). Yowza! I hope you found the journey enticing, exciting, emotional and just a tiny bit magical.

When you're finished reading *Paternal Bonds*, I hope you'll consider writing a review on store sites, reader hubs and/or whatever social media platform you're currently using. Reviews are so important to help authors become visible on the busy, busy landscape. I appreciate each review, ratings, and/or social media share more than I can express.

So what happens next? You can find out as the story comes to its dramatic conclusion in book 6, Powerful Bonds. See you there!

Xo
    Julie

www.ingramcontent.com/pod-product-compliance
Lightning Source LLC
Chambersburg PA
CBHW072037190726
48294CB00005B/1297